JANI
and the
GREAT
PURSUIT

∽

Being an account of certain
events enacted in the Capital of the Empire,
Europe, and elsewhere

and

of various astounding
and life-threatening escapades

as experienced by

a Lady, Miss Janisha Chatterjee.

Also by Eric Brown

ERIC BROWN

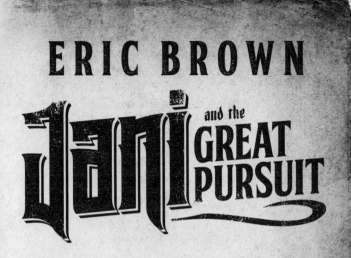

Jani and the
GREAT
PURSUIT

SOLARIS

First published 2016 by Solaris
an imprint of Rebellion Publishing Ltd,
Riverside House, Osney Mead,
Oxford, OX2 0ES, UK

www.solarisbooks.com

ISBN: 978 1 78108 378 9

Copyright © Eric Brown 2016

The right of the author to be identified as the author
of this work has been asserted in accordance with the Copyright,
Designs and Patents Act 1988.

All rights reserved. No part of this publication may be
reproduced, stored in a retrieval system, or transmitted,
in any form or by any means, electronic, mechanical,
photocopying, recording or otherwise, without the
prior permission of the copyright owners.

10 9 8 7 6 5 4 3 2 1

A CIP catalogue record for this book is available
from the British Library.

Designed & typeset by Rebellion Publishing

Printed in the US

For Michael Greenwood
– Fifty years up!

CHAPTER ONE

Aboard the Pride of Edinburgh – *Jani takes tea –*
A security check – Jani is caught out –
"You have some explaining to do..."

JANI WAS ABOARD the *Pride of Edinburgh*, somewhere over northern Greece, when she made the acquaintance of the mechanical dog.

For two days since leaving India, Jani had remained in Lady Eddington's Pullman carriage in the nether regions of the *Edinburgh*'s vast gondola, reluctant to venture out. Lieutenant Alfie Littlebody had tried to reassure her on that score.

"Jani, there's no way the authorities could have linked us with the death of Colonel Smethers–"

She interrupted. "But you commandeered the airship at Annapurnabad under your own name. You told me that. So..."

Alfie sighed. "I had to give my name and rank. Even if the authorities discovered Smethers' body, and even if they linked his death to me and traced the airship to Delhi, there is no way they would know that we boarded the *Edinburgh*."

"Mr Alfie is right," Anand chipped in. "We are safe

aboard the *Edinburgh*. I would like to explore the airship."

The boy was wide-eyed at the thought, and Jani wondered whether the wonders that awaited him in the gilded staterooms and lounges of the vessel were blinding him to the possibility of danger. Or was she being paranoid? She had recently undergone mishap and mayhem sufficient to last a lifetime, and now all she wanted to do was relax until they reached London.

"If you wish to venture out with Alfie, Anand, then by all means do so. While you two are away, I shall draw myself a bath."

That had been yesterday, but now, as the great airship powered its way high above the snow-capped mountains of northern Greece, she was overwhelmed by a feeling of claustrophobia. This was due in part to the environs of the Pullman itself, its narrow confines and its flock wallpaper pressing in on either side. Also the attention of Alfie and Anand was adding to the sense of confinement. If it was not enough that Anand was watching her every move with big, doggy eyes, then Alfie Littlebody was seeking her attention like the overweight, faithful bloodhound he so resembled.

She had discovered a shelf of poetry and novels in the carriage, and attempted to take her mind off what might lie ahead with the distraction of some light reading.

"I am not a novel man myself," Alfie said. "I prefer my reading to be of a factual nature."

"I love Rider Haggard and Jules Verne!" Anand sang, beaming at her.

Jani set aside her Austen. "Each to our own. But I do find that silence is conducive to the appreciation of *whatever* one is reading."

Her remonstrance was too subtle for Alfie, and he went on, "I think we should have a plan of action to hand when we alight at London."

Something turned in her stomach at the thought, as if the ventha-di lodged therein was making its presence known. "On the contrary, we should arrive and *then* make plans." The fact of the matter was that she was frightened of what lay ahead in the Empire's teeming capital, and all she wanted to do was forget the mission on which she found herself.

"And now, if you would kindly allow me to read..."

"One thing I would like to know," Alfie said, "is whether we are availing ourselves of Lady Eddington's hospitality when we reach London. You seemed uncertain when she made the offer of her townhouse."

Jani sighed. "We might very well stay a day or two with Lady Eddington. That remains to be seen."

He reached out and took her hand in his chubby paw. "Janisha, I just want you to know that whatever happens over the course of the next few days, I will remain at your side."

"And so will I!" Anand said. "We are like the Three Musketeers, ah-cha? All for one!"

Alfie squeezed her hand. "And one for all."

She gazed from Alfie to Anand and forced a smile. For all their good intentions, their presence was not unlike the flock wallpaper: all-encompassing and a little overbearing. She slotted *Northanger Abbey* back into the bookcase and announced that, despite her earlier reservations, she was going to take a turn around the upper decks.

Anand jumped to his feet. "And I will accompany you, Jani-ji!" In his brand new leather sandals, creased twill shorts and spanking white shirt, he looked like a pupil from one of the more expensive Delhi finishing schools – not the low-caste houseboy that her father had plucked from the gutters thirteen years ago.

The thought of her father sent a pang of grief through her heart.

Anand was babbling on, "I will give you a conducted tour of the main lounge, Jani-ji. And then we might go to the glittering restaurant!" Yesterday, on his return from the upper-decks with Alfie, Anand had been agog with the experience and eager to recount the wonders of the sumptuous lounge and the restaurant where Alfie had treated him to strawberry sorbet and iced lemonade.

"And I might as well accompany you both," Alfie put in, "considering your concerns yesterday about venturing forth."

She stood quickly and gestured for them to remain seated. "You will do nothing of the sort. If nothing else, the events of the past week should have demonstrated that I am more than capable of looking after myself. And anyway, I need a little time alone."

Alfie indicated her light-beam, standing like a lipstick on the bookshelf. "Perhaps you would be wise to…"

"I will not be needing that, thank you, Alfie. Now, if you would be so kind…"

She swept from the cushioned dining area, leaving Alfie and Anand to exchange puzzled glances, and climbed down from the carriage.

She sighed with relief as she crossed the vast garage, which resembled nothing more than a sidings shed in some cavernous railway stockyard, the great and the good of the Raj being given to transporting their own carriages to and from the subcontinent. Alongside the rolling stock were several pieces of what looked like military hardware: bizarre arrays of golden tubes and gears which she guessed had been found in the alien ship at Annapurnabad and were being ferried to London for further inspection.

As she stepped into the lift and was whisked up to the main deck, she felt a twinge of guilt at running away from Alfie and Anand like this. They meant well, and their devotion to her was touching, even if it was a little cloying – but she feared, certainly in Alfie Littlebody's case, that his unwonted attention in the days ahead might prove awkward. He was a good man, with his heart in the right place, but she thought he was a little out of his depth. After all, thanks to her, he had left behind the safety of his commission in the British army and found himself pitched headlong into a perilous adventure the outcome of which was unknown. Perhaps to compensate, he was fixating his desires upon her. She sighed as the lift bobbed to a halt.

As she moved from the lift and crossed the carpeted deck, she recalled the feeling – from her last journey in an airship – of stepping on to a lighted stage. She was aware of heads turning in her direction. It was not every day that these well-heeled gentlefolk beheld an Indian national outfitted in a summer skirt like a Home Counties memsahib.

On the first day aboard the *Pride of Edinburgh*, Lady Eddington had taken one look at her ripped and scruffy shalwar kameez and pronounced that a change of *couture* was the order of the day. She had returned from the onboard outfitters with parcels full of the latest fashions, dresses and skirts and blouses that must have cost a small fortune. Jani had made her selection – a white dress with appliquéd forget-me-not trim, a yellow linen skirt, three blouses, and four pairs of silk stockings – and the dowager had waved aside her protests that she would one day repay her kindness. "Nonsense, my dear. These are a gift. Now, out of those rags and let's see how beautiful you really are!"

She had dutifully changed and stepped from the bathroom, pleased at the sight of Alfie Littlebody's goggle eyes.

Now she strode across the deck to the café bar, head held upright with pride and, if she were honest with herself, not a little satisfaction that she was contravening the dress code acceptable in the eyes of the ladies and gentlemen sipping their tea on all sides.

She spotted Lady Eddington seated alone before a porthole.

The dowager beamed at Jani and gripped her hand. "My word, but you do look a picture! Hard though it might be to believe, there was a time as a girl when I turned a head or two."

Jani squeezed the old lady's hand and murmured that she could well believe it. In the powdered lineaments of the dowager's lined face she discerned a handsomeness that once must have been beauty.

A waiter approached and Jani ordered mint tea, while Lady Eddington requested more hot water for her pot of Darjeeling.

"And have you thought any more about where you will stay when we reach London?" the dowager asked. "I discerned a distinct reluctance to accept my offer."

"I am sorry. Was it so obvious?"

The old lady's eyes twinkled. "You have a young man awaiting your return?"

Jani felt herself flush. "I thought perhaps I might see Sebastian at some point."

"I understand perfectly, my dear."

"I could stay with you for a day or two, along with Alfie and Anand, and then go my own way."

"Say no more!"

"You see, I think Sebastian might be able to help me. He has friends in high places, you might say, due to his family connections, and if anyone might be able to assist in my finding the Morn, then it is Sebastian."

She stared through the porthole at the crumpled terrain of Greece passing silently by far below, and sighed.

Lady Eddington leaned forward and murmured, "If I were you, Jani, I would not worry too much about Alfie and his heartache."

Jani stared at the old lady and laughed. The wisdom of years, she thought. Was it so obvious? "He's like a faithful dog," she said, "forever following me around. His nose will be put out in no little way when Sebastian and I..." She trailed off, her face hot.

"And Anand, too, Jani. My word, but I dimly recall the days when I too had suitors aplenty."

Jani shook her head. "It's not only that. I mean..." She stared into her tea. "I mean, I feel responsible for Alfie. What he did... he tried to save Jelch's life. He killed his commanding officer – who was an evil piece of work, by all accounts. Alfie burned his bridges and pledged himself to my cause, and... and I don't want to hurt him."

The dowager reached out and squeezed her hand. "Alfie is a grown man, albeit still in part a youth. He needs experiences like this – and I mean experiences of the heart – so that he might come to know himself. He is infatuated with you, Jani, and understandably so. But it is not for you to feel responsibility, or guilt, for the state of his emotions. If he is any man at all, then he will be satisfied with your friendship."

Jani shrugged. "I wonder."

Lady Eddington changed the subject. "At any rate, you have more on your mind than a lovelorn Lieutenant and a besotted houseboy. To think of it! Other realms and aliens and becalmed vessels bearing technological wonders!"

Jani looked up to see a portly man and woman bearing down on Lady Eddington. "Amelia!" shrilled the woman. "I said it was you, didn't I, Cedric? Why, but it must be five years!"

The woman turned a disdainful glance on Jani and peered at her through a pair of lorgnette. "And who is your little Indian friend, Amelia?" she asked in a tone that suggested she didn't really want to know.

Before she could be introduced, Jani squeezed the dowager's hand, murmured that she must dash, nodded to the portly pair and made her escape. She crossed the lounge to the exit.

She stepped on to the bottom tier of a helical elevator and was carried around and around to the observation deck, along with a dozen other passengers. A brass plate declared that the elevator was manufactured by Greenwood and Co., Leeds, West Yorkshire – but Jani suspected that the technology, like everything else that made Britain great these days, was derived from the alien ship that had crash-landed in Nepal fifty years ago.

She found herself deposited in a glass-walled cupola

in the upper reaches of the vast gondola, crossed to the rail and stared out as she considered the child she had been. Growing up in New Delhi, and then from the age of eight boarding in England, she had respected the British – her mother being English, after all – and had assumed that the greatness of the nation was the outward manifestation of some inner quality of national spirit, that there was something inherent within the British which made individuals aspire to greatness and achieve that which other, lesser peoples could hardly hope to mimic.

She had become increasingly less enamoured of the Empire as she matured, and then recently discovered the truth – that what made Britain predominant in world affairs, what made the Empire so valorous and resolute, was not some indefinable inner mettle, but the result of nothing so much as an accident.

Granted, if it had not been the British who had commandeered the Vantissarian vessel and utilised the technological and scientific wonders it contained, then some other nation, the Russians or the Chinese, would have plundered the ship of its technology – and they would have developed machines and weapons with which to subjugate the world. She wondered if the world would have been a worse place if another nation had gained the upper hand. She had been at the mercy of the Russians and the British over the course of the past week, and she admitted that there was little to choose between them – and she suspected that the Chinese would be no better. Come to that, considering the actions of the Hindu priest Durga Das and his accursed henchman Mr Knives, the Indian nation had nothing of which to be proud. There was good in every nation, but it was a truism that the venal and the sadistic were motivated to fight their way to the top in order to secure ultimate power.

It was a depressing thought.

And the Zhell, she wondered? Were the creatures from another realm, bent on invading her world and annihilating its people, even more evil than anything Earth had to offer?

According to Jelch, they certainly were.

Oh, she thought in despair, if only the peoples of Earth, whatever their colour, nationality or ideology, could come together to defeat the threat posed by the aliens! But what realistic chance was there of that, when only she and a handful of others were aware of the Zhell?

Her only hope was to locate the Morn known as Mahran, currently languishing in a London gaol. Perhaps together they might defeat the Zhell. She gripped the rail and thought of her father, tears streaming down her cheeks as she wondered what advice he might have proffered.

Her tears were noticed by a woman and her escort further along the rail. Instead of enquiring what troubled her, the woman murmured something to her partner and they hurried away. Jani wondered whether they would have evinced the same reaction if the colour of her skin had been the same as theirs. She pulled a handkerchief from her cuff and wiped her eyes.

The airship had passed over the mountain range, leaving the snowy summits far behind. Below she made out scattered villages, their terracotta roofs contrasting with the sun-soaked, undulating landscape.

A group of men and women stepped from the helical

elevator, crossed to the rail and admired the view. She moved along the rail a little so as to be quite alone.

It was odd that she had felt out of place in India; she had been aware, when abroad in the teeming streets of Delhi, that she felt – despite knowing that this was *home* – that she no longer really belonged there. And yet she had felt out of place in London, too, despite having lived in England for almost ten years. She was a product of both places, she knew, but the sad fact was that she belonged to neither.

Perhaps the answer would be to live in neither India nor England, but somewhere neutral and in between, like Greece. She laughed at such a silly notion and longed passionately to be held in Sebastian's arms once more.

She turned quickly, aware that someone was standing close by. "Oh," she said, startled, as she saw a young soldier staring at her. He had a thin white face, a tiny toothbrush moustache, and suspicious eyes.

"You all right, Miss?"

"Quite, thank you."

"Only I noticed you crying..." He stared at her dress as if he had never before seen an Indian girl in such attire.

She matched his gaze. "And what, might I ask, is so remarkable about a young woman crying? We do, you know? Cry, that is. I am, after all, human."

She made to move around the soldier before he could reply, but stopped in her tracks as she saw what stood beside him.

She stared, and felt a sudden odd, involuntary spasm of revulsion. "What," she managed at last, "is *that*?"

The soldier smiled at her reaction. "This is Fido," he said with a note of pride.

"How original," Jani said, staring at the creature.

Except, she told herself, it was not a *real* creature. The thing stood perhaps two feet tall at its mechanical shoulder, a dog-like beast assembled from blue-grey slabs of metal, with pistons for legs and a body pocked with orderly rivets, and all of it running with the sheen of machine oil.

The thing emanated an almost palpable sense of threat. Yet, she asked herself, how might that be if it were only a machine?

"Except it's F.I.D.O.," the soldier went on. "It's an ac... an ac—"

"An acronym," she supplied.

"Bet you don't know what it stands for, Miss."

Jani sighed. The last thing she wanted was to play guessing games with a private of the British Army.

"Let me see," she said. "Perhaps it stands for Foolish Ignorant Drooling Oaf?"

The creature regarded her with a pair of red eyes in its triangular head. The hair at the nape of her neck prickled.

The solider looked affronted. "Fido might look like a mindless hound, Miss, but let me tell you that he's one of a kind."

"He is, is he?" She glanced at the private. "Very well, then. Tell me. What does F.I.D.O. stand for?"

The soldier puffed his chest. "Feral Intelligent Diligence Operative."

She stared at him. "And what, in plain English, does that mean?"

He looked downcast. "Don't rightly know meself, Miss. That's what me commanding officer told me when he paired me up with Fido, y'see."

"And what does Fido do, if I might ask?"

The soldier smiled, on safer ground now. "He obeys my every thought, he does."

Jani's apprehension redoubled. "Your every *thought*?"

"That's right, Miss. I think a command, and hey-presto Fido leaps to it. But not only that – he's intelligent, see? He can think for hisself."

It could only be yet another device salvaged from the Vantissarian ship, a mind-reading mechanical intelligence. She wondered if there was a living, biological brain buried under all that armour plating. The idea made her shiver.

"Fido's been my dog for six months. That's how long it takes for our brains to... to attune to each other." The soldier leaned close to Jani and whispered, "Here, I'll give you a demonstration. What do you want it to do? Tell me, and I'll order it by the power of me mind alone."

She glanced at the beast. "Very well," she said. "Command it to walk around the helical elevator and come back to you."

The soldier grinned. "Easy as pie," he said, turned and stared at the creature.

Instantly Fido trotted off in the direction of the elevator, circumambulated it, and returned to its handler's side.

"So what do you think of that, Miss?"

She stared at the beast. "Impressive," she allowed – and frightening, she added to herself.

The soldier raised his hand to his forelock in a quick salute. "My pleasure, Miss, and good day to you."

He marched off, the burly mechanical dog trotting obediently alongside.

Jani remained on the observation deck for a time, watching the sere Greek terrain unfurling far below, then decided that she was hungry and would take tea and cake in one of the small tea rooms that flanked the main lounge.

She rode the down elevator back to the lounge, crossed an expanse of deep pile carpeting dotted with potted palms and aspidistra, and found a quiet tea room. She chose a booth beside a porthole and ordered Assam tea and a chocolate éclair.

London awaited her. It seemed an age since she was last in the capital, though in fact less than a fortnight had elapsed. She considered the many wonders of the city, and knew that she would look upon them with different eyes now that she was aware of the provenance of the science and technology that made London the jewel of the Empire's crown.

The monorail system that connected the boroughs of the city was not the brainchild of British boffins, she knew now, but derived from technology developed by alien minds; likewise the Illuminatory Arrays that brought daylight, and warmth, to the capital and other cities in the depths of night and mid-winter. The hover ferries that plied the Thames were not the brainchild of the British but were driven by other-worldly technology, along with the caterpillar omnibuses that carried commuters along all the main thoroughfares of the capital. Though the names of British inventors and homeland companies had been applied to these wonders and many more beside, that was no more than a ruse to delude an oblivious, patriotic populace.

She bit into her éclair, squirting cream over the back of her hand, and licked it clean.

She looked around to ensure that her breach of etiquette had not been observed, and saw three soldiers push through the swing door at the far end of the tea room. Something about the way they moved, and paused to scan the patrons, suggested that they were not here to sample the café's finest tisane.

The trio split up and approached separate tables, and it was obvious from the response of the diners that they were being asked to produce their identity papers.

Jani swallowed a mouthful of éclair, feeling sick.

She glanced over her shoulder. There was another entrance a few yards away. If she rose casually, perhaps glancing through a porthole on the way, she might essay an exit without arousing undue suspicion.

She took a sip of tea and considered the éclair, her appetite gone. The soldiers were making their slow way towards her table, chatting amiably with the diners. Jani dabbed her mouth with a napkin, rose and moved from the table. To give her exit a casual air, she paused briefly to peer through the porthole, then continued towards the swing-door. Her heart hammered fearfully and she broke out in a hot sweat.

She would make her way to the Pullman, she told herself, and remain there for the duration of the journey. As she approached the door, safety within reach, she wondered why the soldiers were suddenly checking the passengers' identity papers. She had never heard of such bureaucratic punctiliousness before; certainly on the journey out no such checks had been undertaken. With a catch of her breath she wondered if the authorities were aware that she was aboard the *Edinburgh*, and were searching for her.

She reached out and pushed open the swing door, only

for it to come up against someone coming the other way. She stepped back, exclaiming, as a soldier emerged through the entrance and touched the peak of his cap.

"'Scuse me, Miss. Very sorry to bother you, but if I could just have a quick look at your passport."

Her heart sank. Her passport, along with all her other personal possessions, she had left behind in Delhi a fortnight ago.

"Why," she temporised, "of course."

She reached to the pocket of her dress, then feigned annoyance. "Oh, bother. I *am* sorry. I must have left it in my cabin."

"No trouble at all, Miss. If you'll allow me to accompany you. Which deck is it?"

He stood aside, holding open the door, and Jani passed through. "C deck," she said, naming the deck furthest from the main lounge – giving herself, she hoped, plenty of time to evade the young man.

"Having a pleasant trip, are we?" the soldier asked as they walked side by side along the corridor towards the nearest lift.

"Very pleasant, thank you."

"Been to London before, have you, Miss?"

"I was educated in the capital," she told him, "and I am due to resume my studies at Cambridge on my return."

She wondered, as she paced the carpeted corridor, whether in bragging like this she had in fact vouchsafed too much information.

But surely, she thought with relief, if they were looking for her specifically, they would hardly have instituted a passport check on *all* the passengers?

Heartened, she arrived at the lift and paused. The

soldier pressed the call stud and they waited side by side, Jani wondering how she might possibly make her escape.

To run away would call attention to herself. She would have to play the absentminded young thing, once they arrived outside 'her' cabin.

As they stepped inside the lift and the soldier pressed the stud for C deck and the doors sighed shut, Jani asked, "Is there a specific reason for the security check, sir?"

He glanced at her, smiling. She could see that he was discommoded by the paradox she presented; a dark-skinned Indian in Western dress, yet conversing with him in a Home Counties accent.

The lift ascended at speed.

"Just a routine precaution, ever since what happened to the *Kipling*. You heard about that, of course?"

It was on her lips to say that she been aboard the very same ship when it had come crashing from the sky. Instead she said, "But I thought the *Kipling* was fired on by Russians from the ground. How might a security check now prevent another such occurrence?"

The private shrugged, frowning at the obvious logic of her question. "Don't rightly know about that, Miss. Just following orders."

The lift bobbed and the doors swished open to reveal a sumptuous corridor. The soldier gestured for her to precede him, and Jani stepped out with a heavy heart. She turned left and approached cabin 25, the same number she had occupied aboard the *Rudyard Kipling* on the journey out to India.

It would take all her skill at amateur dramatics, in the minutes that followed, to convince the soldier of her story.

They came to the cabin door just as a young couple rounded the corner, the blonde woman laughing at something her blazered beau had whispered in her ear. The couple came to a halt and stared from Jani to the soldier.

"Can we help you?" the young man asked, producing a key and approaching the door of cabin 25.

The soldier stared at Jani. "But I thought you said this was *your* cabin?"

Jani placed a hand before her mouth, thinking furiously. "How silly of me? Did I say C deck? I meant D deck. I'm so sorry."

Jani and the soldier turned, watched by the young couple. The blonde woman's laughter bubbled in the air.

The private summoned the lift and they were soon being whisked up to the next deck. "My memory," Jani said. "It must be the altitude!"

"Quite, Miss..."

The lift halted and they stepped out. Jani led the way along the corridor, her heart pounding. How much longer would she be able to carry out the dissimulation before the private became suspicious?

They halted beside the cabin door and Jani reached into her pocket. She gasped. "Oh! My word..." She turned a despairing glance upon the soldier and gasped, "You might find this hard to believe, but I seem to have misplaced my key. Now, where might I have left it?"

The soldier eyed her dubiously. "Perhaps it's in your room," he said. "One sec, and I'll contact the purser."

"Oh," Jani said in despair as the soldier touched a small, golden device lodged behind his right ear and spoke into the air. "Reg, Private Jones here. Put me through to Clive, would you?"

Jani swallowed, thinking fast. What would she do when the master key arrived and she was let into the strange room? How might she continue the deception?

In the event, she was found out before the key arrived. The door before the pair opened quickly and a middle-aged, moustachioed gentleman peered out. "Can I help you?" he asked, staring at the pair.

Private Jones looked from Jani to the man and asked stiffly, "Do you happen to know this young woman, sir?"

"What?" The man looked affronted as he eyed Jani with distaste. "Never clapped eyes on the girl in my life!"

Jani felt an iron-tight grip on her upper-arm. "I think," Private Jones whispered in her ear, "you'd better come along with me. You have some explaining to do. Very sorry, sir," he apologised over his shoulder as he frog-marched Jani back towards the lift.

"I can explain!" Jani yelped.

"You certainly can," said Jones. "To my commanding officer, Miss. In we go!"

In desperation, Jani reached out, gripped Private Jones by the lapel of his uniform and tugged. Jones, caught by surprise and off balance, pitched forward over Jani's outstretched leg and tumbled into the lift. While he attempted to scramble to his feet, cursing her, Jani turned and fled.

CHAPTER
TWO

~∾~

Jani pursued – A chase through the garage –
Cornered by the mechanical hound –
"The landing is likely to be a trifle bumpy..."

SHE CAME TO a corner and careered around it, unable to stop her headlong flight as she crashed into a serving trolley. She rolled over the rattling contraption headfirst, tumbled to the floor and picked herself up in one fluid movement. Then she was sprinting down the corridor, and when she chanced a glance over her shoulder she was momentarily heartened that the upturned trolley, cutlery and spilled desserts – not to mention a stunned waiter – had created an obstacle course for the pursuing Private Jones. He barrelled around the corner, slipped on a blancmange and fell on top of the hapless waiter. Jani saw no more. She turned another corner and jumped into an open lift.

She slammed a palm against the door controls and scanned the lighted panel. The lift descended only as far as the main lounge. She would have to alight there, cross the deck and board another lift for the garage gondola.

She willed the doors to shut before Jones caught up with her, and, ever so slowly, they did so.

The lift jerked and began its descent. She wondered if Jones would take the stairs and arrive at the main lounge before her? More likely he'd utilise his new-fangled communications device – yet another invention plundered from the alien ship? – and summon help.

Her heart leapt as the lift bobbed to a halt and the door eased open. The scene thus presented was orderly and unhurried. Men and women crossed the carpeted lounge arm in arm. A band played a selection of romantic melodies, accompanied by the chink of cutlery and the murmur of polite conversation. Jani composed herself, drew a deep breath, and stepped from the lift.

Soon, she told herself, she would be plummeting towards the garage and the sanctuary of Lady Eddington's Pullman carriage. Surely there she, Alfie and Anand would be safe. She would gladly suffer all their puppy-like devotion if it meant escaping the attention of the British authorities.

"There she is!"

The cry froze her blood, but not her progress across the lounge. She looked swiftly over her shoulder and felt sick at what met her eyes.

The soldier in charge of the mechanical hound was pointing at her – but, more alarmingly, the armour-plated, oleaginous beast was racing across the lounge towards her, scattering gentlefolk as it went.

Jani stifled a scream and rushed towards another lift. Fortune favoured her and the doors eased open – allowing a startled young man to exit – and she dived inside. She slammed a hand against the controls and sank back against the far wall. The doors came together, but slowly, and through them she watched the headlong charge of the metal monstrosity.

Just as she thought the hound would leap through the narrowing gap and be upon her, the doors banged shut and rang with the deafening impact of the metal dog's collision.

Jani whimpered, then realised that she hadn't directed the lift to take her to the garage level. She scrambled to her feet and hit the controls. The lift halted at the garage only, so her pursuers would know exactly where she was bound.

The lift stopped and the doors opened, presenting the garage, replete with rolling stock and alien apparatus. She ran out and hurried across the chamber. She heard shouts coming from behind her, ducked down beside a golden missile launcher and looked back at the way she had come. A dozen soldiers pushed through a door beside the lift and moved towards the first of the dozen Pullman carriages. As she watched, they spread out and searched each carriage in turn.

Lady Eddington's Pullman was situated in the centre of the garage. She judged that she might just reach it before the soldiers.

She ducked under the couplings between two carriages and paused, squatting and staring across the chamber to Lady Eddington's carriage. The shouts were growing louder, and in counterpoint she made out the rhythmic clank of metal feet on the decking – the mechanical hound?

Twenty yards separated her from the Pullman. She would alert Alfie and Anand, so that they all might flee, hide elsewhere, and return to the Pullman when the coast was clear.

She moved from the cover of the carriages and approached the Pullman.

A face appeared at the lace-curtained window and peered out at her – Anand! She gestured for him to come to the door, then leaped on to the metal steps. The door swung open and Jani hissed, "Go and fetch Alfie! We need to get away from here!"

"Why–?" Anand began.

"Get Alfie!" she cried.

Anand vanished. The soldiers' footfalls were moving ever closer. She wondered if the hound was with them, and how good its sense of smell might be. Indeed did it, like its flesh and blood counterpart, possess heightened olfactory sensibilities – or even abilities way beyond Jani's comprehension?

Anand appeared with Alfie. "The British are searching the garage," she said. "They found me but I manage to get away. Follow me."

She jumped from the steps, Alfie and Anand in her wake, hurried over to a pair of coaches and ducked under the couplings.

"So much for my assurance that the authorities couldn't have linked us to Smethers' death," Alfie began dolefully as he crouched beside her.

"I don't think it was anything to do with that." She hesitated. "It was my fault. They were conducting a security check and wanted to examine my passport."

"So what do we do now, Jani-ji?" Anand asked.

"I think it best to leave the garage. Then, when they have gone, perhaps we could return to the Pullman. Follow me."

She ducked under the couplings and emerged on the far side, scanning the shadowy cavern. This end of the chamber seemed free from soldiers, though their shouted commands were growing louder. It would be a mistake, she thought, to attempt to exit the garage via the lift – but beside it was a door that stood ajar. She would make for this, and hope that it might lead to safety.

"This way!" She ran, doubled up, from the cover of the coach and led the way across a series of tracks. She wondered where the dog might be, and was troubled by its silence.

She reached the door, hauled it open and pushed Alfie and Anand through before her. She was about to follow them when, from across the chamber, she heard a cry. She turned and stared. The young dog-handler appeared from behind a coach and saw her, the mind-reading hound at his side. It took off, eating up the yards with great leaps of its piston-like legs.

Jani slipped through the hatch and pulled the door shut after her. Unfortunately it did not possess a locking mechanism. She was in a long, narrow corridor, hung with hanks of electrical cable and stinking of machine oil. Alfie and Anand were dim figures in the shadows twenty yards ahead of her. She ran after them.

In her wake she heard the hound collide with the door, and was thankful that the hatch opened outwards; inwards, and the beast would have been through in a trice. As it was, she gained precious seconds while the handler commanded the dog to back off and hauled open the hatch himself. "Stop!" he yelled at her.

Up ahead, Alfie and Anand pushed through another hatch. Alfie took off to the right, Anand sprinted straight ahead. Jani caught up with them and veered left, hugging the outer wall of the sepulchral chamber, this one clearly a store room. The stench of grease and oil pinched her adenoids like smelling salts. Lumpish machinery hulked in the gloom, sending inky shadows across a sawdust-scattered floor.

She dodged between bits of machinery in various stages of repair, putting them between her and her pursuers. The deafening thrum of the multiple Hawker Siddeley engines grew louder. She wondered if the reek of machine oil might mask her scent – then wondered again if the mechanical hound had senses other than that of smell with which to track her. Would it be a mistake to take refuge in one of the many empty packing crates that were strewn across the chamber, and pray that the dog would not trace her?

She looked over her shoulder. There was no sign of the soldier and his hound, and the din of the engines drowned out the sound of her pursuers.

She moved away from the outer wall of the gondola and crossed the floor, weaving between lathes and perpendicular drills. Ahead she made out a bulkhead. She wondered if she had reached the foremost wall of the great gondola. She looked around for somewhere she might conceal herself, and at that second the dog showed itself.

It stood a matter of yards away, having rounded the propeller housing of a dismantled engine. The beast came slowly, as if taunting Jani, creeping almost on its belly like a real, live, fur and muscle hound, its red eyes devilish in the gloom.

She backed away, came up against the bulkhead with a start, and stared at the thing crouching before her. If only she had taken Alfie's suggestion and brought her light-beam with her, then she would have been able to face the dog with confidence.

Her right hand, pressed against the wall, came up

against something. An array of tools hung from pegs on the bulkhead. She grasped an ugly-looking hammer and held it before her.

"If you come any closer," she said, "I'll beat your clockwork brain to pieces!"

She wondered if the beast could read her thoughts, intuit her fear, or if its alien brain was attuned only to the mind of its owner. Speaking of whom... She looked beyond the stationary dog, but there was no sign of the young soldier in the gloom of the machine shop. Also, to her relief, she discerned no evidence of the other soldiers.

The hound crouched, staring at her intently. It had her where it wanted her, until its handler arrived.

Perhaps she should attack it now, beat it over its monstrous, wedge-shaped head. She saw movement beyond the beast, in the shadows between the arched engine nacelle and a lathe. The handler stepped forward, perhaps ten yards away.

"If I were you I'd give meself up nice and quiet, missy. I'll call off Fido, okay, if you'll come with me and answer a few questions."

At the sound of its name, as if encouraged, the dog edged forward, on its belly. Its tail whipping back and forth, it looked to Jani as if it were about to leap for her throat.

She cried out in alarm and flung the hammer at the hound. The tool flew through the air, head over shaft, missed the dog by a yard and struck the deck – bouncing up and striking the advancing handler a glancing blow on the side of his head. He gave an abbreviated cry of shock and staggered backwards, collapsing to the floor.

The dog never took its crimson eyes from Jani but,

evidently aware of the fate of its handler, opened its mechanical jaws and gave vent to a blood-curdling screech – more like the howl of an ape than the bark of a dog.

Jani glanced to her left. At intervals in the bulkhead she made out a number of small doors. The nearest one was perhaps two yards away. If she could reach it, slip through before the dog reacted...

She looked beyond the dog. Its handler lay on the deck, unconscious but still breathing. At least she hadn't dealt him a mortal blow, but she wished that her aim had been more accurate and she had accounted for his accursed beast.

She crept, little by little, along the bulkhead. The dog's glowing eyes followed her. She reached out, her left hand fumbling for the lever that would open the hatch.

The dog stirred on its haunches, its tail flicking.

Jani reached out, her hand encountering the lever. She pulled it towards her, then yanked it all the way. The hatch swung open and Jani backed inside.

But before she could shut the door behind her, the dog leapt.

The full weight of the beast struck her in the chest and she tumbled backwards into a small chamber. She rolled over, gained a sitting position and scrambled across the floor so as to be as far away from the hound as possible.

The creature failed to make good its advantage and attack her. It sat on its metal haunches just inside the door, staring at her. The only sound came from the chamber beyond the hatch. She looked around and made out a series of bulky objects lining the wall. She was evidently in some kind of storage room, but one of strange dimensions, ten feet long by three wide, with a cambered ceiling only inches above where she crouched. She looked around for a means of exit, but saw none.

The hound stared at her, unmoving. It had won, had her cornered. She felt an ache like despair rise up in her chest.

She wondered how long it might take the dog-handler to come to his senses and summon reinforcements. It was only a matter of time, now, before she was captured. And then? The British knew about the ventha-di, but not that she harboured it within her. They would question her ever so civilly, to begin with...

The dog remained staring fixedly at her, unmoving, and its very immobility filled her with panic.

She felt a surge of the revulsion she had sensed on her first encounter with the beast. It rose in a wave like a nausea of the mind, engulfing her.

She looked around in desperation for something to use as a weapon. If she could attack the hound, perhaps even disable it, and escape from here before its owner came to his senses...

She felt suddenly dizzy. The sensation was like tendrils, alien tendrils, crawling through her head, fingering her thoughts, and leaving a terrible sense of dread in their wake. A minute elapsed, or was it longer? She lost all sense of duration. What was the creature doing as it stared at her, stared with its terrible crimson, penetrating eyes, bored into her very soul?

She saw movement outside the hatch, and two faces peered in. At that second she would have welcomed any intervention that might have rescued her from the mental attention of the alien dog – even the arrival of the British. But the faces she beheld framed in the rectangular hatch were none other than those of Alfie and Anand.

"We saw you enter here, Jani-ji," Anand said. "But what is that?" he went on, staring at the dog.

She felt a surge of relief, but knew that the appearance of her friends would not forestall her inevitable capture.

"Quick!" Alfie cried. "They've seen us!"

He pushed Anand. The boy tumbled headfirst into the confines of the room, barely missing the mechanical hound. Alfie squeezed his tubby frame in after him, turned and brought down a great lever that locked the hatch.

The gloom was relieved now by slits of light slanting in from Jani's right, and by the hound's red eyes which glowed like coals.

She made out Alfie crouching at the far end of the chamber beyond the dog, fumbling for something on the wall. Anand scrambled across to her and she held him tight.

She heard a cacophony of shouted commands, accompanied by the frenzied thumping of fists on the outer hatch. "Open up! In the name of the King, give yourselves up!"

Jani said, "We're cornered. Perhaps we should do as they say?"

The alien dog sat silently on its haunches, staring at her.

"If you don't open up, then we'll fire. I'll give you ten seconds, nine..."

"Alfie," Jani said, "perhaps now is the time to give up gracefully."

Alfie Littlebody turned in the gloom and smiled across at her. "Give up? Give ourselves up to their dubious mercy, when we can give them the slip? Think again, my dear!"

"But they have us cornered! We're trapped."

Alfie laughed. "Trapped? What nonsense, girl! Now hold on tight!"

She was about to ask him what on earth he might be talking about, when Alfie hauled on a U-shaped lever on the far wall, then hit a red button with his fist.

She was deafened by a series of concussive blasts. The chamber rocked, and her stomach seemed to part company with her torso. If she didn't know better, she could have sworn that the chamber in which she huddled, along with Alfie and Anand – and not forgetting the mechanical hound – was rapidly falling.

Bright light flooded the space, and she made out a series of portholes to her right, interspersed with the objects she had noted earlier – life-jackets. She stared through the nearest porthole in utter disbelief and made out, far below, the green hills of northern Greece rising to meet them.

"A lifeboat!" Alfie yelled.

Her stomach jumped and the lifeboat jerked again as something impeded its fall. Alfie explained, "Parachutes, Jani. Even so, my friends, I'd hold on tight if I were you. The landing is likely to be a trifle bumpy."

Gripping Anand to her and laughing with panicky relief, Jani peered through the porthole. Far above them, beyond the blooming parachutes, she saw the vast and silent shape of the *Pride of Edinburgh* diminishing into the cloudy distance.

CHAPTER THREE

⚬

Das in pursuit – Extraordinary powers –
Mr Knives is healed – Landing in Greece –
"You can do what you will with the girl..."

DURGA DAS WAS on a mission to rid the world of the British.

He was ensconced in a vast armchair in the lounge of the two-man airship that carried him towards London. Through the porthole he could see the *Pride of Edinburgh*: the passenger 'ship carrying Janisha Chatterjee and her cohorts was a distant speck over the mountains of northern Greece. He smiled to himself and contemplated his glorious future.

His ire at being thwarted by the upstart Janisha Chatterjee was beginning to abate. She might have got the better of him in Nepal – and lopped off Mr Knives' hands to boot – but she would pay for her crimes when he caught up with her. More, she would give up the tithra-kuñjī she carried, after which he would obtain the third one from the Morn. And then, according to Kali, he would be able to open a portal to the heavens and allow Kali unlimited access to this world, whereupon his goddess and her minions would wipe the planet clean of the despicable British.

And he, Durga Das, would be elevated to the position of Kali's High Priest on Earth.

For all his adult life he had worked to undermine the presence of the Raj in India. He had followed in the footsteps of his father, a leading Nationalist figure and a priest himself, and on his death had taken over as the head priest of the temple in north Delhi. Das enjoyed a loyal following in Uttar Pradesh and beyond, and more importantly had powerful politicians and policemen in his pay. He had never ceased to be amazed at how a combination of religious prestige and great wealth – donated to his cause by the faithful over the years – had brought him untold power. The one thing he had been unable to buy, however, were the British.

His father had told him, "Kali came to Earth and bestowed upon my grandfather the gift of the coin, and explained its significance. It has been in our family ever since. The coin is called a tithra-kuñjī, a holy amulet that allows access between Heaven and Earth, and when the time is right Kali will step forth. Recite this mantra when the moon is as full as a pregnant belly, and, when the time is auspicious, then Kali will come forth."

For thirty years, on the occasion of every full moon, Das had chanted the holy words, hoping that one day his devotion would reap dividends. "*Anghra dah tanthara, yangra bahl, somithra tal zhell.*"

And then, one day two weeks ago, Kali had manifested herself to him and announced that he, Durga Das, was to be her servant.

"The time of change is upon us," the goddess had intoned. "The portal between the worlds will open anon. You will be called upon to leave your city and head east, into another country. You seek the second tithra-kuñjī, and after that the third. The success of my coming to your world is entirely dependent upon the success of *your* actions."

He had indeed headed east, and done his best to obtain the second tithra-kuñjī, defeated in his goal only by the resourcefulness of Janisha Chatterjee. But Kali had shown herself to be a beneficent and merciful task-mistress, allowing him another chance to obtain the second and third tithra-kuñjī.

"You will hire an airship and follow Janisha Chatterjee to London, where you will obtain from her the tithra-kuñjī she carries. Then with my assistance you will locate the Morn, Mahran. He knows the whereabouts of the third tithra-kuñjī."

Das had hurried from Annapurnabad to Delhi, and there hired the latest Rolls Royce two-man airship, operated by something called an 'automated pilot' – thus doing away with the necessity of a pilot who would have been an unwelcome presence on the journey west.

And the goddess, in her largesse, had endowed him with an extraordinary power.

Back in Delhi, Das had laid his hand on the nasty gash that bisected his belly, thanks to the light-beam wielded by the Chutney Mary, Chatterjee. He had felt a warmth radiate from his palm, and watched in awe as the bloody flesh beneath his hand became a scab, and then no more than a scar that might have been years old.

Now Durga Das closed his eyes and dozed lightly, dreaming of the power he would possess when Kali had expelled the British from his land. He would return to India, oust feeble and corrupt politicians from power, and with Kali at his side would woo the electorate and rule his country according to the precepts of Hindu tradition going back centuries.

He would be invincible.

And the only person standing between himself and ultimate power was Janisha Chatterjee.

He was awoken a little later by a sound issuing from behind a small door at the far end of the lounge. The door opened and Mr Knives, staring at the ugly stumps of his arms – one severed at the wrist, the other below the elbow – tottered out.

The young man sat on the carpet at Das's feet, cross-legged, and stared up at his master with tears in his eyes. "Baba-ji, I recall the woman, Chatterjee, and what she did to me, and I chased her and climbed the rope ladder to her airship, and she kicked out and I fell. And that is the last thing I can remember, Baba-ji!"

"You have been unconscious for more than two days," Durga Das said, "recuperating from your many injuries. When you fell from the rope ladder, you broke your collarbone."

The thin-faced street thug open his eyes wide in disbelief, at the same time rotating first his left arm, and then his right as if doubting Das's words. "But, Baba-ji, I feel no pain!"

"Of course you feel no pain, you fool. And do you feel pain from those ugly stumps, boy?"

With a woebegone expression on his face, Mr Knives stared at the butchered stumps of meat and shook his head. "No pain at all, Baba-ji!"

"And do your arms look as though they were chopped just days ago?"

"No, sir. They look... healed."

"And why do you think that is?"

The youth shook his head. "You have given me powerful drugs?" He bowed his head and brought his stumps together in a terrible travesty of a traditional *namaste*. "Thank you, Baba-ji!"

"Drugs? Do you think someone as powerful as I needs drugs to banish pain? Think again!"

The young man shook his head. "Potions of your own devising, improvements on ayurvedic med–?"

But Durga Das stopped him. "No, no, no!" A thought occurred to him, beautiful in its simplicity. Smiling, he said, "Fetch me one of your knives, Mr Knives."

The youth blinked. "Sir?" He looked around the airborne lounge. "Where might they be?"

"I rescued your precious knives from the valley in Nepal," Das said. "They are on the bureau."

He smiled to himself as the young man crossed the room and clamped one of the knives between his stumps. He carried it back to Durga Das, who took the knife and gestured the youth to sit down.

Das tested the blade. He would give the youth this: he'd kept his beloved blades razor sharp.

"Hold out your arm, Mr Knives."

The young man looked fearful. "Baba-ji?"

"Your arm, Mr Knives, and I will show you how I effected your cure."

Tremulously, Mr Knives proffered his right stump, wincing in anticipation.

Durga Das slashed the knife swiftly through the air. Blood spurted across the lounge in a beautifully geometric arc. Mr Knives howled in pain and pressed the gashed stump to his white shirt, the linen blotting the fluid in a great spreading stain.

"Now hold out the wound!"

"No!" Mr Knives howled, wide-eyed.

"I do not intend to cut you again, you fool! Quite the reverse, in fact. Now, your arm."

Uncertainly, the young man moved the lacerated stump closer to Das, blood dripping on to the carpet. Ignoring the unpleasantly warm tackiness, Das reached out and laid a palm over the pulsing slit.

He closed his eyes and concentrated, as Kali had instructed him to do. He felt a warmth course through his body, spread down his arm and pass through his right hand.

Mr Knives gasped.

Das said, "Do you feel anything?"

"But Baba-ji! Sir, the pain – the pain is no more!"

Das smiled in satisfaction. He raised his hand, and saw that the wound had ceased bleeding. He applied his palm once more to the gash, then closed his eyes and remained like this for five minutes.

When he next examined his handiwork, the wound was scabbing over, and Mr Knives was shaking his head in wonder. "But Baba-ji!"

"Blessed are those who work with the goddess Kali, who has rewarded me for that good work with the power of healing!"

Mr Knives cried out and, from his cross-legged position, scrambled on to his knees and salaamed before Durga Das.

The priest laid a hand upon the boy's head. "Now, on the table over there."

"Sir?"

"A present."

"A present? A present for me, Baba-ji?"

"I see no one else aboard the ship, do you? Now quickly."

Mr Knives hurried across the lounge and picked up the gift from the table-top. He carried the implements over to Das. "But what are they, Baba-ji?"

"What do they look like?"

"Knives, but knives attached to a belt."

"I had these made before we set off, so that you might regain some of your usefulness. Because, without hands, you must admit that your effectiveness as my... assistant... is somewhat impaired. Or should I say, 'without *knives*'?"

Das took the first belt, instructed Mr Knives to hold out his right arm, and proceeded to fasten the belt around the stump. Now two long-bladed, lethal-looking silver knives protruded from the cuffs of Mr Knives' white shirt. Das affixed the second belt to the youth's left stump.

"There, what do you think?"

Mr Knives climbed to his feet, and Das watched like an indulgent parent as the young man danced around the lounge, slashing at an imaginary opponent. The blades, two on each belt, flashed in the light slanting in through the portholes.

The young man grinned. "Baba-ji, I feel whole again!" He raised an arm, admiring the weapons, then looked at Das. "But where are we going, Baba-ji?"

"Would you believe, Mr Knives, that we are bound for London?"

"London?" Mr Knives' eyes grew round. "*London?*"

"On the trail of the Chutney Mary, Mr Knives. And this time, when we apprehend her, we shall not be as lenient as last time."

"Baba-ji?"

"I recall telling you, a week ago, that we would spare the girl when we finally got what we wanted. Well, in light of her actions in Nepal, I have revised my plan of action. Now, when we have obtained the tithra-kuñjī, I will allow you to kill Janisha Chatterjee."

Mr Knives' eyes positively glowed as he considered the notion.

Durga Das waved. "Now, back to your room, Mr Knives, and leave me to my meditations."

The youth backed from the lounge, bowing all the way.

Durga Das was dozing, a little later, when he was stirred by a blue light. He sat up quickly, coming to himself after dreams of naked nautch girls, and stared at the light as a face materialised in the air before him.

"Kali!" He pressed his palms together and fell to his knees.

The blue-faced goddess looked down at the priest. "There have been developments, Das. The Chatterjee girl is no longer aboard the airship."

Das shook his head, attempting to assimilate the impossibility of this statement. "What?"

"Get yourself into the control cabin."

The blue light moved off like a comet, trailing a blur behind itself, and passed through the hatch to the smaller room. Das squeezed himself through after his goddess.

"Observe."

Das stared through the viewscreen. The *Pride of Edinburgh* was a tiny speck in the distance.

"A lifeboat jettisoned from the airship one hour ago," Kali explained. "It carries Chatterjee and her cohorts. You will circle the area until you locate it, then apprehend her upon my instructions."

"And obtain the tithra-kuñjī?"

"And obtain the tithra-kuñjī," Kali said. "After which we will proceed to London, where I will direct you to the Morn."

"And the girl? I had planned to dispense with her once we have the tithra-kuñjī."

The lapis lazuli visage regarded him without a flicker of human emotion. "You can do what you will with the girl," said Kali, "once we have the tithra-kuñjī in our possession."

The goddess faded from sight, and Durga Das bowed.

He turned to the controls and instructed the automated pilot to bring the airship down over the foothills.

CHAPTER
FOUR

∽

On foot to the sea –
A following airship – Das and Knives, again –
Anand faces death –
"To think that soon we will be in England...!"

THE LIFEBOAT HIT the ground with a bone-jarring crash
and slid down the hillside like a toboggan. Jani gripped a
handle on the wall with one hand and held on to Anand
with the other. Through the porthole she watched trees
and shrubbery pass in a verdant blur, deafened by the
din of metal scraping across rock. Alfie Littlebody sat at
the far end of the vessel, bracing himself in the entrance,
nose to nose with the mechanical dog.

Then the rush of greenery outside came to a halt along
with the screech of metal. The lifeboat was suddenly
very still and a profound silence settled, which Jani was
loath to break. The dazzling sunlight dimmed as a fog
enveloped the craft – no, not a fog, Jani realised as she
peered through the porthole, but the parachutes settling
over the lifeboat like a shroud.

Anand was hugging her, his tousled head pressed to
her breast. She eased him from her, smiling at him in the
half-light. At the bottom end of the vessel, Alfie pulled

himself into a sitting position and regarded the dog, which was sitting on its haunches, absolutely motionless.

"Well," he said, "We seemed to have survived that little adventure."

Jani whispered, "The dog...?"

"Strange looking beast," Alfie opined. "It seems to have run out of power."

"But look at its eyes!" Anand pointed out. "They are still glowing."

"It is obviously Vantissarian technology," Jani said. "Moreover, it can read thoughts."

Alfie stared at her. "A mind-reading dog?"

Jani explained what its handler had told her, and Alfie said, "Well, I suggest we get out of here and lock it inside before it comes to life again."

He reached for the handle on the hatch and pulled it towards him. The door cracked, admitting sunlight and the rich scent of crushed shrubbery. He swung the door open. "After you."

She slithered down the inclined deck of the lifeboat and eased herself past the immobile hound with care. Alfie took her hand and she climbed out on to Greek soil and ducked out from under the veiling parachute. The hound made no move to follow. She watched Anand jump out and Alfie close the hatch, imprisoning the alien dog, and felt a surge of relief.

The lifeboat had fetched up against an outcropping of rock on a gently sloping hillside. The land rose in a series of foothills towards a range of snowy mountain peaks; downhill, the terrain eased into an expanse of pastures, sun-parched farmland dotted with tiny stone-built villages. From this elevation, Jani made out stippled fields of olive groves.

To the west she made out the tiny shape of the *Pride of Edinburgh*. It showed no sign of slowing down or turning. "Do you think they'll come after us?" she asked Alfie.

He stood on a rock, shielding his eyes with one hand, and gazed at the retreating airship. "They might have smaller craft which they could send after us."

Anand gazed into the sky. "I can't see any smaller vessels," he reported.

Alfie gestured towards the parachute-shrouded lifeboat. "From the air this would stand out like the proverbial sore thumb," he said. "I think it would be wise to camouflage the lifeboat as best we can."

They pulled off the two multi-coloured parachutes, bundled them beneath a bush, then set to work gathering branches and foliage and piling them across the lifeboat.

"That should do the trick," Alfie said when the job was done, dusting his hands. "Of course, if the vessel has some kind of device capable of being tracked..."

"Perhaps," Jani said, "we should make haste and leave the area."

Her initial exultation at having evaded the clutches of the British was abating now, to be replaced with the cold, hard facts of their situation. They were stranded in a foreign land, hundreds of miles from their destination, with no food, precious little money – and what good would a handful of rupees be in Greece, anyway? – and no means of making headway north-west, save travelling on foot.

"What do we do now?" she asked, trying to keep a note of desperation from her enquiry.

Anand had joined Alfie on the high rock, and side by side they looked like a pair of intrepid explorers scanning the lie of the land. Her heart swelled; and to think that mere hours ago she had been bemoaning their attention.

"I must admit," she went on, "that my knowledge of Greece and its political affiliations is scant. Are we likely to be welcomed?"

Alfie stared down at her, and his expression clouded. Jani guessed the reason for his indecision: how could he tell her that a British officer might be treated with deference here, but that a dusky pair of Indians would more likely be disparaged as gypsies?

"The Greeks are on our side," Alfie said. "In fact, we have garrisons at Athens and Thessalonica. The Russians have great influence in the Slavic states north of here, and the Greek government is understandably fearful of communist unrest on its soil. This is a double-edged sword. While the Greeks themselves might be amenable to my uniform, it does mean that the British have quite a presence here – they are likely to despatch a search party for us forthwith, once the *Edinburgh* has alerted them as to the situation."

"And how far away might be the nearest British outpost?"

Alfie scanned the horizon. "I know for certain they have a station at Ioannina, which I'd guess is a hundred miles or so east of here."

"So if they did send out an airship?"

"Two hours or so could see them overhead."

Pointing to the nearest tiny village, Anand said, "Perhaps we should seek help there? Perhaps we could hire a rickshaw–"

Jani smiled. "We are not in India now, Anand. They don't have rickshaws here. A taxi, perhaps – but then they are unlikely to accept rupees."

Alfie pulled out a wallet, riffled through its contents, and frowned. "I have two five pound notes," he said glumly, "which is hardly likely to buy our way across Europe." He scanned the terrain and pointed to the west, where Jani made out a line of blue on the far horizon.

"I think we should make for the coast," Alfie said.

"And then?" she asked.

"Perhaps we might hire a boat to take us to the south of France."

They set off down the hillside, favouring the shade of trees. The heat of the midday sun was punishing. "It's a great pity that I didn't foresee our sudden flight," she laughed at one point. "Or I would have packed sandwiches and water."

"Oh, Jani," Anand said, "I could eat a masala dosa now!"

"I'm sure we'll be able to find something to eat along the way," Alfie said.

They were brought up short by a noise from further up the hillside – a peculiar, high screeching sound. "The lifeboat!" Alfie cried, alarmed. "It's become dislodged."

He took Jani's arm and hurried her at right angles across the slope, but Jani withdrew her arm and silenced him. "Shh! Listen. It's not the lifeboat."

She recognised the sound, having heard it once before aboard the *Edinburgh*: a whining screech, the product of a mechanical throat.

"What is it?" Anand said, his eyes wide.

The screeching was joined by another sound, the scraping of metal on metal.

"I think it's..."

The noise stopped suddenly. All three looked up the slope. They heard a rattle of scree, the clanking sound of metal feet on rock – and through the trees appeared the oiled, gunmetal-grey carapace of the mechanical hound.

Jani backed away. Alfie fumbled in his pocket and withdrew a cylinder – his Vantissarian light-beam. He turned its base and a rod of brilliant light sprang forth.

He stepped forward, brandishing the weapon – but it was clear that the hound did not intend to attack. It approached to with a couple of yards of the trio, settled on its haunches and stared up at Jani.

Alfie lowered the light-beam and, as the hound remained seated, he deactivated the weapon. The light disappeared and Alfie returned the device to his pocket.

"It appears," Jani said, staring at the motionless dog, "that it's at a loss without its handler."

"The danger is," Alfie said, "if it's transmitting its whereabouts as–"

He stopped as the dog moved. Jani started, fearing an attack – but the hound sprang to its feet, turned, and bolted away from them across the hillside. Within seconds it had disappeared from sight beyond the olive trees.

"Very strange," Alfie said to himself.

They continued down the incline and paused to stare down the slope to a shaded lane snaking along the valley bottom.

Jani glanced up into the cloudless sky. The sun was merciless, the air dry; it reminded Jani of high summer in Delhi. She looked west, but there was no sign of the *Edinburgh*. She considered Lady Eddington, and knew that the dowager would worry herself senseless at their mysterious disappearance.

She would reach London, Jani thought with resolve, assure Lady Eddington that she was well, and continue her mission to contact the Morn. And after that? Well, she should not get ahead of herself; first there was the small matter of effecting transport from this country.

They descended to the lane and walked west, their progress shaded by a line of poplars.

"I have never seen the sea," Anand said. "Aboard the *Edinburgh*, I tried to see the Indian ocean as we passed over the coast, but it was dark and I saw nothing. Have you ever seen the sea, Jani-ji?"

She nodded. "I went to Brighton one day with Sebastian. A day trip." She saw Anand look away at the sound of the Englishman's name. "I walked along the pier – that's a long metal and timber construction built out over the sea..." She trailed off, recalling the meal they'd shared that evening at the Grand Hotel.

To think... Now Sebastian would be on summer break from Cambridge, and knowing him his thoughts would be on anything but his studies. She wondered whether he was thinking of her.

She sighed and stared at the distant, snow-capped mountains.

Anand said, beaming at her, "It is a great pity that we don't have Mel now."

Jani laughed as she recalled the mechanical elephant; those days in northern India, fleeing the British and the Russians alike, seemed so far away in time and space.

Anand pulled a glum face. "Jani-ji?"

"What is it?"

"The letter I was writing to Mr Clockwork aboard the *Edinburgh*. I never finished it. I wanted to tell him where I left Mel and Max, and apologise for running away as I did! Mr Clockwork will hate me."

Jani reached out and squeezed his hand. "We will

send a telegram to Mr Clockwork when we reach London," she said. "We'll explain the situation and Mr Clockwork will be proud of you. Just as I am, Anand-ji," she added.

This had the effect of bringing an instant, foolish grin to the boy's face.

On either side of the lane, the land rose gently to distant mountains. Olive groves covered the fields to the left, and to the right dense forest. For a mile, a silver twinkling stream paralleled the track.

A little later Anand said, "I'm hot and hungry, Jani-ji!"

She smiled. "We all are, Anand. I'm sure we'll find somewhere soon where we can rest and buy food."

The dumpy little Englishman, striding ahead before them, turned and said, "We should find somewhere to sleep when the sun goes down, and resume our trek at dawn. We should reach the coast by sunset tomorrow. We'll find a room for the night, and while you sleep I'll attempt to find a willing boat owner."

"And I'll come with you, Mr Alfie!" Anand offered.

Alfie smiled. "We'll see."

Jani scanned the skies. "At least there's no sign of British airships."

"They'd have little chance of finding us now," Alfie opined, "even if they did locate the lifeboat. And in a day or so, with luck, we'll be out on the high seas."

She made out a quick flash of dark grey between foliage at the side of the track. She wondered if it were a predatory animal, biding its time before it attacked.

"Alfie," she said, "forgive my ignorance, but are you likely to find... dangerous animals in Greece?"

He turned and stared at her. "What an odd question. Why do you ask?"

"I was just wondering."

He shrugged. "Dangerous? Well, this isn't Africa. You won't find man-eating lions and tigers here. Maybe the odd wolf; I don't know." He smiled his reassurance at her. "But I wouldn't worry if I were you. We're perfectly safe here." He patted his pants' pocket. "I have my light-beam, after all."

She nodded, but nevertheless kept an eye on the undergrowth as they walked.

An hour elapsed and she saw nothing more, and her nervousness abated. She told herself that she had nothing to fear from a shy but curious animal; perhaps, in the wake of all that had happened aboard the *Edinburgh*, she was being over-cautious.

Ahead, Alfie paused, his head cocked to one side. "Do you hear that?"

Alarmed, she listened intently. A low drone was coming and going in waves.

She peered into the cloudless sky, searching for the source of the sound. The drone grew louder, a definite engine noise now that could be neither denied nor ignored.

"There!" Anand called out, pointing. High in the east, a mere fly-speck against the fleeceless azure heavens, Jani made out what could only be an airship.

As they watched, the 'ship lost altitude as it came over the foothills. Alfie said, "A Rolls, by the sound of the engine. Don't worry, they're common in Europe. You even have a few in India."

"But might it be the British, searching for us?"

Alfie shook his head, whether to reassure Jani or because he was genuinely unconcerned, she could not tell. "I doubt it. The RAF prefer Sopwiths and de Havillands.

And anyway we're probably too far away for them to make us out."

She nodded, far from reassured.

She watched the airship as it tracked across the bright blue sky, seemingly following them. She thought it might be wise to conceal themselves beneath the boughs of a tree, at least until the airship had passed by, and suggested this to Alfie.

He hesitated, clearly thinking her alarmist, but conceded anyway. "Very well," he said, pointing along the lane.

Ahead, beside the stream, a vast oak tree spread its branches halfway across the lane. They hurried into its shade and looked up.

The airship had lost altitude, following the line of the valley. It passed overhead, a bulbous two-man affair. Jani was confident that, even if its pilot was searching for them, they would no longer be visible beneath the tree.

She squinted up at the 'ship's envelope, grasped Alfie's arm and hissed, "But look! Isn't that the Indian flag?"

She pointed to the tri-colour painted on the nose of the envelope, the tangerine, white and green rectangle tiny but recognisable even at this distance.

"You're right," he said, frowning. "But..."

"It can't be coincidence!" she cried. "What is the likelihood of an Indian airship flying over northern Greece, if it were not searching for us?"

He shook his head. "Impossible," he said, more to himself. "No one from India could possibly know where we are."

"I think Mr Alfie is right," Anand said.

She wanted to believe that the presence of the Indian airship was indeed no more than a coincidence, but she feared that the ill-fortune that had dogged her steps across northern India was stalking her still.

The airship beat its way west, twin engines thrumming. Jani held her breath, hardly daring to hope that the 'ship would continue on its way. As the minutes elapsed, however, the vessel did just that. The thrumming diminished and the 'ship dwindled to a point, then passed from view beyond a line of distant trees.

A quiet reigned, broken only by the rasp of cicadas.

Jani smiled at Alfie, who said, "There, what did I tell you?"

"We should wait here a while," she said, "until we're absolutely sure." She looked at the silver stream chuckling over rocks and boulders. "I think I'll take the opportunity to cool down."

"You do that. I'll keep watch."

Anand settled himself in the oak's gnarled root system protruding above ground. "I'm so tired I could sleep for a week."

Jani moved to the water's edge and peered into the swirling shallows. She removed her shoes, then sat on a rock and unrolled her stockings, stuffing the balls into the pocket of her dress.

She dipped a toe in the water and gasped; straight from the snow-capped mountains, it was icy cold. She placed both feet in the stream and stood up, wading through the braided silver water, small pebbles and mud oozing between her toes. She lifted her dress and waded further out.

A large boulder protruded from the stream by the far bank, and she made her way across to it and sat down, pulling her feet from the water and placing them on the stone's sun-warmed flank.

She wondered how long it might be before they arrived in England. Had things gone to plan, they would have docked in London tomorrow evening. Now it would be days at least, and probably weeks, before they reached the capital. She pressed a hand to her belly, recalling her audience with the alien entity in the Vantissarian ship. Lodged within her was the ventha-di, containing one of the three venthas, the discs which – when all three were placed within the ventha-di – would allow passage from this world to the next.

What had the alien entity told her aboard the Vantissarian ship, that reality was a great book? "*Imagine that everything you know of your world is in fact but a page of this vast book, separated from the next page, or reality, by nothing more than a complex weft and weave of sub-atomic particles or strings – a curtain, if you like.*"

And the fact that the British – and others – would stop at nothing to get their hands on the ventha-di, lent veracity to the fantastical story.

She had the first ventha, and Mahran – imprisoned in London – possessed the second; the plan was to facilitate his rescue (quite how she would not dwell on now), and with him attempt to locate the third, and so enable a portal between the worlds to be opened. And then? Well, Mahran would know how the Zhell might be defeated, she hoped.

She looked across the river at the meadow which sloped towards the foothills. The grass was long, and laced with a hundred colourful wildflowers. She stood, strode through the water and climbed out. She let her dress fall about her wet legs and walked through the grass, putting all thoughts of the immediate future from her mind.

She happened, then, to glance to her left, down the valley, and stopped in her tracks. What she saw there turned her stomach.

Perhaps a mile along the valley, swaying gently in the breeze above a line of trees, was the Indian airship.

She turned back to the river, panic seizing her. There could be no doubting now that the airship, or rather whoever piloted it, was here in search of herself, Alfie and Anand.

She was starting down the slope towards the river when she heard the first gunshot. Alfie, a tiny figure far below, ducked behind the trunk of the oak and drew his light-beam.

She scanned the track, or the little of it she could make out behind the line of trees, her heart hammering. A second shot detonated; Alfie ducked and the tree trunk splintered a foot above his head.

Anand had leapt from his impromptu bed amid the tree's roots. In fright or confusion, he sprinted away from the tree, across the track and into the cover of the shrubbery on the far side of the lane. Jani saw someone dash along the track in pursuit of the boy – the figure too far away for her to make out with any clarity. But she was convinced, as she stared down impotently from her vantage point, that the man had been an Indian.

Alfie turned and looked across the river, seeing Jani and waving for her to get down. She obeyed, ducking into the long grass and peering out. Another bullet split the trunk of the oak. Jani judged that the shot had come from further along the lane. Which meant that there were at least two attackers: the individual who had followed Anand, and the gunman.

A hundred yards along the lane, to the west, she made

out a flicker of lapis lazuli through the trees, a shimmering glow she recognised from somewhere but was unable to place. It might have been the silver-blue reflection of the sun in a mirror – it coruscated with the same dazzling intensity – but she thought not. She had seen the brilliant blue light somewhere before, and recently... and then she suddenly knew where. Her stomach flipped sickeningly.

"No!"

Alfie looked up at the meadow and, with the tree trunk between himself and the gunman, decided that he could make good his retreat. He darted, his dumpy little figure doubled up, splashed across the stream and attained the protective custody of the meadow's waist-high grass, diving into it and disappearing from sight.

Jani watched as a swathe of grass was displaced by his progress towards her; she felt relief but at the same time anxious for Anand's safety.

"Jani! Get down!"

She fell on her side and Alfie parted a stand of grass, his moon face, beet-red with exertion, staring out at her.

"You forgot these," he said, passing her shoes through the grass.

She took them and slipped them on, then grasped his arm. "It's the priest, Durga Das!" she said.

Alfie nodded. "I wouldn't have believed it possible, if I hadn't seen him with my own eyes."

She recounted Anand's dash across the lane into the undergrowth, pursued by someone who could only be Mr Knives. "But how could they have followed us so far around the world?"

Alfie shook his head. "It's hard to credit..."

"And Mr Knives!" she said. "I thought I'd killed him." Fighting for her life, back in Nepal, she had cut off his right hand and half of his left arm. She recalled the monstrous devil's head framed in the blue light, exhorting Mr Knives to kill her. But how had Mr Knives possibly survived the double amputation?

She increased her grip on Alfie's arm, making him wince. "What do we do? Knives went after Anand!"

"If only I had my revolver! This..." He held up the shaft of the deactivated light-beam, "is worse than useless against someone armed with a pistol."

"Alfie, we must do something to save Anand."

Alfie closed his eyes, funk clearly doing battle with his sense of duty. "Perhaps he managed to evade Knives?"

"But we don't know that!" she wailed. "I owe it to Anand. If it were not for me, getting us into this mess..." She held out a hand. "Give me the light-beam."

"What?"

"The light-beam. I'm going down there. If I can reach the far side of the track without being seen..."

"Madness! The priest will pick you off as soon as he sees you."

Jani stared at the quaking Lieutenant. "Then what do you suggest?"

He chewed his bottom lip, torn by indecision. "I don't know. I really don't. Perhaps... perhaps Anand will evade Knives and make his way..."

"To where? He doesn't know where we are."

Alfie shook his head. "Good point. But if you're going down there, I won't let you go alone. I'm coming with you."

Jani smiled, her heart leaping. She could have kissed the pusillanimous Englishman.

"Very well," she said, readying herself to raise her ahead above the grass and scan the lie of the land.

In the event, she was spared endangering herself in pursuit of Anand when a voice cut through the afternoon calm.

"We know you can hear us!" The sing-song Indian voice was stentorian, wheedling and threatening at the same time: Durga Das.

She peered cautiously through the grass and made out, on the lane beyond the oak, the vast saffron-robed belly of the Hindu priest, his greasy grey beard and over-fed face. At his shoulder, hovering in mid-air, was the blue light coruscating around the hideous devil's face.

"Janisha Chatterjee! I know you can hear me. We have some unfinished business to conduct. Now, listen carefully to me." He paused, obviously relishing what he had to say next, and then called out, "We have your little friend, Anand Doshi."

He fell silent, the better for Jani to appreciate the awful fact of his statement. She closed her eyes, a sob filling her throat.

Das went on, "But we are not unreasonable people, Janisha Chatterjee. We have Anand Doshi, and you have *something* I wish to possess. Thus, the makings of a deal. We can achieve, through rational and sensible negotiation, an outcome mutually beneficial to both of us."

Jani stared at Alfie. "I don't trust him!"

Das's baritone boomed out again. "If you don't believe me, Janisha Chatterjee..."

She looked up, over the fringe of grass, and stared down the incline towards the priest on the far side of the river. He gestured, signalling to someone, and as Jani stared, horrified, Mr Knives carried a kicking and struggling Anand from the cover of the tree and stood beside Durga Das.

In the place of hands, she saw, Mr Knives now wore on each arm a leather cuff from which projected a pair of shining, silver blades.

Knives dumped the boy at the feet of Durga Das, who proceeded to gag Anand and bind his wrists behind his back. To his credit, Anand struggled and kicked out, earning a blow to the head for his pain. Quelled, he sagged and the priest completed binding his ankles.

Durga Das beamed down at his handiwork, then called out, "We will return to the airship now, Janisha Chatterjee, and allow you to dwell upon my proposition. But I warn you, time is of the essence. Our mercy, let's say, has its duration, and if you delay too long..."

He let his threat hang in the air, then bundled Anand over his shoulder and moved off down the track. Soon they were lost to sight behind a line of trees.

Jani said in a small voice, "But they wouldn't kill Anand, would they? They want what I have, don't they? The ventha-di. They wouldn't kill Anand!"

Alfie took her hand and avoided her gaze. "Come. We'll take the high ground, climb the incline so we can look down on the airship. Then..."

"Yes?" she said, tearful with hope.

He squeezed her hand. "Then we'll do our best to rescue the lad."

He gestured her to follow him, and then set off through the tall grass.

As she went, Jani recalled watching the boy striding along the lane at her side, his face childlike and innocent, his mop of hair as unruly as a storm cloud. He had been so full of wonder at their adventure... and she could only imagine his terror now.

They emerged from the long grass of the meadow and

came to the margin of the forest. Alfie ran doubled up into the shadow of the trees. Jani followed.

Alfie pointed west and they set off, climbing the sloping, forested incline. They trod carefully, but even so twigs and dry undergrowth snapped and rustled underfoot. Jani hoped the sound wouldn't travel far.

When they had been climbing for around five minutes, Alfie paused and turned to her, a finger to his lips. They came together and he whispered, "We're probably halfway there. I estimate the airship was about a mile from the meadow."

"But what do we do when we reach...?"

"Assess the situation," he said. "Work out where they are holding Anand and where Das and Knives are positioned. Remember, there are two of them and two of us. We have this," he held out the deactivated light-beam, "and the element of surprise. Have confidence, Jani. We'll rescue Anand."

"I hope you're right." She gripped his arm before he could set off again. "One thing. How did Durga Das know where we were?"

Alfie shook his head. "I honestly can't imagine."

She bit her lip, looking the dumpy Lieutenant in the eye. "I wonder..."

"Jani?"

"The blue light. Did you see it, and the face within the light?"

He nodded. "What about it?"

"When I confronted Knives in the clearing back in Nepal, the devilish face within the light seemed to be... I don't know... exhorting Knives to action, *instructing* him. I could hear it speaking, but not well enough to make out the words."

"And?"

"And I wondered whether this creature might somehow have tracked us from India."

They set off again, Jani dodging through the close-packed trees in the Lieutenant's wake.

The heat of the afternoon seemed to intensify. Jani pulled at the neckline of her dress and blew downwards to cool her chest. Cicadas thrummed deafeningly and the scent of pine resin filled the air; she recalled travelling through the jungle of northern India, what seemed an age ago, accompanied by birdsong, exotic blooms and scents altogether different from those around her now. She thought of Epping Forest, and her walks there arm in arm with Sebastian.

They slowed, and Alfie pointed. Through the treetops, far down the slope, she made out the orange, green and white flag on the nose of the Indian airship. She judged it to be perhaps a hundred yards away, moored above the track that wound along the valley bottom. The bulbous balloon swayed from side to side in the slight wind.

Alfie gestured along the incline and crept forward. Heart thumping, Jani followed him.

Within a minute they were level with the airship. Alfie gestured that they should move, circumspectly, down the slope. He led the way. Through the treetops Jani could see the airship, swaying in the breeze.

They came to a tangle of shrubbery and Alfie dropped into a crouch and edged forward, Jani at his side. He parted a fan of leaves and peered through.

Jani gasped at what she saw.

"But what are they doing?" she whispered.

Alfie shook his head as he stared down the hillside.

The airship hung twenty yards above the ground. Guy ropes, attached to thick tree trunks, secured the vessel fore and aft. In the inky shadow of the craft, Durga Das was tying a length of rope to the rope already securing Anand's ankles.

The boy sat on the ground, unmoving, his head bowed. Something tightened in Jani's chest and it was all she could do to stop herself from sobbing.

Mr Knives stood to attention beside the priest, keeping watch. Jani searched the air for the devil's face within the blue light, but it was nowhere to be seen.

When the priest had secured the rope to Anand's shackles, he tied the other end of it to a nearby tree trunk, thus further ensuring the boy's imprisonment; that, at any rate, was Jani's assumption: Durga Das would now turn his attention to negotiating with her.

However, the priest picked up another length of rope and proceeded to fasten it to the rope binding Anand's wrists.

"What is he doing?" she whispered.

Durga Das walked away from Anand, holding the rope attached to the boy's wrists. She was at a loss to work out what the fat priest intended – and even when he approached the rope ladder dangling from the hatch of the airship's gondola, Jani was unable to guess his motives.

Alfie, a second or two ahead of her, swore under his breath.

Durga Das bound the rope to the bottom rung of the rope ladder and Jani felt cold fear rise through her chest. "No!"

The priest spoke to his henchman, and Mr Knives turned and carefully – hampered by the small matter of having no hands – climbed the rope ladder and entered the airship.

Jani recalled Das's claim that 'we are not unreasonable people.' She wanted to rush from her hiding place, career down the hillside and confront the evil priest. Which was perhaps exactly what Durga Das desired.

The priest took something from the folds of his robe. Jani made out a silver revolver.

Durga Das looked around him, searching the undergrowth for any sign of Jani and Alfie. He raised his head as if addressing a crowd. "Janisha Chatterjee," he called out, "the time has come for us to negotiate. You have five minutes in which to show yourself, to emerge and come down here so that we might talk. But be warned!" He paused. "If you should attempt any trickery, if your tame British officer should get into his head the notion that by shooting me he might effect the boy's rescue, think again. I have instructed Mr Knives to power up the engines and lift off if either of you resort to duplicity." He paused again, smiling. "And also, Janisha, he will take off if you fail to show yourself in the next five minutes. So, for the sake of your little friend, I would advise that you emerge from your hiding place and come down here this minute."

Anand looked up. Even seated, bound hand and foot, he managed to strike a pose of heroic – if futile – defiance. He said something to Durga Das, and Jani could well imagine the choice words he unleashed upon the fat priest.

For his part Das chose to ignore him, and moved away from the shackled boy. He stared up the hillside; he appeared to be looking directly at where Jani and Alfie were crouching.

The priest consulted a big wristwatch on his hairy left arm and announced. "Four minutes, Janisha Chatterjee. You have just four minutes to present yourself before me. Otherwise your little friend will be torn limb from limb."

Alfie murmured, "An idle threat, Jani. Anand, as it stands, is the priest's only bargaining chip. He wouldn't be so foolish as to harm the boy."

Jani glanced at Alfie, wondering whether he were saying this merely to comfort her. "I hope so." She shook her head. "But what should we do?"

Alfie licked his lips, lost in thought. "Very well. The only option we have is, for the moment, to go along with what Das says. Go down there and keep the priest talking."

"While you...?"

He hesitated. "While I approach from the blindside of Das. Our first priority is to disarm Das and then cut the ropes that bind Anand before Knives can power up the ship and gain altitude. With the light-beam, that should be achievable." He licked his lips nervously. "It all depends on whether I can approach Das without being seen – either by Das himself or by Knives. Fortunately, it appears that the control room of the gondola is not in the direct line of sight of Das. And even if it were, it would take a good minute for Knives to power up the engines."

"And Knives will be unable to fire at you, without hands," she pointed out.

"What he could do, if he sighted me, would be to call out and alert the priest. Therefore I must emerge from *under* the airship, and still remain on the blindside of Das."

"Can you do it?"

"If you keep Das talking. When you see me on the far side of the airship, then do all you can to move Das so that he faces you, with his back directly to me."

"The difficulty will be prevaricating long enough so as to give you time." She hesitated. "Of course, Das might be lying." The thought sent a spear of dread through her chest.

Alfie glanced at her. "Meaning?"

"He knows that what he wants from me is in here." She indicated her stomach. "I don't know quite how he knows, though I suspect his informant is the creature in the blue light. Not that that matters." She drew a shaky breath. "There is always the possibility, Alfie, that as soon as I show myself, he might shoot me dead in order to get what he wants."

Alfie considered her words. "But he doesn't know," he said, "that I am not carrying my revolver. As far as he is concerned, I cannot shoot him now for fear of risking Anand's life. But if he were to shoot you, then surely he would fear my response, fear that in my rage I'd fire upon him."

She considered the possibilities. "You're right." She took a breath. "But, at some point, as the ventha-di is in here – then he will be planning to open me up."

Alfie reached out and gripped her hand. "Don't even think of that, Jani. I swear I'll never let it happen."

She jumped as Durga Das boomed out, "One minute, Janisha Chatterjee. One minute! Now, for the sake of your little friend here, do the right thing and show yourself."

Alfie gestured for her to wait, then backed from the concealing bush and hurried up the slope.

"Janisha Chatterjee!" the priest called. "Thirty seconds..."

Jani counted to twenty and then, her heart loud in her chest, and feeling a little dizzy, she climbed to her feet and moved slowly down the hillside. Seeing her, Durga Das raised his arms as if greeting a long-lost daughter, a sickening smile spreading like grease across his features.

"So, Janisha," he called out, "we meet again. Come, join me, and we shall talk."

Anand looked up, his face on seeing Jani exhibiting at first joy, quickly followed by fear. "Don't trust him, Jani! The fat priest is evil!"

Das kicked the boy with a sandaled foot. Anand rolled in the dust, restrained by the double binds of the ropes.

Jani concentrated on placing one foot in front of the other as she moved through the grass. She stared at Anand, smiling for his benefit, and raised the hem of the dress as she came to the river and stepped into the cold water.

She waded across the river and climbed the far bank, passing the tree to which Anand was tied and pausing five yards from the boy and Durga Das in the shadow of the airship.

She smiled at Anand, and he returned the expression, a tight grimace that said a lot: that he was bearing up, that he was relieved to see her, that he was fearful for her safety, and, she thought, that he was sorry he had been captured in the first place and had placed them all in this situation.

She squared up to the priest and said, "I will agree to give you what you want only if first you release Anand."

Sweat beaded the priest's great hooked nose. His smile widened, mocking her. "I have fallen for your duplicity once before, Janisha Chatterjee. You are as wily as your traitorous father." He looked around, his beady grey eyes scanning the incline above the river. "Where is the Lieutenant?"

She replied without thinking, "Still aboard the *Edinburgh*. We jettisoned without him."

He laughed. "Wily, traitorous, *and* a liar!" he bellowed. "I know he was with you. Now, if you don't tell Lieutenant Littlebody to show himself, then I shall have no option but to instruct my accomplice to elevate the airship, and the results of that action might, of course, be a little messy. Do it!"

Jani shook her head. "I don't know where Alfie is, honestly!"

"Very well. Mr Knives!" he yelled.

Jani's heart leaped when she heard the airship's engines crescendo from a low drone to a throaty whine. She looked up. The airship pulled on its guy ropes, and the rope attaching Anand to the dangling ladder tightened. Anand was dragged along the ground for a yard or two, yelping in fright.

"Enough, Mr Knives, for now!"

The roar of the engines diminished, the rope tied to Anand slackened, and Jani let out a fraught breath.

Das said, "Now, summon the Lieutenant!"

She said, moving her hand towards her pocket, "Better than that, Das – I can give you the ventha-di."

"Stop!" He raised his pistol and aimed at her.

Jani froze, her hand above the pocket of her dress and her purse concealed here. She had meant to pull it out, throw it at the priest before he could raise the gun, then tussle the weapon from his grasp.

A hopeless plan of action, she realised.

Durga Das smiled. "I seem to recall that the last time you reached into your pocket, you pulled out quite a surprise. I have the scar to show for your treachery."

And I would gladly carve you to little pieces if I had my light-beam to hand, she thought.

"Now," Durga Das said urgently, "call the Lieutenant!"

At that very second Jani caught a glimpse of khaki in the undergrowth beside the track, directly behind Durga Das. Her heart leaped, and to deceive the priest she turned and called across the stream, "Alfie! It's no good. You must show yourself."

She turned back to the priest and stared at him, more than anything wanting to glance over his shoulder in order to gauge Alfie's progress, but knowing that to do so would be a mistake.

"And when Alfie is with us?" she asked.

Anand crouched on the ground, staring up at her.

Durga Das smiled. Jani wondered how the man could invest such an innocent expression with so much malevolence, a rictus at once arrogant and almost ingratiating. She wondered if the priest had practised it while influencing powerful politicians.

"I want the ventha-di, Janisha, and if it means cutting you open to obtain the device, then so be it."

She stared at him, controlling her breathing. She had to keep him talking, at all costs. "How do you know about the...?"

He interrupted. "That need not concern us now."

She recalled what the Morn entity had told her aboard the Vantissarian ship, and made a stab in the dark, "You have the second Ventha, don't you?"

His eyes narrowed. "As I said, that need not–!"

Jani said, "And do you know to what use the venthas can be put?"

"Why do you think I want them, you little fool!"

She shook her head. "I don't know. Power, greed? But I do know that it is you who are the fool. Only by bringing the three venthas together can we hope to avoid the catastrophe that is awaiting the planet."

He laughed at this. "You ignorant heathen! Do you know nothing? Did your father fail in your religious upbringing? Oh, but I quite forgot – your father was a notorious atheist, wasn't he, as well as being a lackey of the Raj!" He controlled his anger and went on, "When I possess all three venthas, Janisha Chatterjee, then I – Durga Das! – shall usher in the Age of Kali, the downfall of the evil British rule of my fine country and the ultimate dominion of the Gods. And I shall be Kali's High Priest on Earth."

Beyond Durga Das, Alfie Littlebody was crossing the track with high-stepping, pantomime caution.

"You're wrong, Das. Your God is a myth. You are being used!"

"You ignorant fool!" Das spat. He leaned forward, aiming the pistol at her chest. "And when I have the second ventha, and you lie bleeding to death, I will make my way to London and there obtain the third from the Morn known as Mahran."

He smiled at her shocked reaction. "But evidently you were unaware that I knew about the Morn and its ventha?" He shook his head, and the weapon twitched in his hand. "Now call for Littlebody!"

Jani turned towards the river and called out, "Alfie! Please, show yourself!"

She turned back to the priest. Alfie was directly below

the bulbous envelope of the airship now, perhaps twenty yards from Durga Das and creeping upon him slowly. In his right hand Alfie had the deactivated light-beam, evidently loath to activate the weapon lest its effulgent glow give him away.

Jani held her breath. All it would take now was for Mr Knives to come to the hatch of the gondola, look down and behold Alfie's advance. She prayed that Knives would remain at the controls, the henchman hoping for another command to elevate the airship and so pull Anand to pieces.

In the end, Alfie's downfall came not from a vigilant Mr Knives, but from another source entirely.

A yard above Durga Das's right shoulder, the air began to shimmer like a heat haze above the ground on a blazing day. Jani stared as a blue light appeared in the shape of an ellipse – and within the lapis lazuli portal a monstrous devil's face stared out at her, all horns and fangs and red, staring eyes. The creature hissed something which Jani did not catch. Das, alerted, spun with a nimbleness surprising in a man of his gargantuan girth, saw Alfie and fired his pistol.

Alfie fell to the ground, clutching his left arm. Between his clasping fingers, blood welled, trickling over his knuckles and staining the earth.

"Alfie!" she cried.

"I'm okay, Jani..." he gasped, grimacing.

Durga Das flung back his head and laughed. "Kali looks upon and favours the righteous, you heathen! Now do you believe me when I say that I have the gods on my side!"

Jani shook her head, staring at the fanged monster framed in the blue light. "I don't know what it is, Das

– but it isn't Kali."

"You infidel!" Das almost screamed.

The blue light faded and the devil disappeared from view.

High above, Mr Knives appeared in the hatch of the gondola and looked down. Durga Das backed away from her so that he had both Alfie and Jani covered. His eyes were huge as he stared at Jani. "Oh, your friend's little game was foolish. You will pay for this!"

Alfie stared at her, wincing through his pain. He mouthed, "I'm sorry, Jani."

She shook her head, despairing at the hopelessness of their situation. On the ground, Anand struggled futilely against the ropes that bound his arms and legs.

Durga Das looked from Alfie to Jani. "Now, who shall die first?" He laughed to himself. "I will leave you, Janisha, until last. You will have the supreme torture of watching your friends die first. Mr Knives!" he called out.

"Yes, sir?" said Knives from the hatch of the airship.

"Take the ship up, Mr Knives, and do not stop until the boy is torn to bloody pieces!"

"No!" Jani cried, launching herself at the priest. She hit his solid bulk and rebounded. She landed painfully on her bottom, her hands to either side. Her right hand touched something, and when she looked down she saw a sizable rock. Without thinking she snatched it up and ran at the priest.

He sprang forward and, with the butt of his pistol, coshed her across the brow. She dropped the rock and staggered backwards, attempting to remain on her feet but failing and falling to the ground. She touched her head, her fingers coming away slick with blood.

"You unmitigated coward!" Alfie Littlebody cried, pulling something from his pocket. Dazed, Jani saw with a sudden surge of hope that he was clutching his light-beam, still deactivated. If only he could activate the weapon, swing it at the priest...

But Durga Das sprang forward and kicked out, punting the light-beam from Alfie's fingers. It went skittering across the lane and into the undergrowth.

Alfie slumped back, holding his bloody upper arm.

Mr Knives was no longer in the hatch of the gondola. The airship's engines droned and the vessel rose. The rope ladder stretched, and with it the rope that bound Anand's wrists. The boy was pulled off the ground, stretched between the two ropes. Jani scrambled across to him, her head throbbing. She reached out and grasped at the boy's white shirt.

Anand was in the air now, turning with the torsion of the ropes like a spitted pig. He stared at Jani with huge eyes, but to his credit pursed his lips and kept his terror internalised.

The boy rose further, the ropes straining on his ankles and outstretched arms, and Jani lost her grip on her handful of shirt. She cried out, watching hopelessly as the boy was carried from her, borne higher into the air. He was six feet off the ground now, his expression one of petrified alarm.

Durga Das stood back, chortling at the sight.

"Higher, Mr Knives!" he exhorted, though Jani doubted that Knives could hear the command above the din of the engines. The order was for her and Alfie's benefit only, a verbal exhibition of the power he wielded. "Higher! And do not stop until the boy is bloody meat!"

The airship climbed, and the rope connected to Anand tightened ever further, and for the first time the boy cried out in pain. The rope cut into the flesh of his ankles and wrists, drawing blood.

Jani could take no more. Crying out and fighting the pain that surged through her head like a hundred migraines, she scrambled to her feet and ran towards the fat priest yet again. She might be weaponless, but she would tear his eyes out with her fingernails.

He dodged her, kicked out a foot and sent her flying to the dusty ground. He swung, aiming the pistol at her. "One more move. Janisha, and I will shoot you dead."

She was directly beneath Anand now, lying on her back and staring up at the boy as he was stretched between the ropes, his blood dripping down across her chest.

Anand screamed in pain as the ropes bit and his joints stretched.

Then Jani saw movement to her left, on the far side of the track. She made out a blue-grey blur – a wild boar? – as the animal moved through the undergrowth. Her first notion was that it had been attracted by the scent of blood, that the ignominy of Anand's death would be compounded when the beast helped itself to his remains.

The animal leapt from the shrubbery and charged across the track, and Jani did not believe what she was seeing. Alfie cried out in alarm as the creature sprang from the ground and snapped the rope a foot above Anand's wrists with its metal jaw. Mechanical dog and Anand landed on the ground with a double thump, and the hound, with a swift twist, was upon the priest, its jaws snapping down on his gun hand. The pistol fell to the ground, followed by the priest. Jani snatched up the gun and rolled away. The hound pounced on the holy man and clamped its jaws around his throat. Das screamed, blood siphoning from his jugular and across the ground in great throbbing pulses.

The mechanical hound had not yet finished its rescue mission. With a leap that was miraculous, the creature took off and in one bound cleared the thirty feet between the ground and the hatch of the gondola.

The dog vanished into the airship and Jani heard a startled cry. Mr Knives appeared on the lip of the hatch, his face contorted with fear. He looked down, then looked quickly over his shoulder, and chose the least terrible option. He leapt, screaming, hit the ground with a sickening thud, and lay very still.

A strange Sargasso of silence and stillness followed in the aftermath of so much noise and action. Durga Das lay unconscious, his life blood pumping from his lacerated neck into the Greek soil. Mr Knives lay face down, his left leg bent at an unnatural angle and blood seeping from his chest.

Above all this, the mechanical hound sat on its haunches in the entrance to the gondola, staring directly down at Jani. Had it been a real dog, she thought, it would have been panting at its exertions and hoping for a reward.

She climbed to her feet, dazed, crossed to Alfie and knelt beside him.

"I'll be fine." He removed his hand from his upper arm and inspected the wound. "Despite all the blood, it's superficial. In fact, it's no longer bleeding." He shrugged. "I'm sorry, Jani. Fat lot of good I was."

"We tried, which is all that matters."

They moved to where Anand was slowly sitting up.

Jani sat beside him while Alfie took a pen-knife from his pocket and sliced the ropes binding the boy's hands and feet. Anand winced, then smiled through his pain.

Jani looked up at the mechanical dog, high above. "I wonder."

Alfie looked up, too. "Yes?"

"Why?" she asked.

"While it was with you in the lifeboat," Alfie said, "before we arrived. Perhaps, then, away from its handler, it had time to... I don't know... to fixate upon you, empathise with you. See you as its... its new commander. You said it could read thoughts. Well, now it read yours, and did what it could to save you."

"I don't know. You see, the handler told me that it took months for him to bond with the dog, until it came to obey his every thought."

"Then..." Alfie shrugged, "perhaps it just read your thoughts, your desperation, and it knew good from bad, and saved us."

She laughed at this. "Good from bad?" But why not, she asked herself. This was Vantissarian technology, and therefore way beyond present human understanding, or at least her understanding.

The dog leapt, and Jani winced lest it smash itself to pieces on the ground. But it landed like a gymnast and trotted over to where she knelt beside Alfie. It sat down and stared at her, and Alfie laughed. "You've made a friend for life. What's the phrase? Don't look a gift dog in the mouth, or something like that?"

She reached out, tentatively, and touched the dog's wedge-shaped head. It tilted its head to one side, nuzzling her palm. "Thank you," she whispered.

Alfie nodded up to the airship. "Well, we were

wondering how we might make it back to Blighty," he said. "And now we know. It'll certainly be quicker than finding a boat to France."

"You can pilot the vessel?"

"Once I get this strapped up, Jani, and with a little help from Anand, then I'll fly us home in no time."

Jani examined the abrasions on Anand's wrists and ankles. "We'll get you fixed up," she said. "There should be a first-aid box aboard the airship."

"And you?" Anand asked. "How is your head?"

She touched her brow and felt a nasty bump, sticky with drying blood. "I'll be fine."

They crossed to the huge, recumbent form of Durga Das. The priest lay very still, his eyes open and staring sightlessly into the heavens.

Alfie knelt and examined him. "Dead," he said, redundantly.

Jani stared down at the man who had taunted her. "Your God couldn't save you this time, could it?" she murmured.

She fell to her knees and searched through the priest's voluminous robe.

"Jani?"

"Das wanted my ventha. But why? As I said earlier, does he himself possess one of the three?"

She turned out the priest's pockets, but aside from a money pouch and a miniature painting of his goddess, Kali, she found nothing. She saw a cord around his bloody neck, and grimacing pulled it free. It was not the ventha, however, but the Hindu swastika symbol of good fortune.

Alfie touched her arm. "We'll search the airship, Jani."

They crossed to where Mr Knives lay face down on the ground in a spreading pool of blood, his blades beneath his body. Alfie knelt beside him and felt for a pulse. "He's barely alive," he pronounced. "I don't think he'll last much longer."

He moved across the lane, searched through the undergrowth until he found his light-beam, and slipped it into his trouser pocket.

They crossed to the dangling ladder and Alfie climbed carefully. Anand followed him and Jani brought up the rear.

She looked down. The mechanical dog sat on its haunches, staring up at her. Then it moved, lightning fast, and Jani stepped back as it landed beside her and trotted into the airship.

She found a medical kit in a storage unit and cleaned and bandaged the flesh wound on Alfie's arm, then attended to Anand's rope burns. Alfie returned the compliment and applied salve and a sticking plaster to her forehead.

They searched the lounge of the 'ship for the priest's ventha, turning out drawers and cupboards, and riffling through Das's travelling chest, to no avail.

"There is always the possibility that he didn't possess a ventha," Alfie said. "Or left it for safe-keeping back in India."

Reluctantly Jani agree that he might be right.

"But look what I have found!" Anand cried, opening a hamper containing a half a dozen tiffin tins and a dozen samosas wrapped in greaseproof paper.

"Well done," Alfie said. "I don't know about you two, but I'm famished."

One hour later, when Alfie had familiarised himself

with the controls, Anand climbed from the 'ship and untied the guy ropes from the trees on either side of the lane. Then he scrambled back up the rope ladder, as nimble as a monkey, and hauled it up after him.

Alfie set a course north-west to London, left the 'ship on auto-pilot and joined Jani and Anand in the lounge.

Jani dipped a puri into a bowl of mutter masala and chewed the delicacy with relish.

Anand, ensconced in a huge armchair, beamed across at Jani. "To think that soon we will be in England!" he said, chomping on a samosa. "Jani, I have only read about England in books! The home of Rider Haggard and Kipling and Wells!"

"And in a day or so you'll be setting foot on British soil for the first time," Alfie said. "You'll be seeing the country at its finest, in summer. I fancy wintertime would be a little too bracing for you."

Jani shivered at the thought. "I found my first few winters there almost unbearable!" she said. "It wasn't only the cold I found so hard to bear, but the unremitting greyness, the constant rain and fog!"

"Pea-soupers!" Anand carolled. "Will we be there long enough to see a pea-souper?" he asked.

Jani smiled. "Who knows?"

"When we get to London," Anand went on, "I would like to go to the New Great Exhibition. I've read so much about it in Delhi."

"And I'll come with you," Alfie said.

Jani sat back and considered their arrival in London, and wondered at Lady Eddington's reaction when they turned up, bedraggled, on her doorstep.

CHAPTER FIVE

∽

At the Burgundy Club – A meeting with Korolov –
A filthy suggestion from Felicity –
"My place or yours...?"

SEBASTIAN TOOK A taxi from his father's mansion in Richmond to the Burgundy Club in the West End, arriving shortly before midnight.

The owners of the nightclub changed the interior décor every few months, and now it was done out like the palatial lounge of a great airship, its potted palms, brass rails and portholes a nod towards both novelty (for how many other nightclubs in London could lavish so much time and expense on such ephemera?) and nostalgia, as the heyday of the intercontinental airship would soon be a thing of the past. In just two days the first sub-orbital rocket would leave London bound for New York, ushering in a new age of super-fast global travel.

The padded booths situated around the dance floor of the Burgundy reflected an earlier, golden age, and the revellers tonight were similarly outfitted in mock-Victorian garb.

Sebastian was in no mood to dress up, however; the club's airship get-up was an unpleasant enough reminder of both Janisha and his unfaithfulness.

He knocked back his second gin sling and slumped in his booth. He had heard the radio report of the attack on the *Rudyard Kipling* two weeks ago, and his blood had run cold. That the authorities suspected the airship had been brought down by Russian artillery only compounded his pain. A day later he'd received the miraculous news that Jani had survived the crash, via a cable sent from the office of a Brigadier investigating the outrage. Then nothing... though the silence had been explained when he read in the *Times* a report on the death of her father, Kapil Dev Chatterjee, the Indian Minister of Security. The obituary had been fulsome in its praise of Chatterjee, the first Indian to hold office in the Raj government, and Sebastian had wished Jani might phone him so that he could extend his condolences.

At the same time, perhaps it was just as well that she hadn't contacted him; he would have felt hypocritical in assuring her of his affections.

He ordered a third gin from the waiter, knocked it back in one and tried, for perhaps the hundredth time since Jani had left for India, to assess his sentiments towards the girl.

There were times when he thought he loved her for the many amazing qualities she possessed, quite apart from her exotic good looks and droll sense of humour. Then at other times he felt a profound sense of dissatisfaction with Jani, and was sure that their relationship was going nowhere. They were living in modern times, for God's sake, an era of equality and abandon – and yet Janisha Chatterjee still upheld the virtuous feminine principles of an earlier age. Her idea of passion was a single drink and a quick kiss goodnight before she slipped away, leaving his heart thudding and his desires unconsummated. He supposed he should expect nothing else; she was, after all, the product of another, more chaste culture, even though her mother had been British; her father had been a strict moralist – despite having been politically liberal – who had upheld the values of the Victorian age in which he had been raised.

The damnable thing was that, despite his feelings for Jani, the pleasures on offer at the moment were a lure too delightful to resist. He suffered pangs of guilt for the pain he knew he would cause Janisha if she ever learned of his waywardness, and yet his resolve to forego other women was always transitory; he could resist the temptations only for so long.

He had come to the Burgundy in order to drink himself into oblivion, but not before attempting to fathom the contradiction between Russia's avowal of world peace and their hostile actions in bringing down the *Rudyard Kipling*, a passenger ship carrying more than a thousand innocent men, women and children.

Now, however, his head was full of Janisha Chatterjee, half a world away and grieving for her dead father – and when he saw Felicity Travers shimmy past he slipped down further into his seat and attempted to conceal himself behind a fortuitously positioned aspidistra.

To his relief she failed to see him, more intent on performing the Black Bottom with her beau for the night – a moon-faced youth up from Eton, by the look of him.

He was in for another shock, soon after, when he espied Dmitri Korolov ordering drinks at the bar; worse, the dogsbody at the Russian embassy had spotted Sebastian and was making a bee-line towards him across the dance floor.

"What the hell are you doing here!" Sebastian hissed as

the young man slid into the booth and pressed a double whisky into his hand.

"What do you think, my friend? Why do most people come here? To enjoy themselves, of course! Do you think that I, after a long day toiling at the embassy, should not be allowed to, how do you say, 'let my hair down'?"

"It's a bloody foolish stunt," Sebastian went on, livid. "What if someone saw us together?"

"My friend, but you should not worry. Do you think your bosses frequent places like the Burgundy? Look around you, Sebastian. These are young people, having a good time, no? Do you see any stuffed shirts from Westminster or the Foreign Office here?"

"That's hardly the point. People talk, word gets around."

"You are being needlessly apprehensive, my friend. Now drink up! Other than to enjoy myself, I came here to see you about certain matters, yes?"

Sebastian clutched the whisky and took a mouthful. He could guess what one of these 'matters' might be – the blessed plans of the sub-orbital, as ever. He waved this away and said, "Anyway, seeing as how you're here, *I* need to talk to *you* about something."

The suave young man smiled. "You see, our little meeting is not such a bad idea, after all." He lowered his voice to a whisper. "About the plans, I trust?"

Sebastian sighed. "As I told you last week, Korolov, I'll have them presently."

"But your English term 'presently' is such an imprecise word for a language that prides itself on its accuracy of definition."

"For God's sake, man, I can't rush things and arouse the suspicion of my superiors. I'm not even in the same department."

"But you have access to the offices where details of the sub-orbital are kept, no?"

"I have, yes. Limited access. But I don't want to show my hand by snooping around in there too often."

"You have the camera?"

"Of course. And I'll use it, once I can assure myself that I won't be disturbed while looking through the details."

"I cannot impress upon you too much how important these plans are to the cause, Sebastian. If the launch is successful, and the British develop many more of these rockets..." He shrugged. "I need not dwell on the consequences, no?"

"Of course not," Sebastian said. "I'll have the plans tomorrow and I'll arrange a rendezvous then."

Korolov smiled. "Excellent, my friend. Now, you said you wanted to talk to me?"

"Yes – about the *Rudyard Kipling*."

The Russian chose to misconstrue Sebastian's words. "A fine British writer, yes, even if he could be accused of imperialism."

"I mean," Sebastian interrupted, "the airship."

"I know. I was being, what is the word, mischievous?"

"'Mischievous'?" Sebastian repeated. "Your blasé attitude towards the death of over a thousand innocents appals me, Korolov."

"The end," replied the Russian, "justifies the means. Anyway, I too wanted to talk to you about the *Kipling*."

Sebastian blinked at the Russian, surprised. "You did?" he said, then repeated, "The end justifies the means? What do you mean by that?" He shook his head, feeling too drunk to be having a serious conversation. "What justifiable end do you think was achieved by such a barbarous act?"

Korolov looked around him, as if to ensure they were not being observed, and leaned closer. "The downing of the *Kipling* was a necessary, if unpleasant, action."

"'Unpleasant'? Your grasp of English is inadequate for the job, Korolov. Was it merely 'unpleasant' for the thousand who died in agony when the 'ship was brought down?"

The Russian shrugged, dismissing the correction. "I repeat, it was—"

Sebastian interrupted. "Damn it all, Dmitri. I threw in my lot with you people because I believed in the cause. I believe in world peace and egalitarianism, and the rights of the worker and what have you. I also believe in common human decency and honour, and—"

Korolov stopped him with a raised hand. "All the values you English are so fond of... what is the phrase... 'paying lip service' to? Look at your own colonial record before you begin to condemn the actions of a state determined to bring about global equality, Sebastian."

"For Christ's sake, Korolov, I'm on your side! I don't need lectures on the perfidy of the Empire! But don't you see how it looks to people around the world when the British can spout about the evil of the Bolsheviks and point to the downing of the *Kipling*?"

The young man shrugged. "Sebastian, until you are in full possession of the facts, until you are in a position of authority and can assess the true political situation, until then you cannot judge our actions. I will tell you something." The Russian paused, saw that Sebastian's glass was empty, and said, "But your drink is finished, my friend. Please allow me to..."

And before Sebastian could protest that he'd had far

too much already, Korolov snagged a passing waiter and ordered a further pair of double whiskies.

When they were nursing their drinks, Korolov leaned close and whispered, "The *Kipling* was transporting a prisoner the British had 'rescued' from us, Sebastian. That is, he was in our custody until he escaped and fled south from Russia into Greece, where he was picked up by the British."

"A prisoner?" Sebastian said, wondering at the importance of such a person if the Russians thought his death worth the lives of so many innocents. "Who was he?"

The young man shook his head, his thin lips pursed around a mouthful of Scotch. "That I cannot say, Sebastian. I cannot say because I do not know. I am, after all, as I am so fond of using the English expression, a dogsbody. I am not told everything by my superiors. However..."

"Yes?"

"An acquaintance of yours, shall we say, was aboard the *Rudyard Kipling*. One Janisha Chatterjee."

Sebastian blinked. His thoughts were muddled with drink and he was having difficulty focussing on the Russian. "What about her?"

"I am pleased to say that she survived the incident."

The 'incident', Sebastian thought bitterly. "That's no thanks to..."

Korolov waved him into silence. "That is not all, my friend. Not only did she survive the impact, along with a few other lucky souls, but the prisoner, the all important erstwhile prisoner of the British, survived also."

Sebastian stared at the Russian, wondering where all this might be leading. "And?"

"And I am led to believe, by my superiors, that your little friend, this Janisha Chatterjee, had contact with the prisoner just before he fled and evaded a Russian follow-up mission."

This was getting more fantastical by the second. Sebastian cursed the effects of the alcohol, shook his head as if to clear it, and said, "Contact? What do you mean, contact?"

"I understand that the prisoner might very well have passed a certain item on to your Indian girlfriend. However, as to the precise nature of this item I, in my lowly capacity at the embassy, have not been informed."

"I find all this very hard to believe, Korolov."

The Russian shrugged. "A fantastic story it might be, but I have it on good authority that it is true. Now, needless to say, we are eager to gain possession of this mysterious item. To this end our agents have been pursuing Chatterjee across India."

Sebastian sat up. He felt like taking Korolov by the lapels and shaking him. "Pursuing her? I'm warning you, if your agents harm so much as a hair on her head...!"

"You will, I think, be pleased to know that she evaded capture unscathed and, so I understand, is making her way from India back to England."

"She is? How do you know?"

The young man smiled. "We have our ways and means," he said. "Now, if and when she does arrive on these shores, it is of course of vital importance that we are notified."

Sebastian nodded, hardly hearing the Russian's words. If Jani was heading back to England, then why hadn't she contacted him with the news?

"We think it highly probable that Janisha will at some point seek to see you. Needless to say, when she does so, we would be exceedingly grateful if you could notify us of the fact, yes?" Korolov held up a hand. "And you have my assurance that we will not, as you say, harm a hair on her head."

"I find all this amazing," Sebastian managed at last.

"Amazing it might be," Korolov said, "but the fact remains that Janisha Chatterjee is in possession of an item of vital strategic interest to my government. And, I need not point out, to the cause to which you have pledged yourself."

"I understand. Very well, if she does contact me..."

Korolov beamed. "Excellent, my friend! Now, I really must be wending my way homewards, and as I pass the bar I shall order you a nightcap. Good night, my friend."

Korolov rose and crossed the dance floor.

So Janisha was on her way back to England, in possession of an item of vital importance to the Russians. He found the idea, in his drunkenness, hard to fathom.

A waiter delivered the promised whisky and, too drunk to care now, Sebastian hugged the tumbler to his chest and closed his eyes.

"So this is where you're hiding yourself, you naughty boy!"

Sebastian jumped, almost spilling his drink. Felicity Travers was swaying over the table, regarding him with a mock-reproving expression. She was dressed, in the spirit of tonight's theme, as a Victorian governess – an outfit that contradicted her bountiful blonde curls and excessive make up. She grasped the hand of a pretty young woman dressed as a scullery maid, whose low-cut bodice left little to the imagination. She introduced the girl as Sophie, "A dancer," Felicity went on, "starring at the Piccadilly, isn't that right, Soph?"

Sophie smiled shyly as both women shuffled into the booth on either side of Sebastian.

"What have you done," he asked, "with the schoolboy I saw you with earlier?"

Felicity smiled. "Oh, him? He ran off to the little boy's room, and anyway what we want tonight, me and Soph, is a *real* man."

"Well, I'm sorry. But not tonight, Felicity." He raised his glass. "This isn't the first."

She pulled a face. "But that's never stopped you in the past, Sebastian!"

He felt a hand on his thigh, rubbing: Sophie smiled up at him. Felicity leaned close and made an incredibly filthy suggestion regarding what a man like himself might do in order to pleasure two willing young women.

"So," she finished, "my place or yours?"

He found his arm around Felicity, his fingers tracing the curve of her hip. He groaned inwardly and knew he was about to give in. Sophie's expert ministrations had climbed from his thigh.

"Not mine," he said. "I'm still at my father's place until I find somewhere in London."

Felicity beamed. "I heard on the grapevine that you'd left university. Sent down, were you? Not for buggery, I hope?"

He assured her otherwise, and Felicity kissed his cheek. "Excellent! Now drink up and let's all have a little dance before we go, shall we?"

CHAPTER SIX

~∞~

The last thoughts of Durga Das – Resurrection! –
Invincible powers – Onward to London –
"Kali resides within me now..."

ONE OF DURGA Das's last thoughts, as he lay dying, was that Janisha Chatterjee had thwarted him yet again.

He relived the moment the dog-like beast leapt at him and tore at his throat; he relived the pain and the shock and the knowledge that this was the end. And yet, as he lay on his back and felt the lifeblood seep from his jugular, he seemed a long time dying.

Those who claimed that a dying man experienced the past events of his life were wrong, he realised: you lived through the final terrible moments. He saw Janisha Chatterjee standing before him, proud and defiant, and he hated her with a passion. He saw the dog-beast run towards him and take a flying leap. He felt the pain, and the terrible knowledge that his mission had ended on failure, and that the faith his goddess Kali had invested in him had been misplaced.

But he had lived a virtuous life in the service of the gods, and he knew he would be rewarded in his next incarnation.

He waited to die, and to be reborn.

He felt the sunlight on his face, dappled as it slanted through the tree high above him; he heard birdsong and the thrum of crickets. Then the awareness of his immediate surroundings faded. The pain in his torn throat abated, and he knew that he was undergoing the transition from death to rebirth, from one life to the next. He awaited his reawakening with anticipation.

His one regret was that he would be unable to avenge himself for Janisha Chatterjee's having thwarted him yet again. If only he had lived long enough to obtain the tithra-kuñjī and see her die...

He wondered when his memories, his awareness of his old self, would pass; the wise men had it that one was reborn anew, with no memory of one's past life. The physical body of Durga Das would die, be cast off, and the spirit would inhabit a new, pristine form. And yet... and yet his memories persisted. He wondered if he was to be blessed, like a very few pious souls before him, by being allowed to carry a past identity, replete with all his memories, into his new life? Perhaps this was to be his reward for so diligently serving Kali?

The notion filled him with jubilation – perhaps he was being reincarnated with all his memories intact so that he might continue his mission, continue his work for the goddess?

At last he opened his eyes and blinked up at the fitful sunlight, mystified.

He was lying where he had fallen, beneath the spreading boughs of the oak tree, in some anonymous dusty track in northern Greece.

He had not been reborn; he had survived – and his initial reaction was disappointment, for he had assumed he was being reincarnated with all his memories as a reward.

And yet he was certain that the attack of the dog had killed him, for it had been ferocious and unremitting, and he had felt the meat of his throat being torn out of his neck, felt the blood spurt from his severed jugular.

If he had survived the attack, then he could only have done so with the intervention of his goddess – which in turn meant that he was, indeed, being rewarded. She had brought him back to life so that he might continue his mission!

Tentatively he reached up to his neck and touched the flesh. He expected to feel a mess of blood and gore; instead his probing fingers encountered a bulge of skin, and above it his flowing beard. There was no wound, no blood. He examined his right wrist, which the dog had crunched, but it too had been healed. He sat up slowly and stared down the front of his robe – which was indeed stained crimson with his blood. The attack had happened, the dog had killed him, and truly he had been brought back to life.

He rolled over on to all fours, then pushed himself on to his knees, stared up at the heavens and clasped his hands together in prayerful supplication. "*Anghra dah tanthara, yangra bahl, somithra tal zhell!*" he intoned.

A thought occurred to him. The Chatterjee girl suspected that he had a tithra-kuñjī – but had she searched him as he lay dead in the lane and taken it? Frantically he dug beneath his robes and slipped a hand beneath his bulging stomach and into the crease of his groin where the disc was concealed. He found the cord and pulled. With a shuddering sense of relief he unfolded the small square of cloth and saw, sitting there, the tithra-kuñjī.

He willed his goddess to appear before him so that he might thank her, and assure her that her faith, this time, had not been misplaced; that he would serve her with all his guile and intelligence, and track down the Chatterjee girl and wrest from her the second tithra-kuñjī and the third, in the possession of the Morn.

But the horned and fanged blue face of the deity did not show itself. Instead, something far more amazing happened.

His goddess spoke in his head. *Durga Das.*

"Kali?" he said, looking around.

Stand, my servant.

Quickly he scrambled to his feet. "But I see you not, Kali. And yet I hear you."

That is because I was forced, in desperation at your incompetence, to take extreme measures. I was forced to undo what your enemies had done, so that your quest might continue.

"Oh, Kali – this time, I promise, I will not fail–"

Silence! And listen to me.

Durga Das sank to his knees. "I listen, Kali!"

I am part of you now, Durga Das. Your every thought is open to me, your every action directed by me. You are inhabited by your goddess, so that this time you will not fail me. Do you understand?

That small part of the holy man, cowed by the goddess's stinging criticism of him, was overridden by his ego: Kali had chosen him, him alone from the millions of other human beings on Earth, to carry out her wishes. Truly he was blessed!

"I understand!"

From this time forth we will work as a team. I will ride you, unseen, and guide you through the various pitfalls and dangers to which, alone, you might succumb. The prize of our mission is such that we cannot risk failure.

To this end I have endowed you with powers that go beyond the paltry one of healing.

"Powers?" Durga Das almost fainted at the thought.

Powers that will make you, Durga Das, invincible. Later, once we are in London, I will demonstrate.

For the first time Das looked across to where the airship had been moored, then saw that it was no longer riding in the air above the oak.

Chatterjee and her minions took it, said Kali.

"Then how...?"

Kali curtailed the thought. *Twenty miles south of here you will find a small town and a railway station. You will take a train to the city of Thessalonica. At the airship terminus there you will book passage to London.*

"Twenty miles?" Durga Das began.

You will walk.

"Walk? Twenty miles?" The very idea struck fear into the holy man's heart.

The exercise will benefit you, and ready you for the task ahead.

He bowed. "I will walk, Kali." He looked across the lane at Mr Knives, who lay crumpled and bloody from where he had fallen from the hatch of the airship.

"Is he dead?" he asked.

He is dead – but he will live, after your ministrations. Tend to him now, and then we will be on our way.

Durga Das crossed to the young man who lay on his stomach, his left leg twisted horribly. His blades had punctured his chest, lacerating the flesh.

Turn him over and heal him, Das.

The holy man knelt and, grunting with the effort, rolled the youth on to his back. The wounds on his chest were an inch deep, and Das's stomach turned. He parted the material of the shirt, then reached out a hand, closed his eyes and applied his palm to the wounds. He felt heat course through him and down his arm; he moved his hand back and forth over the young man's chest.

Within fifteen minutes the gash had scabbed over, and Das turned his attention to the broken left leg. He rested his hand on the swelling around the upper femur and closed his eyes. The healing took almost thirty minutes, during which Das entered a trance state and was hardly aware of the passage of time.

As he worked, Mr Knives' body gave a galvanic jerk, startling Das. The young man began breathing evenly, and Das gave thanks to his goddess and marvelled at the miraculous powers she had conferred on him.

He heard a sound and opened his eyes.

An old man with a wrinkled face tanned to the shade of ancient leather had halted in the lane, leaning on a staff and staring at him. Das allowed that he must have presented a strange sight indeed: an overweight Hindu gentleman kneeling beside the prostrate form of an obviously injured young man.

The old man stepped forward, his expression suspicious, and spoke in a flow of Greek as mellifluous as honey.

Das, not wanting to enter into protracted conversation with the man, decided not to enquire whether he spoke English. He rose to his feet and released a stream of Hindi.

The old man shook his head and stepped closer, peering down at Mr Knives. *He suspects*, Das thought, *that I was robbing him.*

The Greek took in the strange arrangement of blades affixed to the stumps of the youth's arms, and his eyes widened in alarm.

Make him go away, said the voice in his head.

"And how might...?" Das began.

Like this, said Kali, and Das felt himself propelled forward, clearly under the motive power of the goddess in his head.

The old Greek looked up in alarm at Durga Das, stared at him in shock, and backed away, gibbering something in his own language. He turned and hobbled off along the lane.

Mystified at the old man's reaction, Das returned to Mr Knives and knelt beside him.

He laid a hand over a contusion on the youth's forehead, and presently the bruise cleared and the swelling abated – and Mr Knives blinked up at Das in confusion.

"The dog! I was attacked!"

"Calm down. The dog has gone. We are safe now."

"I fell! I fell from the airship! How did I...?" He looked around. "Where is the ship?"

Durga Das explained, and said that now they would set off for the train station, bound thereafter for Thessalonica and London.

Mr Knives climbed to his feet and stared down at his lacerated shirtfront. Then he looked up at Durga Das and shook his head. "I have had enough of all this," he said.

"What?"

"First Chatterjee maims me in Nepal, and now this. A wild beast saves her life and attacks us. Fate is not on our side, Baba-ji!"

Durga Das laughed. "The gods are on our side, you coward. Do you not recall the demonstration of my powers aboard the airship? And how do you think you are able to walk now, after breaking your leg in the fall?"

"You...?" Mr Knives began.

Durga Das bobbed his head from side to side, hitting his chest with plump fingers. "Ah-cha! I healed you! Now follow me!"

But the youth remained defiant. "No, Baba-ji. I have followed you here, but no more. I will make my own way back to India."

Rage consumed Durga Das. He stepped forward, aware that he was propelled by more than just his own anger. He was aware of a heat in his head – not unlike the warmth of healing – and he leaned forward and screamed, "No one disobeys the commands of Durga Das!"

Mr Knives' eyes widened and he screamed in terror. "Your face!" he cried.

Das laughed. "My face? What of it?"

The youth backed away, pointing. "Your... your face, Baba-ji! It... it was... it was Kali!"

Durga Das swelled to his full height, puffed out his great chest and thrust his belly forward. "That is because the goddess Kali resides within me now, Mr Knives! Do you hear me? The Chatterjee girl had me killed – by the same beast that attacked you – and I lay dead on the ground with my throat torn out, and Kali – the great and munificent goddess Kali – saw fit to enter me and heal me and bring me back to life, so that I might continue the mission to wreak revenge on Janisha Chatterjee! And you *will* accompany me to London!"

Mr Knives fell to his knees, weeping now. "Ah-cha, Baba-ji! You saved my life, I will come."

Durga Das turned imperiously and set off along the lane, and Mr Knives scrambled to his feet and scurried after him.

CHAPTER
SEVEN

*Battenberg and rocketships – Lady Eddington is overwhelmed –
Jani makes plans – Alfie is objectionable –
"You're a special woman, Jani..."*

JANI, ALFIE AND Anand sat at a small circular table in the
window of the Blue Horizon café on the corner of Park
Street and Mount Street. They had demolished plates
of salmon and cucumber sandwiches and were making
inroads into a selection of cakes. Anand declared
Battenberg cake far superior to any burfi he'd sampled
back in India, and helped himself to a third thick slice.

Under the table, Alfie's hand found Jani's and squeezed.

Their flight over Europe had been uneventful, and Jani
had taken the opportunity to sleep for most of it. The
encounter with Durga Das and Mr Knives had exhausted
her mentally and physically, and it was still hard to credit
that they were dead; there would be no need to worry
herself about the threat from *that* direction in future.

On arriving in England, Alfie had set the airship down
beside a forest in Kent half a mile from a small town on
the train line to London, and an hour later the trio had
boarded a bullet train to the capital. Jani had wondered
how they might explain the presence of the mechanical

dog, but Fido – as if reading her concern – had taken to its heels as they emerged from the wood and hared off over the horizon, leaving Jani to wonder when, or if, they might ever see the hound again.

She had half expected a police reception to be awaiting her at Victoria, but the only official on hand to meet the alighting passengers was a cheery ticket collector. Jani had hurried from the station and made for the taxi rank, Alfie and Anand hurrying on her heels.

From Victoria they had boarded a taxi for Mayfair and Lady Eddington's address, only to learn from a maid that the dowager was not at home, and that she was expected back at six.

It was Anand who had spotted the Blue Horizon, opposite the terrace of imposing townhouses where Lady Eddington had her London domicile.

It was now approaching six and Jani kept an eye out for the return of the dowager.

Sleek cars slid by in the wide street; bulky Georgian coachwork, all the rage ten years ago when Jani first came to London, was giving way to a more futuristic, streamlined design, and golden livery was becoming ever more popular.

Vehicle design was not all that was new in the city. His cheeks bulging with Battenberg, Anand indicated a wall-poster advertising tours around the Ealing Common Rocket Station: it showed a vast webwork of girders and gantries, and the towering golden needle of a rocketship.

"The world's very first rocket station," Alfie said. "We should visit it during the course of the next few days."

Anand's eyes bulged. "We can?" he spluttered, spitting pink crumbs and marzipan.

"The country's latest invention – or rather re-invention

– is the sub-orbital rocket liner," Alfie said. "A fleet is on the drawing-board at the de Havilland HQ, and the prototype is due to leave London for New York in a day or so."

Jani said, "And of course the rocket will be of Vantissarian origin."

Alfie nodded. "Amazing to think that we are among the few civilians in the land to know the truth of the Empire's amazing technological prowess."

Jani stared at her cup of Darjeeling and murmured, "And perhaps that alone would be enough for the authorities to desire our silence on the matter."

Anand stopped chewing and frowned. "But the Empire is still great, no, Jani-ji? I mean, to be able to use the alien technology – to be able to *understand* it in the first place – this must take great scientific prowess!"

Jani smiled at the boy. He was young, and brought up in the household of a distinguished man – her father – to believe that everything about the British Empire was great and good. His education was just beginning, and over the next few months she suspected that he would learn a lot about the might, and otherwise, of the Empire.

But for the time being she was loath to disabuse him of the notion. "Of course it takes great scientific ability to work out how to utilise the alien technology," she said.

"It's called reverse engineering," Alfie put in. "You have an end result, an object never seen before on this planet, and you take it apart and see how it works, strip it back and work out first principles. It takes a bit of gumption to be able to do that, Anand."

Across the road a black cab pulled up outside Lady Eddington's townhouse. Jani sat up, no longer hearing Alfie and Anand as they chattered about the rocket liner.

As she watched, the tall, upright figure of the dowager alighted, limped around the cab with the aid of a stick, and climbed the steps to the royal blue front door. Jani smiled to herself as she anticipated Lady Eddington's reaction when they turned up on her doorstep.

She interrupted their chatter. "Lady Eddington has returned. Shall we settle the bill and be on our way?"

Alfie paid the waitress and they stepped out into the warm summer's evening. Jani recoiled in shock as a police constable strolled by, raised three fingers to the brim of his domed helmet, and said, "Evening, Miss."

She gathered her breath and hurried across the road.

The maid answered the door and, behind her, Lady Eddington stood and stared in shock. "Oh, my word! Jani, do come here!"

Tearful, Jani hurried into the hallway and fell into Lady Eddington's outstretched arms, inhaling the scent of the old lady's face powder and *eau de cologne*.

"But I thought the worst! I heard about the launch of the lifeboat, and then discovered you missing! Idle gossip aboard the *Edinburgh* was that someone had seen the lifeboat crash into the mountains! Oh, how I wept. But here you are!" She pulled away and examined Jani at arm's length. "And young Anand and Lieutenant Littlebody! I'm quite overcome! You must be exhausted, and you look as though you have been through the wars, and here I am crying like a chorus girl. Eliza, bring the tea things through to the library."

"It's so good to see you again, Lady Eddington," Jani said.

"Please, call me Amelia, child. I think we've know each other long enough now to dispense with formalities. Amelia – 'always improving', as my mother used to say, more in hope, I might add! But come."

Soon they were ensconced on sumptuous sofas in the library and drinking yet more china cups of tea, Earl Grey this time. Anand, despite eating his fill in the café, helped himself to shortbread biscuits and Crawford's chocolate wafers.

Lady Eddington dabbed her eyes with a lace kerchief and declared herself overcome. "I had convinced myself that you'd met your end. And then you appear on the doorstep like a vision!"

Jani smiled. "You don't know how thankful we are to be here, Amelia."

"But how on earth did you make your way from Greece to London with such alacrity, my dear?"

"Where to begin?" Jani laughed. "The very recollection is enough to exhaust me. Alfie, perhaps you should recount all our adventures."

The Lieutenant rested his cup on his khaki knee and began, "Well, even I find some of the events hard to believe." And he proceeded to regale the dowager with a detailed account of their many escapades.

Thirty minutes later Lady Eddington, having punctuated Alfie's tale with many gasps, exclamations and expressions of horror, pressed a hand to her chest and declared, "Why, but merely listening to your travails is exhausting. I said on first meeting you, Jani, that you were a remarkable young woman, and I was not wrong."

"I was aided by two of the bravest and most stalwart young men anyone could wish to have as companions," Jani said. "I could not have survived without both of you," she went on, favouring Anand and Alfie with a heartfelt smile.

"But I was useless when Mr Knives captured me!" Anand said modestly.

"And my attempt at sneaking up on Durga Das was incompetent, and earned me a flesh wound. Still, it might have been worse."

Jani said, "Alfie piloted us across Europe and evaded RAF patrols, Amelia, ably assisted by Anand."

"But if it hadn't been for the mechanical hound back in Greece..." Alfie put in.

"Ah," said Lady Eddington, "the hound. Now, tell me more. Where might the creature be now?"

"He really can read minds!" Jani said. "I was worrying how we might travel to London accompanied by such a creature without arousing undue attention – and instantly Fido looked me in the eye and took off across the countryside."

"My guess, and hope," Alfie said, "is that he will turn up when we most need him."

"Amen to that!" Lady Eddington sang. "Now, by the looks of you, you all need a good bath and a rest. Perhaps an evening meal at eight would suit." She tugged on a bell-pull to summon the maid. "Eliza, inform cook that we have guests for the next few days, and we will be dining at home this evening. And have Dobson show my friends to the guest rooms. Hmm," she said, peering censoriously at the bedraggled trio. "I can see that a change of clothes or two would be in order. I never got rid of some of my late husband's clothing, Lieutenant, and I think it would be wise to divest you of your uniform as soon as possible. I'll have Dobson bring a change of clothing to your room. As for you two," she went on, smiling at Jani and Anand, "perhaps I should send out for clothing in the morning." She clapped her hands. "But that is quite enough for now. I have had an exhausting day and intend to rest before dinner. Over which, my friends, we have much to discuss and much planning to do."

A butler appeared at the door and showed the trio to their respective rooms, and Jani smiled at Anand's wide-eyed, incredulous expression as Dobson addressed the diminutive former houseboy as 'sir' and led them up the curling, marble staircase.

AFTER DINNER, WHICH consisted of mulligatawny soup, steamed trout and treacle pudding – all of which Anand downed as if he had not eaten for a week – they repaired to the lounge where a fire was burning. Despite the earlier heat of the late summer's day, the evening was cool and Jani was grateful for the blaze. She sat back in an armchair, feeling wonderful after having soaked for an hour in a hot bath. Opposite her, Anand looked minuscule, enthroned in a vast wingback armchair. Alfie sat beside Lady Eddington on a *chaise longue*. Dobson had served drinks, hot chocolate for Jani and Anand, and a brandy for the Lieutenant and Lady Eddington.

"And now," the dowager declared, business-like, "there is but the small matter of the immediate future to discuss, and your mission to effect the rescue of Mahran. You told me aboard the *Edinburgh* that you had a plan, Jani?"

Jani cupped her hot chocolate, frowning. "Well, I'm not so sure than I'd use the word plan. That is, the idea of rescuing Mahran was all very well when considered at a remove of days. But now that the time has come, and so soon after our recent contretemps..."

"I can well appreciate your circumspection," Lady Eddington said, a be-ringed hand to her powdered cheek. "Of course, the first thing we need to ascertain is the precise whereabouts of the Morn."

"I was told by the entity on the Vantissarian ship that Mahran was incarcerated in Newgate gaol." Jani shrugged hopelessly. "Of course we can't just walk in there and..."

Alfie said, "The task of springing him from prison will be made all the more difficult by the fact that he will be held under conditions of maximum security. Mahran, and the knowledge he possesses, is considered a threat to national security. If it were not that the authorities presumably wish to elicit more information from the fellow, I suspect he would have been eliminated by now."

The dowager made an expression of distaste. "I wonder if I might have connections who would know something of the prisoner? Perhaps a discreet word in the right ear?"

"That would certainly be of some help," Alfie said.

"Aboard the *Edinburgh*," Lady Eddington said, "you mentioned that you might be able to use your medical contacts to establish communications with Mahran."

Jani shook her head. "Wishful thinking. I know one or two high-up doctors and a professor at Cambridge who might be able to make enquiries, but now I'm not so sure." She hesitated, then went on, "My initial thought was that I might contact them and ask if they might enquire about a prisoner called Mahran, to at least establish his exact whereabouts. But I think this idea is hopeless now."

"And why is that?"

"For two reasons. The authorities are aware of me,

and I think they will have put two and two together by now and come to the conclusion that I am in Britain."

"You sound certain of this, Jani," the dowager said.

"I presume the authorities know by now that an Indian airship transgressed 'sovereign airspace'. It will only be a matter of time before they trace the ship back to India, and the fact that it was hired by one Durga Das. And when they find his body in northern Greece, with the lifeboat nearby..." She shrugged.

Lady Eddington frowned. "You are probably correct in your assumptions."

"The authorities will have alerts out for me," Jani said, "and I suspect they will put all my former acquaintances under surveillance. Also, I was muddleheaded in thinking that Mahran's gaolers would give away any information concerning their prisoner, even to distinguished Cambridge professors."

"In other words," Alfie said, swirling his brandy, "you think the situation hopeless?" His eyes twinkled; she smiled, knowing that he was goading her.

She had been thinking about Mahran, and the difficulty of springing him from Newgate, on and off for days – in between attempting to save her own skin, that was. All along, at the back of her mind, had been an idea that at first she had been loath to mention.

She considered her next words. "I wonder... and this is only an idea... I wonder if it is not time to place everything we know, about the ventha-di and the planned invasion of the Zhell, in the hands of the British authorities. I know we have been running from them until now, but my notion is not that I give myself up to the military, but that I go to the very top and present myself, and my story, and enlist their aid. If I am believed, then they will corroborate my story with what Mahran knows, and free him. Together, we – myself, Mahran, and the British – can work out how to defeat the Zhell."

She looked around at the staring faces illuminated in the flickering firelight. Alfie was regarding her as if she had taken leave of her senses. Anand had a semi-circular smile of hot chocolate plastered on the lower half of his face, the clownish parabola contrasting with his down-turned lips.

Only Lady Eddington, perhaps guessing something of her intentions, did not evince censure. "Interesting," she said, "and when you say 'go to the very top', you mean...?"

"I mean that perhaps I should present the facts to none other than the Prime Minister, Mr Trenchard."

Alfie almost choked on a mouthful of brandy. "You can't be serious? Trenchant Trenchard? But the man is a ruthless, power-mongering ignoramus!"

"He nevertheless holds the reins of power, and by confiding in him we would be getting what we wanted, which is the release and co-operation of Mahran, after all."

Alfie laughed, but without humour. "And how do you propose to gain Trenchard's ear? Waltz up to him as he comes out of Number Ten and buttonhole the old duffer?"

Lady Eddington smiled, "I think Jani's approach will be more subtle than that, am I not correct, my dear?"

Jani smiled. "I happen to know someone who serves in Trenchard's cabinet," she said.

"And who might this Tory be?" Alfie wanted to know.

"Lord Percival Consett," she said. "If I were to present the case to Lord Consett, stating all I know and the danger to the Empire, indeed to the world, then I am sure he would move Heaven and Earth to effect Mahran's release." She wondered, as she said the words, if she were not over-stating the case; he was, after all, a politician, with his own agenda and his own paymasters. What guarantee did she have that her story – fantastic as she admitted it to be – would be believed?

"And how do you know this Tory cabinet minister?" Alfie asked.

She sighed. "His son is Sebastian," she said. "As you know, we were at Cambridge together."

She knew that her flushed cheeks were not caused by the flames in the hearth. She regarded her fingers and murmured, "I think I mentioned that we were close, Alfie."

"I recall you mentioning nothing of your friendship with a Tory scion," he said.

"In that case it must have been Anand to whom I mentioned Sebastian."

The boy stared into the remains of his hot chocolate and said nothing.

"Be that as it may," Lady Eddington stepped in, "the fact remains that the situation is rather delicate. The last thing we want is for Jani to 'spill the beans', as I think the saying goes, and be arrested for her pains, her story disbelieved."

Jani looked at the faces regarding her, and said, "That is why I will confer with Sebastian before I approach Lord Consett."

She stopped, even hotter than before, and ran a finger around the collar of her blouse.

"But Jani-ji," Anand said, "are you sure he can be trusted?"

She felt a flash of impatience bordering on anger. "Of course he can be trusted! He is not merely a casual acquaintance, Anand, some Johnny-come-lately I picked up in the street!" As soon as the words were out, she regretted them. She sighed. "I will seek him out in the morning, sketch the main details of the story and ask him to arrange a meeting with his father."

She smiled sweetly at her friends, and to counter their silence, went on, "Well, do any of you have any better ideas?"

Alfie puffed out his cheeks, torn between expostulation and the admission that he was unable to present a counter plan. Anand remained frowning at his empty mug, clearly upset.

Jani had the guilty feeling that she had kicked two faithful mutts in the rump.

"In that case, in the morning I will..."

Alfie interrupted. "Excuse me, but have you thought this through, Jani? I mean, you admitted yourself that very soon the authorities will be on the lookout for you. Is it safe to go abroad, present yourself to this young man? Think about it – what if you were to be arrested? What then?"

Jani smiled sweetly. "I appreciate your concern, Alfie. But I have thought about the consequences. And even if I were to be arrested, I would appeal to Lord Consett to hear my story."

"I wouldn't put it past them," Alfie muttered, "to have you thrown in a cell and forgotten about."

"I think you are being sensationalist in that assessment, Lieutenant," she said.

Alfie appealed to Lady Eddington. "What do you think? Shouldn't we be more cautious, at least until...?"

The dowager smiled. "I am tempted, all things considered, to agree with Jani that the best course of action, at the present time, is to approach her young beau and attempt to assess, as the saying goes, the lie of the land. If he can arrange for you to have a word with Lord Consett, then all to the good. I think we need, at this juncture, to lay our cards on the table. Earth faces a perilous threat, and those in charge need to be made aware of the fact."

Alfie remained to be convinced. "But those in charge chose to disbelieve what both Mahran and Jelch told them. What makes you think that they will believe you now, a young slip of a..."

Jani stared at him. "So that is the basis of your objection, is it? That the information should come from a mere 'slip of a girl'? Would it be more credible, Lieutenant, if it were to come from your own lips, perchance?"

He waved her words away. "I didn't mean it like that," he said, flustered.

Jani set aside her cup and saucer and smiled at Lady Eddington. "Thank you again for your hospitality, and for a wonderful dinner. But it has been a long and exhausting day, and I really must turn in. I think I could sleep for a week."

Lady Eddington reached out and took her hand. "And you will find your bed of the utmost comfort. You see, my late husband owned many concerns, and one was the Sleepwell Mattress Company. It is one of the few businesses I kept on after his death, and I supervise the quality control of the products myself. Well, goodnight, my dear. Breakfast at nine-thirty."

"Goodnight, Amelia. Goodnight, gentlemen," Jani

said, inclining her head to Alfie and Anand, who murmured their goodnights almost inaudibly.

As she swept from the room, Jani was unable to say whether she felt like laughing or crying.

SHE AWOKE AT nine on Friday morning to brilliant sunlight streaming in through the window, as she had been too tired to draw the curtains the night before.

She lay in the impossibly comfortable bed. The last thing she recalled was her head hitting the pillow; from then, around ten o'clock, until now she had slept without interruption on one of Lady Eddington's truly heavenly Sleepwell mattresses.

She recalled the contretemps with Alfie last night, and felt a twinge of guilt: after everything he had done for her over the course of the last few days, she had treated him churlishly. But, she told herself in her own defence, he shouldn't have been so priggish in his objections.

She determined to apologise to him over her outburst; and, if he were the person she thought he was, she would expect an apology in return.

Someone knocked on the door and, when she replied, the maid entered bearing a pile of new clothes. "Just in from Harrods, Miss, with Lady Eddington's compliments."

Eliza slipped from the room, and Jani climbed out of bed and examined the clothes with excitement: two floral-patterned summer dresses, two pleated skirts with matching blouses – and a rather swish trouser suit that was the height of fashion with young debs these days.

She bathed in the adjoining bathroom, then returned and selected one of the summer dresses; Lady Eddington had even thought to supply underwear and stockings.

When she had dressed, and twirled to admire the result in the full length mirror, Jani admitted that she had never felt as fashionable in her life.

Then she sat on the bed and recalled her promise of the night before, to meet Sebastian and seek an audience with his father. She faced the prospect with not a little apprehension, tinged with anticipation. It would be wonderful to see Sebastian again. They might have been parted for less than three weeks, but it was as if ten times that long had elapsed. She missed him, missed his easy conversation, his courteous attention, his wit and wisdom – and the way he made her feel like the most beautiful, the most cherished girl in the world.

She was eager to feel his arms around her again, but at the same time she could not easily dismiss Alfie's concerns – that her rashness might indeed lead to her incarceration.

She told herself not to be so pessimistic. There was really no other way to go about effecting Mahran's release; she must inform the authorities, one way or another. And to do so through the agency of Sebastian would be to kill two birds with one stone.

She was considering going down to breakfast when there was another knock on the door.

"Come in," she called out.

The door opened and a shy face appeared in the gap. "Jani? I say, are you decent? I'm terribly sorry, but I really must see you."

"Alfie." She stood, facing him. "Very well, do come in and shut the door behind you."

She smiled as he entered and closed the door, for he was outfitted, bizarrely, in the deceased Lord Eddington's tweed plus-fours and jacket.

She covered her mouth to stifle a laugh, "Why, Alfie..."

He looked down at his attire and grinned sheepishly. "I know. I do look a bit of a twerp, don't I?"

"Well, I wouldn't quite say that, but after the uniform..."

"At least it will serve as a jolly decent disguise." He smiled across at her, reddening. "Anyway, I just thought I should apologise for what I said last night."

Her heart felt light. "And I was going to apologise to you, too."

He looked surprised. "For what?"

She leaned against the wall and crossed her arms. "For being insistent that mine was the only way, for riding roughshod over your doubts. I do appreciate your concern, you know?"

"Thank you." Alfie blushed. "And I just wanted to say sorry for demeaning you. I... I didn't mean to say that you wouldn't be listened to just because... because you're... you're who and what you are."

"Why, thank you," she said. *Who and what I am*?

"It just came out," he said.

Shut up, she thought, *before you incriminate yourself even more*.

"Apologies accepted," she said. "We all say things we don't mean to say. I've forgotten all about it. And now, Alfie, shall we go down to breakfast?"

He remained by the door, kicking his heels and staring at the carpet.

"Well?" she said.

He could not bring himself to look her in the eye, and he was obviously having difficulty framing his next words. "Jani, I meant what I said last night, about the dangers involved. Have you really thought through what you intend to do this morning?"

"I have considered every possibility, and judge that the course of action I'm about to take is the best possible way of securing the release of Mahran."

"At considerable risk to yourself."

She sighed. "Alfie, we've discussed this. Even if I were to be arrested..."

He interrupted. "If I may say so, Jani, I don't think you've had much experience of the perfidy of the British ruling class."

"Meaning?"

"Meaning that I think you are mistaken if you think that getting yourself arrested might be one way of attracting the attention of the Prime Minister. There is a reason that Mahran has been ignored – his story, taken at face value, is preposterous."

"In that case, with my story to corroborate his..."

"The British are ruthless!" Alfie expostulated. "Trenchard will have you clapped in gaol along with Mahran and that's the last we'll ever hear from you!"

"Alfie," Jani said after a few seconds, "is my safety what this is all about?"

He stared at her. "Of course. Your safety is paramount. After all we've been through together, do you think I could stand by and..."

"Or are you more concerned about my meeting Sebastian again?"

"No! I mean... Dash it all, Jani – of course I'm jealous, jealous as all hell! I don't mind admitting that. But if you think that is what's motivating me now, then you're wrong. I don't want to see you endangered."

"And I appreciate your concern," she said.

He stared at the carpet, then looked up. "I just want to say that what I feel for you, I've never felt for anyone else.

When you took my hand on the train to London... you don't realise how wonderful that made me feel! You're a special woman, Jani, and you mean the world to me."

It was her turn to stare at the carpet now, and redden. "Why..."

"You must have realised?"

She gestured non-commitally. Of course she had been aware of his devotion, his affection, his puppy-like adoration. "I just assumed that we were very good friends, Alfie."

"You're more to me than just a friend, Jani. Much more. I know, I know. I'm much older than you. We are separated by what...? Fourteen years? But..."

"Yes?"

"I just want you to know that I love you, and that I'll respect you and cherish your friendship even if... even if you decide to... even if you and Sebastian..." Unable to finish the sentence, he shook his head and looked wretched.

"And I thank you for that, Alfie. You're a good man, and I will value your friendship for ever."

He looked up and smiled at her, but despite her promise – or perhaps because of it – he still wore the expression of a kicked puppy.

She said, "And now shall we go down to breakfast, Alfie, and see what the day brings?"

CHAPTER
EIGHT

∽

At Ealing Common – The wondrous rocketship –
Alfie is wretched – Wise words from Anand
Mr Clockwork's Fabulous Emporium! –
"I will even help them fight the Zhell..."

TWICE AS TALL as St Paul's Cathedral, the golden sub-orbital rocket towered over the supporting gantry, its needle-point nose piercing the blue sky. The viewing concourse, fifty yards from the base of the rocketship, was thronged with sightseers craning their necks to take in the wonder of the Empire's latest, greatest invention.

Alfie and Anand crossed the concourse, took a crowded lift to the first gallery of the encircling gantry and squeezed out on to the elevated walkway. They made their way from the crowd and moved clockwise around the circular gallery, Anand wide-eyed at the rocket and Alfie impressed despite his current wretched mood.

The voice of the tour guide drifted their way. "Weighing some two hundred tons, and over fifteen years in development, the rocketship will make the journey from London to New York in a little over two hours."

Alfie heard gasps from the crowd, but at the moment all he wanted was to be alone with his thoughts.

He clutched the gallery rail and gazed at the scintillating flank of the vessel, its sleek body and tripod of flaring fins. Seen this close, the skin of the ship was not one seamless golden expanse; the curved surface was marked with a thousand tiny insignia and hatches large and small, fuel inlets and ports connected to the gantry by hanks of what he supposed were electrical cables.

Despite all this being derived from Vantissarian technology, he told himself, what was nevertheless impressive was the work done by British scientists and technicians to come to some understanding of the alien technology. Beside him, Anand was agog.

Alfie's own wonder at the ship, however, was short-lived, and soon he was swamped by the melancholia that had gripped him since the previous evening.

Until now he had thought little about his future; he had pledged himself to help Jani in any way he could, to remain faithful to her cause and ensure that she did not fall into the hands of the British, the Russians, and whoever else might be on her trail. He had prayed that Jani, seeing his faithfulness, and admiring what she might see as his sterling qualities of bravery and loyalty, might find it in her heart to reciprocate his affection in some way.

After their little tête-à-tête last night and this morning, however – and especially after his wrong-headed avowal of his love this morning, the mere thought of which made his face burn – he had little hope of this. Her heart was won by Sebastian (and Alfie felt a stab of mental pain at the very thought of his name), and he,

Alfie, was resigned to accepting that he would remain no more than a mere friend.

And his future? On the run from the British, AWOL, without a passport or papers... and no doubt suspected of the murder of Colonel Smethers... what would become of him over the course of the next few weeks?

They made a circle of the ship and arrived back at the lift. "Shall we go back down, Mr Alfie?" Anand asked. "I saw a little café on the Broadway selling delicious-looking cakes."

Alfie smiled. "Do you think of nothing but your stomach, boy?"

They descended in silence, left the rocket station and made their way across the common to the café. Five minutes later they were seated at a window table with a pot of Darjeeling tea, salmon paste sandwiches and a selection of éclairs, vanilla slices and Bakewell tarts.

Alfie bit into a sandwich without much appetite.

"You're very quiet, Mr Alfie," Anand observed, popping a second sandwich into his mouth.

"Oh!" Alfie sighed, and was surprised at how despairing he sounded. He shook his head. "I've been dwelling lately on what I did back in Nepal."

Colonel Smethers had killed the alien, Jelch, and Alfie had no doubt that he would have done the same to Anand, had he not intervened. Acting on reflex, he had run the colonel through with his light-beam almost before realising what he'd done.

He had killed a man, a fellow British officer, and despite telling himself that it had been for the greater good, no amount of retroactive self-justification would expunge the terrible sense of guilt that weighed upon his soul.

He asked himself if he would rather he had never met Janisha Chatterjee, had never allowed himself to be drawn into the complex tangle of intrigue and danger, but admitted that his life was richer, and that he had come to know himself a little better, thanks to Jani.

If only he'd not fallen head-over-heels for the girl!

Anand was frowning. "But you saved my life, and helped Jani also."

"And I wouldn't have done anything any differently," he assured the boy. "It's just... What I did, killing a man, was a terrible thing. But it's done now." He shook his head again, gazing down at the neat bite he had taken from the small triangle of white bread.

Into the following silence, Anand said, "Mr Alfie, I think that one of your problems is an affair of the heart, no?"

Alfie looked up. "And what do you mean by that?"

"Meaning, you are sad that Jani-ji loves another and not yourself."

Alfie stared at the lad, and his instinct was to deny the charge. He sighed. "You're very right, young Anand."

The boy looked up from the éclair he was about to slip into his mouth and smiled at Alfie. "I recognise your feelings because I too, until just a few days ago, felt sad also."

"You did? And what eased that sadness?"

The boy shrugged, chomped on the éclair, then said, wiping his lips with the back of his hand, "I looked at the situation with realistic eyes, Mr Alfie. I thought to myself: why would Jani-ji think romantic thoughts about a lowly houseboy when she is in love with a rich, handsome, aristocratic Englishman? Do you know that for years and years I harboured very very fond feelings for Jani-ji? All the while she was in England I was dreaming of the time she would return. And then she did, and we had many adventures, and a little piece of my heart did wonder at the possibility of..." He stopped, looking abashed, then went on, "But I must be realistic and know my place!"

Alfie smiled to himself and murmured, "And what is that, Anand?"

The boy straightened his spine. "I think of nothing but my duty, which is to serve Jani-ji, with no thought of reward. I will do what is right for her; I will save her from the British, from the Russians and from everyone else, and I will help her find Mahran. I will even help them fight the Zhell!"

Alfie gazed at the boy and felt a deep well of shame opening up within him. "That's very commendable," he said.

"And if you were wise, Mr Alfie, you too would forget the painful yearnings in your heart and dedicate yourself to assisting Jani and nothing else."

Alfie pushed aside his plate. "Oh, I assure you that I will not be deflected from being there for Jani and doing all I can to aid her in her mission. But at the same time I cannot dispel the heartache."

Anand smiled in sympathy and pushed the plate of cakes across the table. "Have an éclair and think of other things, Mr Alfie!"

Laughing, Alfie took an éclair and tried to obey the boy's advice.

After lunch, as planned, they left Ealing and took the monotrain to Crystal Palace and strolled around the New Great Exhibition, opened just last year and containing the many wondrous technologies of the Empire.

If anything, the marvels in the vast house of glass were even more awe-inspiring than the sub-orbital rocketship. Alfie took in exhibit after exhibit, impressed by the sheer diversity of the inventions; for brief periods he even managed, somehow, to forget the likelihood that Jani was now in the arms of her lover.

Here, behind cordons of braided maroon rope, were devices that defied identification until he read the captions describing each one: a silver contraption that resembled a giant silver tarantula was the innards of a telephonic relay system; what looked like a spinning gyroscope within an aquarium was a machine that transmitted coded messages to the other side of the world in a fraction of a second. Alfie watched two uniformed nurses who were demonstrating – on an actor with a realistic-looking leg wound – a tubular device that applied salve to the wound, closed the gash with synthetic flesh ties, then bandaged the limb in a process lasting no more than two minutes. He looked around at the hundreds of milling sightseers and marvelled that he and Anand, alone amongst all these souls, knew the truth behind the provenance of these inventions. He considered what the alien creators of these wonders might have made of the appropriation.

Anand, like a child in a sweetshop, said that he would meet Alfie at a nearby café in one hour and scurried off into the crowd.

Alfie strolled from exhibit to exhibit, his sense of wonder soon overcome by the sheer plethora of inventions.

Inevitably, perhaps, his thoughts turned to Jani and his thwarted love, and an almost palpable heartache gripped his chest. He considered Anand's wise words, and wished he could apply them to his own situation.

But the fact was that he could not *merely* serve Jani – though he would do his best to do so; he craved her love and affection. The thought of her conjured her image in his head. He had watched her at breakfast, eating toast with grace and decorum, her long-fingered hands and full lips, and those huge, liquid brown eyes! – and the vision of her in his mind's eye made him want to groan out loud. He was a lovesick fool and he wondered if there might be any cure.

"Mr Alfie! Mr Alfie!" Anand appeared at his side, tugging at his sleeve. "There you are. I have been searching for you all over! Come and see what I have found!"

Alfie allowed the boy to lead him by the hand through the surging crowd to the far end of the great palace. "There!" Anand announced, pointing to a display of what looked like clockwork automata.

"What?" Alfie said, wondering at the boy's excitement – and then he saw the mechanical elephant.

"Mr Clockwork told me that there was another mechanical elephant in London," Anand said. "But I didn't know that he had an emporium here also! Look."

Anand indicated a poster advertising Mr Clockwork's Fabulous Mechanical Emporium – 55 Earl Street, Putney, London.

"Can we go there now!" the boy said.

Alfie consulted his watch. "It's knocking on," he said. "And we did say that we'd be back at Amelia's by five. I'll tell you what, why don't we visit Mr Clockwork's Emporium tomorrow, if Jani isn't in need of our services?"

"Ah-cha," Anand nodded. "But can we have another half an hour here, Mr Alfie?"

"Half an hour, and then we'll catch the monotrain back to Mayfair," Alfie said, and with a heavy heart followed the boy down the crowded aisle.

CHAPTER
NINE

∽

Jani seeks Sebastian – In his arms again –
About the threat – A dinner date –
"Who's for more wine...?"

JANI TOOK THE monorail to Richmond where Lord Consett kept a Georgian mansion in immaculate grounds beside the river. Sebastian would still be on summer break from Cambridge, and if Jani knew him at all then she guessed that, rather than devote the morning to study, he would still be abed at eleven o'clock.

If there was one thing about him that she found a little annoying it was that he possessed the aristocrat's assumption that the best things in the world would come to him as by right and without having to work for them. He had been negligent, not to say downright lazy, in his studies at Cambridge, missing lectures and even seminars and offering up feeble excuses for his many absences. When she took him to task about it, he'd responded with an annoying flippancy and claimed that he was bright enough to get by without scurrying along to every lecture like an obedient sheep.

Against this, however, were his liberal attitudes, his passionate political concern for the underclasses, and his disdain for British rule in India. She supposed that his egalitarianism was the result of having rebelled against the influences of his upbringing; he refused to accept that just because he had been born into aristocracy, he should necessarily reap the rewards.

"But I detect a certain contradiction, Sebastian," she had said one day while strolling along the Thames at Richmond. "You disdain your studies and think that the world will fall at your feet, and yet you are set against inheriting your family's wealth – a stance I find eminently commendable, by the way."

He had turned his blonde head to regard her, smiling his charming smile. "There is no contradiction at all, Jani. I've told my father that I don't need his millions, and nor will I take advantage of his contacts in order to 'better' myself. At the same time, I don't see why I should kill myself studying that which I consider superfluous to my future."

His attitude astounded her; she had felt privileged to be accepted at Cambridge, and was determined to do her very best in her medical studies, for her own sake and to reward the expectations of her father... who now would never see those expectations fulfilled.

She had asked Sebastian what he saw as his future, and he had been maddeningly vague on the subject. "Oh," he had waved, "I am sure something will turn up."

Jani smiled at the recollection, and her heart swelled at the thought of seeing him again. She stared down at the busy London streets as the silver bullet of the monotrain carried her west.

She had done her best to lighten the mood at breakfast that morning, though after their little discussion in her room Alfie had been largely silent. Even Anand, normally so voluble, had been quiet; she wondered if he too resented her meeting Sebastian today. Alfie had finally elicited a smile of enthusiasm from the boy when he promised to take Anand to the rocket station at Ealing that morning, and in the afternoon to the New Great Exhibition at the Crystal Palace.

Lady Eddington had buttonholed Jani just before she left the house and slipped a crisp five pound note into her hand, warning her against drawing any monies from her own account. "The authorities have the banks in their pocket, my dear, and if they get confirmation that you've entered the country..."

Jani had arranged to meet Lady Eddington back at the house after four that afternoon, and hurried out.

Now the monotrain eased into Richmond station and Jani alighted with a dozen other passengers. She attracted the occasional glance as she left the station, being the only brown-skinned person in sight, but the police officer patrolling the platform failed to give her a second glance. Breathing a little easier, Jani left the station, crossed the road, and took the riverside path towards Consett House.

She wondered if she should feel guilty at Alfie's proclamation of love for her this morning. She had never considered herself vain, but she admitted to feeling a certain stirring in her heart at the thought of his affection. Was that terrible of her? She was devoted to Sebastian, after all, and yet could not deny – despite her protestations that morning – feeling not a little reciprocal affection towards the young Lieutenant. The feel of his hand in hers on the train journey to London yesterday had set her heart aflutter.

Her head was a whirl of conflict, not unlike the confusion she felt when she considered the problem of her identity. English or Indian? At times she felt one, and then the other, and then a little of both – and sometimes even, she admitted, neither!

Life was, she told herself, often a muddle through which one navigated one's way guided by the fickle rudder of instinct.

And her instinct told her that what she was doing now, in seeking out Sebastian and his father, and perhaps even the Prime Minister, was the right course of action.

She would slip into the grounds of Consett House, sneak through the garden and, rather than present herself at the front door, tap on the window of Sebastian's ground-floor room. How surprised he would be to see her! His face would be a picture.

She was contemplating this when she noticed, across the river, a young man strolling along a path in the Park, and her heart surged.

It was Sebastian, slim and upright and very blond, in a summer blazer and flannels.

She had the urge to call out, but restrained herself. She would cross the river and sneak up behind him. She hurried to the next bridge, a hundred yards further along the river, and crossed it to the Park.

Sebastian was two hundred yards ahead of her by now, strolling along with his hands in his pockets. She wondered if he had turned a new leaf – rising early, for him, before getting down to his studies. But she doubted it.

Jani increased her pace, relishing the duration before springing her surprise. As far as Sebastian was aware, she was still in Delhi, mourning the passing of her father.

A hundred yards ahead of her now, he turned from the path and crossed a rising greensward flanked by oak trees. At the crest of the hill, silhouetted against the blue sky, was a park bench. Sebastian sat down and stretched his arms along its back in a characteristic pose she recalled so well.

She would move to the oaks, hurry from one to the other until she was near the bench, then watch him until his sixth sense alerted him to her presence. She felt the pressure of excitement rise in her chest as she crossed the grass to the first oak, then moved on to the next.

She was behind the second oak tree from the park bench when she saw, coming from the opposite direction, a tall man in a dark suit and homburg, who strolled up the rise and took the seat next to Sebastian.

Jani peered around the tree trunk at the two men seated with their backs to her. This was evidently a pre-arranged meeting, as Sebastian and the stranger were now engaged in earnest discussion, Sebastian gesturing from time to time. At one point he drew a long, buff envelope from an inner pocket of his blazer and passed it to the man. Two minutes later the meeting was over; the tall, dark suited stranger rose, tipped his homburg, and strolled off down the hill, soon disappearing from sight.

Jani spent a minute speculating about the man; a theatrical agent, perhaps, who had accepted one of Sebastian's plays? Or had Sebastian started reviewing on the side, and rather than expend effort in going into London had arranged to hand over the copy closer to home?

Her heart tripped with anticipation as she moved around the tree and approached the park bench.

She considered clasping her hands over his eyes and saying, "Guess who?" but as she tiptoed towards the bench, Sebastian heard her and turned his head.

He leapt to his feet, his face the epitome of shock.

"Good God!"

"Well," she laughed, "are you pleased to see me, Sebastian?"

"Jani?" he said incredulously, a mop of blond hair falling over his eyes. He swept it back with the careless gesture she loved so much. "Good God, but what are you doing here?"

"Why, I'm here to see you, of course."

"Jani!" He sounded desperate, and his gaze swept the surrounding hillside wildly as if ascertaining whether their conversation was being observed. "Jani..."

"Is that all you're going to say?" she teased him. "Anyway, who was your friend?"

"Who?" He looked puzzled. "Oh, Jefferson? He... he was employed by my father until recently, until he was forced to leave. He's fallen on hard times and I'm helping him out."

She smiled at him. "You're a kind man, Sebastian," she said. "Well, are you going to stand there all day, staring at me as if I'm a ghost, or do you intend to give me a hug?"

He glanced down at the bench that separated them, then vaulted it in one leap like a triumphant tennis player and pulled her to him. "Jani... This is impossible! How on earth did you get here?"

She laughed, luxuriating in the feel of his arms around her. They kissed. "It's a long story," she said when her lips were free, "and one you're unlikely to believe."

He pulled away and stared at her at arm's length, like an art dealer examining an old master. "But... you do realise that half the world is searching for you?"

Her stomach turned. "They are?"

"Well, every damned figure of authority in the Empire, that is."

She stared at him, feeling horribly endangered. "They've contacted you, quizzed you as to my whereabouts?"

He escorted her around the bench and sat her down. Facing her, he said, "I found out from another source... At Westminster."

"Ah, your father told you?"

He licked his lips. "My father said nothing to me. You see, I work now as a secretary for Cecil Palmer, the MP."

She stared at him, mystified. "A secretary? But Cambridge...?"

"I couldn't hack the damned place. Hated the people, the lectures." He stroked her cheek with his knuckles. "So I decided to get out and do something worthwhile."

"Like work for a Tory MP?" she asked.

"How might I learn to subvert that which I despise if I don't know how the system works, Jani?"

"I still don't understand how you came to find out about me."

He pressed a finger to her lips, a gesture he had used before, and which she found annoying. "Shhh. Listen to me. I came across a memo. Confidential. I only had time to read it briefly. Imagine my shock when I found out that its subject was you."

She was glad she was sitting down, or she might have collapsed. "What did it say?"

"Just that you were in possession of something, and that you must be apprehended at all costs. You met with someone in India. The last thing the report mentioned was that you were expected to make your way back to Britain and that the authorities must be placed on the highest alert." He stared at her. "Jani, what the blazes is going on?"

She clutched his hand. "Sebastian, you might find this

hard to believe. I know I would, but please believe me when I say that everything I am about to tell you is true." She took a deep breath. "Very well..."

She began with the attack on the *Rudyard Kipling* and recounted her survival and meeting with the creature called Jelch, a Morn.

Sebastian listened in silence, not even interjecting with questions when her story became a confusion of names and places. She told him about being chased across northern India and into Nepal by the British and Russians, how Jelch had being killed by a madman named Colonel Smethers, and how Smethers had been killed in turn by the man who had acted as a staunch ally, one Lieutenant Alfie Littlebody.

She told Sebastian about the ventha-di now lodged in her stomach, and her audience with the Morn-entity aboard the Vantissarian ship, and how the British were plundering the ship for its advanced technology – and, most importantly, she warned Sebastian of the threat from the Zhell and her mission to free Mahran, the Morn, from Newgate in order to prevent the Zhell's invasion of Earth.

He shook his head. "A ventha-di?" he said, the word sounding odd on his lips.

"It is a small triangular object, wafer thin, with circular holes at the three corners. Into each of these holes fits a ventha, like a small coin. I have one ventha already in the ventha-di. The second is in the possession of the Morn imprisoned by the British – or at least he knows of its whereabouts. No-one knows where the third ventha might be."

Even to her ears the story sounded fantastical – even she found the notion of the alien threat somewhat abstract – and she could only wonder how it might seem to Sebastian. Would he think her mad, having lost her wits in the aftermath of the crash-landing and the death of her beloved father?

He stared down at her hand in his, then raised his eyes to hers. She said, "You do believe me, Sebastian? You don't think me insane?"

He squeezed her hand and looked away from her, staring across the park. He seemed to be lost in thought, his gaze seeing something far, far distant.

"Well, Sebastian?"

"And you need my help to secure the release of this creature, this Mahran, from Newgate?"

Her heart leapt. "So you do believe me!"

He shook his head. "I must admit I find it all hard to believe. But... but I ask myself, why should you make up such a fantastical tale? And I suppose it explains why the authorities are looking for you."

She looked around, as if squads of police might at this very minute be encircling the park. "And will you help me? You will approach your father?"

"What do you think?" he said, kissing her lips again.

She felt a pain in her abdomen, which she knew to be love, or passion, or something similar, and wanted to fall into his arms and weep with relief.

Sebastian shook his head again, in wonderment. "And to think that all the technology which the Empire would have us believe is the result of Great British invention, is no more than the scraps from an alien table. What delicious irony!" He looked at her, then remembered himself. "But you're in danger here," he went on, clutching her hands. "Dash it all, come back to the house."

"But won't your mother and father–?"

"They're away for a few days, visiting the country seat in Warwickshire. We need to talk; there's so much to catch up on. I was so sorry, Jani, to hear about your father."

She bit her bottom lip and stared at him through eyes brimming with unshed tears, then said, "At least... at least I was with him at the end."

They hurried down the hill, hand in hand.

"And you must be very careful when you leave," he said. "Where are you staying at the moment?"

She told him that Lady Eddington was kindly lodging herself, Lieutenant Littlebody and Anand Doshi, at her townhouse for the duration.

He cast her a dubious glance. "Eddington? The widow of Charles Eddington, that vile Empire builder?"

"The same, but let me assure you that Lady Eddington is a wonderful person. Without her we might never have been able to escape from India."

"And this Littlebody character?"

"A sweet little man who has assisted me selflessly, putting his life on the line to do so, along with Anand. You must recall me talking about my childhood play-mate, the houseboy Anand Doshi?"

"Quite a little team you have yourself there. I hope their intentions are honourable."

"Sebastian, they have given up everything they have for me and the mission to locate Mahran. They are good people."

He indicated a path that led to the imposing Georgian pile half a mile away beside the river. They hurried through a stand of elm trees.

"And you say you're all lodging with Lady Eddington in Mayfair? Where exactly?"

"Mount Street, number 15. But why–?"

He slipped an arm around her waist. "So that I know where to find you, of course, Though, on second thoughts, it might be wisest to find alternative accommodation."

She glanced at him, alarmed. "Do you think–?"

"Tongues wag. If neighbours saw a beautiful Indian girl enter and leave the house, accompanied by a soldierly type and a young Indian... And if the authorities started asking questions..."

They came to the gates of Consett House and hurried up the drive. Minutes later they crossed the ornate marble hallway to the west wing, where Sebastian had a suite of rooms overlooking an emerald lawn as neat as a swathe of baize.

In the small living room he poured himself a brandy and offered her the same.

"Tonic water for me, please."

"You don't mind if I...? All this comes as something of a shock, after all."

They crossed to a chesterfield and sat side by side. He took her hand. "So you came to me so that I might broach this with my father, see what he says about coming clean to Trenchard?"

"That was the idea, yes. It seemed," she said, despairing, "the only possible way forward." She stared into his face, trying to assess by his expression what he thought of the plan.

"Well?" she prompted.

"Trenchard is a rogue. The stories I've heard about his quelling of the revolt in Kenya... The man is an out-and-out militaristic Imperialist with no conscience. He believes every race to be lesser than the British and assumes that this gives him carte blanche to annihilate them. Oh–" he went on at her wide-eyed reaction, "I use the term advisedly. *Annihilate*. He's instituted a shoot-first policy in South Africa and Malaya."

"So you think I should not consider approaching him?"

He pursed his lips around a mouthful of brandy, then nodded. "Perhaps it would be a mistake."

"But surely he'd listen to me? If my story tallies with Mahran's..." She leaned forward. "According to Jelch, the only way the Zhell might be countered is if Mahran possessed all three venthas. Then he might be able to effect some kind of seal or... Oh, I don't know exactly what he could do! But Jelch said that the Zhell are merciless, and we must do something. You do believe me, don't you?"

"I do, of course I do. But the question is, would Trenchard? The man suspects spies in every room. By all accounts he's half-mad with paranoia."

"Then what should I do?" she asked in desperation. "Surely your father might intercede on my behalf, approach Trenchard–"

Sebastian nodded. "This is what I'll do. I'll contact father, explain the situation. I'm sure he'll see reason. For a dyed-in-the-wool Tory, the old duffer is a reasonable man. I'll phone him this evening and get back to you."

She let out a sigh of relief and sat back. "Do you know, I worried that you wouldn't believe me? I worried that you would think me half-mad."

He stroked her cheek. "Only half-mad, what with you spouting a tale of alien beings and invading hordes? By rights I should think you stark, staring crazy, so far gone down Queer Street, as Doyle would have it, that you couldn't find your way back."

She kissed his fingers. "Oh, Sebastian! You cannot imagine how I've missed you!"

"And me, you. One solitary telegram from some Brigadier's secretary assuring me that you'd survived the crash-landing with minor injuries, and then nothing at all, not a dickey-bird."

"But I was being chased across half of India by the Raj and crazed Russians," she laughed.

"Christ, Jani, how beautiful you are when you laugh!"

"*Only* when I laugh?"

"Even more so when you laugh. You're the most beautiful woman in the world. Come here!"

She was in his arms, kissing him with a passion she thought herself incapable of; his fingers traced the line of her ribs, cupped her left breast and made her gasp. She felt that spasm in her lower abdomen again, knew it to be lust and wondered – maddeningly – what her father might say.

She pulled away, took a breath, arranged her hair and found her tonic water. "And you, have you not fallen in love with some pretty secretary at the House of Commons?"

"Oh, there are one or two who have their eye on me."

"Just like those serving girls at King's?" she said.

"Oh, much prettier," he laughed.

"I'm upset."

"Don't be. They're none as beautiful, nor as intelligent, as you."

"You're just saying that,"

"I mean it." He reached out and grabbed her hand. "Jani, stay the night, please. Share my bed."

She stood quickly, spilling a little of her drink. "Sebastian..."

He looked up at her with imploring eyes. "You have no idea how much I desire you, Jani."

She felt a little dizzy, as if it were she who had partaken of the brandy, and lots of it. Her vision swam and her abdomen ached. She wanted to fall into his arms, allow him to carry her to his bed, undress her slowly...

She closed her eyes. "No. I'm sorry. It... it wouldn't be proper. Oh, Sebastian. I love you so, but now is not the right time."

"When might be the right time, then?"

"Soon, I promise. Once... once I have found my bearings, once things have sorted themselves out. You do understand, don't you?"

He smiled at her, eased himself back on the chesterfield and sipped his brandy. "Of course I do. What do you take me for, a rake? I'll wait for as long as you like. I love you, too, Jani."

Her heart swelled, and the thought of alien invasion, of menace from a realm beyond this one, seemed an impossible notion beside the real, hard fact of her love for this young Englishman.

They talked on and on, missing lunch, Jani filling in the details of her adventures while Sebastian spoke disparagingly of his work in the Commons and the fossilised Tories to whom he was obliged to kow-tow.

It was after three when she looked up and noticed the carriage clock on the mantel-shelf. She told Sebastian that she must fly, as she had promised Lady Eddington that she would return by four. He insisted that she travel back by taxi, rather than risk being spotted by a vigilant bobby aboard the monorail to Mayfair.

They parted with kisses at the front door, Sebastian promising he would telephone his father that evening and be in touch with her forthwith. As the taxi whisked her away and east through the busy streets of London,

Jani sat back and wondered whether, despite everything, she had ever been as happy in all her life.

OVER DINNER THAT evening she informed Lady Eddington, Alfie and Anand that her meeting with Sebastian had proved successful. "He agreed with me that it would be wise to approach his father, Lord Consett, about the matter before taking it to the Prime Minister."

"And Sebastian believed your story about the crash-landed vessel, creatures from other realms, and invading alien hordes?" Alfie asked.

"But of course."

"He wasn't at all sceptical?"

"Not at all. He believed me. I am not in the habit of telling lies to Sebastian, you see."

Alfie shrugged. "I would have thought he would have found it all a bit far-fetched, that's all."

Jani smiled, recalling what Sebastian had told her. "The story was so incredible that it just had to be true – I think that was his reasoning, along with the fact that I had no reason to lie to him."

"Exactly so," Lady Eddington put in. "More wine, my dear?"

As Jani sipped her wine, she wondered at Sebastian's acceptance of her fabulous story – and told herself that it could mean only one thing: that he did love her, and trusted her every word.

Alfie asked, with manifest insincerity, "And how was Sebastian?"

"He is well, and working as a secretary in the House of Commons."

"I thought he was at Cambridge?"

"He was," Jani replied. "But he decided to... to leave and find employment more suited to his temperament."

"Did he leave, or was he sent down?"

Jani's face flared with heat, and she was casting around for a suitably cutting reply when Lady Eddington said, "And how was your day, Anand?"

"The sub-orbital rocket was astounding," the boy said. "But even better was the Great Exhibition. Did you know that Mr Clockwork has an emporium in London? Mr Alfie said we might visit it tomorrow or the day after."

The butler ghosted up to Lady Eddington and whispered in her ear. She turned to Jani and said, "A phone call for you, Jani. From Sebastian. Dobson will take you to the library."

Jani dabbed her lips with a napkin, excused herself and hurried from the room. Dobson indicated the library, and Jani crossed to the phone and snatched up the receiver. "Sebastian?"

"Jani, my sweet Indian princess. You can't imagine how wonderful it was to see you today."

"I think I can, Sebastian, as I felt the very same."

"Well, I contacted pater earlier this evening—"

"And?"

"And, without mentioning your name, I put it to him that I was in contact with someone who could corroborate the story of the prisoner held in Newgate."

Jani pressed the receiver to her ear. "What did he say?"

Sebastian hesitated. "He saw through me, and asked if you'd been in contact. I admitted as much, Jani, though claimed that you'd phoned me."

"And his reaction?" Jani held her breath.

"He said that it would be in your best interests if you were to give yourself up right away."

"Mmm. So we aren't much further forward."

"I'm sorry. I rather bungled it. But I'll talk to him tomorrow, explain the situation and make him see the danger we're all in. But in the meantime..."

"Yes?"

"It would be wonderful to see you again. I know you must be careful, but I thought perhaps we could meet tomorrow evening? I know just the place, a restaurant in Whitechapel."

"Whitechapel?" she laughed. "How romantic!"

"I'm sorry, Jani. I'd much rather take you to the Ritz, in a perfect world. But I know the most wonderful Indian restaurant called Wahlid's, on Watson Road."

"The perfect habitat for a girl of my complexion," she said.

"You aren't angry with me?"

"Of course not!" she hastened to reassure him. "I want to see you, and the venue doesn't matter at all. And it will be nice to eat Indian food."

"We can discuss all this business about approaching my father, and how to go about it, and the prisoner in Newgate and all that."

"I'll look forward to seeing you, Sebastian."

He suggested meeting at the restaurant at eight, and advised Jani to take a taxi directly to Whitechapel. She said goodbye, replaced the receiver, and returned to the dining room.

"Well?" Anand asked as she took her seat at the table.

"Lord Consett said that it would be wise if I were to hand myself in to the authorities," she said, somewhat paraphrasing Sebastian's message.

"But did he give you any reassurance that you would be unharmed?" Alfie wanted to know.

"He said no more than that. I am meeting Sebastian tomorrow, in Whitechapel, to discuss the matter further and plan the way forward."

Anand stared at her with a spoonful of treacle pudding halfway to his mouth. "Perhaps Alfie and I should come too," he said, "seeing as how every bobby in London will be looking out for you."

Alfie said, "I think Jani will want to be alone when she meets her young man, Anand."

Jani avoided his eyes, and recalled something that Sebastian had said earlier that day. "And I was wondering," she said, "whether it is safe for us to remain here with you, Lady Eddington. If there is an alert out for me, and they are looking also for Alfie and Anand, and if we have been seen coming and going from here..."

Lady Eddington pursed her thin lips, considering. "I know a little place in Highgate, owned by a friend. I will look into your staying there, my dear."

"I was thinking," Jani said, "that I would not want our presence to land you in trouble with the authorities."

The dowager laughed. "My child, I am old enough not to care about the retribution of the authorities! It is your safety that is my concern! Now, who's for more wine?"

Jani accepted a second glass, and then a third, and she was quite tipsy by the time she made her way to bed.

CHAPTER
TEN

❧

Sebastian meets his handler – On the Triangle Line –
Rostov shows his hand – Blackmail! –
"I know where the device is..."

SEBASTIAN SPENT A miserable two hours in the House
of Commons library the following morning. Cecil
Palmer, MP, had instructed him to go through Hansard
in search of a speech given by some Liberal member on
the Kenyan revolt last year, Palmer hoping to wrong-
foot the Liberal on some policy matter – but Sebastian
was unable to concentrate. His mind was full of Jani,
his shame at his recent conduct with Felicity and others,
and the dilemma in which he now found himself.

The sight of her yesterday, the feel of her in his arms,
her obvious love for him... despite her coy demurral
when he asked her to stay the night... had all served
to convince him that he felt for Janisha what he
had felt for no other. Physical intimacy with Felicity
and her like was all very well, but while undeniably
pleasurable was ultimately meaningless. When in
Jani's company he felt uplifted, in awe not only of
her beauty, and her intelligence, but her personality
– her pluck and humour and occasional, intense

seriousness. The mere thought of her now sent his heart thumping.

And her fantastic story of alien ships, otherworldly beings, a device which she carried in her stomach and portals to other realms? As outlandish as it all sounded in the cold light of day, he believed her. He knew Jani Chatterjee, knew that she was not one to make up such fantastical tales, for any reason. She really did carry an alien device secreted in her person, which the British authorities, along with the Russians and Indians, were at pains to possess.

He had told Jani last night that he had mentioned 'someone' to his father; but this had been a holding tactic, as he had not spoken to his father and had no intention of doing anything of the sort.

At the same time, he was loath to tell the Russians of their meeting, or where she was now hiding.

How could he betray Jani in her hour of need?

The problem was, what to do?

As the clock approached midday, he scribbled down a few notes from Hansard, outlining the Liberal's speech, and decided to take a stroll along the river, perhaps have lunch, and think about what to do next.

He escaped the dusty library and emerged blinking into brilliant sunlight. It appeared that all London shared his idea, for the riverbank path was busy with strolling sightseers. A jet-powered catamaran sped past on the Thames, offering tours of the river, and overhead a swollen blimp sailed by advertising Camp Coffee.

Sebastian bought a pot of tea and a Cornish pasty from a tearoom and decided to sit at an outside table overlooking the river.

As he ate, without really tasting the pasty, he considered Jani and what he should do about her.

The obvious course of action was to continue stalling her on the question of approaching his father. When he met her at Wahlid's this evening he would say that his father had yet to broach the matter with the PM; a lie, but a necessary one. It would buy him time. As for the Russians... he would ensure that he was not followed when he rendezvoused with her, and exhort her to extreme caution.

He sipped his tea and stared across the sparkling river, and a thought occurred to him.

Her mission in coming back to Britain was to locate this prisoner, Mahran, give him the device and locate two others which, all together, she thought might act as some sort of seal or barrier between the worlds.

Sebastian's obvious course of action was to assist her in this, of course; perhaps, if Jani passed on the ventha-di to the alien, then her part in the affair would be finished. The authorities might examine her all they wished, but she could either claim ignorance or tell the truth, that Mahran now possessed the device.

Of course, if the alien were incarcerated in Newgate gaol, then contacting him would be easier said than done.

Why, he thought, couldn't life be simple?

He was smiling at the memory of kissing Jani yesterday when a street urchin hurried up to his table, dropped an envelope beside his plate and muttered, "Note from Mr Rostov, sir."

His heart sinking, Sebastian gave the lad tuppence, waited until he'd run off, then opened the envelope with shaking fingers.

The note was succinct: *Hyde Park, three o'clock.*

Rostov was his contact at the Russian embassy – Dmitri Korolov's immediate superior – and a summons from Rostov was so rare that Sebastian's mental alarm bells were set ringing.

He pushed his half-eaten pasty aside; he no longer felt hungry. The sunlight, the gay crowds of tourists, the perky dance band tune drifting from the tearoom's radio, all served to point up his abject melancholia.

As he made his way from the café, he wondered if his chance meeting yesterday with Jani in Richmond Park had been witnessed by his contact. The thought turned his stomach.

Back at the library, he tried to push all thoughts of Jani and his meeting with Rostov from his mind and concentrate on the Liberal's speech. The minutes ticked by with agonising slowness and first images of Jani, kissing him, strayed into his head, quickly followed by Rostov's stolid Muscovite visage. His contact was a soul peculiarly devoid of humour, smalltalk, or any of the finer human virtues. Sebastian had met him only twice before, on both occasions being reprimanded for not producing what was required.

At two-thirty he left his report on Palmer's desk and hurried out.

Perhaps, he told himself as he went, the meeting might not concern Jani at all.

And, as his father was fond of saying, porcine creatures might emulate airships.

He arrived at Hyde Park at three. Rostov was five minutes late, and this time the stocky, barrel-chested Russian didn't sit down on the bench beside Sebastian.

He paused, ostensibly to light a cigarette, and as he

did so muttered, "The three-twenty monotrain from Hyde Park, coach three," and strolled on.

Sebastian watched him go, his heart pounding and his face running with sweat. The meeting on the Triangle Line could mean only one thing, that Rostov wanted more than just a brief discussion with him. Their interview was to be protracted, in some quiet compartment aboard the monotrain, as the train made its endless equilateral journey around London.

Sebastian waited until his contact had waddled out of sight, then made his way to the monorail station, feeling more than a little sick. He was sure now that the Russians were aware of his having met Jani.

But what line should he take if they confronted him with the fact?

He entered the station, bought a day ticket and, when the monotrain slid up to the platform, stepped aboard the third coach and found an empty compartment. He sat down beside the window and stared out as the train eased itself from the station. He watched the Thames pass by below and drew a nervous breath, his apprehension mounting.

He started as a shadow fell across him, and he looked up to see Rostov staring down at him unsmilingly. The Russian took the seat opposite Sebastian, a short, fat man dressed in a fraying grey suit. His face was pale, his nose almost purple, as if back in his motherland he had existed on a diet of cabbage and vodka.

"It has been a long time, no, since our last meeting? Six months?" Rostov gestured with a wave, as if absolving Sebastian from the need to reply.

"I trust the plans I obtained were satisfactory?"

"The plans? Oh, the plans! Very good. Well done, my

friend." He waved again, dismissively. "But I come not about the plans, my friend."

Sebastian nodded, his mouth drying out suddenly. "Then?"

"I come about the girl, Janisha Chatterjee. Your – how do you English say it? – your old fire."

"Flame," Sebastian corrected.

"You English have such turns of phrase! 'Old flame'. Which suggests that these people, these women, might at any moment be extinguished, no?"

Was this, Sebastian wondered, a coded threat? "I don't think it suggests this at all," he said. "And anyway, Jani isn't–"

"Yes?"

"An old flame." He found himself reddening.

The Russian frowned. "But you and her were once upon a time...?" Rostov made an obscene gesture: pumping a fat forefinger into a circle formed by the thumb and forefinger of his left hand. "No?"

"No," Sebastian muttered. He stared out of the window. They were passing Kensington High Street, the pavements packed with busy shoppers. How Sebastian wished he was amongst them.

"I am disappointed, Sebastian," Rostov said. "Very disappointed. You see, you were seen yesterday, in Richmond Park, with this girl, this Janisha Chatterjee. Now Mr Korolov reports that he spoke with you the other evening, and told you about Chatterjee. Mr Korolov reports that he asked you to contact us if the girl came to see you, no?"

Sebastian gave his most disarming smile. "I assure you that you have no reason to be disappointed. I wanted a little time alone with Jani before I alerted you."

"So all is well!" the Russian beamed at him. "You saw the girl, and she told you where she is staying in London, no?"

Sebastian shook his head, thinking fast. "No. No, she didn't. I asked, of course, but she thought it wise not to say, in the circumstances."

"She cannot suspect that you...?"

"I'm sure she suspects nothing of the kind," Sebastian reassured him.

"That is good–"

Sebastian interrupted. "But don't *you* know where she is staying? If you saw us together in the Park, I presume you had her followed?"

The Russian made his characteristic, dismissive wave again. "Agh! But the fool who followed her taxi lost her in traffic. So you see, it is imperative we find the girl." Rostov hesitated, then went on, "She told you why the British, and we Russians, are pursuing her, yes?"

"No. She said nothing about this. We had other things to talk about. But the other evening Korolov said something about a certain item."

"The details need not bother us, my friend. Suffice to say, she has something that we want."

"Something?"

"Something, an item, which I cannot discuss with you. Let me say, though, that it is important to the security of the motherland, yes? And therefore, my good comrade, its importance is your concern also."

Sebastian nodded. "I see."

"So I need hardly state that you should arrange to meet the Chatterjee girl again, and thereafter we shall conduct a little conversation with her."

"And do you think she will give you this item, just like that?"

Rostov smiled, and the expression did not sit well on a face hitherto unaccustomed to accommodating such jollity. "I think we might be able to *persuade* her to do just that, my friend."

"'Persuade her'?" Sebastian was aware of sweat trickling down his chest. He stared at the Russian. "I'm sorry. I can't be party to the torture of someone I love."

"Commendable sentiments!" Rostov cried with unusual animation. "I suspected you might take this line." He reached into an inner pocket of his grey suit jacket. "But I feel sure that I can persuade you to see reason."

Sebastian felt sick as the Russian pulled a long manila envelope from his pocket and, with difficulty, inserted two fat fingers and tweezered out what appeared to be a photograph.

Rostov regarded the photograph for a minute, smiling to himself, occasionally turning the snapshot this way and that, the better to appreciate whatever was represented.

"Now I wonder if your employer, or your father, or even the Chatterjee girl herself, would care to peruse what I have here, my friend?" And watching Sebastian closely, he passed him the photograph.

Sebastian took it with shaking fingers. He gagged, sure that he was about to vomit. It took a few seconds for him to make complete sense of the tangle of limbs, and to register that the figures in the picture were himself and Felicity Travers. He had never seen anything quite so graphic, but the photograph – the frozen representation of such intimacy – made carnal and animalistic an act he recalled as being exquisitely pleasurable... if, in retrospect, tainted with the bitter corrosive of guilt.

He swallowed a mouthful of bile and passed the photograph back to Rostov, who smiled and, with an expression of surprise, declared, "And here we have another one!"

This photograph showed Sebastian with a girl whose name eluded him. If anything, it was even more revealing than the first, his face in very close proximity to the blonde's *derrière*.

"And yet another!" Rostov said, pulling a third picture from the envelope with the élan of a magician producing a rabbit from a hat. "My word, but you exhibit an appetite that I, as an old man, find enviable!"

Sebastian barely glanced at the photograph, wincing, and almost flung it back at the Russian. "These women... Felicity and the others... they were working for you?"

"Not directly, so that they would know who employed them. But yes, we paid them to..." Rostov raised the pictures in the air before inserting them back into the envelope. "But let me keep these safe, for we would not want them falling into the wrong hands, would we?"

Sebastian thought back a few nights to the Burgundy Club and events at Felicity's apartment with the two women – and he experienced a quick stab of disappointment at the fact that they had been paid to seduce him.

"What do you want?" he muttered.

"Merely what I stated earlier. Arrange to meet the Chatterjee girl. We will take it from there."

Sebastian closed his eyes, near to tears. If the photographs got out, came into the possession of his father and mother, or Jani... It would be over with Jani, of course, and his parents would be destroyed.

But the alternative, betraying Jani and leaving her to the cruel mercy of the Russians, to be tortured until she revealed the whereabouts of the ventha-di...

He stared out of the window as the train drew up at Holland Park station. A little girl, her hair in blonde pig-tails, skipped along clutching her mother's hand, and both mother and daughter were laughing joyously. The vision was so beautiful, so innocent, that it brought tears to Sebastian's eyes.

As the train pulled from the station, Sebastian knew what he must do.

He turned to Rostov and said, "What I said earlier, about not knowing where the device is. I was lying. Jani told me."

The Russian leaned over his little pot-belly. "She did?" Rostov smiled. "And you will... how shall I say?... assist us in this matter?"

Sebastian felt ill. "I... I have an idea, a scheme to retrieve it. But," he rushed on, "I want your assurances that Jani will come to no harm. Do you agree to that?"

"Very well, my friend." Rostov narrowed his piggy-eyes. "Tell me."

He told Rostov about his arrangement to meet Janisha at Wahlid's tonight, and thinking on his feet outlined his scheme to retrieve the device. The Russian listened attentively, nodding occasionally.

Sebastian finished speaking and leaned back. Rostov smiled and offered Sebastian his chubby hand. They shook.

"I knew I could rely on you, my friend."

"But remember – Jani is not to be harmed!"

"You have my assurances that we will harm not a hair on her head," Rostov said. "I will see you later this evening, yes, and we will raise glass of vodka to our ingenuity!"

"And when you have the device..." Sebastian began.

"Yes?"

He relayed to the Russian what Jani had told him about the threat of the Zhell, and the importance of the Morn languishing in Newgate gaol – the story sounding bizarre and far-fetched as he tried to convince the Russian.

"So you see," he said, "it is vital that we should work with this Morn, Mahran, to defend the planet."

Rostov said "An amazing story, my friend."

"But you believe me?"

Rostov's expression remained impassive. "We knew already about the alien prisoner of the British," he said. "And when we have the device, and have succeeded in liberating the Morn, then we shall be in a better position to assess this... this alien threat, no?"

The train pulled into the next station and Rostov climbed to his feet.

Sebastian reached out, imploring. "And the photographs?"

Rostov smiled. "All in good time, my friend. All in good time!"

He nodded a terse farewell and hurried from the compartment.

As the train accelerated from the station, Sebastian swore to himself, sat back in his seat and closed his eyes.

CHAPTER
ELEVEN

～

Dining at Wahlid's – A stroll through the market –
Sebastian has a plan – Pursuit! –
"You really are imagining things!"

THE PRESS OF humanity passing up and down the street made it impossible for the taxi to drop Jani directly outside Wahlid's, so it braked on the corner and she climbed out. "A hundred yards down the street on your right, duck," the driver said as Jani paid him.

She had last seen crowds like this in Old Delhi on leaving the hospital following her father's death. She had wandered for a while, losing herself in the familiar scents and sounds and recalling the times she and her father had strolled down the narrow streets of the capital. Now she was in a district of London that looked like part of the sub-continent relocated halfway around the world, though there were fewer Indians amongst the crowd than Bangladeshis and Nepalese. Most of them were in traditional dress, the women in saris and the men in shalwar kameez, and Jani felt a little out of place in her summer dress and powder blue cashmere cardigan.

She had spent the day at Lady Eddington's, reading Jane Austen and taking afternoon tea with the dowager.

Alfie and Anand had taken themselves off to explore London, and they were still out at half-past seven when Jani took the taxi.

Now she hurried along the street, dodging through the crowds and keeping an eye out for officers of the law.

The buildings on either side were little more than slums, red brick back-to-back hovels, which in many cases had been knocked into one to form larger shops. She passed jewellers and sari merchants, premises selling rugs and travel agents offering airship excursions to all corners of the world. In between was the occasional restaurant, and the scent of cooking spices wafting out on the warm night air whetted Jani's appetite. Above the higgledy-piggledy rooftops of the slum, as if to throw the tumbledown condition of the buildings into relief, sleek silver monotrains raced by on raised tracks, and gaudy Illuminatory Arrays lighted the packed thoroughfares.

She found Wahlid's restaurant – its brightly-lit shop front setting it apart from its more dowdy neighbours – and was met by a turbaned *maitre'd* in the foyer. She gave Sebastian's name, and he bowed and led her into a long, low-lighted room to a booth at the rear, where Sebastian looked up from studying a menu and rose to greet her.

Jani smiled, her heart skipping. He kissed her cheek and Jani slipped into the seat opposite.

Jani looked around, taking in the Asian diners and the far fewer Londoners served by a platoon of liveried waiters. "I take it you've been here before?" she said.

"Once or twice. The food is excellent. I thought you'd feel more at home here."

She looked at him. "Amongst Bangladeshis and Nepalese?"

"I'm sorry, I should have said... What I meant is that you're less likely to be spotted by anyone on the lookout for..."

She reached out and took his hand, prepared to forgive his ignorance. "This is lovely, Sebastian. But what is even better is seeing you again."

"Well..." he began, and Jani thought he was about to impart some news when a waiter appeared at the table.

"I always judge a new restaurant by the quality of its dal," Jani said, "so I will have a dal palak, please, with three chapattis."

"And a murgh biryani for me," Sebastian said.

"And any drinks?"

"Just water, please," Jani said, and Sebastian ordered a jug of iced water.

When the waiter had taken their order and departed, Sebastian said, "Father rang me today—"

"And?"

"Apparently he spoke with the PM this morning. My father relayed what I'd told him, about the threat of the Zhell, and that Mahran would back up your claims." Sebastian frowned. "Trenchard merely told my father that you should give yourself up, 'for the good of the Empire'."

"That's all very well, but did your father or Trenchard agree to asking Mahran to corroborate my claims?"

"That's the damnable thing," Sebastian said. "I pleaded with my father to approach the Morn, but apparently Trenchard would give no assurances."

"But that doesn't make sense!" Jani said furiously.

"It's almost as if they don't believe what you say about the Zhell," Sebastian went on. "They probably think your story too fantastic."

Jani hit the table. "But Sebastian, the British have the Vantissarian ship in their possession. They have their hands on a thousand and one amazing devices. The very fact that the Vantissarian vessel exists should have made them more amenable to listening to fantastic stories!"

"But you must admit, stories of invading alien hordes...? If you hadn't had it from the horse's mouth, so to speak, then would you have believed it?"

She rocked her head from side to side, non-committal. The waiter arrived bearing steaming bowls of dal palak and murgh biryani.

Jani waited until he'd departed, then said, "But there *is* a way they can corroborate my story. You see, one of the devices the British found aboard the Vantissarian vessel was a CWAD, as they call it. Or if they didn't find the device as such, they developed it from Vantissarian technology."

He repeated the acronym. "Which is?"

"A Cognitive Wave Amplification Device." She scooped up a helping of dal on a scrap of chapatti and chewed.

"Sorry, none the wiser. In plain English, please."

"It's a device – a series of pinions that are inserted, or rather screwed, into one's facial bones–"

Sebastian winced. "To what end?"

"So that the CWAD's operator can read one's mind."

"What?"

"Do you see these?" She touched the tiny pin-prick scars on her brow, cheek and jaw. "That's where the Russian spies attached the CWAD back in India, so that they could read my thoughts."

He set aside his fork and touched her brow, then cupped her cheek. "My princess."

"So," she went on, resuming her meal, "if Mahran is agreeable to having his thoughts read, Trenchard *will* be able to corroborate my story."

"It all sounds rather painful."

"They could always sedate him," she said. "And it would be in his interests to undergo the process."

"I wonder why they haven't used the device on Mahran before now?"

"I was thinking the very same thing." She shrugged. "Perhaps they've only just developed the technology, and haven't yet got round to using it on Mahran." She sighed. "Let's face it, Sebastian, he's been languishing in gaol now for decades – perhaps the authorities have forgotten all about him."

"I'll contact my father again," Sebastian said. "I'll mention the CWAD and see if he'll see reason."

"Oh, if only he would! If only all this was sorted out. I'm rather sick of being on the run, of suspecting everyone and jumping at every shadow. I just hope..."

"Yes?"

"I hope that when Trenchard has all the facts in his possession, when Mahran and I have told him of the threat from the Zhell... well, that he'll allow Mahran the freedom to do what he has to do."

Sebastian popped a chunk of curried chicken into his mouth. "Which is?"

Jani sat back, her meal finished. "Well, to be perfectly honest. I don't know. It is vital that he has the three venthas, so that he can..." She shook her head. "As I said before, I don't really know what he will do, then. The Morn entity aboard the Vantissarian vessel was vague. It merely said that I had to locate Mahran and then help him find the third ventha. Mahran will know what to do, of course, once he's in possession of the third one."

Sebastian was staring at her in silence. He gripped her hand across the table. "The important thing is your safety. I will make it my duty to ensure that you come to no harm."

They held hands across the table for what seemed like an age.

"And now?" he asked. "Coffee? Dessert?"

"Neither for me, unless you'd like coffee."

"What I would really like," he said, "is to wander through the streets with you, hand in hand."

"That sounds wonderful." She beamed at him. "I just want to be with you, Sebastian, to feel safe with the man I love."

"You romantic," he laughed. "And why not? We could stroll through the night-market; I know an odd little pub tucked away down an alley not far from the market."

He settled the bill and they left the restaurant and joined the crowds milling down the street. The night was warm, the sun westering and laying down layers of tangerine and carmine over the city. Far to the west, the golden glow of Ealing Common Rocket Station lighted the sky, silhouetting the jumble of spavined rooftops and lopsided chimney-pots.

They strolled down the busy street and entered a cobbled square given over to stalls and small stages where hawkers, performers and self-proclaimed technical-wizards entertained the crowds.

The Whitechapel night-market sold not fruit or vegetables, or run-of-the-mill merchandise as might be found at any ordinary market, but the flotsam and

jetsam – in other words the cast-offs – of this wondrous
technological age. Jani and Sebastian passed stalls piled
high with scraps of metal that resembled so many tangled
callipers, the innards of complex machines, pumps and
pistons, and destitute dials and dismembered switches.
In amongst this treasure trove of superannuated junk,
performers rigged out like metal men proclaimed
messianic verses on the makeshift podia of scrapped
road-engines. Gymnasts, spread-eagled like da Vinci's
Vitruvian Man inside spinning gyroscopes, some got up
as automata, others in Pierrot costume, rolled through
knots of gawping onlookers. Loud music played, an
ear-splitting discord from a hurdy-gurdy interspersed
with electrical bleeps and blares.

Jani laughed and squeezed Sebastian's hand,
forgetting herself, her worries and cares, carried along
with the strange, weird and wonderful phantasmagoria
of the passing show.

They stopped before a raised dais on which a
puppeteer controlled stuffed animals, badgers and
foxes and weasels, seemingly without the use of strings.
Jani could only guess that the animals themselves were
automata – they certainly were not alive, as their
threadbare pelts moved with unsettling, jerky starts.

Next was a woman who swallowed a white,
phosphorescent substance – exhorted the crowd to
wait for an instant, her outstretched digits counting
off the seconds – and then exhaled above her head a
huge white cloud in which the multi-coloured image
of a fairy-tale castle could be seen before the cloud
dissipated into thin air.

They moved around the square, taking in marvel
after marvel.

"I always wondered," Sebastian said, "at the rate of technological progress over the course of the past twenty to thirty years. It was a second industrial revolution, fuelled by the pre-eminence of British scientific innovation – or so our leaders led us to believe. But something struck me as odd – the *rate* of the progress. No sooner had one new product hit the market than it was superseded by another, better one." He shrugged. "Of course you could put this down to the innate need of a capitalistic society to be constantly upgrading its products, beguiling the populace with new, desirable gewgaws. But it seemed that new things were constantly coming on to the market almost before traders could profit from their arrival. Now, of course, all is explained. Our scientists discovered untold wonders aboard the alien ship, and at first our scientific and technological understanding was incapable of coming to terms with all but the most rudimentary of these devices. So initially we came up with novelties, many of which you see around here. Then, when our scientists came to understand the principles of the alien technology, they were able to take bigger and better things from the ship and put them to use – the strange power-source that fuels the electrical generation stations, and which will soon power the sub-orbital rocketships, all of which make the Empire the global power it is today."

"I have wondered, " Jani replied, "since learning the truth of our pre-eminence, what the world might have been like if the secret of the Vantissarian ship had fallen into the hands of the Chinese, say, or the Russians."

He looked at her as they strolled along. "And have you come to any conclusion?"

"Human beings are human beings, the world over. Had the Russians discovered the ship, then they would have put what they found therein to work for them, making great their empire, making their leaders rich. The same with the Chinese – and with the Indians: I am under no illusion about that. I have personal experience, lately, of the perfidy of the Russians, but I have no doubt of the depths the British would sink to in order to attain their desires."

"Mmm," Sebastian said, staring into the distance. "I would like to think the Russians, seeing as how they espouse a free and egalitarian society, would put the Vantissarian technology to work to better the lot of the average man, the worker."

She glanced up at him. "In theory, maybe so," she said. "In reality, I don't know. What did Lord Acton say about absolute power? I have little doubt that the rulers in Russia are just as mendacious and self-aggrandising as rulers the world over."

"I don't know about that."

She laughed. "Perhaps that's your failing, Sebastian. You are too naïve."

"And you, Miss Cynical? Where is the innocent student I met six months ago, her head full of the Romantics, with dreams of qualifying as a doctor and returning to her own country to better the lot of the oppressed and the diseased out there?"

"The two are not mutually exclusive, Sebastian. I can be hard-headed about the ways of the world, and wary of those in power, and yet still harbour the dream that I, personally, can do something to help the poor and the oppressed."

He slipped an arm around her waist and pulled her to

him as they walked. "And that's what I like about you, Jani: your dreams are untainted by your pragmatism."

"I'll take that as a compliment," she laughed.

They stood on the edge of the square, taking in the hustle and bustle of the night-market, the music and the noise. "And now I think I'd like that drink you suggested earlier," she said. "Perhaps a glass of Bordeaux might be nice."

"And you've taken to drink since I last saw you."

"Lady Eddington says that her husband left a fine cellar, and that it's her duty to consume it before she 'falls off her perch'. I sampled the finest wine from France last night."

"What decadent taste!" he taunted. "I'll be satisfied with a pint of ale. This way."

They left the square and moved down a narrow street thronged with pedestrians. The sun was going down and a rich magenta glow had settled over the rooftops. Jani leaned into Sebastian and wondered when she had last been so happy.

"Tell me about these stalwart companions of yours," Sebastian asked. "I'd like to meet them, and thank them for seeing you through some tough times."

She glanced at him, wondering if he were fishing. "Well, I've told you about Anand. He was my father's houseboy, rescued from the streets when he was three. He was like a younger brother to me before I left India at the age of eight. He's fiercely loyal, bright and curious."

"And this Alfie Lightbody?"

"Littlebody," she corrected. "Alfie is older than me, over thirty, small and dumpy and round-faced." She considered the Lieutenant, then went on, "He combines innate circumspection with moments of rash impulse –

almost as if he must prove to himself that he isn't the staid, middle-class choir-boy he perhaps once thought himself to be. He's just as loyal as Anand, and..."

"Yes?"

She shook her head. "Nothing." She had been about to say, 'And he is a little in love with me', but stopped herself; it would be unworthy of her, both to taunt Sebastian like this, and to so flagrantly flaunt Alfie's confidences.

"No, tell me."

"Well, I had been about to say that he would risk his life for me," she temporised. "Which I suppose, in a rash moment, he would do."

"They sound," he said, "just like the kind of companions a girl needs to protect her in hard times."

"They are fine companions, and we worked well together to reach Britain – abetted in no small measure by good fortune, I might add."

He steered her left, along a narrow cobbled alley winding between ancient buildings which leaned over the thoroughfare like confabulating old crones, the peaked bonnets of their roofs almost touching overhead. The sound of the night-market's music grew ever fainter.

Jani held on to Sebastian's arm as they hurried on.

He was saying something about the character of this district of old London, when Jani said, "Shhh!"

"What is it?"

Her heart thudded. "I thought I heard footsteps," she said, turning and peering into the shadows behind them.

"No one there," Sebastian said, "and even if there had been..."

"I know. I'm being paranoid. I'm sorry."

"As I was saying," he went on, "for all this area's character, and occasional places of architectural interest, it's a slum that really has seen better days. In a fair world it would be demolished and its inhabitants re-housed in brighter, better dwellings."

"Well, now that you are on the first rung of a political career, Sebastian, you can plan ahead to the time when you might effect such change."

"I'm a lowly secretary, Jani. It will be years yet before I know enough to stand as a parliamentary candidate."

She tugged his arm. "And very unlikely that you would be elected on a Socialist ticket."

"You never know," he said to himself.

There it was again, she thought, fear leaping to her throat. This time when she turned quickly and peered into the twilight, she thought she saw a dark figure pull back into a doorway.

"Jani? You really are imagining things."

"I don't know," she said, hurrying on and pulling Sebastian after her. "How far away are we from the public house?"

"Not far at all; a few hundred yards. We're nearly there. And even if we are being followed, what of it? More people than ourselves are abroad tonight–"

"People who conceal themselves out of sight in doorways when I turn to look?" she countered. She felt a little sick; until now the evening had been wonderful, and she had been able to forget the fears and worries that had beset her of late. Now, all at once in a terrible rush, she was dogged by the possibility that one of her many enemies had at last tracked her down, and her fear was made all the worse for not knowing the identity of those in pursuit.

At least she had Sebastian at her side, she thought, and gripped his arm ever tighter.

"This way," he said, indicating a turning. They hurried right, moving down an even narrower passage than the last. "A short cut," he explained.

Jani nodded. Soon they would be in the bright lights and bustle of a friendly pub, and later, from there, she would ring for a taxi to take her straight home.

She turned and glanced over her shoulder. She detected no sounds of pursuit, saw no shadowy figures. She allowed herself a deep breath and admitted that perhaps paranoia had got the better of her.

Then, just as she was beginning to relax, she heard a rush of running footsteps at her back, and suddenly Sebastian grunted and was falling. Jani turned and lashed out, screaming, and connected with Sebastian's assailant – a black-garbed man who cursed in a language familiar to Jani, but a language not English. She reached out to pull Sebastian to his feet and urged him to run, and then she too was running, conscious of Sebastian's footfalls a little behind her. She turned a corner, and turned again, desperately hoping to find herself on a wider, lighted lane that might at last lead to reassuring crowds and illuminated shop fronts – but each turning she made led her down ever narrower and meaner alleys, and the light grew dimmer around her, with only the stars above to feebly light her way.

"Sebastian?" she said with rising panic, as she turned and saw that he was no longer behind her. "Sebastian!"

She heard footsteps and her heart skipped with relief – and then the nascent joy corroded to heart-stopping panic when she saw the dark shape of her former assailant. She turned and ran, sprinting down the narrow alley with no idea where she was or how she might get away but with only one desire in her head – to escape her pursuer.

If she ran and ran then surely, soon, she would reach civilisation?

But what of Sebastian? She was leaving him, deserting him. Already he might be in the clutches of those who followed, suffering who knew what at their hands.

She thought of Alfie's light-beam, and knew she had been rash in refusing his offer that she should take it along tonight. But she had been going out with Sebastian for a quiet meal. What need might she have for such a lethal weapon? Oh, how she wanted it now, so that she might turn on her pursuer and surprise him – just as she had surprised Durga Das and Mr Knives, back in Nepal – with a few well-aimed slashes.

The footsteps at her back were growing louder. She heard the laboured breathing of her pursuer. Up ahead, in the dwindling perspective of the alleyway, someone appeared – and she almost wept with relief. The figure was tall, and wore a cape, and it could only be a uniformed London Bobby.

She cried out and sprinted towards the distant figure, almost laughing now at the thought of salvation.

Her relief turned to panic when she came within yards of the tall, caped figure and she realised that he was not a policeman at all – the cape had been a terrible decoy. The man spread his arms and blocked her way.

She skidded to a halt, turned and ran. Someone appeared from the shadows before her, his pale potato face topped by a bowler hat. Weeping now but determined not to give in without a fight, she lowered her shoulder and charged, and hit what felt like a brick wall. The man grunted, then laughed, and strong arms embraced her despite her frantic struggles. She kicked out, to no avail. She heard a voice – the caped man issuing instructions in Russian.

She screamed as she smelled an overwhelming chemical reek, and then something wet was pressed to her face. She tried not to breathe, but that was impossible, and she felt suddenly dizzy and sick. As her vision swam, she caught a glimpse of the taller man's face in the starlight, and instantly knew that she had seen him, somewhere, before. But where?

Her last thought was relief that at least Sebastian had managed to get away, and then she was unconscious.

CHAPTER
TWELVE

~

Anand is concerned – Jani has not returned –
To Mr Clockwork's Emporium – The Mechanical Man –
"Breathless and flushed with passion..."

AT BREAKFAST NEXT morning Anand buttered his first piece of toast and smothered it in thick-cut orange marmalade.

Last night after dinner, while Jani had been meeting with her beau, Anand had told Mr Alfie and Lady Eddington that he would like to get some fresh air before he went to bed. He'd taken a turn around a nearby square, then considered the advisability of making his way to Whitechapel and Wahlid's restaurant. He was curious about this Sebastian character, and wanted to see the young man who had won Jani's heart. In the end, on reflection, he'd decided against the idea of following her: after all, if Jani found out she would be displeased and might accuse him of spying on her.

He looked up as Mr Alfie and Lady Eddington entered the room, speaking to each other in hushed tones. He thought Alfie looked worried about something, and as they took their places at the table and Dobson poured them cups of Earl Grey, Anand said, "Will Jani be joining us soon?"

Lady Eddington cleared her throat, glanced at Mr Alfie, then said to Anand, "Janisha did not return last night."

Anand stopped chewing. He swallowed and said, "What?"

"Surely you heard," Alfie said, somewhat shortly. "Amelia said that Jani did not return here last night."

Anand pushed his chair away from the table, alarmed. "Then we must do something!"

"I think that will be unnecessary," Lady Eddington began.

Alfie said, "We have no cause for concern. She was out with her friend, Sebastian, after all. She probably decided to..." He reddened suddenly and fell to buttering his toast with excess vigour.

"Janisha is old enough to take care of herself," Lady Eddington said, though Anand thought he detected a slight tremor in her tone.

He took a contemplative bite of his toast. "But she would have phoned to tell us, surely. It is not like Jani-ji not to tell us of her plans."

Mr Alfie sighed. "She no doubt had other things on her mind," he said, and changed the subject. "Are you ready to visit Mr Clockwork's Fabulous Emporium? There's a monotrain from Mayfair at eleven."

At ten forty-five they left the townhouse and hurried to the station, Anand still concerned over Jani's absence. He tried to broach the subject with Mr Alfie as they stood waiting for the train, but the Lieutenant wouldn't have any of it. "Jani is her own woman," he muttered. "If she chooses..."

They made the journey to Putney in silence, Anand staring out as they crossed the Thames. All manner of strange craft jetted up and down the river, but Anand's appetite for wonder was not whetted this morning: he was too busy regretting his decision not to follow Jani last night. If only he'd kept her under surveillance, followed her back to wherever Sebastian lived and thus reassured himself of her safety... Not knowing what had become of her was like a storm cloud on a summer's day.

Obviously Mr Alfie was allowing his romantic inclinations towards Jani-ji to influence his reasoning. He was so jealous of Sebastian that he could only assume that Jani had spent the night with the young man, and was blinded to the obvious danger: that either the British or the Russians had kidnapped her. Mr Alfie, for all his education and the fact that he was a soldier of His Majesty's army – or rather *had been* a soldier – could be remarkably pig-headed at times.

At some point during their airship journey to Britain, Anand had managed to overcome his dreams of one day winning Jani-ji's heart. Later he had listened to her telling Lady Eddington about Sebastian, had heard her sighs and seen the dreamy look enter her big brown eyes. She was in love with an aristocratic Englishman, so what chance had he, harijan Anand Doshi, of ever winning her heart?

He had to be practical about his relationship with his childhood friend. If he could not love her – or rather, if he could not have his love reciprocated – then he would serve her and bask in whatever gratitude she deigned to show him. He looked ahead to when all this chasing about and hullabaloo was over with, to when Jani would settle down in a big English country house and start a family. He would offer his services as a faithful retainer, a butler or odd job man. This way he would be with her for the rest of his days. The thought gave him comfort.

If only she would return safe and sound; perhaps, when they returned to Lady Eddington's later that afternoon, he would find Jani-ji taking afternoon tea and crumpets with the dowager.

"Penny for them?" Mr Alfie said as they left the train station at Putney and made their way to Mr Clockwork's Fabulous Emporium.

"I am thinking about Jani, and the house she and Sebastian will live in one day." He smiled up at the Englishman. "They could employ us, Mr Alfie. I could be a butler and you a footman, perhaps."

Mr Alfie gave him an odd look. "Or I could work in the kitchen as a scullery maid," he said.

Anand ignored what he thought might be Mr Alfie's attempt at sarcasm and pointed to a great painted sign above a shop front across the road. "Look, Mr Clockwork's Fabulous Emporium! I wonder if it will be like the one where I worked in Delhi?"

Mr Alfie smiled, perhaps glad Anand had changed the subject. "Well, let's go across and see, hm?"

They joined the queue to enter the Emporium and in due course paid the sixpence entry fee.

For the next hour, Anand was in wonderland. The chamber was packed with a hundred amazing exhibits, from automata that were so lifelike they resembled real people, to giant simulated beetles and jewelled crabs and fantastical clockwork animals. Mr Alfie was impressed, too, and Anand took a proprietary pride in escorting the little Englishman down aisle after aisle of exhibits.

Anand was transported back to the workshop of Mr Clockwork's Fabulous Emporium in Old Delhi, working with the master himself, watching the magician – for that was how Anand thought of him – building and repairing engines and cogwheels and motors and passing on his expertise to Anand. Now he felt a small twinge of regret that all that was in the past, but only a *small* twinge. His future was with Jani, serving her, after all.

They turned a corner together and stopped in their tracks – for standing before them, in pride of place at the end of the chamber, was a giant mechanical man.

Anand opened his mouth, then laughed, and moved slowly towards the Mech-Man.

"Max," he breathed.

Alfie said, "Or one very much like him."

On closer inspection, Anand saw the many differences from the mechanical man he had taken from the Emporium in Old Delhi in order to save Jani. This one was enamelled green, not black, and its chest was more barrel-shaped than the other's squarish trunk. Also, this one was smaller, perhaps ten feet high, and its head was domed rather than square.

"I wonder if the owner would let me have a test ride, Mr Alfie?"

His friend laughed. "That I very much doubt."

"Well, in that case I'll take a closer look," Anand said, and with a glance over his shoulder to ensure he was unobserved, stepped over the cordon and walked around the towering Mech-Man.

"Its access hatch is in its back," he reported back to Mr Alfie. "You entered ours in India by tipping back his shoulders and head, which I always thought an awkward arrangement." He saw a plate bolted to the thigh of the giant, and bent closer to read the spec. "According to this, Mr Alfie, this Max is watertight, weighs almost half a ton, and has its own internal tanks to supply air to the driver!"

Anand reached out, touched the cold metal of Max's thick leg, and felt a thrill rush through him. What he would give now to climb aboard and test-drive Max around the streets of London!

They spent another hour in the Emporium, before Anand thought of Jani and suggested they make their way back to Mayfair. He nipped back to take one last look at the giant, silent Mech-Man before joining a morose Mr Alfie at the exit.

"I hope Jani-ji has returned by the time we get back," Anand said as they made their way to the station. "Mr Alfie, do you think she will be there?"

The little Englishman sighed. "I'm sure she will," he muttered to himself. "Breathless and flushed with passion."

CHAPTER
THIRTEEN

∽

A prisoner of the Russians? – Jani's relief –
Sebastian's reassurances – Betrayal! –
Jani has a plan –
"A few Bolshevik agents hold no fear for me..."

JANI AWOKE SLOWLY.

Her first confused thought was that she was in a cage in the taxidermist's warehouse back in Delhi, and that soon an evil pair of Russians would enter the chamber and taunt her – for the language she had heard her assailants use last night was the ugly, guttural tongue of Russia. But no... the taxidermist's warehouse had been weeks ago, on another continent. And *that* Russian pair were dead.

But she had been apprehended again by another set of Russian agents, and she could expect to be subjected to the same routine of interrogation and torture if she did not give them what they wanted.

She was in a bed in a smart room with a window looking out on to a blue sky. So she had been unconscious for hours, evidently. She tried to raise her head and look around, but the after-effects of whatever they had used to render her unconscious now made her head throb like a beaten drum. All she could see was a white door, tiled walls and a plastered ceiling with a central, shaded bulb.

She wondered if she was in some kind of hospital room.

She looked at the window again. There were no bars with which to keep someone imprisoned; a simple lever would open the window inwards. Perhaps, once she had regained her strength, she could move to the window and see how high up her room was; if it were on the ground floor, then escape would be simple – if higher up, then perhaps there would be a drainpipe nearby. She smiled as she realised that she was indulging in wishful thinking.

Sebastian? Had he managed to get away from the Russians, or had they captured him, too?

She considered the caped agent who had rendered her unconscious last night. She had seen him before, recognised his face, and yet was unable to recall where.

She moved her right hand to her chest, and discovered two things at the same time. One, that she was no longer wearing the summer dress Lady Eddington had bought her; and two, that her right forearm was wrapped tightly in a beige crepe bandage. As soon as she saw her arm, she felt a throb of pain at the wrist. She must have injured herself when she fell to the ground.

She lay very still and took deep breaths. The room, and whatever lay beyond it, was in silence. She wondered when whoever had abducted her would show themselves and make their demands. The Russians knew she possessed the ventha-di, but they had no way of knowing that it was lodged in her stomach. She could play for time, claim ignorance, or send them searching for it on a wild goose chase across London.

She considered the CWAD the Russians in India had possessed, and fervently hoped that their London comrades were not so well equipped.

She raised herself from the bed, drew aside the covers, and sat up. She was wearing a short cotton slip. The base of her skull throbbed as if she'd been coshed, but the nausea soon passed. A small cabinet stood beside the bed, and when she pulled open the door she found all her clothing, neatly folded. She experienced a quick stab of outrage that they had undressed her. Which, she thought, was a minor crime beside the fact that they had rendered her unconscious, abducted and imprisoned her. Still, the sense of violation irrationally angered her more than anything else.

Taking a breath and glancing at the door, she stood and took three strides across to the window.

She peered out and discovered why the window was not barred: the room was two floors up, with a drop of twenty feet to the side-road below. She tried the lever, pressed it down and pulled, and the window swung open, admitting a warm breeze and the muted hum of London traffic. She leaned out and looked right and left. As she had feared, there were no obligingly handy drainpipes or ledges which might have facilitated her escape. Not that she would have fancied edging along a ledge, or shinning down a drainpipe, as the drop was sheer and vertiginous.

She would have to consider some alternative means of escape, in that case.

She was about to move to the door, open it and peer out, when she heard voices beyond. She closed the window, hurried back to bed, and was arranging the sheets over her when the door opened and a matronly, middle-aged nurse bustled in, her rosy face wreathed in smiles.

"Miss Chatterjee!" she sang. "How wonderful that you're with us at last! Now, I'll just take your temperature."

She inserted a thermometer beneath Jani's tongue, effectively silencing her questions, then read the result and found it satisfactory. "Now I assume you're thirsty, and could eat a horse? I'll bring you a nice glass of cold water and see what doctor says about solids, hm?"

"Where...?" Jani began, her mouth dry and her tongue sticking. "Where am I? What time is it?"

The nurse smiled and touched Jani's cheek. "You're safe, my dear," she murmured. "You have nothing to worry about. Now lie back and rest." She consulted a watch pinned upside-down on her bib. "It's just after three, Miss."

"In the afternoon?"

The nurse smiled. "In the afternoon."

"Sebastian?" she managed as she sank back into the pillows.

The nurse beamed. "The handsome chap who brought you in? Why, he's chomping at the bit to see you after your little operation."

Her heart surged. Sebastian had brought her in? "Operation? What operation? Where am I?"

"Harley Street, Miss Chatterjee, a private room of Mr Consett's family physician. You broke your arm rather nastily when the brigands tried to drag you off. But Master Sebastian will tell you all about it. I'll tell him you're up to seeing him, shall I?"

Jani almost wept. "Oh, yes! Yes, please!"

"He'll be overjoyed to see you," the nurse said, moving to the door. "I'll fetch him immediately."

Jani closed her eyes, her heart bursting with joy and

relief. With just a few words the nurse had reassured her that not only was she was *not* a captive of the Russians, but that Sebastian was safe and well.

But what had happened? Had Sebastian alerted the police, and had the Russians been apprehended, red-handed, as they were carrying her off? Or had Sebastian fought off his attackers and single-handedly managed to wrest her away from the Bolsheviks?

Whichever, he was free and she was overwhelmed with relief.

The door burst open and Sebastian stood on the threshold, staring in at her. She struggled into a sitting position, weeping and reaching for him. He strode to the bed and they embraced. "Oh, Sebastian! You don't know how..."

"Jani! I was beside myself while you were in theatre. I imagined – oh, I don't know what I imagined."

She stroked his face, staring at his black eye. "You... you saved me?"

"With a little help from a passing constable. They clobbered me and left me unconscious, or so the blighters thought. I heard them running after you and gave chase. As fortune had it I bumped – literally bumped – into a bobby on the way, explained the situation and off we went, following the sound of their footsteps. They were carrying you off when we caught up with them and in the ensuing fisticuffs – my word, you can't imagine how satisfying it was to plant one on the caped chappie – you fell to the floor and injured your arm rather badly. Broken, I'm afraid."

She smiled. "It's nothing. I'm safe, thanks to you, and that's all that matters."

"Unfortunately the blighters ran off, but I was more

bothered about you." He stroked her cheek. "You broke your arm in two places, girl. The earlier op was to set the bone, but the surgeon decided you need a second one tomorrow at midday, so he can insert a pin to straighten it."

"I'll bear up," she said. "You can't imagine the fear I felt on waking up and thinking I was imprisoned by the Russians. It was like a nightmare."

"Well, the nightmare's over. Once you've had the second op and you're fit and well, we'll have you out of here."

"But does your father know what happened to me? Are the authorities–?"

"They're none the wiser. I thought it best to keep mum."

She nodded. "And Lady Eddington, and Alfie and Anand! Sebastian, could you possibly call Lady Eddington and tell her what happened, assure her that I'm well? Or if there is a phone handy, I could ring..."

"I'll do it as soon as I leave here, Jani. No need to worry on that score."

"I'll be glad when all this awful business is over, Sebastian, and I've explained everything to the government, and when Mahran is released and they can get on with saving the world. All I want to do is return to my studies, and..."

"Yes?"

She smiled and squeezed his hand. "And spend lots of time with you."

He kissed her forehead, "I'd like nothing better, Jani. Now, is there anything I can bring you in the morning?"

"A book. I'm reading Jane Austen's *Northanger Abbey* at the moment."

"I'll do that. Now rest, and try to sleep. I'll see you first thing."

As he left the room, she thought that the last thing she felt like doing was going to sleep, what with the relief of discovering that she was no longer in danger.

The door opened and the nurse bustled in, carrying a glass of water. "There you are, and doctor says you can eat whenever you like. Are you up to a light meal?"

"Yes, please."

The nurse had left the door open, and Jani could see out into a long corridor. Sebastian was standing there, chatting with a tall, dark-haired man.

The nurse said, "Then I'll arrange that and bring you something presently," plumped the pillows and swept from the room, closing the door behind her.

Jani lay and stared at the closed door as if frozen. "No," she said to herself, processing what she had seen and attempting to come up with some explanation other than the obvious one. "*No!*"

She felt sick, and wanted to scream aloud, kick out and punch Sebastian and avenge herself. She lay back, closed her eyes and tried to control her breathing.

It came to her that she had to be very careful, very careful indeed. She had to set aside her emotions, her hurt at the betrayal, and think through her next actions with calm and rationality.

The man she had seen Sebastian speaking to in the corridor was the caped Russian agent who had attacked her in Whitechapel. He was also, she realised, the very same man she had seen Sebastian with in Richmond Park two days ago.

A Russian agent.

Which meant that Sebastian was also...

Which meant that he had betrayed her, that all his protestations of love, all his endearments...

No, she must stifle the anger rising within her. Now was not the time for fury or revenge. As she had told herself, she must act with calm.

Her heart thumping, she sat up in bed and called out, "Sebastian! Sebastian, are you still there?"

She called out again, and the door opened and a smiling Sebastian hurried to her bedside. "Jani?"

She forced herself to act normally, to smile at him as if nothing untoward had occurred. She was consumed with rage, with a bitter sense of betrayal, but knew she must not show it.

"Sebastian, I need to see Lady Eddington–"

He smiled. "As I said, I'll phone her, reassure her that you're well."

"No," she said. "Sebastian, I really need to *see* her. I need something... something that I can only discuss with another woman. Please, Sebastian, could you prevail upon her to visit me this afternoon?"

"I'll contact her immediately," he promised.

"She is free in the afternoons, and spends her time at home. Please ask her to come."

"Of course," he said, bending to kiss her forehead. She closed her eyes, wanting more than anything to slap his face, to cry out and accuse him.

"Now sleep," he murmured, and slipped from the room.

Jani took the glass of water from the bedside table, drank it in one go and lay back. She stared up at the ceiling, a great pit of despair opening up in her chest.

Furiously, she tried to think of a scenario which exonerated Sebastian, tried to come up with a perfectly innocent explanation for his speaking with the very man who had abducted her the night before. She was not mistaken – the tall man in the corridor and the caped kidnapper were one and the same, the man Sebastian had met in Richmond Park. He had spoken with an unmistakable Russian accent – and she recalled just last night Sebastian's speaking up for Russian egalitarianism.

So all his avowals of love? His kisses, the look of adoration in his eyes when he stared at her? Did they mean nothing, or did he truly love her and could at the same time serve his Russian paymasters?

But he had betrayed her, effectively sold her into the captivity of the Russians. She gave a gasp as she recalled his telling her about the operation she would undergo tomorrow, to fix a pin in her broken arm.

If he were a Russian agent, then there had been no chase last night, and she had not slipped from her abductor's grip and broken her arm. So the lie about her arm, the charade of the bandage... all this was nothing more than a ruse to get her to accept the operation... which would be to remove the ventha-di from her stomach!

She moaned aloud at the thought of Sebastian's betraying her like this. He would have her undergo an operation, face the danger of its going wrong, all to satisfy his commitment to an ideology?

So his professed love for her meant nothing beside his loyalty to the Russian cause.

But the pain in her arm? She raised it and stared at the bandage. There could be no denying the pain. Her forearm throbbed; she had never broken a bone before, so had no idea what a fracture might feel like.

Glancing at the door, and listening for footsteps, she unknotted the end of the bandage and slowly unwound the beige crepe, ready to slip her arm beneath the covers should someone approach.

She thought she would never get to the end of the bandage: it was like a children's party game of pass-the-parcel, when each successive unwrapping of a layer promised to reveal the prize. Very soon the pain in her forearm eased as the pressure of the bandage lessened, and as she unwound the last layer of crepe she saw why. A six inch length of silver metal, its underside sharply corrugated, pressed into her flesh and left a painful impression. She stared at the metal, tears spilling down her cheeks.

She removed the metal and slipped it under her pillow. Quickly she rewound the bandage, attempting to make it as neat as possible, then tied the knot as best as she was able – not an easy task, one-handed. At least the knot was on the underside of her arm and not visible, and if anyone entered the room she would hide her arm beneath the bed cover.

She lay back and composed her breathing. With luck she would not see Sebastian again before Lady Eddington arrived. She would conspire with the dowager to make her escape. And then? She liked to think that at some point in the near future she would be able, on her own terms, to confront Sebastian and demand an explanation for his treachery – his treachery not so much to his country, but to her.

She panicked at the thought that Lady Eddington might not be at home, even though Jani knew she spent her afternoons reading. What if, today, she had chosen to leave the house and Sebastian was unable to contact her? What chance might there be then of her effecting an escape? She was scheduled to undergo the operation tomorrow. Except, of course, she would do nothing of the kind. She would attack whoever tried to force her to the operating theatre, and run like the wind.

She felt a flutter of panic in her chest as it came to her that Sebastian might have lied to her about contacting the dowager. But why would he do that, she asked herself? To uphold the pretence that she was in some private Harley Street surgery, surely he would allow the visit?

The uncertainty preyed upon her, adding to her mental anguish.

She considered what Sebastian had told her last night about his speaking to his father, and Lord Consett's relaying the information to the Prime Minister. All lies, of course, designed to lull her into a false sense of security.

She considered the operation she was due to undergo at noon tomorrow. How might he have explained that, when she woke after the procedure to find that her stomach had been operated upon, and not her arm?

Unless, of course, the plan was not to have her wake up?

She sobbed quietly; the idea was too horrible to contemplate.

She dried her eyes and stared at the ceiling, breathing deeply and thinking of Alfie and Anand and Lady Eddington – loyal friends she knew she could rely upon. Soon, with luck, she would see the dowager and, if all went to plan, not long after that she would be reunited with the redoubtable Alfie and Anand. Her heart swelled at the thought.

She sat up and found her wrist-watch amongst her clothes in the bedside cabinet. For the next hour she glanced at the watch from time to time, amazed at how slowly the minutes crawled by. Her thoughts performed a maddeningly circular tour of Sebastian's professed love, the fact of his betrayal, the operation and its aftermath – these nightmares punctuated by the thought of what she should do if Lady Eddington failed to arrive.

At four-thirty – Jani had just checked her watch for perhaps the hundredth time – the cheery nurse popped her head around the door and said, "Are you up to seeing someone, my dear?"

Jani smiled through her hatred of the woman – another treacherous actor in this terrible charade! – and said, "Yes, of course."

The door opened further, the nurse stood aside, and the tall, thin, severely upright figure of Lady Amelia Eddington hurried in. "But my dear! The shock of hearing what has happened! At least that young man of yours saved the day, and I must say that I'm impressed with the level of security in here! Your safety is guarded like the crown jewels!"

Instantly Jani was crying. She reached out for the dowager and hugged her thin frame.

"There, there, Jani. You have been through so much of late, and now this, but all is well, my dear."

Over Lady Eddington's shoulder, Jani saw that the door was closed; they were quite alone.

She pulled away and smiled through her tears. "Amelia, you must help me!" she whispered.

"My dear, everything is in hand–"

"No! You don't understand! This... all this," she waved, "it's a lie. A pretence!"

The dowager stared at her as if she were mad. "Jani?"

"Please listen to me, Amelia! Please believe me." She glanced at the door again, expecting someone to enter at any second. She whispered, "Sebastian... Sebastian is a cad. He's in the pay of the Russians. He didn't rescue me last night. He set me up, arranged to have me abducted."

"But this is incredible!" The dowager looked stricken. "How can you be certain?"

Jani explained about the caped kidnapper, and that she'd seen him speaking to Sebastian in the corridor earlier that afternoon. Then she slipped the length of metal from beneath her pillow and explained its significance.

When she'd finished, Lady Eddington looked up from the metal and stared at Jani, silent. Her hand found Jani's and squeezed.

"Oh, you poor, poor dear."

Jani told the dowager about the operation scheduled for tomorrow. "I need to be away from here before then. During the night, if possible."

"But the security," Lady Eddington said, gesturing towards the door. "There are 'heavies', I think the term is, in the corridor. There is no way..."

"I think there *is* a way, Amelia."

"If there is a way, my dear, then I trust you to have found it. Now tell me."

"I will need your help in arranging this, Amelia, and Alfie and Anand to carry it through. There should be little risk, other than to myself. But I have every confidence..."

"Tell me."

Gripping the dowager's frail hand, Jani outlined her

plan, instructing Lady Eddington as to what she needed and how Alfie and Anand should play their part. She went over it again, and the dowager nodded and repeated her role in the operation.

"I'm sure I can do that, and Alfie and Anand will be more than up to the task. But my worry concerns you, my dear."

"Amelia, I have fought off vile Russian assassins, fled from duplicitous Hindu priests and mad, gun-wielding English Colonels. A few Bolshevik agents hold no fear for me. If Alfie and Anand can carry out their part of the operation, then all will go to plan."

Lady Eddington raised Jani's hand to her lips and kissed her fingers. "And then?"

She thought about it. "Have Alfie arrange alternative accommodation from now on, if you would. You have been kindness itself, but it would be foolish for us to return to Mayfair, as well as dangerous for you."

The dowager nodded. "I'll arrange that with Alfie," she promised.

"One more thing, Amelia. Please don't tell Alfie that Sebastian... that he betrayed me. I will broach the subject in my own good time."

"You have my word on that score, my dear."

"And ensure that Alfie doesn't enlist Sebastian's aid in the escape," she added urgently.

"I understand," Lady Eddington said.

"And later," Jani said, summoning a brave smile, "we will meet and have tea and laugh about everything we've been through together."

Lady Eddington smiled and murmured something, which Jani thought might have been, "Remarkable."

"Now I should be on my way." The dowager leaned

forward and kissed Jani's brow. "And fear not, my dear. Be brave!"

She moved to the door, turned and smiled, then slipped from the room.

Jani stared through the window at the afternoon sunlight. She felt a little better for having seen Amelia, and arranging the details of her escape, and tried not to dwell on everything that might go wrong between now and the early hours of the morning.

But what could possibly go wrong, she asked herself? Her operation was scheduled for tomorrow at noon; Sebastian was not due to visit again until tomorrow morning; only the nurse would pop in from time to time, maintaining the pretence.

At five, the nurse entered bearing a tray of food and exhorted Jani to 'Eat it all up like a good girl'. Jani smiled and watched her leave the room, then turned her attention to the plate of food, a slice of ham, overcooked carrots and boiled potatoes. She was famished, but the plate was unappetising to say the least. She picked at the potatoes and carrots and left the undercooked ham.

Despite her nervousness, she dropped off after the meal and awoke, with a start, some hours later. The room was in darkness, illuminated only by a light from the hall shining through a transom above the door. She fumbled for the bedside lamp, found her watch and squinted at it in the glare of the light.

She sank back, relieved. For a second she feared she might have slept through the time of the arranged rendezvous. It was just after twelve; she still had two hours until her plan swung into action.

She slipped from bed and moved across to a door to a small bathroom. She did what she had to do, then washed her hands and face. Back in the bed chamber, she moved to the door; it was closed, and rather than open it and risk alerting whoever might be out there, she knelt and peered through the keyhole. At the end of the corridor, seated on a straight-backed chair, was a fat man in a non-descript suit, leafing through a newspaper.

She moved to the window and looked out. The night was quiet, the side-street illuminated by the stars. There were no lights along the street, which would work in her favour. Her stomach heaved at the thought of what she had to do at two o'clock. She returned to bed.

When she was away from here, and somewhere safe with Alfie and Anand, she would confer with them and plan what to do next. Her idea of confiding in Sebastian to liaise with the PM had proved a spectacular disaster. Of course she could still approach the PM, despite Alfie's reservations – but a far better plan would be to circumvent the middle-men and free Mahran from Newgate gaol. Which was, she thought, easier said than done.

Anyway, all that lay ahead; first she must evade the clutches of the perfidious Bolsheviks.

An hour passed slowly. Each minute seemed to extend itself for an infinite duration. She slipped from the bed and paced the room, back and forth, visited the bathroom again, and peered through the keyhole at the guard. He was still there; his paper read, he was now flipping through a magazine.

When she next looked at her watch it was almost ten to two. Her heart thumping and her hands shaking, she carefully opened the bedside cabinet, withdrew her clothes, and dressed. It felt good to be wearing her familiar summer dress and cardigan again. She pulled on her stockings, slipped her feet into her shoes, then moved to the keyhole.

To her relief, the guard was still absorbed in his magazine.

She returned to the bed and pulled the pillow case from one of the pillows, then moved to the window. Her tongue-tip trapped between her teeth, she eased down the lever and pulled the window open. Fortunately there was little traffic in the area, whose noise might have alerted the guard. She hung the pillowcase over the sill so that it draped down the outer wall and signified her room. Satisfied, she shut the window, trapping its hem.

She returned to the bed, sat down and stared at the minute hand of her watch as it crept towards the hour.

With a minute to go, she wondered if the nurse might look in on her charge at the stroke of two, then reassured herself that this was unlikely. After all, the nurse had not appeared at one o'clock. But what if she did her rounds every two hours?

She told herself that she was being paranoid and tried to control her breathing.

At two o'clock, she rose from the bed and crossed to the window. She pressed her nose against the cold glass and peered out and down the side-street. Her heart jumped at the distant sound of an engine. She waited, too fearful to hope... The engine noise increased, then stopped.

Her hands were shaking uncontrollably as she grasped the lever and pulled it down, easing open the window.

If the guard should hear her now, and investigate...

The pillowcase, released, fluttered down in the darkness like a falling dove.

Jani peered down and there, twenty feet below her,

she made out the dark shape of an high-sided flatbed
lorry, its headlights dimmed.

She had the sudden conviction that she was about to
empty her stomach of the little she had eaten hours ago,
then quelled her nausea and eased her legs one after the
other through the open window. Her breathing coming
in ragged spasms, she sat on the sill and stared down.

She was unable to see into the back of the lorry, but
trusted Alfie and Anand to have considered her landing.
As she had instructed Lady Eddington to tell them, they
had pulled the lorry to within a foot of the wall. She had
a target to aim at of approximately ten feet by twenty-
five – a vast, yawning area, she told herself, and yet it
seemed so small from this elevation.

She heard a sound from the room at her back, the
click of the door opening. She peered over her shoulder.
The nurse, her smiling face transforming comically as
she looked from the bed to where Jani was perched,
called out and advanced. Galvanised, Jani gave a shriek
and jumped.

She fell through the air. The world gyred around her.
Then she hit something, flat on her back, and bounced –
and instantly the lorry started up and sped off. Winded,
her breath coming in great, painful gulps, Jani stared
up and could take little satisfaction in seeing first the
nurse's face at the window, and then the guard's. And
then they were lost to sight as the lorry sped around the
corner, and the pain in Jani's chest turned to elation.

She sat up in the darkness and felt around her,
then laughed aloud. Her landing might have been
uncomfortable, but that was only because she had
landed on her back. Her friends – or rather Lady
Eddington – had come up trumps. The flatbed was

lined, like the padded cell of a lunatic asylum, with a layer of Sleepwell mattresses.

As the lorry jounced through the darkened streets of London, she scrambled on all fours over the piled mattresses. She peered through the wooden slats at the cab, hoping to find a window through which she could signal to Alfie and Anand, but all she made out was a grease-encrusted metal plate.

She had instructed Lady Eddington to tell Alfie and Anand not to stop until they reached their destination, wherever that might be. She had faith in her friends to have found a safe bolt hole, and settled back against the mattresses to enjoy the ride.

There were no sounds of pursuit, and she could only imagine the confusion, chaos and recriminations back at the private surgery. Sebastian would be put out in no small way, and Jani rejoiced at the thought.

Then, unbidden, she was caught in a paroxysm of tears.

She was still weeping when the truck braked suddenly. She heard a shout, the sound of the cab door opening and more shouts. Before she had time to realise what was happening – before she really had time to panic – three black-clad figures swarmed over the side of the truck and approached her. One grabbed her arm, another her torso, and the third advanced upon her with something held high in his outstretched hand.

Jani screamed as a sharp and very painful needle was jabbed down into her shoulder, and then, for the second time in a little over twenty-four hours, she slipped into oblivion.

CHAPTER
FOURTEEN

❦

Back in Harley Street? – A guest of the British –
A meeting with MI5 – Jani does a deal –
"I would like to see Lord Consett..."

JANI'S FIRST NOTION on awakening was that she was back
in the Harley Street surgery, recaptured by the Russians.

She was in a comfortable bed with cool linen sheets
drawn up to her chin. She blinked up at the magnolia-
coloured ceiling, then sat up in panic and stared about
her. She wasn't in the hospital room of old, but in a
sumptuously furnished and decorated bedroom, with a
cream carpet, cream and mauve striped flock wallpaper
and heavy velvet curtains at the bay window. Paintings
by Constable adorned the walls, and an ornate walnut
dresser stood against the wall at the foot of the bed. It
looked like a bedroom in a country house, and through
the window she made out the distant tops of oak trees
and a blue sky.

She swivelled and planted her bare feet in the thick
carpet. She was wearing a plain white nightgown, and
as before her clothes were neatly folded and stacked in
a bedside cabinet. She moved to the window and looked
out.

Indeed she was in a country house, with a gravelled drive bisecting an immaculate lawn. Trees surrounded the garden, beyond which were high stone walls. Through the tall iron gates at the end of the drive she made out farmland alternating with patches of woodland.

She moved to a basin in the corner of the room, feeling woozy with the after-effects of the drug that had knocked her out. She splashed her face and, feeling a little better, returned to the bed and dressed.

She was imprisoned again – but by whom? Had the Russians recaptured her? Or had the British apprehended Alfie and Anand and spirited her away?

At the thought of her friends, her heart leapt. What had become of them in the early hours of the morning, when her abductors had halted the truck? She recalled hearing muffled shouts, the cab door opening, but after that nothing. Had Alfie and Anand managed to get away, or were they imprisoned here too?

She crossed to the door and tried the handle, expecting the door to be locked. She was surprised when the handle turned and the door opened. She peered into a corridor which gave on to a railed landing, furnished with occasional tables bearing sprays of fresh flowers. As in her room, art works lined the walls, this time by Gainsborough and Turner.

Cautiously she stepped from the room, padded along to the landing and peered over the rail. On either side, a grand staircase swept down to a black and white chequered marble hallway; the front door stood open, admitting the summer breeze and birdsong.

A door opened behind her, making her jump, and she turned to see a middle-aged woman in a mauve two-piece with pearls step out and smile at her through a pair of *pince nez*. "Miss Chatterjee, up at last, are we? Excellent. Now, please make yourself at home. Breakfast is being served in the dining room, down the stairs to the right."

And before Jani could open her mouth to ask a question, the woman swept away along the landing and turned into another room. Jani stared after her, her expectations subverted: she was being treated like a guest, not a prisoner. She felt a little like Alice in Wonderland.

She descended the staircase, turned right and found herself in a large dining room, not unlike the restaurant of a country hotel. At the far end was a silver *bain marie*, and the scent of cooked bacon and eggs competed with the aroma of wisteria wafting through an open window.

A small, bald-headed man, looking for all the world like a bank clerk, was tucking into a cooked breakfast to her right. He looked up and beamed at her as she stood uncertainly on the threshold. "Do help yourself, my dear. Jolly good scrambled eggs, I must say."

She moved towards him, hesitated, then said, "Do you work here?"

She smiled up at her. "Occasionally, my dear."

"This might seem a strange question, but where am I?"

"Carmody Hall," he said, still smiling as if finding her question not in the least bit strange. "Surrey. Fine place. Georgian, so I'm told."

Frustrated, she said, "But who runs this place?"

He peered quizzically at her and repeated, "Who runs the place? Why, the nation, of course."

"And why am I here?"

"Ah," he laughed, pointing at her with his fork, "now,

only you will know the answer to that, my dear. I say, but the bacon is first rate too. I'd dig in before it all goes, if I were you."

She looked round at the vacant tables and said, "I don't feel in the least hungry, thank you."

"In that case I recommend a stroll round the grounds to get your appetite up, my dear, and someone will be with you presently."

"They will?"

"Indubitably," he beamed.

As she turned and stepped from the dining room, she wondered whether she had just made the acquaintance of the White Rabbit or the Mad Hatter.

She left the hall and took the steps down to the drive, then crossed to the lawn. She turned and looked back at the building, foursquare and resplendent in the morning sunlight, its façade clad with an extensive coat of ivy. She moved towards the distant wrought-iron gates, wondering if these would be unlocked too.

When she reached the gates, however, she found them securely locked.

She made her way widdershins along a paved walk that circumnavigated the lawn, came to a secluded garden screened off from the rest of the grounds by a series of maze-like privet hedges, and sat down on a bench.

In the distance, presumably to the north over London, the tiny specks of airships moved hither and thither like tropical fish in an aquarium.

She would gather herself, then return to the house and search the rooms in case Alfie and Anand were also imprisoned in Carmody Hall. She appeared to have the run of the place, so she would take advantage of the fact.

She considered Sebastian, and his treachery towards

her, then found the thought too painful and attempted to think of other things.

She started as a young man appeared from behind a wall of privet, smiled at her and sat down on the bench. She gathered her skirts and shuffled away from him.

"Good morning, Miss Chatterjee – and a fine morning it is too. Johnson's the name, *Mister* Johnson, if you please."

He held out a limp hand, which Jani stared at without taking.

The man smiled, shrugged, and withdrew his hand. He reached down to his side and lifted a small briefcase on to his lap.

Jani stared at him and said, "Who are you?"

The man blinked. "Why, Mister Johnson," he began.

"I mean," she said patiently, "who do you work for?"

The man blinked again, as if her question were a complex mathematical conundrum. "Why, the government, of course."

Jani regarded the young man, who looked and sounded so quintessentially British that her suspicions were aroused. "That is a very good answer, *Mister* Johnson," she replied. "But *which* government, if you don't mind my asking?"

"What a very odd question, Miss Chatterjee, if you don't mind *my* saying. Which government do you think?"

"Well, I can think of two or three, at least. I have learned from experience that appearances, *Mister* Johnson, can be deceptive."

The young man sighed. "I was told that you were a feisty character, Miss Chatterjee, as well as intelligent and stubborn."

She bridled. "And who told you that?"

"Why, my superiors."

"Your Moscow paymasters, *Mister* Johnson?"

Johnson laughed and shook his head. "Oh, Miss Chatterjee, you *have* got hold of the wrong end of the stick, haven't you? No, you see, *yesterday* you were in the hands of the Bolsheviks."

"And then my friends intervened to save me," she said. "And where are they, for that matter?"

"They?"

Jani was about to say the names, but thought better of it. "The people who rescued me in the truck last night?"

"I can assure you that they came to no harm at all."

"And where are they now?"

"Oh, I don't know anything about that, Miss Chatterjee. That will be the province of a different department entirely."

"Then what *do* you know? Why are you here, speaking to me?"

"Ah," he said, "*that...*"

He opened the case on his knees, reached into it and pulled something out.

And the sight of the object dangling in his fingers sent a cold wave of dread through her.

He smiled. "I see that you are familiar with the device, Miss Chatterjee?"

She stood up quickly, intending to hurry back to the house and lock herself in her room, if that were possible. As quick as lightning, Mister Johnson's left arm shot out and he grabbed her by the wrist, drawing her back down to the bench beside him.

She winced at the pain, determined not to cry out as she sat down. The young man released his grip on her wrist and smiled. "Excellent. Now." He held up the filigree silver nexus before her, jiggling it a little in a gesture she found intimidating. "Can you recall the name of this ingenious device?"

"If you think I intend to play word games with you, Mister Johnson, then you're mistaken."

"Feisty and stubborn, indeed," he murmured to himself. He shrugged. "Very well, let us dispense with the preliminaries. You know what this is, and what it does, and... how shall I put this?... how painful its application can be? According to my superiors, the Bolsheviks had the temerity to apply one to your physiognomy without the benefit of anaesthetic back in India – but then that's the Russians for you all over, isn't it? They are a nation of barbarians and their methods are commensurately crude."

"What are you trying to say?"

"Merely that you need not fear that we would utilise the CWAD without first anaesthetising you, Miss Chatterjee."

She swallowed, staring at the web of silver wires draped over his right knee. "And why would you do that?"

"Why, so that you would feel no pain."

"No," she said patiently. "I mean, why would you use the device on me?"

"Ah!" he laughed. "I'm with you now. Well, you do possess certain facts that my superiors, in their wisdom, would like to share. And according to our records you have shown a marked inclination in the past to keep these said facts to yourself."

Her stomach turned. They would use the mind-reading device, learn that she carried the ventha-di within her...

If that were not bad enough, she still doubted that Mr Johnson – and everyone else at Carmody Hall – were who or what they said they were. On the face of it, Johnson and his cohorts appeared just too stereotypically British to be true.

She had been deceived once by agents of the Russian state, and she did not intend to be duped for a second time.

"Well, Miss Chatterjee?"

"Yes?"

"Are you inclined to remain characteristically stubborn in the retention of this information, or might you be more accommodating this time?"

"Meaning, will I tell you what you wish to know?"

"Precisely!" Mister Johnson smiled.

"That really depends," she said, "on what you want to know."

"Come, come. There is only one relevant fact, one nugget of vital information, and I know that you know what it is."

"If you wish to know something, Mister Johnson, then I suggest you ask me. I am not, unlike this device of yours, a mind-reader."

Johnson smiled, and made an appreciative face as if he considered her words well said. "Very well, Miss Chatterjee, I will not beat around the bush. Where is the ventha?"

She stared at him. "I don't know where it is," she replied, feeling sick.

"We know you either have it or know where it is, so it would save a lot of trouble, and distress, if you were to tell me."

She held the young man's gaze. "The fact remains,

I cannot be certain yet whether you are indeed in the employ of the British, or the scheming Bolsheviks."

He sighed, but was interrupted before he could reply.

A tall, silver-haired gentleman appeared under a bower of wisteria and stared at Mister Johnson; then the newcomer's gaze fell to the filigree mind-reading device on Johnson's lap, and his expression turned thunderous.

"What in the blue blazes is going on here, Johnson? I thought I told you–"

"But Major Heatherington, I was only..."

"Get yourself out of here, Johnson, and take that infernal device with you!"

Johnson fumbled the CWAD back into his briefcase, snapped it shut and took off through the bower like a frightened rabbit. Wide-eyed and more than a little relieved, Jani watched him flee.

Heatherington sighed. "Take no notice of the young oaf, Miss Chatterjee. I really must apologise on his behalf. Y'see, Johnson is new to the game. Eager, don't you know? Not that that excuses anything, and as for that contraption of his..." Heatherington shook his head in disgust. "There are ways and means, my dear, ways and means – and the use of such implements is not one of them. But allow me to introduce myself. Major Heatherington, formerly of the Royal Gloucestershire regiment, now working for MI5. At your service, as they say."

He sat down beside Jani and patted her hand. "You've been through a lot of late. No wonder you look so bemused. I advise a good long bed-rest."

Jani interrupted. "I'd really like to know what I'm doing here, Major Heatherington," she said. She suspected that the preceding contretemps between the two men had been no more than a charade for her benefit, and she was having none of it.

He stroked his silver moustache with his thumb and forefinger, moving them outwards from his philtrum in a gesture of contemplation. "First off, you're safe here from the Russians, the Chinese, and heaven knows whoever else might wish to do you harm. Your welfare is our ultimate concern, Miss Chatterjee."

"That doesn't really answer my question, with all due respect. Also, I'd like to see my friends. Mister Johnson assured me that they came to no harm last night–"

"They put up a decent fight, by all accounts, before our operatives chased them off."

"So you're not holding them here?"

Heatherington shook his head. "They vanished into the night."

"And how did you find out where the Russians were holding me?"

"We didn't," he said. "I don't s'pose it'll do any harm to tell you. We had Lieutenant Littlebody and his little friend under close surveillance, since one of my men spotted them in Putney the other day." He waved this away and changed the subject. "Anyway, as Johnson might have said, the reason you're here is that we really want to get our hands on the ventha, y'see." He said this with a candour that surprised Jani.

"And why do you want the device?"

He narrowed his eyes at her. "For reasons of national security, of course. For global security, no less."

"So you've finally come round to believing what Mahran told you, all those years ago?"

"Oh, Mahran blathered on about some alien threat –

but we took it with a pinch of salt." The major leaned closer and whispered, "The creature was deranged, y'see. Totally out of its head. Didn't see it myself, but by all accounts it was a slavering wreck, howling about invading aliens, don't you know, and the end of the world!"

"But didn't you use the CWAD on Mahran, to read the truth in his mind?"

"'Course we tried the thing – but apparently all we got was gibberish. Alien mind, y'see. Made no sense at all. But..."

"Yes?"

"But we analysed his every word, back when he was first apprehended and since, and the bods in intelligence've come up with a theory. More than a theory, in fact."

Jani shook her head, non-plussed. "A theory? About what?"

"Why, the venthas, of course. Mahran claimed there were three of them, and that when they came together they... and the records are vague about this... they would help to stop the progress of the Zhell. So," Major Heatherington said, tapping Jani's knee three times in a gesture of triumph, "the creature could only have been talking about a super-weapon, y'see!"

"A super-weapon?" Jani echoed disbelievingly.

"That's what intelligence surmises, and what Trenchard thinks – and that's good enough for me."

"A super-weapon," she said again, more to herself this time.

"So now y'see the reason we need the thing, Miss Chatterjee? And y'see why the damned Russians and the Chinese are so eager to get their hands on you?

My God, but if our enemies got their grubby paws on the thing... God knows what they'd do. Doesn't bear thinking about!" He pointed at her. "We need to ensure Great Britain's military pre-eminence, y'see! Only reason there's been peace in Europe this century is because we're so dashed powerful, don't y'know?"

"And you think I'm in possession of one of the venthas?" she said.

He smiled. "Miss Chatterjee, you told your father about your encounter with the Morn in the wreckage of the *Rudyard Kipling*; you told him that this creature had given you something for safekeeping. Y'see, you were overheard by your father's nurse, who was in the pay of the Russians. Now we picked up this Vikram chappie and interrogated him, and he spilled the proverbial haricots, y'see?"

She stared into the sky while he was telling her this – information which she knew already, thanks to Alfie – and considered how wrong Major Heatherington was, and how typical it was of the British authorities to be so small-minded and nationalistic. The future of the planet was at stake, and they could think only of small-scale national interests.

More than ever now she knew that it would be a terrible mistake to allow the British – or anyone else – to get their hands on the ventha in her possession.

"So you see, my dear, how important it is that we take care of the device, not only to prevent it falling into the hands of our enemies, but so that we maintain the pre-eminence we currently enjoy on the world stage." He paused, then went on, "Surely, as a proud citizen of the Raj, you sympathise with these sentiments?"

She composed herself, and smiled at Heatherington.

She had to be very careful in how she played the wily Major now. She said, "And do you know where the two remaining venthas might be?"

Heatherington scowled. "We're pretty dashed sure that Mahran had one in his possession before we apprehended him, but he wouldn't divulge its whereabouts until the other two came to light."

"And the third?"

"Apparently that was lost somewhere in the Himalayas. There was a rumour that it had fallen into the possession of locals, but if so we haven't found out who." He tapped her knee again. "But rest assured, the search is underway."

"But without the other two, the third one is, effectively, useless."

"Mmm, I can't deny that," Heatherington allowed. "But we'd rather be in possession of even one of the venthas, than risk the Ruskies or the Chinese happening upon it. So, m'dear," he went on, "how about you doing the right thing and telling old Major Heatherington where it is, hm?"

Jani watched a back-heavy bumblebee bounce from bloom to bloom, like an overburdened, miniature airship. The sun was hot, soporific, and this – along perhaps with the sedative still in her system – made her drowsy.

But not so drowsy that she didn't know how to play the major at his own game. "You present an interesting situation, Major. But you have left just one criterion from your analysis."

"And what might that be?"

"You have presumed upon my credulity and belief that you are, indeed, who you say you are."

He bridled. "Why, I can show you me dashed papers, if that'll convince you!"

Jani smiled. "Yesterday I was apprehended by the Russians, and I assumed them for a time to be British. Now, a small part of me – a very small part, admittedly – remains a little sceptical as to who you are, and no amount of paper waving will convince me."

She knew, then, what she would require from Heatherington as proof positive of who he was – or rather who he was representing. "But there is one way I might be convinced," she finished.

The major cocked an eye at her. "There is, is there? And what might that be?"

"I would like to see Lord Consett," she said, and then – as an afterthought she would later wonder at – added, "And also his son, Sebastian."

"The Consetts, hm?"

"I would like to see them here, as soon as possible, and have a private conversation with Lord Consett and his son."

"And this might persuade you to divulge...?"

She inclined her head. "Indeed it might."

The major nibbled at his moustache. "Well, Lord Consett is a busy man, what with his government duties and what have you. But seeing as this is a case of national importance... Tell you what, Miss Chatterjee, I'll put it to his Lordship and see what he says."

"I rather think," she said, "that he will jump at the opportunity, don't you?"

"Quite," Heatherington said, then slapped his thigh. "Right-o. Well, I'd better get to it, what?" He stood and extended his hand, and Jani shook it.

"Those Intelligence bods were dashed right about

you, weren't they? Said you were bright beyond your years, and they weren't wrong. Well, enjoy our hospitality, Miss Chatterjee, and I'll see you later."

She remained seated on the bench, in the sunlight, and watched the major march across the lawn towards the hall – only now questioning herself about why she had asked to see Sebastian as well as his father.

Sebastian would find himself in an odd situation. Disinclined to see her because of his betrayal, he would be unable to refuse his father's request to accompany him in seeing the girl he professed to love – for the good of his country, after all.

Oh, how she would enjoy watching him squirm! She would, she told herself, be in a strong position: he would be beside himself with fear in case she should inform the authorities that he was a lackey of the Bolsheviks; he would be malleable, and willing to do her bidding.

She stood and strolled from the garden.

She returned to the dining room and helped herself to a plate of scrambled eggs and toast and a pot of Darjeeling tea. The little man who had recommended the eggs had been right: they were delicious. There was no one else breakfasting at this late hour – it was almost ten – and she had the vast room to herself.

So the British thought the ventha-di was a weapon! She wondered what the Russians thought it might be. She had told Sebastian what she knew about the threat of the Zhell, but whether he'd believed her or not, and passed her story on to his paymasters, she was unable to say. At any rate, the only people she could trust now were her friends Alfie, Anand and Lady Eddington.

There remained the problem of achieving contact

with Mahran, and the even greater difficulty of freeing him from the grasp of the British.

As for her own situation... She had the first inklings of a plan to get herself away from Carmody Hall and the clutches of the British.

She finished her tea and repaired to her room, lay down on the bed and lost herself in thought.

CHAPTER
FIFTEEN

∽

Das in London – Turning the tide –
The gates of heaven will open! – Summoning Kali –
"I think a demonstration might be required..."

THE FIRST THING Durga Das did on arriving in London, two days earlier, was to make his way – at Kali's suggestion – to Savile Row and purchase for himself and Mr Knives two fine pinstriped suits. He had then found an Indian barber in Bayswater and had his beard trimmed and his long locks cut to just above his collar. He was renting, again at Kali's suggestion, the upper floor of a townhouse in Pimlico, and had found an excellent Gujarati restaurant nearby.

FOR TWO DAYS Kali had been silent on the subject of the Chatterjee girl, allowing Durga Das to see the sights of the capital. He and Mr Knives had taken all the tours, with a special excursion to view the sub-orbital rocket at Ealing Common. Das despised the gleaming new station and the towering golden rocket itself, hated with a passion the arrogant, bustling capital city. It might have been a metropolis of futurity to match any the world over – but then how could it not be? It was founded after all on riches plundered from countries like his own. Even as he rode the monorail high above the leafy borough of Shepherd's Bush on his way back from the rocket station, he reminded himself that the prosperity he could see all around him, from the well-dressed commuters to the gadgets and gewgaws for sale in parade after parade of shops, resulted in part from the rape of his own great nation.

Mr Knives regarded everything with wide-eyed awe, in danger of being beguiled by the superficial attraction of gross materialism. As they pulled away from Acton mono-station, the youth pointed to two immodestly-clad young women of his own age weaving along the broadway on scooters.

"What attracts you, Knives? Their comeliness or their wealth?"

Mr Knives blushed. "Both, Baba-ji!"

"Don't be misled by their immodesty, or their fascination with the latest fads. Both are based on false assumptions. For is it not said that the spirit grows without either the sustenance of the ego or support of the physical?"

Mr Knives frowned, but nodded. "Yes, Baba-ji," he said, sneaking a glance at the bare calves of the young women as they passed by far below.

"Let me tell you that the British Empire is a passing phenomenon, Mr Knives. Soon it will be no more, swept away like a child's sandcastle before the incoming tide. And that tide?" He posed the question, eyebrows arched, and stared at Mr Knives.

"The tide? Do you mean that London will be flooded, Baba-ji?"

Durga Das closed his eyes briefly. "It is true that I plucked you from the street not for your brains, but for your knife skills. The tide to which I refer, my friend, is the tide of the spirit, the tide of righteousness that will sweep the world when Kali and her minions step from heaven and take their rightful place on this benighted plane. Kali will come, and all will worship her, and who will be responsible for this great coming, Mr Knives?"

The youth ventured, "You, Baba-ji?"

"Exactly. I will have opened the gates of heaven and brought forth the gods, and you will have a small part to play at my side, let it be said."

"I will?"

"Soon we will apprehend the Chatterjee girl, and then the Morn, and we shall possess all three tithra-kuñjī."

"But where is the Chatterjee girl, Baba-ji?" Mr Knives asked.

Durga Das shook his head and fell silent as the monotrain carried them east to Pimlico. It was a question he had considered frequently over the course of the past two days. He had petitioned Kali to speak to him with the mantra *Anghra dah tanthara, yangra bahl, somithra tal zhell*, but to no effect, and had tried communicating directly to Kali via his thoughts, *Kali, your most holiness, we need to speak*, again without result. He was tiring of the glut of things vulgar and material that was London, and was impatient to take up the chase once again. He disliked the regard to which he was subjected by most Londoners, who judged him by the colour of his skin, oblivious of the fact that they were in the presence of a venerable holy man. He would be glad to be away from this heathen land, and to bring about its eventual downfall.

That evening they took a taxi to the Jewel of Jaipur – where the grovelling owner did at least accord Durga Das the correct degree of respect – and dined well on saag murgh and keema jalfrezi, followed by an assortment of burfi and milky spiced chai. Mr Knives had dispensed with his impromptu set of lethal blades, and Das had fashioned in their stead a series of forks and spoons affixed to the belt around each stump so that the youth could dine without assistance.

Replete, they caught a taxi back to Pimlico where Mr Knives retired early and Durga Das enthroned himself in a vast padded sofa before a flaring electro-fire. Despite its being high summer, he still found London evenings chilly after the heat of Delhi.

He knew that Kali was maintaining the silence for a reason. She had communicated with him in the past only when necessary, and he knew that she would be monitoring the situation, and Chatterjee's whereabouts, and would command him to action only when she was sure that action on his part was required.

Nevertheless he was curious. He could not help recalling something Kali had vouchsafed to him on the dusty lane in northern Greece, to the effect that she had endowed him with more than just the ability to heal. Now Durga Das was eager to learn what that 'something' was.

He fell to his knees and clasped his hands and intoned, "*Anghra dah tanthara, yangra bahl, somithra tal zhell!*" and, "I beseech you, oh Kali! Please, speak to me."

A profound silence greeted his words, and Das was contemplating the comfort of his king-sized feather bed when a familiar voice spoke in his head.

Your summons coincides with my desire to communicate, Kali said.

Das climbed from his knees, resumed the sofa and made himself comfortable.

"In Greece you said that you had endowed me with 'powers that go beyond the paltry one of healing', and I was wondering, oh Kali, what those powers might be?"

He had the impression of laughter within his head as Kali replied, *I think a demonstration might be required.*

"A demonstration?"

But not tonight. Be patient, Das, and tomorrow we will begin the next phase of our quest.

CHAPTER
SIXTEEN

∽

A meeting with Lord Consett – Jani confronts Sebastian –
The end justifies the means – Jani plans her escape –
"I knew I could rely on you..."

JANI HAD FALLEN asleep after breakfast and was awoken by a light tapping on the door. She sat up, rubbed her eyes, and glanced at her wristwatch. She'd slept for almost three hours; it was now after one o'clock.

She hurried to the door, interrupting the repeated tapping. It was the woman in the twin-set and pearls. "Lord Consett to see you in the library, Miss Chatterjee."

Jani thanked her and said she'd be down in one minute, then washed her face at the basin and combed her hair. Now that the time had come to confront Sebastian with his treachery, she felt more than a little sick.

Always assuming, of course, that he'd agreed to accompany his father.

She left the room and made her way down the stairs. The twin-set woman met her in the hall and escorted her to the west wing and the library.

Jani composed herself before the polished oak door, took a deep breath, squared her shoulders and entered the room.

Lord Consett stood at the far end of the room, his back to the hearth. He was a small man with a big, polished bald head and a walrus moustache, dressed today in tweed plus-fours as if he'd been dragged here directly from the golf course.

On their few previous meetings, Jani had always received the impression that Lord Consett took a dim view of her liaison with his son. He had reputation as a short-tempered martinet, who didn't suffer fools gladly and, according to Sebastian, had few friends.

She paused by the door and said, "And Sebastian?"

"Kicking his heels outside," Consett said gruffly. His speech, indeed his general manner, tended towards the abrupt, which Jani interpreted as a self-defence mechanism maintained to overawe new acquaintances; it had become such a characteristic of the man that he used it now even in the company of family and friends.

She moved to the window and looked out. Sebastian was a small figure on the lawn, hands shoved into his pockets as he strolled back and forth, head down. Her stomach clenched, and she quickly turned away from the window.

"Very good," she said, crossing to the hearth and seating herself on a *chaise longue*.

Lord Consett sat on the edge of an adjacent armchair. "Good to see you again, Janisha. Been through the mill of late, what?"

"You could say that," she agreed.

"Sebastian's not been himself lately. Put it down to worrying about you. Anyway, now you're back, I hope you'll settle him down a bit, hm?"

"That remains to be seen, sir."

He cleared his throat. "Heatherington brought me up

to speed. Explained the situation. 'Course I understand your confusion. Totally understandable. I hope my presence will reassure you. Heatherington might be a bit of an old stickler, but he's a good man. Can be trusted implicitly."

"I'm delighted to hear that," she said non-commitally.

"Well, as I say, old Heathers gave me the gen. Said you wanted reassurances, after which you'd play ball. Now," he went on, leaning forward and staring at her with his tiny, jet black eyes. "I can't begin to stress the delicacy and the importance of this matter. You're no fool, girl – brightest button in the box, in my opinion – so I won't patronise you. We need the venthas for the good of the Empire. We don't want this weapon falling into the wrong hands, you see. I mean to say, you've seen what devils the Russians are. Imagine a super-weapon in their possession, for God's sake!"

She inclined her head, implying she not only understood but agreed with him.

She considered her earlier idea of telling the British about the threat of the Zhell. It was still an option, she thought; but better still would be to meet Mahran and solicit his opinion.

Heatherington said, "So... now you know this set up is all above board and tickety-boo, we really would like to know what you did with the ventha that the Morn – what was his name? Jelch? – gave you back in India."

"You do know," she said, "that the ventha is useless unless all three are united?"

"That's understood, and we're doing all we can to locate them. If only Mahran had done the right thing, come clean and told us the whereabouts of the ventha he had in his possession."

She stared at the diminutive Lord, his use of the past tense alarming her.

Lord Consett said, "So, Janisha – where is the ventha which Jelch gave you?"

Her pulse racing, she said, "Before I divulge that information, sir, it would be wise of me to ascertain Mahran's well-being. Indeed, I should like to meet him. If you would be so good as to bring him here, today."

Lord Consett's reaction surprised her. He leapt to his feet, startling Jani, and crossed to the window. He stared out, his hands clasped behind his back.

"Sir?"

He turned quickly. His brow was creased; he seemed to be in debate with himself. At last he said, "Very well. I think I know you, Janisha. I trust you. You're a good woman, despite... despite your age. The facts of the matter are these. I'm afraid I can't accede to your request to arrange an audience between yourself and the Morn because..." He frowned, and Jani could see that it pained him to admit this: "Because, you see, we no longer have Mahran in our custody."

She shook her head. "You don't...?"

He returned to the fireside and resumed his armchair, flinging himself into its embrace as if in despair. "Between you and me, Janisha, the blasted Bolsheviks sprung him from Newgate last night."

She blinked, attempting to assimilate this latest twist.

"Blew a great ruddy hole in the outer wall, and a dozen of the blighters assaulted the main body of the building, killing half a dozen guards in the process before locating Mahran and absconding with him. We suspect inside help, of course. Bolshevik agents in the gaol itself."

Jani closed her eyes briefly. She had felt, mere minutes ago, that events were playing themselves into her hands.

"And you have no idea at all where he might be?"

"None at all," he admitted. "But we're ruddy well scouring the land. Every police force in Britain is on the alert." He paused, then said, "And of course this means that you yourself are in increased danger. The Ruskies will stop at nothing, now that they have Mahran, of... of adding to their collection, as it were."

Jani turned and looked through the window. Sebastian was a tiny, distant figure kicking daisies on the lawn.

Lord Consett went on, "So you see, if our knowledge of the whereabouts of your ventha was vital before last night, now it is imperative that we locate the device before the Russians happen upon it."

He allowed a pregnant silence to develop. "Janisha, do your duty to the nation and tell me where it is, I beg you."

She sat upright, staring down at her hands clasped in her lap as she considered her next words. "Let me assure you, sir, that the ventha is safe."

"Janisha, we really need to know its whereabouts."

"I appreciate that, sir, but... Before I tell you, I need a little time to myself, in order to... to settle my mind on certain things. Please, if you would give me ten minutes? I would like a little fresh air."

He nodded, exhaling with evident relief. "I'll be waiting here when you return, Janisha."

"I think I shall take a turn around the garden, sir," she said, rising from the *chaise longue* and pacing from the room.

She hurried across the hallway and stepped out into the sunlight, feeling light-headed with what she had just learned and apprehensive at the imminent encounter with Sebastian.

Taking a deep breath, she descended the steps, crossed the gravel drive and made her way across the lawn to the distant figure of Sebastian.

He was standing with his back to her, staring at the bower where, that morning, she had spoken with Mister Johnson and Major Heatherington.

Now that the time had come to confront her betrayer, she felt anger rising within her. She worked to control her rage; anger was a redundant emotion in the present situation, even if it were a valid and entirely reasonable response to his perfidy. She needed to keep a tight rein on her emotions during the forthcoming encounter.

Nevertheless, as she approached Sebastian and cleared her throat, she felt a bolus of rage fill her chest, along with another emotion, that of some hopeless, residual affection for the young man.

He turned quickly.

They stared at each other, separated by three yards which might have been as many miles. She was reminded of her meeting with him two days ago, in Richmond Park, and the surge of love she had felt for Sebastian then.

She felt as if she might collapse in a flood of tears, and fought to remain calm.

"Jani," he began, reaching out a hand to her. He smiled, bluffing, as he said, "What a dashed mix up! There I was, thinking you safe in Harley Street. Imagine my horror when I learned that you'd been captured, and then my relief when..."

"Shut up!" she cried at him. "Don't compound your lies with more lies!" Her throat was sore with the effort of not crying, her eyes drenched with unshed tears. "I know the truth, Sebastian. I saw you with the Russian!"

He feigned an incredulous expression, which enraged her even further. "Janisha?"

"How could you?" she asked, with a calmness that amazed her. "How could you do that to me? Oh, I understand what might have compelled you to side with the Russians, I understand your idealism. But what I cannot begin to comprehend is how you could betray what I thought of as your love for me."

"Jani..."

"But that was my mistake, wasn't it? I thought you loved me, and the fact was – the fact *is* – that you felt, and feel, not a single scintilla of affection for me, admit it!" And she knew that, in asking him this, she was hoping to hear his denial.

He was shaking his head, his expression pleading. "Jani, you're wrong. I *do* love you."

"You liar!" she screamed, wanting more than anything to believe him. "How can you love me and do what you did?" Tears came now, a torrent of the treacherous things, and she dashed them angrily from her cheeks.

He stepped forward, reaching for her.

"Get away!" She stepped back. "Don't you dare touch me! Don't even come near me!"

They stood yards apart, staring at each other, her breath coming in spasms. Sebastian looked wretched.

"You don't understand," he murmured.

"Understand?" she said. "Understand? What is there to *understand*? You sold me out for your ideals. You love your Russian paymasters more than me! You'd have had me operated on, cut open, to get what you wanted. And what then? Did they plan to kill me, to get rid of the evidence?"

"Jani, Jani... You don't understand. Please, let me explain myself."

"Explain? You don't *need* to explain! I understand everything that happened–"

"You understand nothing!" he cried, surprising her with his anger. "I can explain."

He moved to a bench and sat down, resting his elbows on his knees and clasping his hands, hanging his head as he considered his words.

Rubbing tears from her cheeks, Jani moved to a bench a few yards from Sebastian's and sat down. She lodged her feet on the seat and hugged her shins, protectively, and stared at him.

"Well?" she called out.

He looked up at her and said, "I admit that I was working for the Russians. I believed – I *believe* – passionately in what the Russian state stands for. I think Marx is the only truly great political philosopher of our age, and what Lenin and Trotsky have done in transforming the Soviet Union into an egalitarian society, to counter the evil of western capitalism."

"But that doesn't explain why you had to betray our love!" she cried.

"Please, Jani, listen to me. Let me explain." He ran a hand through his blond hair, then stared up into the cloudless sky and said, "They approached me while I was at Cambridge. They knew I was in the Young Socialist League, and they sent someone to sound me out, work out if my idealism was no more than that – or a real, intellectual understanding of what Marx wrote and Lenin brought into being. Anyway," he waved that away, "I was interested, more than interested in joining their cause. It was a way to do something to counter what my father and his friends were doing to the world, a way of fighting the evils of Empire."

She said, "But you told me, in Cambridge, that the only way to effect change was from within, to join the Socialists in Britain and work for change democratically."

"I did believe that, before I understood what a farce democracy is. The Tories are in power, have been for two decades, and will do nothing to relinquish their stranglehold. No, the only way I could serve my ideals was to go over to the Russians."

She suddenly understood something, then. "So *that's* why you left Cambridge?"

He smiled. "Someone in Westminster, a fellow traveller, suggested I leave and apply to work for Palmer. I got the job, with a good word from my father." He laughed at this. "From the inside, I was a valuable asset to the Russians."

"You spied for them?"

"I passed on certain items of information, let's say."

"You betrayed your country, your fellow countrymen. And then, when I returned from India, when I turned up, you betrayed *me* just as willingly."

"I didn't want to betray you, Jani," he said in almost a whisper.

"What?" she said incredulously. "You didn't *want* to? Then why... why on Earth *did* you?"

He looked up from his hands and stared at her. "I was blackmailed, Jani. I *had* to do it."

She shook her head, feeling incredulous and a little sick. "Blackmailed? How...?"

He flung back his head and looked straight up into the sky. "Oh, God. What a mess! What a terrible, stinking mess I've made of everything. What is truly terrible, Jani, is how through the best of intentions you can bring hurt and suffering to those you most love."

"Why were you blackmailed, Sebastian?"

"I... I was indiscreet. This was before we met, Jani. A year or so before. I would never..." he faltered.

Jani said, icily, "*What* 'was before we met'? What did you *do*?"

He could not bring himself to meet her eyes. "I... I had a liaison, a brief affair. I don't know how they found out, or managed to get pictures."

"They photographed you with... with someone?" She felt ill, and the words came only with great effort. "They photographed you, and then when the time came, they used the photographs against you?"

"I was seventeen. Still at Eton. There was this serving girl a little younger than me. It was a silly, stupid fling."

A *serving* girl, she thought; how appropriate!

"I..." He swallowed. "It was over in a month, a brief infatuation." He let the silence stretch, then went on, "Then I went up to Cambridge, and met you, and fell in love—"

"Don't!"

"And then, when you came back to England and told me about the ventha-di—"

"You passed this information on to your paymasters..."

He looked abject. "I told them everything, but only after they had threatened to send the photographs to my father."

"So they made you dupe me. That night in Whitechapel, the night-market, your saying you knew a quiet little public house... And the attack – all set up to get me into the Harley Street surgery, so they could open me up." Revulsion turned in her chest like something alive.

"Jani..." he pleaded.

"And when I came round from the operation with a great scar across my stomach?" she said. "How did you intend to explain *that*?"

He shook his head, abject. "They said they could perform the operation without scarring you. At the same time they would insert a pin in your arm, to make you believe..."

"And later, when I discovered that I no longer carried the ventha-di?"

"I... I would have blamed it on the British, claiming that the Harley Street surgery was a MI5 front."

Jani interrupted him. "I can't believe that you would have *allowed* the Russians to do this to me."

"Jani... Jani, please try to understand my position. There was nothing I could do to prevent them. The photographs..." He shook his head. "You don't think I was happy with what they planned, do you?"

"I don't know, Sebastian. I honestly don't know. After all, with the ventha-di your oh-so enlightened, egalitarian paymasters would have what they wanted, wouldn't they? And all thanks to you. You would have helped the Bolshevik cause a great deal!"

"I was sickened, Jani!" he cried. "I was sickened with the shame of betrayal."

"And now? Do you see what evil, scheming people you're serving? People who would blackmail a fellow comrade to get what they desire. And would you really want a world ruled by these thugs?"

She stopped suddenly, staring at him, then went on

in almost a whisper, "My God, Sebastian. I remember something you once said, when I mentioned the Georgian peasant massacre. You said that in certain cases the end justifies the means. And you *believe* that now, don't you? You might have betrayed me, and a part of you might even truly regret the hurt you've caused me... but another, greater part truly believes the cause you're working towards. *The end justifies the means.*" She was crying again, tears leaking from her eyes and rolling down her cheeks, and this time she did nothing to stop the flow.

"Jani," he said, "you can't begin to understand how... how torn I am. How I believe with all my heart, and all my head, in the Russian cause, and yet how I regret hurting you."

"But the end justifies the means, after all! You believe that, don't you? And don't worry – because whatever hurt you've caused me, I'll get over it, won't I? Time will heal all wounds. I'll grow, mature, and forget you in time. And anyway I'm only a woman, and an Indian at that! Is this what you're telling yourself, Sebastian, in a bid to salve your conscience?"

"Jani, please... please don't torture me like this!"

"*Me* torture *you*? I don't believe I'm hearing this! And you don't think what you've done has tortured *me*?"

He looked at her, and he was weeping. "I know it has, Jani. And I'm truly sorry. I would do anything to be able to undo what I've done. In hindsight I should have let them show my father the pictures... even though that might have driven you from me. At least it would have spared you this hurt. I'm sorry, Jani. I'm so sorry, and I'd do anything at all to make things better between us."

She looked away quickly, not wanting to see his pain,

not wanting to witness his entreaty – not wanting, she admitted, to weaken. She stared at the house, at the windows reflecting the light of the afternoon sun. What with the scent of the flowers, and the warm breeze, the day was idyllic, perfect – and its perfection made her pain all the more intolerable.

After a minute of tortured, intractable silence, she turned to him. "Anything?"

He blinked. "Pardon?"

"I said, 'Anything?' You said you'd do anything to make things better between us."

He gestured hopelessly. "I mean it. I love you, Jani. I want to win back your trust."

She sensed his abject hope, and wondered if she should despise herself for what she was planning. "How could you do that, Sebastian? How on earth do you think I could ever again trust you, after what you did?"

He shrugged, looking forlorn.

She stared at him, letting the silence extend, torturing him. "Your father has just informed me, Sebastian, that your people – the Russians – raided Newgate last night and abducted Mahran."

She could tell from his expression that this was news to him. "So your paymasters kept you in the dark about this, did they?"

"I'm just a low-level informant, nothing more. They wouldn't disclose plans like this to me."

"So this changes things, Sebastian. The Russians have Mahran. My plan was to contact him myself, and somehow effect his release." She leaned forward. "For the security of this planet, Sebastian – not just for some petty ideology! I'm working for *all* humanity, not just for one section of it!"

He opened his mouth to say something, no doubt to claim that his paymasters had been working for all humanity too, but perhaps he thought it best to let it pass.

She said, "You said you'd do anything to win back my trust."

He looked at her, slowly understanding, and then shook his head. "That's impossible! They wouldn't tell me anything like that."

"I want to know where the Russians are holding Mahran, Sebastian. Surely you can find that out for me?"

He spread his hands hopelessly. "But how?"

She smiled at him, sweetly. "That's for you to work out."

"But it's impossible. They'd never divulge his whereabouts."

"Meet your contact, tell him that you know where I'm being held. Say that you might even be able to bring me to where they're holding Mahran."

"Even if I did this, I doubt they'd tell me. And if they knew where you were, wouldn't this endanger you?"

She smiled across at him. "No, because I intend to get away from here... with your help."

"My help?" he echoed.

"I want you to contact Lady Eddington. Tell her to get in touch with Alfie Littlebody and Anand Doshi, and arrange for them to meet you in London with transport."

He stared at her. "And then?"

"And then I want you, Alfie and Anand to drive down here and arrive at one o'clock tomorrow morning. And bring a rope ladder."

"A rope ladder?"

"A long one – long enough to extend over the wall behind you, beyond the oak tree. I seem to have the run of this place, and with luck they won't be keeping a watch on me in the early hours."

"And if they do?"

She shrugged. "Then my little plan will come to nothing, and I'll be forced to think again."

She hoped he wouldn't say that he could do all this himself, without enlisting Alfie and Anand's help. The fact was that, despite all his entreaties, she did not trust him not to deliver her into the hands of his paymasters.

She doubted he would be able to discover Mahran's whereabouts, but it would be enough, for the time being, if he were able to help her escape from this place.

"Very well," he said with determination. "I'll do that, Jani. I'm truly sorry for what I did. You do trust me, don't you?"

She stared into his eyes, unable to tell him that she would never be able to trust him again – despite knowing that, whatever he had done to her, for some reason she still loved him.

"I *might* bring myself to trust you if you succeed in freeing me and locating Mahran," she said. "Now I need to speak with your father, and prevaricate about the location of the device."

She stood and faced Sebastian, who stood also and took a step towards her. She raised a hand, stopping him. "I will see you at one, with luck," she said. "Goodbye, Sebastian."

She turned and made her way back to the hall.

At the door she paused and stared back at the lawn. Sebastian was seated on the bench, holding his head in his hands. Biting her lip, she hurried inside.

She found Lord Consett in the dining room, tucking into a plate of roast beef and mashed potatoes. He stood quickly, dabbing his mouth with a napkin. "Janisha?"

"After due consideration," she said, "I see no reason to keep the whereabouts of the ventha from you and the government."

He almost deflated with relief. "Capital," he said. "I knew I could rely on you."

"While fleeing from the Russians and the British in northern India," she said, "I thought it best to lodge what they were looking for in a place of safekeeping."

Lord Consett nodded, hanging on her every word.

"To this end I concealed the device in a guest house in Rishi Tal. Unfortunately I cannot recall the name of the establishment, nor the room number, but I do remember that it overlooked the lake. I taped the ventha to the underside of the top drawer in the room's only dresser."

"I'll get someone on to the matter immediately," he said, moving towards the door. "Thank you, Janisha."

"I don't suppose," she asked, "that I will be allowed my freedom now?"

He paused before the door and turned to her. "Just as soon as we have the ventha in our possession, Janisha, then I'll see to it personally that you're released from Carmody Hall."

She watched him hurry from the dining room. It would take the British authorities a day at least to scour every guest house in Rishi Tal, and discover that she had sent them on a wild goose chase – and perhaps, by then, she would be far away from here.

She moved to the window and stared across the lawn. Sebastian was seated in the distance, still holding his head in his hands. A surge of sadness threatened to engulf her. She thought of her promise to him, and wondered at her duplicity.

She hurried up the staircase to her room, repeating to herself the phrase, "The end justifies the means," but doubting that, in this case, she agreed with the dictum.

CHAPTER
SEVENTEEN

∽

Conversation with his father –
Sebastian seeks out Lady Eddington –
Captured by the Russians –
"We shall be very careful with your precious little girlfriend..."

SEBASTIAN SAT BESIDE his father in the back of the chauffeur-driven Bentley as they sped north to London.

He felt like a man reprieved from a death sentence. He considered the lies he'd told Jani about the photographs, and persuaded himself that they had been necessary. The truth would have hurt her even more and made the possibility of any rapprochement between them – slim though it was even now – practically impossible. It was a measure of the girl's character, her essential decency and humanity, that she was willing to give him a second chance. And he would grasp the opportunity with both hands, he told himself; not only that, but he vowed that from now on his life of deceit and lies would be a thing of the past.

A little later his father said, "You're quiet, Sebastian."

"Oh, I'm tired, that's all."

"Made up at seeing the young Janisha again, I don't doubt?"

"Rather."

His father cast him a shrewd glance. "What did you talk about, out there in the garden?"

Sebastian shrugged. "Oh, her studies," he temporised, "and how she hoped to get back to them very soon." As he suspected that his father would be expecting the question, he asked, "Just what is Janisha doing at Carmody Hall, father?"

His Lordship harrumphed a little, then said, "Let's just say that she was mixed up in a little intrigue, hm, after the crash-landing, and leave it at that? Nothing serious. She isn't in trouble." He paused. "Didn't mention anything of it to you, did she?"

"Not a thing," he said.

"Well, with luck she'll be out of there in no time."

Sebastian smiled to himself. "That's good to know," he said.

"Quite a girl, Janisha," his father said after a minute. "Quite a catch. What are your intentions in that department, Sebastian?"

He felt himself redden under his father's scrutiny. "Why, I haven't really thought..."

"You could do worse, you know? She not only has beauty and intelligence – attributes not often found together in the fairer sex – but she has a commonsensical approach that bodes well for her future."

"And... the fact that she's Indian?"

His Lordship grunted. "What d'you mean?"

"Last year, when you first found out that she and I were friends, you weren't exactly enamoured of the idea."

Lord Consett shrugged uncomfortably. "Didn't know the girl then, did I? Got to know her a little since then.

And her father was a capital fellow – for an Indian, of course. Served the Raj damned well. And, after all, her mother was one of us."

Sebastian smiled to himself.

"What I'm trying to say," his father said, "is that a girl like that is just the sort to take a young chap in hand and show him what's what, if y'get my drift."

Sebastian stared out at the passing countryside. "Quite, father."

The idea that one day he might settle down with Jani so that she might 'show him what's what' was so far removed from the current situation that its contemplation was painful. First he had to fulfil his part of the bargain and spring Jani from Carmody Hall.

One hour later the car approached Richmond, and Sebastian asked to be let off at the monorail station. "I need to go into town to see someone," he explained to his father as he climbed from the car.

He entered the station and boarded an east-bound monotrain, going over what he would tell Lady Eddington. He just hoped that the woman was at home and not taking high tea with her blue-rinsed Tory friends.

He stepped from the train at Mayfair station and hurried along Mount Street, finding number fifteen and climbing the steps.

His heart thudding, he rang the bell-push. A trout-faced butler answered the door and Sebastian asked to see Lady Eddington.

"And whom should I say is calling, sir?"

Sebastian told him and kicked his heels on the doorstep as the butler retreated.

He returned after a minute. "Her Ladyship will see you in the drawing room. She asked if you would take tea?"

"A stiff brandy if you don't mind," Sebastian said, following the butler into the house and along a corridor to a sumptuous room overlooking a lawned rear garden.

"Her Ladyship will be with you presently, sir."

Sebastian sat on a padded window-seat and gazed out at the lawn; a bower at the far end only reminded him of Jani and his meeting with her, and her recriminations and tears. He turned away bitterly, in time to see Lady Eddington limp into the room with the aid of a stick. She was a tall woman with a kindly, powdered face – which was drawn into lines of concern as she approached and held out her hand.

He introduced himself, adding, "I am a good friend of Janisha Chatterjee."

"I know all about you, young man. But Janisha?" she asked as she sank on to a nearby wicker chair. "I've been worrying myself sick about the girl."

"I've just seen her–"

"You have? But where is she? And who the blazes is holding her? Is she well?"

Sebastian smiled at the barrage of questions. For all she was a dyed-in-the-wool member of the landed gentry, she clearly had Jani's best interests at heart. "She is well, and incarcerated at Carmody Hall – a department of MI5," he explained. "She asked to see my father, Lord Consett, and myself as some part of a deal to inform the British where the ventha is."

Lady Eddington stared at him. "But she doesn't intend to tell them, I take it?"

"No fear. Jani's made of sterner stuff. She plans to escape from the hall this evening, and that's why I'm here. She asked me to enlist your help in getting her out."

The dowager clapped her hands before her flat chest

and exclaimed, "Just like the girl! What spunk! Now tell me what I can do."

"I need to contact Lieutenant Littlebody and Anand Doshi," Sebastian began, and proceeded to outline Jani's plan.

Fifteen minutes later Lady Eddington had her Rolls driven around to the front of the house, and Sebastian assisted her down the steps and into the back of the car. "Highgate, Donald, and take a circuitous route if you please."

"Yes, ma'am," said the chauffeur, pulling out into the street.

"I'd drive the thing myself," she explained to Sebastian, "but my blessed leg is still not quite the ticket, you see."

They took a devious route north, via Kilburn, the dowager turning in her seat to see if they were being followed. "Can't be too careful these days, can one?" she asked, and, smiling to himself, Sebastian agreed that one couldn't.

Presently they pulled up in a lane off the High Street and Lady Eddington led him into a mews and up a flight of stone steps. She rapped on the door and a shock-haired Indian boy, stick-thin and barefoot, pulled it open.

They hurried inside and Lady Eddington made the introductions.

Sebastian found himself in a small but comfortable lounge – with a fire blazing despite the time of year – in the company of Janisha's very unlikely-looking co-conspirators. Lieutenant Littlebody was, despite his surname, a dumpy little man who looked less like an officer in the British Army than some mild-mannered country parson. And Anand Doshi looked very much like the street-urchin-come-houseboy Jani had described, right down to his thin face, massive staring eyes and unruly thatch of jet black hair.

Anand lifted a small table bearing a chess-set away from the hearth and they seated themselves, while Lady Eddington assured Littlebody and Doshi that Janisha was safe and well.

Doshi punched the air and beamed at Littlebody, who flopped into an armchair in evident relief. "We've been sick with worry," he said, "ever since a pair of heavies shanghaied us and dragged Anand and me from the truck last night."

"We thought we'd saved Jani's bacon, sir," Doshi said. "Everything had gone to plan! We were driving away with Jani in the back of the truck when a car pulled up in front of us and four thugs jumped out! We had no time to do anything, did we, Mr Alfie?"

"Not a blessed thing! They set about us with clubs and we were forced to beat a retreat, loath though we were to leave Jani. They drove the truck off before we could do a dashed things about it. Thing was, we couldn't work out who the blazes it was who'd got the better of us. But you say it was the British, Lady Eddington?"

"It was, and they have Jani incarcerated at a place called Carmody Hall," she said, and explained what Sebastian had told him and Jani's scheme to free her in the early hours.

Sebastian caught Littlebody giving him the occasional once-over – as if he were sizing up a potential rival. The trio had shared many adventures, after all, and been confined together aboard the *Edinburgh* since leaving India. Time enough, he thought, for the Lieutenant to form a hopeless attachment to someone as comely as Jani.

He dismissed the thought as uncharitable. After all, Littlebody and Doshi had proved loyal helpmates in Jani's flight from the authorities.

"I can supply you with a car and a rope ladder," Lady Eddington was saying.

"We'll set off just before midnight," Littlebody said.

"I'll accompany you," Sebastian said, "and guide you to the hall. There's a great oak standing just inside the north wall, and Jani said we should throw the rope ladder over the wall there."

Anand Doshi was on the edge of his seat. "It is good, no, to be planning again after sitting on our bottoms for so long? I was becoming tired of beating Mr Alfie at chess!"

Lady Eddington beamed. "Then it is arranged. I shall go forthwith and gather what you need. I'll have the car driven around at eleven-thirty."

Sebastian stood. "I'll return here then. In the meantime I really must go and get something to eat."

Littlebody hesitated, then said, "You're very welcome to stay and dine with us, Sebastian. Anand rustled up a very passable curry earlier."

"That's kind of you," Sebastian said, eager to be away from the cloying heat of the small room, "but I really should be pushing off."

Lady Eddington remained seated, but clutched his hand before he made for the door. "Jani spoke glowingly of you, Sebastian, and I can tell that her estimation was one hundred percent correct."

He forced a smiled, colouring, and moved to the door accompanied by Littlebody. The lieutenant looked awkward and hesitant as he extended a hand on the threshold. "Well, thanks for everything, old chap. See you tonight."

Sebastian shook the Lieutenant's hand. "See you then," he said, and hurried down the steps and out of the mews.

He knew a pleasant little French place around the corner in the High Street, which served an excellent beef bourguignon and kept a fine claret. He felt he would need to be half cut come this evening, and wondered at his reception from Jani when they whisked her away from Carmody Hall.

He was approaching the restaurant when he became aware of someone striding along beside him; before he knew what was happening, or could think to call out, another tall figure was on his left. In an instant they had his upper-arms in a manacle-strong grip.

"What the...!"

Something poked him in the ribs, and he looked down to see a pistol in the hand of the heavy.

"Be quiet, or I will shoot."

A car jerked to a halt at the kerb and the back door swung open. He was bundled inside; the door slammed shut and they accelerated away down the street.

The heavy on his left worked the revolver painfully into his ribs.

Sebastian had had no time to panic, and all he felt now was despair. These people had to be MI5; his liaison with the Russians had been found out.

Then a small man in the passenger seat turned and gave one of his rare smiles, and Sebastian knew he was wrong.

"I am very sorry we had to resort to such crude

tactics," Rostov said, "but it seems that you can no longer be trusted."

Sebastian tried to smile, not knowing whether to feel relief or alarm. "I don't understand," he said, sweating.

"Then allow me to explain. You were seen earlier in the company of Lady Eddington. Now we know that the old crone has links to Janisha Chatterjee, and as the latter has 'disappeared', we suspect that Eddington knows something of her whereabouts. By logical extension, my friend, it is possible that you, too, know where Chatterjee is at this moment."

"That's ridiculous!" Sebastian said, thinking fast. "Of course I saw Lady Eddington – I was trying to find out where Janisha might be!"

The Russian tipped his head to one side as if he might be considering the veracity of Sebastian's claim. "Well, we shall see about that, my friend."

Rostov nodded to the heavy on Sebastian's right, who drew a black hood from his coat pocket, pulled it over Sebastian's head, and tightened a drawstring around his neck. "What the blazes?"

"Merely a precaution," Rostov said.

Sebastian tried not to dwell on the inevitable 'interrogation' that awaited him.

The car slowed, perhaps five minutes later, and came to a stop. He was marched from the car and manhandled up a short flight of steps. He heard a door open and then the sound of old linoleum crackling underfoot as he was frogmarched into a building.

He was pushed up a flight of stairs, almost tripping as he went, and then forced down on to a straight-backed chair while someone bound his hands and feet, securing him to the chair.

The heavies removed the hood and Sebastian blinked in the early evening sunlight slanting through a barred window into a small, bare room.

Seated on a settee, positioned immediately before Sebastian, was Dmitri Korolov.

Rostov positioned himself before the window, smiling at Sebastian.

"Now, my friend," Rostov said. "Where is Janisha Chatterjee?"

"I told you, I don't know."

"Well, as I said earlier, we shall see about that."

He nodded to Korolov and the young man picked up a polished wooden box from the cushion beside him, set it upon his lap and hinged open the lid. He pulled something out very carefully, a silver wire mesh as delicate as a hair-net. He plugged a lead that trailed from the nexus into a socket in the side of the box, then lifted a pair of headphones from the box.

"Do you have any idea what this is?" Rostov asked.

Sebastian shook his head, not sure if he really wanted to know.

"You British call it a CWAD."

"A what?" He recalled Jani's description of the device the other day, and his stomach turned.

"A Cognitive Wave Amplification Device," Rostov said. "They are ingenious machines, one of which we liberated from your people a little while ago."

"Not *my* people," Sebastian snapped.

The Russian smiled. "Well, we shall find out soon where your loyalties truly lie, my friend, along with the whereabouts of Janisha Chatterjee." He looked across at Korolov. "If you would care to explain how the CWAD works, Dmitri."

"My pleasure," Korolov said, removing the headphones and picking up the fine mesh. It hung limply from his fingers, its wires glinting. "The CWAD, when applied to the face of the subject, allows the operator – in this case, myself," he said, gesturing to the headphones on his lap, "to 'read' – or perhaps 'interpret' would be a better description – the thoughts of the subject."

"I don't believe you," Sebastian said, fear clutching his heart.

"To quote your Dr Johnson," Korolov smiled, "'belief is your prerogative'." He nodded to one of the heavies by the door, who stepped forward.

Sebastian saw a needle glinting in his right hand.

Korolov said, "To affix the CWAD to your face, of course, it is necessary that you are unconscious. We wouldn't want you to injure yourself while struggling, would we?"

Sebastian tried to moved away from the advancing needle, but the ropes held him tight. He struggled, but the heavy struck his face, then plunged the needle into his upper arm.

Sebastian passed out.

WHEN HE CAME to his senses, the CWAD was pinned to his face and it felt as if a dozen nails had been hammered into his jaw, cheekbones and forehead.

Dmitri Korolov perched on the edge of the settee, the headphones clamped to his head, adjusting controls within the box. He looked up at Rostov and nodded.

"To achieve the best results," Rostov explained, "the subject must be conscious. It is a pleasure to have you back with us, my friend."

The ropes bit into his wrists and ankles. His face throbbed. To add to the pain, his bladder was full to bursting.

Rostov knelt before Sebastian, staring into his eyes. "Now, where is Janisha Chatterjee?"

Sebastian hung his head and wept, "No..."

"Yes!" Korolov exclaimed, touching the earpieces of the headphones as he concentrated. "And what time will...?"

But Sebastian could do nothing to withhold the information about the plan to free Janisha from Carmody Hall.

Korolov looked across at Rostov. "She's at a location in Surrey. Carmody Hall, and... at one o'clock she will be rescued by Lieutenant Littlebody and Anand Doshi. Or that's the plan. Our friend Sebastian would have accompanied them too, except that he will be *otherwise* engaged."

Rostov glanced at his watch. "It's not yet six. Plenty of time." He smiled at Sebastian. "And there I was, thinking that I had recruited a true servant to the cause, someone who might be trusted, who reviled the system from which he himself hailed."

On the settee, Korolov interrupted his comrade; the young man was frowning as he said, "But... that's the odd thing. He really *does* detest the bourgeois iniquity of the Imperialist system, but his feelings for the Chatterjee girl are stronger." He shrugged, as if non-plussed by the fact that someone might allow sentiment to overcome ideology.

Korolov removed the headphones, and Sebastian was thankful that the Russian was no longer reading his most private thoughts.

Rostov addressed the heavies in Russian, and one of them nodded and left the room. Rostov turned to Sebastian, smiling. "Soon, my friend, Janisha Chatterjee will be in our custody. But don't worry yourself. We shall be very careful with your precious little girlfriend."

He snapped something in Russian to the remaining heavy, who for the second time advanced on Sebastian with the hypodermic syringe.

"No!" he cried, and struggled, futilely, as the Russian slipped the needle into his upper arm.

Rostov, Korolov and the heavy left the room and locked the door behind them, and Sebastian hung his head and wept.

As he felt himself slipping into unconsciousness, he wondered if this time the dose might be fatal.

CHAPTER
EIGHTEEN

∽

Escape! – The friends are followed – Alfie to the rescue –
Betrayed again – The mechanical hound –
"I wonder when he'll be back..."

AT SIX THAT evening Jani's pacing back and forth was
interrupted by a soft tapping at the bedroom door. It
was the twin-set and pearls woman, asking if she would
prefer to take dinner in the dining room or to have it
delivered to her room. Jani selected the latter option,
and fifteen minutes later took receipt of a trolley bearing
grilled salmon, asparagus and sautéed new potatoes,
with a crème brûlée dessert, accompanied by a glass of
rosé wine – a far better meal than that provided by the
Russians the previous evening. Jani had had nothing to
eat since breakfast and, despite the sickness that still
lingered at Sebastian's treachery, and apprehension at
her imminent escape attempt, she managed to enjoy the
meal.

Later she drew a hot bath and soaked herself for an
hour, finding the process both mentally and physically
relaxing. She dried herself and dressed, then considered
descending to the library and selecting a book. But she
had no desire to come upon one of her captors and be

forced to indulge in smalltalk, and she doubted she could have concentrated on a book, anyway.

At ten o'clock she heard movement outside her door, and then the sound of a key turning in the lock. She crossed the room and tried the handle. The door was locked. She hurried over to the sash window and found that it slid upwards with ease. She peered down and smiled. The brickwork around the window was sheathed in a thick mat of ivy, which would provide a perfect ladder to facilitate her escape. The sun was going down in the west, filling the summer night with roseate light; there was no one in sight across the extensive lawns and woods surrounding the hall. She closed the window and paced the room.

She would wait until half-past midnight, then climb through the window and conceal herself in the trees beside the outer wall.

The final hour before one o'clock seemed to expand to fill an aeon. She sat on the bed and went over and over her plan; of course the success or otherwise of her escape depended upon Sebastian. He had seemed genuine in his contrition, and in his vow to assist Jani and so regain her trust. But what if, when he considered his options away from her influence, he decided that his loyalties lay not with her but with the Bolshevik cause?

She consulted her watch. It was a minute before half-past twelve. She turned off the bedside light, crossed to the window and peered out. A half moon rode high in a clear sky, illuminating the lawns. She leaned out, a warm breeze lapping her face. The grounds were in silence and she detected no movement below.

She straddled the windowsill and gained her footing in the tenacious raft of ivy below the window. She turned and felt for a lower foothold, gripping the sill until her footing was secure. She kicked into the growth, scrunching the old ivy beneath the new and, little by little, lowered herself down the front of the hall. The descent was easier than she'd imagined, the gnarled roots and tendrils of the ivy providing ready-made hand- and foot-holds. Her only concern was the desiccated dust of dead leaves that threatened to send her into a sneezing fit; she pursed her lips and turned her face away from the dust created by her descent, and a minute later reached the flower bed.

She crouched, very still, and looked right and left along the façade of the hall. There was no sign of movement, and the only sound that interrupted the silence was the occasional hooting of a distant owl.

Rather than head off across the open lawn before the house itself, she crept along the front wall, then crossed the drive to a stretch of topiaried privet. Her heart beating fast, she slipped behind the hedge and paused, listening. She expected to hear shouts and sounds of pursuit, but still the only sound was the lonely ululation of the owl.

She hurried across the lawn in the shadow of the hedge, thinking that so far her escape had been remarkably simple. She wondered at the security measures in place at the hall; apart from locking her door, her captors seemed to have done nothing to prevent her absconding. She wondered if there might be sensors on the outer walls, or even patrolling guards. But if the latter, then she saw no sign of them as she approached the northern wall. She came to the tall oak tree she had singled out to Sebastian, crouched in a nearby rhododendron bush, and peered out.

In the light of the half-moon, she consulted her watch. It was seven minutes to one. She had a clear view of the ridge of the perimeter wall, fifteen feet above her head. She concealed herself in the shrubbery, waited and listened. The owl had ceased its hooting and a perfect silence reigned. The loudest sound she could hear now was her heartbeat, its pulse thumping in her ears.

One o'clock came and went. She listened out for the sound of a car engine, but heard nothing. She told herself that this was to be expected: Alfie would hardly be foolish enough to drive right up to the wall, alerting potential guards.

She considered everything that might have gone wrong to prevent Alfie and Anand from carrying out the rescue: a failure to locate a rope ladder in time; a mechanical breakdown... or had Sebastian been unwilling to contact Lady Eddington?

She was jolted from this pessimistic reverie by a rattling sound high above. She looked up but saw nothing. The rattle sounded again, and this time she made out the serpentine shape of a rope ladder jerk over the ridge and rattle down her side of the wall.

Jani's first impulse was to dash from her hiding place and climb the ladder, but she urged herself to caution. She had no guarantee that her friends were on the other side; what if Sebastian had betrayed her again, and the Russians awaited her?

Her best course of action, she reasoned, was inaction. She crouched on her haunches, hugging her shins, and stared up at the ladder slung over the wall.

A minute passed, then two. Whoever awaited her beyond the wall would sooner or later wonder at her non-appearance, scale the ladder and show themselves.

All she had to do was sit tight and wait.

Another minute elapsed and Jani was frantic with impatience. What if there were a patrolling guard, and he chose this very moment to do his rounds, discovered the ladder and Jani crouching there...?

She was wondering whether she should discount her own wise counsel and scale the ladder anyway when she heard a faint sound. She moved her head, listening. Someone was scrambling up the outer wall, his breathing stertorous.

Jani backed further into the protection of the flopping rhododendron bush in case a Russian head should show itself. She moved aside a fan of leaves and peered upwards, holding her breath.

She made out the top of a head, and then the head itself rose above the ridge of the wall like a miniature full moon – and Alfie Littlebody peered down into the grounds.

Faint with joy, Jani rose from her hiding place and waved up at Alfie. He raised an arm and waved back, then disappeared from sight. Jani hurried to the wall and gripped the ladder, looking over her shoulder. The façade of the hall showed through the trees, moonlight glinting from its hundred windows.

Jani began climbing, finding the ascent far more difficult than the descent from her room. Though she could grip the rungs with her hands well enough – albeit scraping her knuckles once or twice – the ladder's rounded rungs were hard up against the brickwork and she could only gain limited purchase with her toes on the rungs. It fell to her arms to take her weight and haul herself up the face of the wall, and she was panting with exhaustion by the time she reached the ridge.

She lay on her stomach along the top of the wall and peered down, hear heart quickening at the sight of Alfie and Anand standing below, waving up at her.

The descent was much easier, thanks to Alfie holding the ladder away from the wall. She lodged her feet on rung after rung and climbed down in seconds.

She hugged Alfie to her, almost weeping with relief, and then embraced Anand's scrawny frame. "It's so good to see you again!"

"Jani-ji!" was all Anand could say, his face streaked with tears in the moonlight.

Alfie hauled the rope ladder back over the wall and bundled it under his arm. "This way," he said, indicating a rutted lane with high hedges on either side.

Anand led the way, Jani following. Alfie whispered, "I left the car on the lane half a mile away. We'll be in London within the hour."

Even now, as she hurried along in the company of the people she most trusted in all the world, she expected a belated pursuit – fearing alarm bells or shouts to sound in their wake. Her escape had passed in textbook fashion, and a part of her was disbelieving that it could have gone so well.

Presently she made out the dark, boxy shape of a Riley Tourer in the shade of a beech tree. Only when they were driving away from the hall, she told herself, would she feel wholly at ease.

She had expected to see Sebastian in the driving seat, prepared for a quick getaway – but Alfie slipped in behind the wheel and Anand opened the passenger door and waved her in. He jumped into the back seat. "Now full speed ahead, Mr Alfie!"

As Alfie started the engine and the car lurched from under the tree and along the lane, Jani looked around the car, her stomach turning sickeningly. "But where is Sebastian?"

Hunched over the wheel, Alfie glanced at her. "He and Lady Eddington met us this afternoon and we made plans to rescue you. He said he'd meet us this evening and come along, but he never turned up."

"We waited for fifteen minutes, Jani-ji," Anand said, "but feared we might be late, so we set off."

Jani's heart sank, and she wondered at his motivations in not meeting Alfie and Anand. Surely, to show his loyalty, he would have obeyed her request to be here tonight. She tried to persuade herself that there was some innocent explanation for his absence.

She turned to Alfie, then smiled over her shoulder at Anand. "You weren't hurt when the British stopped the lorry?"

Anand laughed. "We put up a fight, Jani-ji, but the thugs were armed with clubs. They pulled us from the cab and chased us off while others drove you away."

"The only thing that hurt," Alfie said, "was our pride. And of course we were beside ourselves with fear for your safety."

"But all's well that ends well!" Anand cried out. "All we have to do now is help Mahran escape from gaol."

"On that score," Jani said as the Riley tore along the darkened country lane, "I have news. The Russians have captured Mahran." And she relayed what Lord Consett had reported yesterday.

"If the task of rescuing Mahran from Newgate was hard enough," Alfie grunted, gripping the wheel, "then it's all the harder now. He might be anywhere."

"Do you think they might have taken him out of Britain?" Jani asked.

Alfie thought about it. "Impossible to say. They want the three ventha, and preferably all together. They know that you possess one of them, and that Mahran knows where the second is. They might have smuggled Mahran from the country for safekeeping, or then again holed up somewhere until, they hope, they can apprehend you."

"It means that we must protect Jani with our lives," Anand said in almost a whisper.

"And I have every faith in you," she said. She sat back and, in a flight of fancy, dreamed that the reason for Sebastian's non-appearance was that he was too busy trying to trace the whereabouts of the abducted alien.

"The main thing is that we return to the safety of London and rest," Alfie said. "We've all been through a lot of late. We need to consider the matter with clear heads."

Anand told Jani, "Lady Eddington gave Alfie the keys to her friend's flat in Highgate."

She looked from Anand to Alfie. "But is it safe? If the authorities–"

Alfie interrupted. "Lady Eddington assured us that it's quite safe."

Jani sank lower into the seat and stared ahead at the rushing countryside illuminated in the double cone of the car's headlights. The thought of a comfortable bed and a long sleep was delicious.

Alfie glanced at the rear-view mirror, frowning.

Jani looked at him. "What is it?"

"Oh, nothing. Just another vehicle, I think."

Anand turned around on the back seat and peered out.

"But its lights are not white," he reported, "but red."

Jani turned and peered through the rear window. She made out the distant pair of crimson lights, but it was hard to tell just how far away the vehicle might be.

"Probably one of the new-fangled roadsters that are coming on to the market now," Alfie said.

"How far are we from London, Alfie?" she asked.

"Another forty minutes should see us in Highgate."

Anand reported, "Now there is another vehicle behind the first one. And the car with the red lights..." He paused. "It must have turned off the road because I can't see it now."

The wash of the new car's headlights illuminated the interior of their own car. Jani peered through the rear window; the vehicle was perhaps thirty yards behind them, but coming no closer. She told herself that they had no cause for concern.

As if reading her thoughts, Alfie said, "There are bound to be other cars on the road, Jani, even at this hour." But he sounded far from sure about this, and she noticed that he'd increased speed.

Five minutes elapsed and the following car drew no closer, and Jani began to relax. When they eventually reached Highgate she would sleep till noon, then consume a huge breakfast and later, over coffee, discuss the situation with her friends.

"Hello, what's this?" Alfie said, surprised.

Jani looked up. One hundred yards ahead, the lane was blocked by a car that had evidently skidded and slewed sideways.

Alfie slowed down, peering ahead.

"The car behind us has stopped," Anand reported, "and... Mr Alfie, two men are climbing out."

Jani reached out and gripped Alfie's tweed sleeve. "Look."

She indicated the car blocking the lane. The front door had opened and two men, muffled in greatcoats despite the summer weather, eased themselves out and stood in the lane side by side.

Jani whispered, "I don't like this at all."

She stared at the tall figure approaching their car, and her heart skipped a beat. "The Russian," she hissed.

"What?"

"It's the Russian I saw in the Harley Street surgery the other day!" she said. "Alfie, do you have your light-beam?"

He nodded, tight-lipped. "But I have a better idea," he said. "Jani, Anand – hold on tight and get down!"

"But what–?" Jani began, ducking, as Alfie revved the engine and the car surged forward. Anand let out an excited yelp. Jani heard a gunshot. Alfie was crouching low over the steering wheel, an expression of determination on his usually bland features. The car swerved, and through the quarter-light on the driver's side she made out the blur of an overcoated figure leaping out of the way.

She remembered the car blocking the lane, and was about to point this out to Alfie when their car struck something with a glancing blow, and she knew they'd winged the Russian's vehicle. The jolt sent her crashing painfully against the door. The Riley careered off the road and whipped through undergrowth, Alfie cursing under his breath as he fought to control the vehicle. She heard another shot, then another, and the rear window exploded with a loud detonation.

"Anand!" she cried, twisting in her seat.

A tousled head popped up, grinning. "I'm still alive and kicking, Jani-ji!"

"Get down!" she commanded, and the boy vanished from sight instantly.

She peered through the windscreen. Alfie had manhandled the car back onto the lane and was accelerating. The headlights cut two dazzling cones in the darkness. She wondered if it were too early to assume they'd successfully eluded the Russians.

Russians, she thought sickeningly.

Anand was kneeling on the back seat now, singing out, "We're leaving them behind, Mr Alfie! The second car is stuck in the ditch!"

She peered through the rear window and made out distant headlights, diminishing rapidly as they tore away from the scene of the intended ambush. Alfie swung the car left at a T-junction, and then took a sharp right turn. Jani glanced at the speedometer: they were nudging sixty miles an hour and the hedges on both sides sped past in blur.

Alfie was breathing hard and sweat sheened his forehead. He turned and grinned at her. "I think we've eluded them, Jani!"

"Excellent driving, Mr Alfie!" Anand cried.

Jani found herself reaching out and gripping Alfie's thigh. "Well done," she said.

Alfie slowed the car and sat back, releasing a long, pent-up breath. "I'll take a longer, alternative route into London," he said. "I don't think they stand a chance of tracing us now, but to be on the safe side..."

Anand said, "But how did the Russians know where we were, Jani-ji? I am sure that we were not followed from London."

She shook her head in the darkness, glad that neither Anand nor Alfie could see her pained expression. She sat back in her seat, going over and over her conversation with Sebastian the previous day and wondering at his lies, his treachery.

She gripped the edge of her seat and tried not to cry.

Five minutes later Anand tapped her shoulder. "Jani-ji, I think you should know – we are being followed again."

Her heart jumped as she turned and peered through the rear window. She made out the pair of red lights they had seen earlier. "But what on Earth could it be?" she said.

"At least it's not the Russians," Alfie said.

As she watched, the red lights approached at speed, and the vehicle – or whatever it was – sped past their car in a small, dark blur.

Alfie stamped on the brakes and swore.

Jani was flung forward, bracing her arms against the dashboard as the Riley came to a sudden halt. She stared through the windscreen at the object that had planted itself foursquare in the middle of the road before the car.

Jani found herself laughing with almost hysterical relief.

Anand hung between the front seats and joined in her laughter. "But it's Fido!" he cried.

The mechanical hound rose from its haunches and approached the car.

"Open your door and let it in, Anand," Jani ordered.

"Ah-cha!" he said, opening the rear door.

Jani turned and watched as the hound jumped up onto the backseat, its bulk dwarfing the boy in the cramped interior and its weight making the car rock.

Anand reached out tentatively and patted the hound's metal flank. "I never thanked you for saving my life in Greece, Fido."

Jani stared at the mechanical hound. "Have you been following us all the way from Kent?" she asked. "And what might you have done had the Russians succeeded in stopping us?"

Alfie glanced at her. "It's my guess that Fido would have intervened – and to the detriment of the Russians," he added.

"But why is it following us?" Anand asked. "What does it want?"

"I don't know," she said. The hound's crimson eyes stared at her, its peculiar reek of hot metal and engine oil filling the car. "But I think that before long we'll find out."

Alfie started the engine and accelerated along the road.

A combination of the heat from the dog, and the rocking motion of the car as it sped along the country road, lulled Jani into a troubled slumber. Within seconds a host of dream images were crossing her mind: a dark church, its spire spearing a star-filled night sky; then Jelch, the elongated man-thing from the race known as the Morn. He was bound hand and foot, and curled in the corner of a whitewashed room. The image of church and Morn seemed in some way connected, but in her dream Jani could not work out how. Then she was running through the church, towards Jelch, but it seemed that no matter how fast she ran in a bid to reach him, he moved further and further away.

She woke with a start and looked about her.

They were on the outskirts of London, evidently: small

red-brick houses passed on either side, interspersed with warehouses and factories. Oddly, the image of the church persisted in her mind's eye. She still felt incredibly drowsy.

"How long...?" she began, slurring the words.

"You've been asleep more than half an hour, Jani."

"That long?" It seemed as if only minutes had elapsed. "I feel terrible."

"Well, after what you've been through..." Alfie smiled at her.

In the back, Anand had wound down the window and stuck his head out to cool himself, his hair flapping in the headwind. Beside him, the dog stared at Jani, its crimson gaze intense.

She looked away, uneasy.

Her vision swam, and she could not banish the vision of the dark church.

She recalled the minutes she had spent in the lifeboat with the mechanical hound back in Greece, before Alfie and Anand had discovered her. The dog had stared at her then, disorientating her mentally – as if looking into her mind.

It was doing the same thing now, and she wondered if the visions in her dream – of the church and Jelch – had been planted there by the creature.

They were passing through darkened streets, still south of the Thames, and Jani was overtaken by the sudden notion that they should not cross the river. When they came to a junction and Alfie slowed down, Jani said, "No, turn right."

"But Highgate is to the north, over the bridge," Alfie said.

She shook her head. "I know this might sound

fantastic, but I think Fido doesn't want us to go there. Or rather..." She stopped.

"Go on," Alfie said, obeying her and turning right.

"I think he wants us to go somewhere south of the river." She turned and stared at the dog, uneasy at the idea of its reading her thoughts. "I'm right, aren't I? We should keep to the south of the river?"

The dog stared at her, then lifted its right paw, reached through the gap between the seats, and rested it on her shoulder. The paw was the weight of a gold ingot. She shrugged it off with difficulty. "This has something to do with the church, right?"

"The church?" Alfie said, glancing at her.

She explained about the visions. "And Jelch?" she said, staring into the hound's eyes.

The image of the Morn, bound and incarcerated, entered her head again, and Jani understood. "No, it's not Jelch," she murmured to herself. "It's not Jelch, it's Mahran! Am I right?"

Again the dog lifted its club-like paw and lodged it on her shoulder.

"Jani-ji," Anand said. "What does it mean?"

She pushed the paw from her shoulder. "I don't know. Unless..." As the vision of the Morn persisted, she knew she was right. "I think Fido knows where Mahran is, and is leading us towards him."

The dog lifted its paw between the seats again and dropped it on to her left shoulder like a deadweight.

"The church!" she cried, suddenly realising. "The Russians are holding Mahran in a church!"

The red eyes drilled into her consciousness, and she knew she was correct.

Alfie glanced at her. "It's reading your mind?"

"More than that, Alfie. It's... it's implanting visions, giving me what seem like *intuitions*. I *feel* we need to be heading east, that Mahran is being held..." She closed her eyes, concentrating. She saw the church again, and next to it a line of elm trees and an open space. "He's being held in a church next to a park. I'm sure I'll know where it is – or rather Fido will instruct me – when we're closer."

They came to a junction and Alfie glanced at her.

"Straight on, and then veer left, towards the river."

"We're approaching Battersea. There's a park there."

Jani stared out at darkened houses and shop fronts; there was no other traffic on the road and the streets were eerily quiet. They came to another junction and Jani indicated left, and shortly after that she pointed right, bizarrely navigating her way through a section of city she had never seen before.

They passed open parkland on their right, flanked by dark trees. A hundred yards up ahead she made out, with a strange jolt of recognition, the spire of a church against the stars.

"There!" she cried out, pointing.

Alfie slowed and drew the car to a halt at the side of the road, fifty yards from the church. Jani turned to the hound and said, "Mahran is there, in the church, isn't he?"

Again Fido lifted his paw and flopped it on to her shoulder, where it sat like a weighty epaulette. A wash of affirmation surged through her head.

"What now?" Alfie said.

Jani stared at the church. "I intend to take a closer look."

"Is that wise?"

"Just a look," she told him, "to reconnoitre. We need to work out exactly where Mahran is being held."

"*If* he's being held there," Alfie said.

"I'm certain he is." She pointed. "I'll cut through the park and approach the church from the side."

"I'll come with you," Alfie said.

"Me too," Anand chipped in.

"Very well." She opened the door and climbed out, joined on the pavement by Alfie and Anand. The mechanical hound chose to remain in the car, and Jani was unsure how she felt about this. It would have been comforting to have had the hound by her side.

They found a gate in the railings and hurried across the grass. The church cut a black silhouette against the night sky, like a great ship on a becalmed and darkened ocean. Jani felt her pulse quicken as they came to a hedge that flanked the churchyard, hurrying along its length until she reached a painted timber gate. She turned a circular metal catch and pushed, then slipped through followed by Alfie and Anand.

A series of headstones stood like lop-sided dominoes in a swathe of unkempt grass. Jani crossed to a table-stone in the lee of the building and crouched. She could tell, from the state of the windows along the side of the church, that it had long since been deconsecrated and given over to other uses: some windows were boarded over, the stained glass in others pocked with dark holes.

She was about to suggest to Alfie and Anand, crouching beside her, that they should cross to the building and attempt to peer inside, when a noise froze the words on her lips. They ducked down as the sound of a door opening was followed by voices. They grew louder, passing along the side of the church perhaps ten yards from where Jani was concealed. She peered up and over the stone slab when she judged the men had passed, and made out a tall figure beside a smaller, barrel-chested man.

She looked at Alfie. "*Russians!*" she whispered.

The men passed from sight around the front of the building. She heard the sound of an engine starting up and a vehicle driving away. The pair had come from a small annexe at the back of the church. She pointed to it and led the way across the graveyard.

The solid timber door was locked, and a window to its right was barred on the outside. Jani stood on her tiptoes and tried to peer in. She made out, through the dusty, cobwebbed panes, a dark interior, its far wall illuminated by a shaft of moonlight.

She felt that strange, cerebral jolt of recognition again as she made out a whitewashed wall. But she was unable to see if the room contained Mahran.

"What now?" Anand asked.

"It will be light soon," she said. "We don't have the time, or the means, to do anything now."

"I suggest we repair to Highgate," Alfie said, "and consider how to proceed when we've slept and have a good meal inside us."

Jani led the way across the graveyard, through the gate and across the park. When they approached the car, Jani saw that the rear door was wide open and swinging on its hinges.

Jani peered inside, but there was no sign of the mechanical dog.

"Well, he did his duty in leading us here," she said, "and now he's gone off on his own errands. I wonder when he'll be back."

"Or *if* he'll be back," Alfie said. He examined the shattered locking mechanism, then managed to lodge the door shut.

"Oh, I somehow think we'll see the hound again," she said.

They climbed into the car and Alfie set off north, across the Thames to Highgate.

They were silent for a time, before Anand hung between the front seats and said, "I've been thinking, Jani, Mr Alfie."

"About?" she asked.

"About how to free Mahran," he said. "I was about to tell you earlier about my plan to free him from Newgate gaol. Well," he went on proudly, "the church certainly isn't Newgate, so I think my idea will work even better!"

Jani stared at the boy. "Tell us," she said.

He beamed at her. "When we have reached Highgate," he said, "over a pot of Earl Grey tea."

CHAPTER
NINETEEN

∽

Jani chastises Anand –
Alfie learns of Sebastian's betrayal –
His heart leaps –
"You're a good man, Alfie Littlebody..."

IT WAS ALMOST three when they arrived at Highgate and
Alfie led his friends up the steps to the flat and unlocked
the door. Anand repaired to the kitchen to brew a pot
of tea, and Jani flopped down on the sofa before the
fire. There was a chill in the room, and Alfie stirred the
embers in the grate, added pieces of kindling and coal,
and soon had a fire blazing.

He sat in an armchair and smiled across at Jani. He
thought, despite her unkempt hair and tired eyes, that
she had never looked more beautiful. His stomach ached
with unrequited passion. "You look all in," he said.

"I feel all in, Alfie. All this chasing from pillar to post
has exhausted me. I want to do nothing but go to bed
and sleep for a day."

"And so you shall, once Anand has had his say."

She shook her head and rested her brow on her hand,
staring at the fire with dead eyes.

"Jani, is everything alright?"

She drew a heartfelt sigh, gazing at Alfie as if about to tell him something – but at that second a smiling Anand marched into the living room with a tea tray.

The boy poured three china cups of Earl Grey and sat in the armchair before the fire, looking right and left at Alfie and Jani.

Alfie sipped his tea. "Well, if your idea is as good as this brew, we'll have Mahran out of the grasp of the Russians in no time."

"My plan is even better than this tea," Anand said. "It is foolproof and cannot fail. It is all the better for having the element of surprise. Whatever the Russians will be expecting us to do, it will not be this."

Jani looked up from the fire, her elegant fingers still propping up her head. "I'm very tired, Anand. Will you please outline your plan so that I can get to bed?"

Undeterred by her tone, Anand sipped his tea and smiled from Jani to Alfie. "You see, I know the plan will work because it has worked before. Recall your incarceration in the Old Delhi warehouse, Jani-ji, and how I rescued you from there?"

Jani sat up, staring at him. "But..."

"Yes! I plan to take the Mech-Man from Mr Clockwork's Fabulous Emporium in Putney and storm the church where Mahran is imprisoned. Mr Alfie, while I am away, you will go to Lady Eddington, tell her about my plan and request that she furnish us with weapons – she was telling me just the other day that she had contacts who could supply whatever we needed, in respect of breaking Mahran from Newgate gaol."

Jani was shaking her head. If anything, she looked even more tired. "So you intend to storm the church, all guns blazing, and rescue Mahran single-handedly?"

Her tone was scathing.

Anand shook his head. "No, Jani-ji. You see, I will storm the church, yes, surprising the Russians within, and you and Mr Alfie, armed with the weapons supplied by Lady Eddington, will take advantage of the confusion, follow me in and mop up the Russians."

Alfie opened his mouth to veto the idea, but Jani got there before him. "Ridiculous," she said. "The idea is absurd. I'm sorry to be the one to pour cold water on your delusions, Anand, but your scheme is littered with flaws from beginning to end."

The boy looked crest-fallen. "But Jani-ji!–" he began.

"No!" Jani snapped. "I'm not having it. Your hare-brained scheme will not only endanger yourself, but place Alfie and me in untold danger too. And to be frank, speaking personally I've had enough close shaves over the course of the past couple of weeks to last a lifetime."

"But Jani-ji, I've thought through every aspect of the rescue mission!" Anand pleaded.

"No, Anand. In your dreams you've fantasized about rescuing Mahran and playing the little hero, but you haven't really thought through the dangers. To begin with, what makes you think that a) you can break into the emporium and simply drive the Mech-Man from there without being detected, let alone seen by a thousand passers-by? And b)..."

"But I have thought of that! I will go now, before dawn, and take the Mech-Man before daylight. So you see, I will not be detected or observed."

"And b)," Jani went on, "the Mech-Man is not an easy object to conceal without half of London being aware of his presence. How on Earth–?"

"But I have thought of that, too," Anand said, looking very pleased with himself. "You see, the Mech-Man is watertight, and equipped with its own air supply. So what I plan is that when I have broken out of the emporium, under cover of darkness, I will take him directly to the Thames, which is only a hundred yards away, and submerge him in the river – emerging only in the early hours of tomorrow morning."

"And then you will stride through Battersea, storm into the church, find exactly where the Russians are holding Mahran... and then, while the Russians are firing at you, you expect Alfie and myself to follow you in armed to the teeth." She shook her head and glared at the boy. "You've been reading too many adventure stories, Anand. Your scheme is insane. I don't want to see you dead, and for my part I am far from happy about risking my neck." She looked across at Alfie and said, "Alfie? What is your opinion on the matter?"

He looked across at the expectant boy and shook his head. "Jani is speaking eminent sense, Anand. Your plan, while commendable in its aims, is strewn with too many imponderables. Before we rescue Mahran, we need to think long and hard about how we might go about it."

Anand looked deflated and stared from Alfie to Jani with pained eyes. "And what is your plan, then, Jani-ji?"

Jani, to Alfie's surprise, lost control of her temper. "Oh, for God's sake! How do I know? I'm tired, Anand! Tired of everything! I didn't ask to go on this fool mission to deliver strange devices to alien creatures. I didn't ask to have my life placed in danger at every turn. My father died two weeks ago, and I've hardly had time to... to..." She shook her head. "And on top of all that..."

Alfie looked across at Jani and saw that she was weeping; pearly tears rolled down her dusky cheek, to be dashed away by the back of her hand.

Anand sat very still, staring at his fingers. "I'm sorry, Jani-ji."

"And so you should be. Now go to bed before I really lose my temper!"

Alfie watched Anand slide from the armchair and cross the room, slip through a door and close it quietly behind him.

After a short interval, Alfie ventured, "Don't you think you were a trifle harsh on the boy?"

Jani glared at him. "No, I don't. Of all the stupid, brainless ideas!"

Alfie shrugged. "But he meant well."

Jani sighed. "I know he did, but... Oh, Alfie!"

And then she gave in and wept anew, leaning forward and pressing both hands against her face and sobbing uncontrollably. Alfie dithered, wondering whether to go to her and take her hand. He supposed that the cumulative events of late had finally taken their toll, and this was the result.

He rose, took two steps across the rug, and knelt. Hesitantly he reached out and touched her elbow. "Jani."

This had the effect of producing a fervent wail from her. "Oh, Alfie! How *could* he?"

Alfie shrugged. "He's only a boy, Jani. All this is one big adventure to him–"

She removed her hands from before her face and blubbered a laugh at him through her tears. "Not Anand, silly. I mean Sebastian."

He shook his head, non-plussed. "Sebastian?"

She found a balled handkerchief in the cuff of her cardigan and blotted her eyes. "It was Sebastian who betrayed my escape from... from Carmody Hall to the Russians. You see, he's working for them."

He stared at her, trying to take in her words. "Working for them?" he echoed fatuously.

"He's a spy, Alfie, recruited at Cambridge. At the hall, I told him of my plan to contact you via Lady Eddington and rescue me... And... and – oh, Alfie! He betrayed me to the Russians! And I really, truly, thought he loved me!"

She fell forward and he embraced her as she sobbed on his shoulder. He found himself ineffectually patting her back and saying, "There, there," over and over, as if comforting a child who had scraped her knee.

"I'm so sorry, Jani."

She pulled away and looked at him. "Are you, Alfie?"

He wanted to reach out and stroke her wet cheek, then pull her to him and kiss her on the lips. "I desire more than anything to see you happy," he murmured, and felt guilty for the tiny spark of joy that leapt in his heart at the thought of Sebastian's betrayal.

Jani smiled. "You're a good man, Alfie Littlebody. And I'm lucky indeed to have friends like you and Anand."

He patted her shoulder, his heart skipping. "If I were you," he said paternally, "I'd go to bed and get a good rest. I'll cook breakfast when you wake up and we'll have a day or so of doing absolutely nothing before we consider what to do next, hmm?"

She nodded. "That sounds like a capital idea, Alfie."

When Jani had taken herself off to bed, Alfie sat in the

armchair before the fire, nursing a glass of brandy and considering the events of the night.

He told himself that he dare not invest too much hope in his reawakened dreams. Sebastian had proved himself a cad, unfit to hold sentiments for someone as sweet and good as Jani, and now the way was clear for him, Alfie, to show Janisha Chatterjee the love she deserved.

But the damnable thing was that he was on the run from the British, in all likelihood with a murder charge hanging over his head.

If it were possible, then he was all the more determined now to work for the success of their mission, for success would achieve a double outcome: if they could locate the Morn and persuade the authorities of the danger posed by the Zhell, then his superiors might see their way to exonerating him of what he could claim was an act of self-defence in killing Smethers.

And also, if they succeeded in their mission, then he would surely win Jani's undying affection...

He refilled his brandy and tried to set aside these thoughts and concentrate on the immediate future. For the next two or three days he would relax with Jani, and might even suggest that he show her around Highgate. His father had been incumbent at St Christopher's, many moons ago, and Alfie had fond memories of growing up in the district. He would show Jani his old haunts, and take her to the churchyard where his father was buried.

He felt a wonderful warmth in his chest, which had nothing to do with the alcohol, as he thought of the beautiful young woman sleeping not a dozen paces from where he sat.

Later, a little tipsy and more than a little euphoric, Alfie took himself off to bed.

CHAPTER
TWENTY

❧

Anand has a plan – His letter – Off he goes to Putney –
The Mechanical Man! – Under the Thames –
"Sit tight and wait..."

IT WAS JUST after four o'clock when Anand heard Mr
Alfie's bedroom door click shut, then opened his own
door a fraction and peered out. The sitting room was in
darkness, but for the red glow of the fire's embers.

Holding his breath, he tiptoed from his room and
crossed to the table, where he placed the letter he'd
written over the course of the last half hour. He moved
towards the hallway, releasing his pent-up breath as he
turned the lock, opened the front door and slipped out
into the night.

Jani-ji's rejection of his plan to rescue Mahran was all
the more painful because he'd expected that she would
greet his idea with gratitude and enthusiasm. Time was
of the essence – who knew what the evil Russians would
do to Mahran, or how long they might hold him in the
church? He had to resort to desperate measures to save
the Morn. Jani had refused to countenance his plan, he
reasoned, because she was exhausted after her double
imprisonment; all she wanted was to rest for a while.

Well, he – houseboy Anand Doshi – would win her respect and gratitude when he led the charge into the church, routed the Russians and found the Morn.

All he had to do, before all that, was to successfully liberate the Mech-Man from Mr Clockwork's Fabulous Emporium.

From Highgate he took a taxi south to Putney, using the pound note Lady Eddington had given him on his first day out in London. He had sufficient change from the fare, when the taxi had dropped him off, to buy a few provisions from a café frequented by workers at the nearby night market. He bought two pork pies and a bottle of milk, but when he asked if they stocked chocolate éclairs the fat man behind the counter laughed uproariously.

Anand fled the premises, and soon was in a dark alley behind the emporium. The day before yesterday on his trip here with Mr Alfie, he'd conceived the idea that at some point soon the Mech-Man might be a useful ally, and had slipped to the loo before leaving. In a jiffy he'd snapped the bar-catch on the window and arranged the broken mechanism so that it would appear intact to a casual observer.

He heard a sound from further along the alleyway and stepped back into the shadows of a doorway. He held his breath as someone came strolling past – a burly figure Anand guessed was a night-watchman. The man passed along the alley and turned the corner, and Anand let out a long breath.

He approached the wall of the Emporium and placed the bottle of milk, and the brown paper bag containing his pies, on the window ledge and climbed up beside them. He pushed open the upper window, retrieved his milk and pies, and leaned through the opening. He lodged the bottle and the bag on top of a cistern to his right, then squirmed through the window and landed like a gymnast on the wet tiles.

Retrieving his breakfast, he felt his way from the toilet, along a pitch-black corridor, and entered the main showroom of the Emporium. Silvery moonlight slanted through three high skylights in the sloping roof, illuminating a hundred glittering gold and silver objects. Anand made his way along the aisle to where the Mech-Man stood, proud and imperious like some great metal Ozymandias.

Now that the time had come to put his plan into action, he considered Jani's objections. A lot could go wrong, he conceded – but, as he'd stated in his letter to Alfie, there came a point when it was important to act. There was danger in crossing the street, but that did not mean that one should not endeavour to get to the other side. Mahran needed their help – the Zhell had to be defeated – and the only way he could see of rescuing the Morn was by storming the church with the Mech-Man.

Placing his milk and pies on the floor, he scaled the back of the mechanical man and turned the lever on the hatch in the giant's back. The solid door swung open, revealing a dark interior and the control seat, for all the world like a dentist's chair. He returned for his provisions, tucking them under his shirt, and climbed back up into the cab. Closing the door behind him, he stowed the milk and pies under the seat and sat down with a sigh of relief.

He was sweating and his pulse was racing. So far all had gone to plan, but there was still a long way to go. He found the cab's light and switched it on, then scanned the arrayed controls. To his relief they matched those of the Mech-Man he'd piloted back in Delhi, with only a few dials and levers in different positions.

Of course, if the primary motor was deactivated and he could not even start the Mech-Man, then all would be for nothing. He would be forced to scurry back to Highgate with his metaphorical tail between his legs, and hope that neither Jani nor Alfie had risen early and discovered his letter.

He reached out a tentative finger, hovered it over the big red starter button, then pressed. Instantly the engine grumbled into life; the control room vibrated, shaking Anand in his seat. He laughed like a maniac and grabbed the controls. Now that he'd started the process, there was no going back. He must be quick and exit the building before any neighbouring busybodies heard the engine and called the police.

Through the viewscreen set into the chest of the Mech-Man, Anand peered out at the moonlit emporium. He grasped the motive lever, turned the directional dial, and walked the Mech-Man from its position at the rear of the showroom. He turned it left, towards the eastern wall which gave on to the alleyway. The wall was constructed of red brick, not stone, and would be no match for the might of a striding mechanical giant.

Gripping the accelerator, Anand pushed it forward and gritted his teeth. The Mech-Man strode towards the wall and crashed through the flimsy brickwork as if tearing through tissue. Anand heard the crash of falling masonry and for a second the viewscreen was obscured by a whirlwind of plaster dust; then the scene cleared to reveal the moon-washed alley.

He steered the Mech-Man over a pile of rubble,

crunching bricks underfoot, then turned down the alley towards the bank of the Thames.

The important thing now was to be away from the scene of the break-out as quickly as possible. The chances were that the cacophony had woken neighbours and alerted the night-watchman. He had banked on attracting some attention, but reasoned that any witnesses could do nothing to apprehend him once he had gained the river and submerged the Mech-Man. Then he would be able to move at leisure under the water and wait the day out until the early hours of tomorrow morning.

He clanked over the cobbles, making enough noise to wake the dead. He emerged from the alley and turned down a street towards the river, passing warehouses on one side and a row of terraced houses on the other. Ahead he saw a council truck brake in the street and disgorge half a dozen workers. They stared at the Mech-Man's relentless approach, their cigarette ends glowing in the twilight. As he drew near and passed by, some pressed themselves against a wall while others scurried behind their truck. Anand laughed to himself, concentrating on his footing as he turned a corner, stepped up the kerb and approached the bevelled grass embankment.

He concentrated on the controls as he walked the Mech-Man up the slope, canting the giant forward as Mr Clockwork had taught him to do back in Delhi. Having safely gained the summit of the embankment, Anand swivelled the mechanical man to look back at the way he had come.

There was quite a little crowd of sightseers in his wake, comprising the council workmen, a few porters from the market, and a raggle-taggle band of street urchins, all gesticulating and pointing at the Mech-Man. Unable to resist the urge, Anand activated the lever to move the Mech-Man's right arm.

To his delight, many of the onlookers waved back.

Then he turned the Mech-Man and stared down at the river. The sun was rising over the skyline to the east, turning the Thames into a swathe of molten tangerine like flowing magma. He peered down at the mechanical man's feet, checking the evenness of the surface that sloped towards the river. The grass continued until it reached the capstones of a retaining wall.

Anand eased the Mech-Man forward and down the slope, then lowered the giant into a sitting position on the wall, dangling its legs into the river like any common or garden bather. He pressed the great hands down against the wall on either side and pushed off, slipping into the river. The water came up to the Mech-Man's midriff.

Pulling levers and pressing pedals, Anand took a careful step forward, then another. Then, gaining confidence, he steered the Mech-Man out into the middle of the river. The water crept up the giant's body, soon covering the viewscreen. Anand strode on, seeing little through the murky water. He found the controls for the headlamp and turned it on, and a bright white light cut through the aqueous brown murk.

Anand turned and strode away from where the onlookers had seen him enter the river, lest the police decide to investigate. He headed east, towards Battersea, and ten minutes later halted the Mech-Man and lowered it into a sitting position to avoid the keels of passing boats.

He switched on the air supply and sat back in the seat,

relaxing now that the initial stage of the rescue plan was complete. Of course, all his hard work to date would come to nothing if Alfie did not obey his instructions as set out in the letter. But he trusted the barrel-shaped little Englishman to do the right thing.

"And all that remains now," he said to himself, "is to sit tight and wait."

As the occasional fish swam up to the viewscreen and peered at the curious specimen of humanity within, Anand retrieved his milk and pies from under the seat and ate his breakfast.

CHAPTER
TWENTY-ONE

∽

Alien weapons – Anand's letter –
A fool's errand –
"I think you're wonderful..."

JANI AWOKE AND stared at the bedside clock. It was almost five in the afternoon; she had slept solidly since four o'clock that morning.

She considered the evidence of Sebastian's treachery, and contrasted her feelings now with those on that day in Richmond Park when she had seen him for the first time in weeks. She had felt jubilant with love, light-headed with the knowledge that her sentiments were reciprocated. Now she felt wretched.

And though they had discovered where the Russians were holding Mahran, they were no closer coming up with a plan to rescue the alien.

She looked around the small, beautifully furnished room. On a chair beside the dressing table was a pile of new clothing and underwear, and Jani smiled as she realised that the dowager had thought of everything.

She moved to the adjacent bathroom, drew a hot bath and soaked herself for half an hour, then dressed in fresh clothing and stepped out into the small lounge.

The first thing she saw, after noticing that there was no one in the room, was the circular mahogany dining table, and what was upon it.

They appeared to be weapons, but of a decidedly alien design: three sleek, golden rifles with studs instead of triggers and what looked like bloated gemstones at the end of their barrels. Next to these were half a dozen small, silver objects that looked like miniature pineapples, and which she guessed were some kind of bomb.

"Vantissarian technology," Alfie said, peering from around the ears of a large armchair before the hearth.

"But how did you obtain these?" she asked in wonder.

"How else? With Lady Eddington's funding and contacts. I left while you were asleep and made my way to Mayfair. I explained the situation and Amelia gave me the details of a 'certain little man' I should contact." He shrugged. "I was against Anand's idea, like you, but I rather think he's forced our hand." He passed her a sheet of note-paper. "Read this."

She took the note, seated herself in the chair opposite Alfie, and read the signature at the foot of the page.

"It's from Anand," she said.

Alfie nodded, tight-lipped.

Apprehensive, Jani began reading.

Dear Mr Alfie,

I am very sorry you did not agree to my plan to rescue Mahran, and I am very sorry as well that I must do what I must do. In all the books I have read, there is a time when the hero must ACT. He must forget the dangers and do what he knows to be the right thing. When I saw the mechanical man in the emporium, I knew what I had to do. It worked once when I rescued Jani from the Russians in Old Delhi, so I know it can work again. I might be small, and you and Jani might think me nothing more than a lowly houseboy, but with Max I am big, and I can achieve great things. Please don't try to stop me – you must do what I said earlier when I told you about my plan. Lady Eddington can obtain the weapons she told us about, so contact her and explain the situation. I will get Max just as I told you earlier, and at two o'clock tomorrow morning I will smash through the west wall of the church and rescue Mahran.

You must do this, Mr Alfie: when I have entered the building, come in after me and launch the stun-bulbs. These will knock out the Russians. In case any Russians are not knocked out, stun them with the Vantissarian electro-rifle that Lady Eddington told us about. When I have rescued Mahran, we will get away in the car, leaving Max in the church and a great mystery behind us. Mr Alfie, this is important: Jani must not be allowed to go with you. Not only is she a woman who must be protected, but also the Russians are looking for her and we do not want her to fall into their hands if something goes wrong tonight. Explain this to her. I think she will understand. I will see you later, Mr Alfie.

Your good friend, Anand.

Jani looked up, tears in her eyes. "I don't think of him as nothing more than a lowly houseboy," she said.

"I know you don't," he murmured.

"Thank you for showing me this. We must stop him, of course." She glanced at the armoury on the table.

He said, "As soon as I read the letter, when I awoke

at noon, I made my way to the emporium. I thought he would wait until darkness tonight before trying to break Max from the premises."

"And?"

Alfie shook his head. "And there was a vast hole in the side of the building. I elicited information from a witness that in the early hours a giant mechanical man had burst from the building. He saw the Mech-Man stride into the Thames beside Putney bridge and vanish from sight." He smiled. "I'll give Anand this, he's a clever little tyke. We'd never find him in a month of searching!"

"But when he emerges in the early hours, surely then we could...?"

Alfie shrugged. "Emerges where? He might come out in any of a hundred stretches of the river near Battersea Park. And even if we were lucky and did spot him, how could the two of us stop the might of the mechanical man?"

Jani stared at the weapons on the table. "So you intend to go along with his plan?"

"I must say, for a sixteen year-old houseboy with relatively little experience of the world outside of Delhi – and with only adventure novels as his inspiration – Anand is quite remarkable. He's thought of everything."

She looked down at the letter and read out loud, *"Alfie, this is important: Jani must not be allowed to go with you. Not only is she a woman who must be protected,"* she looked up at Alfie as she read this and pulled a face, *"but also the Russians are looking for her and we do not want her to fall into their hands if something goes wrong tonight. Explain this to her. I think she will understand."*

She said, "I take it that the reason you let me see this is that you knew very well that I would certainly *not* understand?"

He held her gaze. "For all his nous, Jani, I think Anand doesn't know you that well. Or perhaps it would be better to say that his cultural prejudices preclude the idea that you need no protection."

"And you, Alfie? You speak of 'cultural prejudices', but don't such prejudices maintain in British society, too?"

He tipped his head in acknowledgement. "Perhaps, yes, but Jani..." He hesitated, then went on, "I've come to know and respect you. I've watched you over the time we've been together; I think I've come to understand the kind of woman you are, if that is not a presumption too far. I know that the other day I..." He looked down at his hands, his plump face colouring, "I professed my profound sentiments towards you, and this was no idle claim, but genuine emotions based on considered observation of you, and of my own responses to you."

"So you will allow me to accompany you on this fool's errand tonight, Alfie, even though just hours ago I was dead set against the plan?"

"There is no question of 'my allowing you' to do anything, Jani. You are your own agent, and have shown the fortitude of a legion before now. As for it's being a 'fool's errand'... maybe so, but he was right in one thing – he will have the element of surprise. It will be the early hours of the morning; the Russians will not be expecting a ten foot metal automaton to come barging in through the wall of the church, and if we follow up Anand's initial assault with a barrage of stun-bulbs and, after half a minute, proceed cautiously, armed with the

Vantissarian electro-rifles..." He shrugged. "I think fortune might be on our side, and we will effect the rescue of the alien."

"I don't know. You shower me with attributes of fortitude, Alfie, but to be quite frank I feel anything but brave at this very moment, considering what we must do."

"We are all a little apprehensive before such trials, but you've proved yourself equal to the challenge again and again, and tonight will be no different."

She read through the letter once again, considering Anand's plan and attempting to work out what possibly might go wrong. "It would take only one Russian, with a gun, to survive the stun-bulbs and fire at you or me..."

"We would go in only when we are certain that the bulbs have done their work," he countered.

"And what if the Russians have moved Mahran?"

He smiled at her. "In that case, I think Fido might have let us know about it," he said. "He obviously has an uncanny ability to discern the whereabouts of the Morn."

Jani sat, lost in thought for a minute. "I wonder why?" she mused. "I mean, why is the hound assisting us like this?"

"Who knows? It – he – is Vantissarian technology, from the same ship which brought Jelch and Mahran here. Perhaps they were known to each other, fifty years ago."

"And perhaps, when we have rescued Mahran, we might learn the truth," she said.

"So you will accompany me?"

She nodded resolutely. "How could I allow you and Anand to go alone?" she asked. "I would be beside myself with worry for you."

He looked away, reddening.

She went on, "And anyway..."

"Yes?"

"I despise the Russians and everything they stand for. They are even worse than the British, who wish to obtain the ventha because they think it a super-weapon." She recounted what Heatherington had told her yesterday, then went on, "Oh, Alfie, what hope is there for the human race when we are governed by such limited, nationalistic prejudices? Just think what might be achieved if we were to set aside our hostilities and work together? You smile; you think me naïve?"

He shook his head. "Oh, no, Jani. I think you're wonderful, and I think that as long as the human race possesses individuals like you, individuals combining optimism and humanity, then there is hope."

She gestured. "Again, with all modesty, you shower me with attributes I think I barely deserve. I wonder, looking into my heart and being honest, if not a little of my motivation in agreeing to accompany you tonight, is not fuelled by the desire for revenge."

"Revenge?"

She sighed, and in a small voice said, "Alfie, I thought I loved Sebastian, and he me. Recent events have worked to show me how deluded I was, and the pain of betrayal is terrible. I wish to show Sebastian, and his paymasters, that I can overcome adversity and defeat their small-minded, nationalistic goals." She smiled. "Oh, listen to me, listen to my high-flown words! I'm beginning to sound like a long-winded politician."

Alfie said, "I'm sorry, Jani, about what happened last night, Sebastian's betrayal..."

She stared at him. "Are you *really*, Alfie?"

He held her gaze. "Truly," he said. "I don't like to see you so upset, and I understand your pain."

She smiled. "Thank you, Alfie. Now," she said, changing the subject, "I've slept all day and I am famished."

"Lady Eddington has provided a well-stocked larder, and as I'm hungry too I suggest I prepare a meal of bacon, eggs and toast. We have quite a night in prospect, and we need the fuel of a square meal within us."

CHAPTER
TWENTY-TWO

∽

Battersea bound – A wait in a churchyard –
Arms at the ready – The Mechanical Man –
"This is it..."

AT ONE O'CLOCK in the morning, Jani watched as Alfie placed four stun-bulbs into the knapsack Lady Eddington had provided, then passed another four to her, which she slipped into the pockets of her coat. He took the three electro-rifles from the table and placed them on the floor. Jani was about to ask him he was doing, when he began rolling the weapons in the rug and explained, "Chances are we won't be seen on the way to the car, but if we are..."

He glanced at his watch, then at Jani. "All set?"

Tight-lipped, she nodded.

They left the flat and descended the stairs to the mews. Alfie had left the Riley parked on the High Street, and as they rounded the corner and hurried along the street, he said, "As coincidence would have it, my father had his first parish here. I was brought up in Highgate until I was eight, when we moved to the country. This is my old stamping ground." He laughed.

"What?" Jani asked, glancing at him.

"I just remembered something. Me and my best friend, Jimmy Padget, played British and Boers on these very streets, fashioning rifles from twigs."

"And now you're carrying Vantissarian weaponry on a mission to save an alien from Russian spies."

"Who would have thought it?" he mused.

"I often pinch myself, to ensure I'm not dreaming. I feel swept along by the events of the past few weeks, almost as if I have no say in the matter."

She considered what Alfie had said earlier about her attributes of fortitude, optimism and humanity; but perhaps most women, in her circumstances, would have acted as she had? She glanced at the dumpy little man almost running at her side, and wondered how she might have fared without his loyalty and resolve to see her through the bad times.

They came to the car and Alfie started the engine and pulled from the kerb, turned and headed south towards the river.

In the hours after their meal, Alfie had gone through the plan of attack. When Anand had burst into the building through the wall, all would be chaos for a while. She and Alfie would take the opportunity to lob stun-bulbs into the melee, and then, when they had ascertained that the Russians were stunned and all was quiet within the church, they would enter and attempt to locate Mahran. He would be affected by the stun-bulbs, too, and it would be beholden upon them to carry the alien from the ruins. It was at this point, Jani pointed out, that they would be at their most vulnerable to a counter-attack from any Russians who might have come round from being stunned. Alfie said that he hoped Anand would have climbed down from Max at this point and would cover their retreat; the third electro-rifle was his.

"And when we have Mahran safely in our custody?" he asked as he drove over Albert Bridge.

"We will be in possession of two of the three venthas," Jani said, "or almost. Only Mahran knows where the second one is secreted. Then we must locate the third."

"Which might be anywhere."

"Perhaps Mahran might have some idea as to its whereabouts."

She fully intended, once they had rescued Mahran, to hide up somewhere and rest for a day or two; no more chasing about the country, pursued by vengeful enemy agents or the British.

They drove through the silent, moon-silvered London streets. To the west, Ealing Common Rocket Station glowed against the stars. The rocket itself was a towering golden pinnacle three hundred feet high, illuminated by spotlights, its tail fins flaring and its tapered nose pointing towards the heavens.

"Look," she told Alfie, pointing. "When is it scheduled to launch?"

"The big day is just two days away," he said. "It would be wonderful if we were around to watch the take-off."

"Well, maybe we will be able to do that," she said. "It would be something to tell our grandchildren, and Anand will certainly want to watch the launch."

"Witnessing the launch of the first sub-orbital rocket will be nothing beside the many other stories we'll be able to tell our grandchildren, Jani."

"Isn't it odd, but events, no matter how fantastic

they might seem before they actually happen, when lived through are always somewhat – I don't know what the right word is – mundane? Commonplace?"

He glanced at her. "Even happening upon an alien creature in the wreckage of an airship?" he asked.

She nodded vehemently. "Even that," she said. "You see, it only seems fantastic in retrospect. At the time I was more bothered about finding food and water, and medicaments for Lady Eddington's broken leg. Take what we're doing now, Alfie – crossing London armed with alien weapons, on our way to save an alien who might himself be able to prevent an alien invasion of our world. I mean, it's just *too* fantastic to be true. Therefore it seems mundane."

He laughed. "A philosopher as well," he said.

"Or perhaps I'm gibbering away like this in order to settle my nerves."

"We'll be fine, Jani. I have a feeling that everything will work out for the best."

"I hope you're right," she said, settling back into her seat.

Five minutes later Alfie turned left and approached Battersea. In due course the buildings gave way to the dark, open space of the park. A cold weight of apprehension settled in her stomach. The stun-bulbs felt heavy in her pockets.

Alfie cut the engine and rolled the Riley to the side of the road. They sat in silence for a minute, neither of them speaking. Alfie glanced at his watch. "One-thirty," he murmured.

"I wonder where Anand is now?"

"Perhaps still under the Thames."

"Oh, I hope the mechanical man *is* watertight, and

doesn't lose its footing on the riverbed, and I hope a hundred and one other disasters don't befall the stupid boy."

"Stupid?"

She shook her head. "Forgive me. I don't know what to think. A part of me resents him for pitching us into this situation. However, if we succeed tonight, then I'll be the first to praise him."

"Perhaps it will take a moment of madness, or rashness, to bring us success. We might have dithered for days about the right thing to do to rescue Mahran. Come on," he said, "I could sit here chattering all night rather than do what we have to do."

He climbed from the car, looked up and down the street to ensure there was no one about, then eased open the rear door. He passed Jani the first electro-rifle, then took the remaining two. Jani shut the door and followed Alfie into the park.

They paused and looked east. The darkened church spire rose against the stars a hundred yards away, a miniature version of the sub-orbital rocket to the west. The only sound was that of the wind soughing through the elms surrounding the churchyard. Jani expected to hear the clanking din of the mechanical man at any second. She just hoped that its approach, when it did eventually occur, would not alert the Russians.

Gripping the rifle to her chest, she followed Alfie across the park.

They came to the high wooden gate and Alfie turned the metal handle and pushed, slipping into the churchyard. Jani followed, experiencing fear and exultation in equal measure.

They hurried over to the table-stone they had hid

behind almost twenty-four hours ago, and Alfie checked his watch again. "Ten to two," he whispered.

"Anand can't be far away."

Alfie pointed north. "The river is in that direction. He'll have to cross the road, enter through the front gate – I hope it's wide enough – and round the church to this wall."

"I just hope he can make the thing walk on its tip-toes," Jani said, trying to inject a note of levity.

"Even if the Russians hear its approach," Alfie said, "I'm confident we'll cope. If anyone from the church shows themselves before Max enters, we'll stun them with these." He held up his rifle.

Jani nodded. She clutched her electro-rifle, its weight reassuring.

She glanced at the church. Its long windows were in darkness. She hoped that whoever was within the building was now fast asleep.

Earlier that evening Alfie had given her a crash course in the use of the electro-rifles and the stun bulbs. "The bulbs are easy," he'd said. "Depress the red stud, followed two seconds later by the green, then throw. They're timed to go off six seconds after the green stud is activated. Make sure you're out of their blast range once you've thrown them – duck behind the masonry or a gravestone or something. You don't want to stun yourself. And the rifles are even easier to use. Aim down the length of the barrel, and when the target is in the sights, press the red stud once. An energy beam will lance from the weapon and find its target."

Now they crouched in the lee of the table-stone and waited. Alfie whispered, "I've set the rifles to maximum stun, so we won't be killing anyone tonight."

"I'm pleased to hear that."

"With luck, though, the stun-bulbs will do their job and we won't have to use the rifles."

She nodded and pulled two stun-bulbs from her coat pocket.

Alfie consulted his watch again. "It's one minute to two."

The only thing Jani could hear now was the thumping of her heart. She stared at the darkened wall of the church, at the broken and boarded-up windows. Not a flicker of light showed, and she told herself that this could only be a good thing.

"Two minutes past," Alfie reported.

Jani nodded, nervous. "I just hope..." she began.

"What?"

"That Anand's okay. That everything went according to plan. I just hope some bobby hasn't seen the mechanical man stride from the river, called for reinforcements, and..."

"You're finding things to worry about," Alfie reassured her. "He's just taking a little longer than planned, that's all."

"I hope you're right, Alfie," she said, clutching a stun-bulb in her sweating palm.

Jani's heart leapt as she heard a car engine. It approached along the road, grew louder as it came abreast the church, and then stopped. She heard a car door open and slam shut, then a second.

Alfie reached out and gripped her arm. They ducked down behind the table-stone, Jani's mouth suddenly dry as she prayed that Anand would not arrive now with the mechanical man.

She heard voices approaching along the side of the

church. She moved her head a fraction and peered over the bevelled edge of the stone. Two figures – one tall, the other short – strode down the path beside the building, conversing in Russian. She watched them pass where she and Alfie were crouching; they entered the annexe and closed the door after them. Jani heard a key being turned in the lock. A light came on behind the barred window.

"We could have done without that!" Alfie hissed.

Jani could only nod in agreement, too apprehensive to speak.

"It's ten past two now," Alfie said. "I suppose we should be grateful Anand didn't turn up on time."

"I must admit that I wouldn't be sorry if he failed to show up at all," she whispered in return, "though I do hope he's come to no harm."

"What's that!" Alfie hissed, turning.

Behind them, something vast and dark loomed over the hawthorn hedge. As they watched, a section of the hedge bowed forward and two great iron legs, like pistons each as thick as a man, stepped into the graveyard. The mechanical man's torso, like some vast, barrel-shaped vat, swelled above where Jani and Alfie cowered, and its domed head swung back and forth. What amazed Jani was how Anand had managed to bring the mechanical man so close to the church with so little noise. She had expected its clanking progress to be heard from streets away, but the boy had wisely chosen a quiet route across the grass of the park. Now its progress towards the church was littered with an obstacle course of headstones and grave-tables, and she wondered how Anand would negotiate the final ten yards without alerting the Russians.

The mechanical man bowed, as if inspecting Jani and Alfie, then raised a girder-like arm in acknowledgement that Anand had seen them. Alfie hoisted a rifle in response.

The Mech-Man straightened up and faced the church, and Jani felt suddenly tense with apprehension.

Beside her, Alfie breathed, "This is it!"

CHAPTER
TWENTY-THREE

In conversation with Kali –
Through the streets of London – A meeting with a Bobby –
"I'll be wishing you good night..."

DURGA DAS SLIPPED from the apartment and stepped out into the clear, moonlit evening. The night was warm; no other pedestrians were abroad.

He trembled with excitement at the thought of the 'demonstration' about to take place.

Kali spoke in his head, *When you reach the far side of the square, take the lane towards the river.*

Das came to the street and turned left, wondering where Kali might be leading him.

"Can you tell me where we are going, Kali?"

We are merely taking a stroll.

"And the Chatterjee girl?"

What about her?

"You have traced her to London?"

I have matters in hand, Das. Chatterjee cannot escape my attention.

"And might I ask how you have traced her so far?"

She carries the ventha upon her person, and through this I can trace her.

"And now? This demonstration?"

Das was impatient to find out where this midnight stroll might be leading him, and the nature of the 'demonstration' at its conclusion.

As I said in Greece, Das, I have endowed you with certain powers, so that your efficacy in aiding me and my task might be ameliorated.

"Powers?" Das felt a little dizzy at the thought of what those powers might be.

You will find out presently, Das. Be patient.

"Certainly, oh Kali!"

Presently they came to the Thames. The riverbank was lined with the curved, glowing columns of light – the so-called Illuminatory Arrays – which illuminated the streets of the capital city, and the broad river was busy with all manner of strange and wonderful vessels: catamarans and hydrofoils and great double-decker ferries taking sight-seers on late night tours of the Thames. Late night promenaders strolled back and forth along the riverbank, availing themselves of refreshments and snacks from stalls and kiosks.

Turn right and head west, Kali instructed, *and keep to this side of the street.*

Das did so, wondering what might lie ahead.

The occasional vehicle passed by as he strolled along, everything from the scooters so popular in the city to long, sleek silver cars and the less frequent open-topped tour bus.

Observe, Das – fifty yards ahead.

"A policeman?" Das whispered. "Should I cross the road?"

On the contrary. Follow him.

"Follow?" Das asked, perturbed.

That is what I said. Follow the constable, at a distance. He must not be aware of your presence, to begin with.

"And then?" Das said.

You will see, said Kali.

Wondering what he might be called upon to do, but telling himself that he was following the instructions of his goddess, Das strolled after the bobby.

They passed from a busy section of the river, and the caped constable turned right along a narrow, cobbled lane.

"And now?" Das asked.

Continue to follow him.

He came to the corner and peered into the shadows. The constable was a dark shape fifty yards ahead, already disappearing into the inky gloom.

Das followed him down the alleyway.

The policeman came to a small square surrounded by stately elms and, hands clasped behind his back beneath his cape, proceeded upon his beat around the quadrangle.

Follow at a distance, Kali said.

Aware of his heartbeat, and the perspiration that had gathered around his tight collar after such unaccustomed exertion, Das followed the bobby around the square.

What is your considered opinion of the police of this land? Kali asked.

The question surprised Das. "My considered opinion? I'm not sure that I have..."

They are, after all, the enforcers of laws which, in extension, keep your own people under subjugation.

"I consider all British rule, to a varying extent, an evil to be vanquished."

Just so, said Kali. *And tonight you will do your little bit to vanquish that evil.*

"I will?" His heartbeat increased.

You will kill the constable.

"I will?" he said again.

What? You demur?

"No. No, not at all. If Kali commands... But," he went on, "might I not be endangering myself – and my ongoing mission vis-à-vis the Chatterjee girl?"

This will be a necessary demonstration of your new powers – powers you will employ in the apprehension of Janisha Chatterjee.

"And how might I go about...?"

The killing of the constable did not cause him undue concern – the man was no more than a minion of a greater evil, after all, and would pass on through the great cycle of life – but the manner in which Das might be called upon to do the deed unsettled his finer sensibilities. He was unarmed, after all, and he doubted his ability to strangle the man.

Approach the constable, stretch out your right arm towards him, and think *him dead. I will do the rest.*

Das shook his head in wonder. "Merely point at him?" he murmured. "*Think* him dead?"

As I said, I have invested you with miraculous powers. Now do as I say!

Das had slowed his pace during this interior dialogue, and the constable had increased his distance from the holy man. Das hurried after him, propelled by excitement and a growing sense of power; he was carrying out the commands of Kali, a goddess come to Earth. What finer duty might a mortal wish to accomplish?

He was five yards from the strolling bobby when, alerted by his footsteps, the policeman turned.

"Evening, sir. Fine night."

"The finest," Das said, coming to a halt and staring at the man. He wondered if he should raise his hand now, and will the bobby dead.

"Can I be helping you, sir?"

"No, no. I was just enjoying a quiet constitutional."

The constable peered at Das. "From India, sir?"

"New Delhi," Das replied.

"My word. Do you know, sir, I served in Delhi twenty years back with the Colonial Force, and fine times they were, too. A wonderful country you have there, sir."

"Truly wonderful," Das agreed.

"Of course, the Nationalists were getting a bit uppity and we had to keep them in line, sir."

"Quite," Das responded, now relishing the task ahead of him.

"Well, nice talking to you, sir, and I'll be wishing you good night." The constable raised two fingers to the rim of his domed helmet, nodded to Das and turned.

Now, commanded Kali.

Das allowed the bobby to proceed a few yards, then raised his right hand and pointed at the man's caped back. "Die," he murmured to himself.

He was startled by what happened next. A dazzling blue light emanated from his fingertips, sizzling through the air, and hit the constable between the shoulder blades. Instantly the bobby was a blazing torch, every inch of his person consumed in a blinding orange conflagration. Das stepped back, covering his nose and mouth against the stench of roasting flesh, and wishing he could just as easily close his ears against the man's dying screams.

The bobby dropped to his knees, arms aloft, then fell forward on to his face and lay still, the flames licking greedily over his blackened corpse.

Das turned and hurried from the square, his heart hammering with the thrill of the execution.

You acquitted yourself in exemplary fashion! Kali said, and the commendation was music to Das's ears.

And soon we will proceed to apprehend Janisha Chatterjee.

"Soon?" His heart leapt at the thought. Oh, how he would delight in watching Chatterjee dance to her death wreathed in flames of his own devising... once he had obtained the tithra-kun⁻jī.

Return to the apartment, wake Mr Knives, and call a taxi, Kali told him. *We are heading south of the river to Battersea.*

CHAPTER
TWENTY-FOUR

∽

Imprisoned by the Russians – Sebastian turns violent –
The chase is on –
"For the love of Jani..."

SEBASTIAN CAME TO his senses slowly, the drug still in his system making his thoughts sluggish. So the Russians hadn't killed him. He wondered if he had that to look forward to, or if they considered that he might still be of some use to their cause.

It was dark in the room, with only the moon illuminating a patch of bare floorboards. He was still lashed to the dining chair. He tried rocking it, but found that its legs were attached to the floor by L-brackets he could just discern in the moonlight.

He wondered how long he'd been imprisoned here. He had a vague recollection that he'd surfaced from the drug-induced coma hours ago, and the sun had been shining. This led him to believe that he'd been here for twenty-four hours. If he could free his hands, then he'd be able to consult his wristwatch.

He thought of Jani, and wondered if she'd managed to escape from Carmody Hall – and if the Russians had succeeded in apprehending her. He felt a terrible sense of helplessness.

He rocked the chair again, in desperation this time, and was encouraged as the wood creaked. He threw all his weight back and forth, then from side to side. The chair rocked and he felt something give. He threw himself to the right and left, ignoring the pain in his wrists as the rope bit into his flesh. Something snapped and the chair teetered. He threw himself the other way and with a rending crack the chair disintegrated beneath him and he slammed to the floor.

He lay panting amid the debris of the chair, his arms still pinioned behind his back. He moved his hands, but found them still securely bound. He looked around the room, saw the window and formed a plan. Taking a breath, he shook off the debris of the chair, rolled himself across the bare floorboards towards the window and, grunting with exertion, managed to stand.

He worked his left elbow between the bars and applied pressure to the window frame. He tried again, more forcefully this time, and felt the wood give a little; he elbowed the frame again, ignoring the pain, and this time the timber spar snapped and the pane shattered.

In the moonlight he made out shards of glass still secured in the frame. Turning his back to the window, and careful not to slice himself, he pushed his wrists between the bars and moved the rope towards a fang of glass, felt its contact, and worked his hands carefully up and down. The rope gave and slackened; he pulled his hands free of the remaining cords and bent to the knotted rope securing his ankles.

The knot proved too tight to undo with his fingers, but picking up a shard of glass from the floor, he managed to slice through the rope and free himself.

He reached up and touched his face. The Russians had removed the CWAD, leaving the flesh swollen and painful.

He moved to the door and tried the handle, finding it locked, then applied his shoulder to the timber; but it was solid on its hinges and didn't move a fraction. He returned to the window, tilting the face of his watch in order to catch the moonlight. It was two o'clock in the morning. He thought again of Jani. One way or the other, her fate would now be sealed.

He gripped the bars of the window, but they were embedded and immovable. He peered out at the building opposite, desperately hoping that the place was inhabited and he could attract the attention of an occupant. But his hopes on that score were dashed: his prison looked out across the moon-lit alley on to the blank red-brick wall of a warehouse.

He heard a sound beyond the door; footsteps, followed by a key turning in the lock. He had a split second to decide what to do next: hide behind the door and hope to surprise the Russian when he entered – or move to the settee and lie doggo.

Fear got the better of him and he fell on to the settee, but not before snatching up a length of rope from the floor and concealing it behind his back as he lay down. He slit his eyes and had a blurred view of the door opening, and for a second entertained the absurd fantasy of seeing Janisha being pushed into the room.

But the only person who entered was a heavy he hadn't seen before.

His cheek pressed against the material of the settee arm, he watched as the Russian fumbled for the light switch. Dim light flooded the room. The heavy was armed with a pistol, but he lowered it when he saw that his prisoner was still unconscious.

The Russian crossed to the sofa, knelt before Sebastian and reached out with his free hand, prizing open Sebastian's left eyelid. Sebastian suffered the examination, feigning continued unconsciousness, while calculating when might be the best time to launch his attack.

The heavy stood and turned, only then noticing the debris of the chair on the floor. Before he could react, Sebastian leapt to his feet and looped the rope around the Russian's neck. He pulled and twisted with all his strength, amazing himself with the ferocity of his attack. The heavy tried to reach behind him with his revolver, and acting on instinct Sebastian pushed the Russian forward and rammed his head against the doorframe. The heavy grunted and sagged to his knees, but Sebastian was loath to loosen his grip on the rope. He pushed the Russian to the floor and stamped on his gun hand, feeling the crunch of metacarpal bones, then reached down and pulled the pistol from the man's slackened grip.

The Russian lay face down on the floor, groaning. Sebastian pulled the rope from around the man's neck, bound his wrists behind his back, and rolled him across to the radiator beneath the window. With a second length of rope from the chair, he tied the Russian's wrists to the radiator.

He picked up the revolver, his heart thumping in fear, and knelt before the groaning Russian.

He could always have taken off then, fled the erstwhile prison and saved himself, but the thought of Jani would not allow him to take the easy option.

He levelled the pistol at the man's forehead. "The girl!" he said. "Janisha Chatterjee?"

"Girl?" The Russian stared at him, wide-eyed.

"Did you get the girl, Janisha Chatterjee?"

Fear showed in the heavy's eyes. "The girl?"

"Janisha Chatterjee. Where is she?"

The Russian tried to struggle, but the ropes held. Sebastian pressed the pistol against the man's temple. "I swear, if you don't tell me, you bastard, I'll happily blow your brains out!"

"The girl... I don't know if..." the heavy trailed off.

"You don't know if they've got her?"

"*Da.* I don't know."

Sebastian felt a surge of despair. "Where were they taking her?" He had an inspiration. "Mahran – the Morn you sprang from gaol. Where are you holding the Morn?"

"Ah, the Morn."

"Where is he?"

A defiant look entered the man's eyes.

Sebastian raised the revolver and screwed it into the flesh of the man's forehead. "Now tell me where you're keeping the Morn, or I'll blow your brains through the back of your cretinous Russian skull!"

He had never seen terror in the eyes of a human being until then, and he found it in himself to experience a fleeting second of pity for the man. Then a phrase crossed his mind – *the end justifies the means* – and he increased his pressure on the trigger and yelled, "Tell me where the Morn is!"

He lashed out with the butt of the pistol and smashed it against the Russian's temple. The heavy rocked and moaned something. He said the word again, and Sebastian made out what might have been, "Church!"

"A church? Where?"

The man groaned. "Battersea. Battersea Park."

"The name of the church?"

The heavy closed his eyes, either in pain or in an attempt to dredge the name from his memory. "Saint..." he said, "St Mary's."

"And that's where they're holding the Morn?"

The man nodded, his eyes wide in fright.

Sebastian lowered the pistol and nodded. "If I find you're lying, by God I swear I'll come back and finish the job!"

He pushed himself to his feet and hurried from the room. He ran down the corridor, came to a flight of linoleum-covered stairs, and descended at speed. He appeared to be in a building that had once housed offices, vacated and rundown now.

He arrived at the ground floor, moonlight slanting through a broken window.

He paused to examine the chamber of the pistol. Six brass bullets reflected the moonlight.

"For the love of Jani," he said to himself.

He pushed through a pair of loading doors and found himself in the alleyway. The sound of distant traffic drew him to the right, and presently he came out on a busy street – but not before slipping the revolver into his blazer pocket.

He flagged down a taxi and collapsed into the backseat. "St Mary's Church, Battersea Park," he said, and closed his eyes as the taxi sped through the anonymous London streets.

CHAPTER
TWENTY-FIVE

∽

The attack commences – The Mech-Man does its job –
Anand is captured – The Russians make a demand –
"Or the boy will die..."

JANI WATCHED THE Mech-Man stride towards the church.

"Prepare yourself," Alfie whispered at her side.

Anand, no doubt well aware of the noise the headstones would make when trampled by the Mech-Man, chose haste rather than circumspection. Jani heard the whir of its motors, revving up – and then the automaton strode forward flattening headstones and crunching them underfoot. In seconds he reached the wall of the church and didn't slow down: one instant the wall that had stood for centuries was a solid, buttressed bastion of sooty brickwork, and the next – with a deafening explosion of metal on masonry – the walls collapsed and windows shattered, and the Mech-Man disappeared into the shadows. "Follow me!" Alfie cried, dashing forward.

They ran through the broken remains of headstones and paused before the yawning rent in the wall. Jani heard cries from within and the sound of the Mech-Man's progress as it crunched through pews. She primed her first stun-bulb, then pressed the green stud and lobbed it into the darkness, and, soon after, Alfie did the same. She ducked behind a pile of tumbled masonry as the double detonation sent a concussive shockwave back out of the church and above their heads.

Alfie counted down a minute, then sprinted, scrambling over piled bricks and firing his electro-rifle; its azure glare lit up a scene of chaos, the Mech-Man stomping through the matchwood of broken pews and swiping at staggering figures. Jani was about to follow Alfie into the melee when to her right the door of the annexe burst open and two Russians came staggering out. Instantly she lifted her rifle, took aim and fired. The energy beam briefly connected her rifle to the figures, the men dancing a galvanised jig before falling to the ground. The light was still on in the annexe, and through the open door she made out a whitewashed wall, a chair, and the outline of a trapdoor in the floor. Attached to the chair was a pair of handcuffs, which suggested that someone had indeed been held there.

She raced after Alfie into the nave of the church. Anand had activated a great searchlight on the headpiece of the Mech-Man, and this illuminated a scene of upended pews, a tumbled altar and scattered stonework, as if the church had suffered an intense, localised hurricane. The iron giant stood in the middle of the devastation, its torso twisting to the right and left as Anand sought out their enemies. Jani ducked as a bullet ricocheted off the Mech-Man's body and others thudded into the bricks above her head.

She scanned the chaos for any sign of the Morn, but made out nothing other than splintered timber, broken bricks and settling dust – and the occasional inert and unconscious Russian agent. She came to Alfie, crouching behind the toppled altar, and he reached into his pocket for another stun-bulb, activated it and threw. They ducked as its detonation blasted through the air. Jani expected the gunfire to cease, but if anything it increased, a machine-gun rattle of bullets chipping the stones a foot above their heads. The Mech-Man started up again, stomping towards where the gunmen were barricaded behind a pillar. Jani lobbed another stun-bulb and ducked.

"Mahran wasn't in the annexe," she reported.

"And he doesn't seem to be in the church itself. They might have taken him away earlier. Or..."

"Yes?"

"If the church has a crypt, it would make sense to hold a prisoner there." He paused. "I've used all my stun-bulbs. You?"

"Two left. Here." She passed them to Alfie.

Percussive shots were still ringing out, deafening in the confines. Jani was flat on her belly, too afraid to raise her head and peer over the altar. Alfie was not so cautious, and from time to time bobbed up to release a beam of electro energy across the chamber.

The Mech-Man homed in on the pillar behind which the Russians held out, its huge feet crunching pews. From where she lay, through a pile of kneelers and hymn books, Jani watched the Mech-Man's domed headpiece turn back and forth as it marched. The giant came to the pillar and stopped dead, and at first Jani feared that one of the bullets had somehow struck home.

The firing had stopped, and a ringing silence reigned.

Cautiously Jani raised her head and peered down the aisle of the devastated church. All was in semi-darkness other than the brilliant cone of white light that shone from the Mech-Man's headpiece. She made out swirling dust beyond the silent iron automaton, which was bent at the waist as if to peer down at what it had found.

"What is he doing?" Jani hissed.

Alfie was about to reply when the Mech-Man started up again, the rumble of its engine and the clashing of its gears deafening. Jani watched as the automaton stepped forward, rounding the pillar. She expected to hear the rattle of gunfire in response, but none came.

Alfie gripped her arm and swore as the Mech-Man stumbled. At first Jani assumed it had caught one of its great feet on a piece of debris, but the giant didn't fall flat on its face; instead it canted sideways. She heard an explosion – or rather a crumbling cacophony of stonework, and the Mech-Man pitched to its right and rapidly vanished from sight.

"I was right!" Alfie hissed in her ear. "The church does have a crypt – and the Mech-Man has fallen into it!"

The percussive rattle of gunfire sounded from down below, ricocheting off the iron man's carapace.

Alfie signalled that they should advance, and she followed him cautiously through the wreckage and around the pillar. Before them was a great ragged hole in the floor, and the remains of a big timber trapdoor. Down below Jani made out the erratic light of the Mech-Man's headlamp.

Alfie activated a stun-bulb and tossed it down into the crypt. He pulled her to the floor as the blast boomed in the crypt.

They peered at each other, Jani biting her bottom lip, as the gunfire stopped and the silence stretched.

Half a minute elapsed.

She heard a faint sound. "The Mech-Man's hatch opening?" she asked Alfie.

He nodded. They waited with bated breath for the boy to emerge.

"Come on," Alfie hissed, "come on!"

"What can he be doing?"

Alfie shook his head. "Investigating? Looking for Mahran?"

Jani strained her hearing but made out not a single sound from below. Perhaps Anand had emerged from the Mech-Man and was proceeding cautiously through the crypt, wary of hidden Russians – but why hadn't he returned to them and reported that the way was clear instead of going off on his own errand?

"What's that?" Alfie hissed, staring at her.

They heard the faint sound of a struggle, shoes scrabbling on stone slabs, followed by a grunt.

Jani had the urge to call out, to reassure herself that the boy was unharmed.

Then someone yelled in heavily accented tones, "We have the boy, yes? We will kill him if you do not show yourself."

Jani leaned towards Alfie and whispered, "'*Yourself*'? They cannot know how many of us there might be. I have an idea."

Alfie listened while she outlined her plan, then nodded.

The guttural Russian voice came again. "I said we have the boy. If you want him to live, come down here very slowly."

"Very well," Alfie said. "I'm coming."

"Where is the girl?" the Russian called.

Alfie hesitated, then called out, "What girl?"

"'What girl'?" The voice was mocking. "The blessed Virgin Mary, who do you think? Janisha Chatterjee is who! Where is she?"

Alfie licked his lips. "Do you think we'd be foolish enough to have her come along with us?" He looked at Jani and winked.

"Come down here," the Russian called. "You will lead us to the girl, yes, or the boy will die."

Alfie smiled at Jani, then called out, "Very well, I'm coming."

Jani gripped his arm quickly, as if to forestall his progress. Alfie unhooked her fingers, squeezed her hand, and moved off.

He stepped towards the hole in the floor, picking his way through the debris and peering into the crypt to assess the best way down. Cautiously he stepped forward, picking his way over the rubble, and disappeared from sight.

Jani looked back along the ruined length of the church. Holding her breath, and careful not to make a sound, she crept back along the nave towards the gaping hole in the side of the church.

Halfway there, she heard the Russian call out again. "Put down the rifle, and the grenade, or the boy dies!"

"Very well," Alfie said.

"Excellent," the Russian said. "Now, come this way and..." The rest was lost as the Russian lowered his voice on Alfie's approach.

Jani made her way through the wreckage of the church.

CHAPTER
TWENTY-SIX

❧

Jani to the rescue – The Morn, at last –
Mayhem and murder in the crypt –
The return of Durga Das –
"Please, Jani, believe me..."

SHE CLAMBERED OVER the piled rubble, approached the lighted annexe, and crept inside.

She crossed the room and carefully lifted the chair away from the outline of the trapdoor. Fearing that it might be locked from underneath, she knelt and took hold of the iron ring handle. She looked up at the naked bulb hanging from the ceiling, then stood and found the light switch. She turned off the light and felt her way back to the trapdoor, her heart pounding at the mistake she had almost made. If she'd opened the trapdoor with the light still on, alerting the Russians to her presence...

She shut out the thought, gripped the iron ring and pulled, easing the trapdoor up little by little, wincing as the hinges creaked. In the scant light from the moon outside, she made out a flight of worn stone stairs. Beyond was a faint light from the Mech-Man's headlamp. She opened the trapdoor to its full extent and, gripping her rifle in readiness, descended cautiously.

She was in a small ante-room to the crypt proper, with whitewashed walls and a curved ceiling. A door before her stood half open. Her heart pounding, she crept to the door and peered into the crypt.

The first thing she saw was the automaton at the far end of the chamber, lying on its side. Alfie stood beside the Mech-Man, his arms in the air. Jani made out two Russians standing between herself and Alfie. The taller man had an elbow crooked around Anand's neck and held a revolver to his temple.

The second Russian, the small fat man with silver hair, gripped a revolver in his right hand and aimed it at Alfie.

Only then did she make out the figure secured by manacles and leg-irons to the wall to the right of the Russians – a figure spread-eagled like the cartoon captive in some mediaeval dungeon.

It was the Morn, Mahran.

She was so much reminded of Jelch, her dead alien friend, that it was painful. The creature was tall and attenuated, his flesh a dirty grey. He wore prison garb – obviously Newgate's finest – which hung on his undernourished frame in rags. His head was bald, as Jelch's had been, and inhumanly long. He might have passed for human, though an odd, deformed specimen of the race.

From the ends of his long, stick-like fingers, blood dripped, and Jani realised with revulsion that the Russians had removed a number of his fingernails.

Mahran was conscious, his dull eyes staring across at the Russian pair.

On a table beside the spread-eagled Morn, Jani made out the silver filigree nexus of a CWAD. She wondered if the Russians had yet to use the device on Mahran.

She gripped the electro-rifle, her palms slick with sweat.

The Russians were armed, so she would need to bring both of them down in an instant.

The dumpy silver-haired Russian said to Alfie, "The boy will remain here while you take me to Janisha Chatterjee. You will attempt no deception, or the boy will die. Once we have the girl, we will release you both."

"And what do you want with Janisha?" Alfie asked.

"No questions!" the fat Russian snapped.

"But will you let her live?" Alfie persisted, and Jani realised that he was stalling so that she would have time to act.

"I said no questions!" the Russian screamed.

Jani was about to raise her rifle, aim and fire at the Russians in quick succession when the fat man began backing – his pistol still directed at Alfie – towards the room where Jani was concealed. She had mere seconds in which to act.

Anand was in the most immediate danger, gripped by the tall Russian, a pistol to his head. She would fire at him first, and hope he would be too blitzed to pull the trigger. Of course, Anand would suffer the effects of the electric shock, too. But that couldn't be helped.

She raised the rifle, swung its barrel through the opening and aimed at the back of the tall Russian's head. Her pulse pounding, she fired. Instantly, before she could assess the success of her shot, she swung the rifle and fired at the fat Russian as he turned towards her, his mouth open in comical surprise. He lit up with coruscating blue light, jigged and toppled to the floor.

Jani hurried into the room. The tall Russian was

on the floor, spasming. Anand crawled away from his erstwhile captor, unharmed. Jani hugged the boy to her, then held him at arm's length and shook him like a rag-doll. "And that will show you that it is not I who needs protection!" she cried and then, weeping, pulled Anand to her in a fierce hug.

Alfie snatched up his rifle and approached the Russians cautiously, assured himself that they were no longer a threat, then crossed the crypt to the Jani and the boy. "Anand?"

The boy smiled shakily, too overcome to articulate his relief.

"Jani?" Alfie asked.

"I feel as though I might suffer a heart attack at any moment," she managed to laugh. "But otherwise I am fine."

"That was a dashed fine example of shooting, if I might say."

"I had a point to prove," she said, tousling Anand's hair, "quite apart from a scallywag to save."

Startling Jani, a voice called out from across the crypt, "And who, in this sorry farrago of inhumanity, might you be?"

She turned quickly. The Morn hung on the wall, arms outstretched, its long head raised in what might have been a pose of nobility. His voice was oddly accented, but remarkably cultured.

Her throat swelling, Jani stepped away from her friends and approached the alien.

She stopped before him. "I am Janisha Chatterjee," she said, "I am a friend of your compatriot, Jelch, and I have come halfway around the world to save you from the British... and the Russians."

The alien turned his head a little, regarding her slantwise as if with suspicion. "You are not the latest human come to humiliate and torture me?"

She glanced at the creature's bloody fingers and, surprising herself, reached out and touched Mahran's grey cheek with her fingertips. "I said I am a friend of Jelch's – or was, before... before he perished. I have come to you bearing the ventha-di – sent to you by the Morn entity aboard the Vantissarian ship – containing a single ventha. I was told that you know the whereabouts of the second."

The creature stared at her, his narrow eyes widening. His eyes were bright blue, very much as blue as Jelch's.

"You tell the truth?" he murmured. "But Jelch... he is dead?"

"I'm sorry. He was a true friend. But here is not the place to explain. We need to get you away, to a place of safety."

"You will find the keys for these irons in the coat pocket of the tallest Russian," Mahran said.

Alfie knelt and found the keys in the Russian's pocket, then hurried over to the Morn and unfastened first the leg-irons, and then the manacles. Released, the Morn sagged and stumbled, and Jani reached out and held him upright. The creature was stick-thin and light; she and Alfie eased him into a sitting position on the cold slabs of the crypt.

"We'll get him back to the car," Alfie said, "then make straight for Highgate."

"No," the Morn said sharply. "We should make for–"

Anand looked up. "What's that?" he said.

A sound came from above – someone moving through the wrecked church.

Jani was about to suggest they leave immediately when the door swung open and a slight, well-dressed man appeared in the doorway.

Jani stood quickly and faced him, disbelieving. The man was young, and Indian, and in place of hands he had affixed to each stump a set of lethal-looking silver knives. He leaned against the doorframe, smiling at them.

"But he was dead, or dying," Jani said.

"Evidently not," Alfie murmured.

So Durga Das's henchman had continued the quest of the dead priest, and somehow followed them all the way to London. Even though only days had passed since leaving him in northern Greece, he seemed miraculously recovered from his injuries.

After the initial shock, Jani regained her composure. Mr Knives seemed to be unarmed – with anything other than his eponymous knives, of course – and so posed no threat against her electro-rifle.

She raised it and aimed at the Indian. His smile persisted; he seemed not in the least fazed by the weapon.

"Stay where you are, Knives, and don't move!"

She recalled his arrogant habit of paring his fingernails with one of his knives. Well, bereft of hands now, he was unable to perform that annoying gesture. But his snide, lop-sided smile was just as stomach-turning.

"Oh, let me tell you, Miss Chatterjee, that I have no intention of moving. In fact I am very comfortable here." He folded his arms across his chest, the blades glinting in the light from the Mech-Man's headlamp.

Jani shook her head. "What do you want?"

"What do I want? *We* want what *we* have always wanted, Janisha Chatterjee."

We? she thought, a sickening sensation in her stomach.

Anand stepped forward. "Stand aside and let us past, or Jani-ji will make you sorry you followed us all this way!"

Mr Knives smiled. "Oh, Janisha will do nothing of the kind, you little fool."

Alfie raised his rifle and said, "Do as Anand said, Knives. Stand aside or I'll shoot."

Something about the man's nonchalance, and his earlier use of the pronoun 'we', gave Jani a terrible premonition. She chastised herself: they had left Durga Das lying dead in the lane in northern Greece.

"You will shoot no one, Littlebody."

The voice came from behind her and, incredulous, she turned and stared at the speaker. He had entered the crypt via the ruined trapdoor entrance, and now stood, larger than life, beside the sprawling Mech-Man.

Alfie swung his weapon and aimed at Durga Das. "How the...?" he murmured, more to himself.

Das had divested himself of his holy robes and looked incongruous in a pinstriped suit and white shirt. If he had appeared huge in his saffron robe, the city suit had the effect of making him appear even larger: its trousers were voluminous, to accommodate his bloated legs, and the suit jacket was buttoned and straining over the great protuberance of his belly.

"You were dead," Alfie whispered. "Or so I thought." He turned to Jani and murmured, "I'm sorry. I was mistaken. God knows, I should have made sure and finished him off!"

Das interrupted. "No, Littlebody, you were not mistaken. I *was* dead. Very dead. But the beneficence of the gods is bestowed upon the virtuous, and my humble, life-long service to Kali was rewarded."

Jani shook her head. "No, that's impossible."

Das smiled and raised his head, presenting for her inspection the bloated, toad-like expanse of neck which just days ago had been ripped to pieces by the mechanical dog.

Now the odious bulge of flesh was unblemished.

"But how...?" Alfie said.

"Oh, you doubters, you godless heathens!" Durga Das cried. "You ignorant idolaters at the shrine of materialism! Look upon the work of Kali and repent your ignorance!"

Alfie stepped forward, brandishing his rifle. "You forget one thing, Das. We're the ones with the weapons here. Stand aside!"

"If you think I have come all this way, expended so much energy, to be cowed by futile threats, think again! It is you who should obey *my* commands, or suffer the consequences!"

Jani was to recall what happened next for a long, long time, the image haunting her dreams and giving her sleepless nights for weeks.

Durga Das raised his right arm, pointed at the portly Russian lying unconscious on the stone floor, and said, "Behold my powers and obey!"

A coruscating blue light, woven like twines of wire, leapt from the priest's fingers and hit the Russian. His body gave a galvanic twitch and exploded into raging flame. Jani backed away, crying out in horror as the body was consumed in the conflagration.

Durga Das's belly laugh accompanied the crackle of roasting flesh as the priest turned and pointed at Alfie.

Jani looked for a weapon in his hand, wondering how he might have come upon Vantissarian technology; but his outstretched hand appeared empty.

The holy man's forefinger pointed at the Lieutenant. "Now drop your weapon!"

Alfie glanced at Jani, who nodded that he should do as the priest commanded. He let the electro-rifle slip to the floor, then moved towards Jani.

"And you, too, Janisha Chatterjee!" Das commanded. She considered firing her rifle, hoping that she might surprise the priest, but he pointed at Anand and cried out, "Do it!"

She obeyed, curtseying to lay the rifle on the floor. She glanced at Anand, his fists balled in rage, and shook her head minimally to forestall any rash action on his part.

From his seated position on the stone floor, Mahran looked on with weary eyes, impotent.

Durga Das took a step forward, his waddle emphasised by his trousers, the huge hams of his thighs rubbing together like racing dirigibles. He laid a hand on the headpiece of the Mech-Man and smiled across at Jani.

"I really must applaud you in your efforts in overcoming such adversity, and venturing so far on your valiant, if futile, mission. You have shown a level of ingenuity and valour I find almost commendable – and, I must say, in so doing you have made my task a degree easier."

"Your task?" Alfie snarled.

"Why, that of obtaining what you call the ventha, in Janisha's possession," Das purred. "That is all I want. The transaction I suggest is both simple and mutually expedient. I want the ventha – and the second ventha in the possession of the Morn," he said, flicking a glance to the seated alien. "Give them to me and I will allow you to live."

Jani found her voice. "And what makes you think

I still have the ventha? I would be foolish to carry it around with me."

"Silence!" Das spat. "We have played this little game once before, I recall. I know you possess the ventha, and that you carry it within you, because my informant is none other than my goddess, Kali."

Kali, Jani thought – the creature in the blue light she had beheld in India and again in Greece? But where was Kali now?

"You have the option of simply giving up the ventha and saving your life and those of your friends, or dying. Really," Das went on, smiling, "it will make little difference to me."

He hesitated. "But perhaps you need another example of my power, to prove that the first was no mere fluke? Very well." And he reached out and pointed at the second Russian who was lying stunned on the floor.

Blue light cracked from the priest's fingertips, arching across the crypt and hitting the Russian. He bucked, jerking horribly, and burst into flame. This time the horror was intensified by the fact that the Russian had been regaining consciousness, and his high-pitched, dying screams filled the chamber.

Jani covered her ears and stared at the priest, attempting to discern some weaponry concealed in the cuff of the man's jacket.

Das was laughing, his delight grotesque in the flagging orange light of the Bolshevik's immolation. "I hope that little demonstration has convinced you of my power, and my willingness to use it. Now, if you remain intransigent and refuse to give up the ventha, I shall take great pleasure in burning the boy!"

Anand glanced at Jani, and, far from cowering before

the threat, he straightened his spine and stared defiantly at the priest.

Alfie said, "Why do you want the ventha?"

"As I told Chatterjee in Nepal. With the venthas I will usher in the Age of Kali; and I, Durga Das, will be Kali's high priest on Earth when my goddess rules the planet and sweeps the scourge of the British from my land!"

From his hunched, cowed position on the floor, the Morn spoke, "But Das, you do realise, I take it, that individual venthas – even two together – are quite useless? Only with a quorum of three will they function to open the world-portal."

Das turned his arrogant gaze on Mahran. "Janisha has one ventha about her person; you, sir, possess or know the whereabouts of the second."

"And the third?" Jani asked in a tremulous voice, fearing his reply.

He smiled and reached a huge hand into the pocket of his black suit. He withdrew something, a coin that was tiny in the grip of his fat fingers, and held up the silver disc for all to see. "The third ventha," he said, replacing it in his pocket.

Jani glanced at Alfie and shook her head in despair.

"When I possess all three venthas, my goddess will work through me to bring about the opening of the portal to the heavens!" Das cried. "And then Kali will unleash her full power across the face of this benighted planet!"

Mahran looked up at the priest, who loomed over him like some bloated, Savile Row-clad genie. "You speak of your *goddess*," the Morn said with contempt in his voice, "but you fail to realise that gods, of any type, do not exist."

"Have I not proved that I have the power of the gods!" Das cried, pointing to the charred and burning corpses.

"That proves nothing," Mahran replied, "but that you have access to sophisticated Vantissarian technology. Where is this Kali you so arrogantly boast about?"

Das tipped his head, for all the world as if listening to an inner voice. He gave a satisfied smile, his bearded cheeks bulging, and nodded to himself.

"Another demonstration? Is that what you heathens require? Very well, a demonstration is what you will have!"

He gestured like a stage magician, throwing his arms into the air, and at that very second an effulgent blue light emanated from his features – and the fat face, surrounded by curling grey locks, vanished and was replaced by the leering devil's countenance Jani had last seen in Greece. The blue face, all gnarled fangs, sickle horns and crimson, staring eyes, looked out upon the startled audience, its expression one of overweening triumph.

And then, as instantly as the vision had appeared, it vanished and Durga Das laughed at their horrified expressions.

"And now do you dare to doubt my claims?" he cried.

Mahran, alone of the quartet of onlookers, remained unshaken. To Jani's astonishment, the Morn flung back his head and laughed. "Oh, you fool, Das! You poor, misguided dupe!"

"And who are you to doubt my word, you sorry specimen?" Das cried, bringing his outstretched arm to bear on the alien.

Mahran, still seated, leaned forward and said, "Listen

to me, Das – the creature you think of as your goddess is nothing of the kind! It is the incarnation of evil, an alien from another realm. Listen to my words, Das, and think long upon them. The creature controlling you for its own despicable ends is not Kali but a member of a bellicose alien race known as the Zhell!"

Jani stared at Mahran, his face twisted in hatred of Das and his controller. "You are deluded, Das!" the Morn went on. "The Zhell need the venthas to open the world-portal, yes – but not to bring the Age of Kali to Earth, but to initiate their invasion of this realm, just as they have invaded world after innocent world over the centuries!"

Das bellowed, "Silence! Or, I warn you, once I have your ventha I will gladly see you writhe in flames!"

The priest turned to Jani. "And now, your ventha – or the boy dies!"

She hesitated, and the priest stepped forward and pointed at Anand.

She was about to say that she had no way of retrieving the ventha in her stomach when she heard a sound from the room at the far end of the crypt; she suspected that, at last, some curious locals had come to investigate. Would she and her friends have time to take advantage of their arrival, she wondered, and flee from the insane holy man – or would he burn them all in vengeance as they fled?

Then someone burst through the door, coshed Mr Knives on the head before he had time to turn, and caught the slumped figure. The new arrival held the unconscious form of Knives before him as a shield, a gun to the young man's head.

Jani stared and felt weak at the knees.

"If you so much as harm a hair on the head of Jani, Alfie or Anand, then your companion will die!" Sebastian called across the crypt to Durga Das.

The priest stepped forward, his face twisted in rage.

"Sebastian?" Jani said.

Sebastian glanced at her and smiled. "I didn't betray you," he said. "Not this time, Jani. I didn't tell the Russians about your planned escape from Carmody Hall."

She stared at him, more than anything wanting to believe him.

Das bellowed, "Unhand Mr Knives or Jani dies!"

"I told you – if you harm Jani, then *Knives* dies!" He smiled at Jani. "Quickly, get out of here while you can!"

Jani made to move towards the door beyond Sebastian, but found her limbs frozen. How could she leave Sebastian when he had risked his life to save her?

"Come with us," she said desperately. "Back towards the door using Knives as a shield."

"Do not move!" Durga Das commanded.

Sebastian was backing towards the door, dragging Knives with him, when the priest let out a stentorian roar and raised a hand. An arc of brilliant azure light illuminated the crypt, striking Mr Knives and Sebastian just as the latter aimed his revolver and fired off six rapid shots at the holy man.

The first shot punched a hole in the holy man's chest while the second punctured his swollen gut and the third missed and ricocheted off the Mech-Man. Three more bullets gouged bloody divots from the priest's arms and legs. He staggered backwards, tripped and fetched up in a sitting position against the automaton.

Sebastian cried out and dropped the flaming Mr

Knives, his own clothes wreathed in flame. He fell to the floor and rolled, managing to extinguish the fire as Jani raced across the crypt and dropped to her knees. He stared up at her, managing to smile, the left side of his face a slab of bloody meat. Jani took him in her arms and looked down at his torso, sickened by the sight of flesh seared to the bone.

"Please..." Sebastian murmured, almost soundlessly. "Please, Jani, believe me. I..."

"Sebastian!" She fought back her tears.

"*I love you*. Please believe that I didn't... I didn't betray you."

She reached out, weeping now, and touched the bloody pointillism that marked his brow, cheek and jaw. "I believe you, Sebastian."

"They," he said. "They..."

"Hush," she said, and caressed his cheek.

He smiled and murmured her name, then said no more.

Jani hung her head and sobbed. She felt a hand on her shoulder. "Jani..." She looked up at Alfie, who stared down at her with such an expression of pity on his moon-like face that the pain consuming her was redoubled.

Mahran was on his feet and limping, despite his obvious pain, towards the holy man's corpse. The alien knelt slowly, reached into the priest's suit pocket and found the ventha. He hobbled across to Jani. "We must make haste, Janisha. Durga Das is dead, for now – but there is no telling how soon the Zhell might be able to regenerate him."

Jani only half heard his words, unable to comprehend the full import and horror of what he was saying. "But Sebastian... Can't we take him?"

"We have little time. Come, Jani."

She kissed Sebastian's warm brow, then lowered his body gently to the floor.

Alfie helped her to her feet and together, with Anand assisting the feeble Morn, they moved towards the stairs.

At the door, Jani took one last glance back into the crypt, taking in Sebastian's body, the flaming corpse of Mr Knives, and the bullet-riddled Durga Das seated against the Mech-Man.

They climbed the stairs to the annexe and hurried to the outer door. Alfie assisted her, stumbling, across the graveyard and through the gate in the hedge, Anand and the Morn leading the way.

As they hurried from the park, a police car sped by, its flashing blue light washing darkness from the night. Jani considered the chaos of the crypt, the stalled Mech-Man and the corpses, and wondered what the authorities might make of such a hellish scene.

They piled into the car and Alfie started the engine. From the back seat, next to Anand, Mahran said, "To Blackwall, Alfie – and warehouse three at the East India Dock."

Jani closed her eyes and wept as the car accelerated into the night.

CHAPTER
TWENTY-SEVEN

∽

Das pleads for another chance – Kali is implacable –
Das meets his destiny – "Please let me live....!"

DURGA DAS SAT against the flank of the mechanical
man, aware that he had failed Kali yet again.

He felt the bullets that had riddled his limbs and
torso as so many points of localised, thudding pain.
He had been so close to getting what he wanted –
more importantly, getting what Kali wanted – only to
have it snatched away at the last moment. Now he
sprawled on the cusp of death, his energy draining
away. He could only open his eyes minimally and
watch as the Morn approached him, felt in his pocket
and took the tithra-kuñjī. Das tried to move, to raise
a hand and deal a fiery death to the damnable alien;
he willed Kali to help him, but only silence met his
mental pleas.

He saw Janisha Chatterjee weeping over the fallen
man, and the dumpy British soldier help her to her
feet while the Indian street urchin assisted Mahran
from the crypt. If only he could reach out, burn them
as they tried to leave. Perhaps, then, all might not be
in vain. He put all his effort into straining the muscles

of his right arm; he sweated with the exertion and cursed as his arm moved fractionally.

Then they were gone and he was alone in the hellish crypt save for the burning corpses of Mr Knives and two others.

But perhaps, he told himself, perhaps all was not yet lost.

He had been hit in the chest, stomach and limbs, and yet he was still alive. That could only mean Kali, in her omnipotence and wisdom, was working to bring him back to life as she had done in northern Greece.

He would rise from the dead and show the Chatterjee whore and her hangers-on that he was a force to be reckoned with – he and his goddess. He would follow them from the church, wrest from them the tithra-kuñjī they had taken from him, then take Chatterjee's and force the Morn to divulge the location of the third.

The Age of Kali *would* come to Earth, and it would be thanks to him.

"Oh, Kali, wondrous one. Fill me with life, allow me to pursue the heathens!"

You failed me, Durga Das.

"I... I was unlucky, Kali! If not for the appearance of the gunman... I almost had Chatterjee and the Morn."

But 'almost' is not good enough!

"I know, Kali, and I apologise! I failed, but I promise you I will not fail again. The disappointment has fuelled my desire to serve you all the more! Give me strength, Kali, restore me and I will..."

Kali interrupted, *And why should I do that, Das?*

"Why? So that I might pursue the villains, obtain the tithra-kuñjīs. All is not lost, Kali! We might yet..."

The Morn has your tithra-kuñjī, and Chatterjee has

hers, and they are heading towards the location of the third. You have proved yourself inadequate to the task I set you, Durga Das.

"But..." Das babbled, "but we cannot give up, Kali!"

I do not intend to give up in my quest, you fool – but I will continue without your cumbersome presence.

"No! please, no... I can–"

Yes?

"I will serve you in any and every way possible. I am your servant, your abject servant who will do anything, anything to..."

But Das, I have given you several opportunities to assist me, and you failed. I no longer need you.

"But please, I beg you! Let me live, please let me live!"

I have no time to waste on resurrecting you yet again, Durga Das. The effort tires me, and you are worth less than nothing to me now.

"No, please, I beg you!"

And Das...

"Kali?" Das said in desperation.

When you die, you will not be reborn; there will be no resurrection for Durga Das! Your belief system, your ludicrous religion, is a farce. You will die, and you will be dead forever!

A terrible thought occurred to the holy man. *Anghra dah tanthara, yangra bahl, somithra tal zhell.*

Zhell?

"What the Morn said, about you being a... a Zhell?"

He was speaking the truth, Durga Das.

"No!"

Yes!

And Das was aware of the creature's mocking laughter as he died.

CHAPTER
TWENTY-EIGHT

∞

At East India Dock – In the warehouse –
The British attack – In the aerial-car –
"We are going to Tibet..."

ALFIE PULLED UP before the monolithic block of the Thames-side warehouse and cut the engine.

Jani stared out. The area was in darkness, with only a few streetlights to relieve the gloom. She considered Durga Das, and what he had done to Sebastian; and soon, she thought, the unholy priest would be regenerated, thanks to the Zhell. But at least he no longer had the ventha; that was some small comfort.

They climbed from the car and Jani looked into the sky. There seemed to be a lot of airship activity to the south and west; the tiny shapes of a dozen 'ships, illuminated by their running-lights, appeared to be converging on this very location. A coincidence, surely?

As they stood watching, the firefly lights of other airships appeared in the night sky to the north and east. Jani heard the rumble of car engines, drawing closer.

"They can't have followed us, can they?" she asked Alfie.

He came to her side and slipped an arm around her shoulders. "I don't know, Jani. But I think not."

The Morn limped around the car and indicated a narrow cobbled alleyway between the warehouses. "This way."

Assisted by Anand, he set off down the alley, Jani and Alfie following.

A hundred yards further on they came to a recessed entrance, and Mahran stood looking up at the great timber door like a penitent before a locked cathedral.

Alfie said tentatively, "And how do we get in?"

Mahran turned suddenly, so rapidly that Jani started, expecting trouble. She looked down the alleyway. A light appeared at the far end – no, two red lights, and this time she knew where she had seen them before.

The twin crimson points approached, accompanied by the sound of metal on cobbles. Mahran dropped to his knees and the shape of the mechanical hound materialised from the darkness at a run.

Fido approached the kneeling Morn, and Mahran reached out and took its head in his hands. They touched foreheads in a gesture Jani found strangely moving.

Then, to her surprise, the hound turned and trotted away, back up the alley. Fifty yards away he stopped and turned, facing them.

"But what is he doing?" she asked.

"Stand aside and you will see," said Mahran, shepherding them from before the warehouse door.

Jani looked up. An airship passed overhead, sending down a probing antenna of light. The grumble of converging vehicles increased. She whispered, "They *are* coming after us!"

The next sound she heard was the rapid clatter of metal feet on cobbles as Fido charged towards the warehouse. Five yards from the door, the hound leapt and crashed through the timber like a missile.

"Quickly," Mahran said. "Inside."

He stepped through the ragged hole in the door, followed by Alfie and Anand. Jani came last, looking over her shoulder for signs of pursuit. The alleyway was empty, but the din of airship engines was deafening and searchlights crisscrossed in the night sky like duelling swords.

The interior of the warehouse was in darkness save for the meagre illumination of the moon slanting through a dozen evenly spaced skylights high above.

Fido trotted alongside the limping Morn. Jani caught up with the alien and asked, "You know the mechanical hound?"

He turned and sketched a smile at her. "We are old acquaintances, Jani. There were a dozen of them aboard the Vantissarian ship – though in quite a different form than this."

"And they are... living?" she asked.

"Not in the sense that you understand the word. They are MIs."

"MIs?" she echoed.

"Manufactured intelligences, designed to facilitate onboard communications between officers of the vast ship."

"I see," she said, uncertainly. "And they *can* mind-read?"

He smiled again. "That is how they are able to communicate."

"I was aboard the *Pride of Edinburgh*, coming from India, when I first encountered the hound. So it read my mind, my intentions in coming to Britain, and realised that it must help us locate you?"

"Like a Terran hound," Mahran said, "the MI has programmed into it a deep and abiding sense of loyalty and duty. Aboard the Vantissarian vessel, the MI and I were close."

A searchlight swept through a skylight, illuminating the interior of the warehouse. Mahran led the way down an aisle between tiered galleries occupied by huge wooden crates, pausing to scrutinise each stencilled sign at the foot of ladders leading up to higher galleries.

He stopped at last and said, "This one. Up we go."

He climbed the first rung of the ladder, then turned to look down at Fido, who sat on its haunches and gazed up at the Morn. Mahran stared at the MI in silent communication, and then the hound turned and trotted away.

Mahran explained, "I've told it to go and cause as much disruption as possible among those who pursue us."

"So we are being followed! But how?" She thought of the ease with which she had escaped from Carmody Hall, a small voice telling her that she had been allowed to get away; but that still left the question of how the British had followed her so far.

"If they know where we are," she said, "then surely it will be only a matter of time before they find us, no matter how well we conceal ourselves in here?"

But Mahran had resumed his ascent. Jani followed, then Alfie and Anand.

The interior of the warehouse was bright now with the searchlights of the hovering airships; the din of their engines was overpowering. She heard vehicles screech to a halt in the street outside.

They came to a lateral gallery and Mahran turned left, passing a dozen berths filled with crates. At last he came to a weathered, stencilled container the size of a small house.

Anand stared up at the light pouring through the skylights. "I saw someone!" he cried out.

Jani stared at the rectangle of white light.

"They're coming down on ropes, Jani-ji!" the boy called out above the noise of the airships.

She heard multiple thumps on the roof above their heads, and knew that it was only a matter of time before they were captured. Even if they managed to hide within the crate, how long would it be before the authorities combed the building and found them?

But, she asked herself for perhaps the twentieth time in as many minutes, how had they managed to trace her?

Her blood froze at another sound, and Alfie clutched her hand.

A booming voice, amplified through a loud-hailer, called out, "We know you are in there, Janisha Chatterjee. Give yourself up to the authorities now, and you will be treated with lenience. We have your best interests at heart, Janisha. Do your duty to your country!"

Jani smiled bitterly to herself. She recognised the voice as belonging to Major Heatherington and felt a plunging sensation of despair.

"They have us," she said. "Mahran, they have us *and* the venthas! And the one you possessed? It's within the crate, isn't it?"

Mahran, tapping a code into a huge combination lock on the front of the container, merely nodded.

"Then we're leading them to all three!" she said.

"Would I be that foolish?" he said enigmatically.

Mahran pulled away the hasp and opened a small door in the crate. In the half-light Jani made out a second door beyond the Morn, this one made of metal. He reached out and entered a code into that door's locking mechanism, then pulled open the door and called out, "Quickly! Inside."

"Janisha," Heatherington's booming voice filled the warehouse, "come out now or I will send in my troops."

The rest was lost as they stepped into the crate and through the second door. After the glare of the searchlights, all was semi-darkness within. Jani almost lost her footing and grasped Alfie's hand in order to remain upright. Mahran slammed the metal door behind them with a percussive thump – and the darkness became total.

"Mahran?"

"One moment while I find the..." he said, fumbling in the darkness.

The chamber was flooded with light. Jani stared around her in wonder.

They were standing in what looked like an over-furnished boudoir, all velvet upholstery, polished mahogany and brass scrollwork. A great seat was positioned at the far end of the small chamber, and beyond it was a long, shuttered window in a studded brass frame.

"Where are we?" she whispered.

Mahran ignored the question and rounded the great seat, taking something from a recess beneath the shuttered window.

"Wherever we are," Alfie commented, "it's a pretty prison to be found in."

Mahran turned to them and held up a small disc.

"The third ventha," Jani said.

She had come halfway around the world, fulfilling Jelch's wishes, and united all three venthas – only to find herself cornered like a cowering rat.

The Morn slipped the disc into the pocket of his prison rags and lowered himself into the padded seat.

The amplified voice of Major Heatherington sounded again, but too muffled for her to make out individual words.

"They'll be here in seconds!" Anand said.

Mahran swivelled his seat and stared at them. "You will find seats against the far wall. Strap yourselves in and hold on tight."

Jani began to question him, but he gestured urgently at the seats and turned his own to face a sloping console of dials and verniers.

Jani crossed the chamber and strapped herself into a fold-down seat between Alfie and Anand, exchanging a worried glance with the Lieutenant as she did so.

She was alerted by a loud grating sound, and the metal shutter slid open to reveal a window and beyond it the planks of the containing crate. She made out the Morn's bony elbows on either side of the seat-back, moving back and forth industriously.

"Of course!" she said to herself. She thought she understood. The venthas, and this strange contraption in which they found themselves... Could it be that the British were right, all along?

"Mahran," she said, "this is some kind of weapon, isn't it? An iron-clad or some such? And with the venthas it becomes a... a super-weapon?"

The Morn laughed. "It is nothing of the kind, Jani. Sit back and observe."

He reached out, pulled a lever, and the chamber was filled with a growing, rumbling roar. The container shook, rattling the teeth in her head.

"What is this?" cried Alfie.

Jani was thrown back and forth so violently that her vision blurred, and the noise of what sounded like multiple engines deafened her.

Then the chamber seemed to rise precipitously, leaving her stomach behind.

"Mahran!" she yelped.

The chamber *was* rising, the slatted planks of the crate disappearing with a splintering crash. Then they were climbing away from the gallery on which the crate had resided and gaining speed as they did so. The next thing she saw through the viewscreen was the interior of the warehouse, washed in the glare of searchlights.

"Hold on!" Mahran warned, and the chamber rattled as it crashed through something solid. The ceiling of the warehouse, Jani thought, as a thousand confetti-like tiles fluttered beyond the viewscreen.

They were in the air above the warehouse now, careering towards the swelling flank of an airship. Only swift manoeuvring by the Morn, frantically working the controls, avoided a collision. Their own craft tipped and canted away through the night, and the gondola of the airship sped by a matter of yards from the viewscreen. Jani glimpsed startled white faces in the control cabin before they were snatched away.

"I had doubts about its air-worthiness after so long," Mahran said over his shoulder. "But I need not have worried."

"But what is it?" Anand asked.

"Yet another example of Vantissarian technology," the Morn replied. "An approximate translation from my own language would be an 'aerial-car'. It is how I came to Britain, fifty years ago, on my abortive mission to warn the government. I landed in Sussex and had the craft crated up, then made for London and arranged for its safekeeping."

Jani stared through the viewscreen. A dozen airships were manoeuvring to avoid colliding with the aerial-car. She imagined Major Heatherington's consternation as he watched their vessel race away to the east, and she smiled to herself. Ahead, the sun was coming up and the horizon was haemorrhaging bloody light.

"We've escaped," Anand said in barely a whisper. "We've escaped, and I honestly thought we'd had our chips, Jani-ji!"

Jani smiled at the boy, and from his control seat Mahran said, "We have escaped, for now. But the British are not giving up so easily. Look." He reached out and touched a dial, and across the chamber from where she, Alfie and Anand sat side by side, another shuttered viewscreen slid open.

Mahran canted the vessel so that they had a better view.

All London, washed in the pale dawn light, was spread below them, a thousand streets and buildings shot through with the silver serpentine length of the Thames. In the west, Jani made out a brilliant bright light – a pulsing orange flame rising slowly into the sky.

"But what is it?" Anand asked.

Jani stared at the tongue of flame, and thought she could just make out the golden shape of a dart above it.

"It's the British sub-orbital rocket," Mahran said, "and it's coming after us."

Into the following, ominous, silence, Jani asked, "And just where are we heading, Mahran?"

He swivelled his seat so that he was regarding the trio.

"We are going to Tibet," said the Morn.

CHAPTER
TWENTY-NINE

∽

Mahran's story – Towards the nodal point –
A last word with Lady Eddington –
The mechanical hound again –
"Onward..."

"BEFORE I ELUCIDATE further," Mahran said, "first I must ask how you came upon my friend and colleague, Jelch?"

"Oh, it seems such a long time ago now!" Jani said. "I was aboard the *Rudyard Kipling* airship, bound for New Delhi, when the Russians attacked..."

For the next hour she recounted her adventures across India and Nepal, her capture by the Russians and her escape, thanks to Anand, and then her flight from the British, the Russians and the holy man Durga Das – all of them intent of wresting the ventha from her possession.

She told Mahran of Jelch's murder at the hands of Colonel Smethers, and her audience with the Jelch-like 'entity' aboard the Vantissarian ship.

When she came to the end of her story, Mahran nodded and said, sadly, "Jelch was a true friend, and a brave colleague. I am distressed that he suffered at the hands of the Russians, and then the British, just as I was tortured by the latter."

She stared at the Morn. "I must admit that I feared for your health," she said. "I had heard stories that you succumbed, mentally, under the torture of the British."

Mahran stretched his lips in a wry smile. "Perhaps I should not have been so naïve as to assume the authorities would believe my story of other worlds and invading armies. They tortured me, seeking what they termed the 'truth'. I feigned insanity in a bid to stop their ministrations. I lived in the hope that Jelch might..." He shook his head. "But to find out now that my friend has met his end..."

His gaze fell to his mutilated fingertips, and he was silent for a stretch, before looking up and saying, "We complemented each other very well. Jelch was a Morn of action, myself more... cerebral, shall we say? I was – I am – a scientist, Jelch a strategist. We came to Earth to warn your rulers about the threat of the Zhell. Little good did that do! But," he went on, "I am determined to succeed in my mission, and I will dedicate my work to my fallen colleague."

Jani regarded the forlorn Mahran, wishing that she could say something to lighten his burden. But what could she say? How could mere words, now, salve the pain of grief? She thought of Sebastian, and shut her mind to that part of her that had yet to begin the long process of coming to terms with his end, just as she had shut her mind to the contemplation of her father's demise, over two weeks ago. Words were all very well, but what really mattered more than any verbalisation of sympathy was action, the action of those loved and trusted ones – like Alfie and Anand – who she knew would remain loyal to her whatever happened, and her own action: she pledged to do all within her powers to be loyal to Mahran so that he could succeed in his mission.

She looked up and ventured, "So... with all three venthas, Mahran, we can now seal the world-portal, which is the reason we are flying to Tibet?"

He sighed. "To use a crude analogy, Jani: the venthas are a key which can lock and unlock a passage between realms or worlds. However, though a key can lock a door, so another key, in another's possession, can unlock it. That is the situation, now, with the Zhell. You see, the fact the Zhell have achieved what we call a 'minimal breach' of the fabric between realities – you saw it yourself in the miniature portal that followed Durga Das – means that they are close to achieving a major breakthrough; a rent in the fabric which would allow their armies through *en masse*. There was a time when I thought that if Jelch and I could warn the powers of your world of the Zhell, then they would unite and bring all their might – aided by Vantissarian technology – to bear on the invaders."

Jani shook her head. "But now?"

"Now that time is past. Humanity is too divided, too consumed by petty political squabbles and short-term goals to prove an effective, united front against the Zhell."

"But what can we hope to do, if we cannot seal the portal between the worlds, and my people are too ineffective to repulse the Zhell?"

"Simply put, Jani, we can open a breach in the fabric of reality through which I can travel the next 'world' or 'realm'. In time I will enlist the aid of another race

– a race whose scientific prowess and technological wherewithal exceeds even that of the Morn. They are called the Meldoran."

"And with the venthas you can do this?" Alfie asked.

"The venthas enable a traveller to pass into a reality contiguous to the one he or she already inhabits. My plan is to travel to Vantissar and find the nodal point – the 'Tibet', if you like, of that world – and from there travel through the portal to my own world and beyond."

"But how might you reach the world of the Meldoran?" Jani asked. "Because according to the Morn-entity aboard the Vantissarian ship, the world beyond your world – the contiguous world to yours – is the homeworld of the Zhell."

The alien inclined his head again. "Which is precisely the conundrum that faces me, my friends. You see, the question I ask myself is how, thousands of years ago, did my illustrious ancestors manage to locate the world of the Meldoran? History is vague on that point. It might be that Meldora is the world beyond that of the Zhell, or way beyond, and that the Morn expedition had to pass through Zhell at a time when it was not the bellicose threat it is now. At any rate, I intend to find out – and when I do eventually locate the Meldoran, and if they are still the scientifically pre-eminent race they were of yore, then I will petition their aid in combating, in whatever way, the scourge of the Zhell."

Am I really hearing this, Jani asked herself, feeling something stirring, something roused, within her chest.

She considered his words. "But, Mahran, correct me if I am wrong; the Zhell have conquered Vantissar – so won't you be in grave danger in travelling there?"

"That is so, but Vantissar is a vast place, and with luck I can avoid the Zhell."

Jani stared at him. "And Alfie and Anand and I?" she asked.

"Yes?" said the Morn.

"We have come a long way on this mission," she said, "and I for one would not wish to abandon it now."

"Nor me," said Alfie and Anand as one.

"In other words," Jani went on, "we have burned our bridges here on Earth, with everyone out for our scalps. So, can we come with you on this march through other worlds, other realities?"

"The danger will be great, my friends. The Zhell are merciless. They know we possess the ventha-di and all three venthas. They will be searching for us."

Jani looked first at Alfie, and then at Anand, and saw nothing but resolve in their eyes.

She spoke for them both when she said, "We have faced danger again and again over the course of the past weeks, Mahran, and we are ready to face even more."

The Morn smiled. "In all fairness," he said, "how could I deny myself the support of beings who have shown themselves, to date, to be loyal and staunch companions to me and my erstwhile colleague?"

A SHORT WHILE later Mahran, noting Jani's tiredness, pulled down a divan from the wall and suggested she rest. Alfie and Anand, too intrigued by the vessel that carried them rapidly east, joined Mahran at the controls while the Morn explained the workings of the craft.

Jani stretched out on the padded velvet of the divan and within minutes was asleep. Her dreams were a chaos of violent imagery; she was fleeing a fanged, airborne Zhell, which in turn was pursued by a British airship and an Indian 'ship bearing Durga Das – and then, as in the way of dreams, these visions morphed into the crypt where Sebastian lay dead. Then she saw the Russian burning, screaming in pain... And then these violent visions ceased, to be replaced by the image of Lady Eddington, who smiled and called Jani remarkable and wished her God Speed.

She woke with a start, seeing the dowager's kindly, powdered face recede in her mind's eye. She sat up and stretched, blinking at her surroundings. She was reminded of Captain Nemo's *Nautilus*, which she had seen in an old, illustrated edition of Verne's *Twenty Thousand Leagues Under the Sea*.

Mahran sat in the control seat, his attention fixed on something in his long-fingered hands. Jani was surprised to see that he was poring over one of her shoes. "Mahran?"

He held up the shoe, its heel removed to reveal a small recess. In his right hand, Mahran held a tiny silver device.

"Alfie told me about your escape from Carmody Hall," he said. "And I wondered how the British tracked us to the warehouse. Now I know."

Alfie said, "The British implanted a tracking device in your shoe, Jani."

She shook her head. "You know, I wondered at the ease with which I escaped from the hall. They *allowed* me to get away."

"So that you might in time lead them in time to the ventha-di," Mahran said.

Jani crossed to the viewscreen and stood beside

Alfie, placing a hand on his shoulder. He reached up and tapped her fingers. She peered through the screen, seeing an expanse of featureless dun foothills rolling by silently below.

"Where are we?"

"Coming over eastern Afghanistan," Mahran said.

"Afghanistan? So quickly?"

Anand explained. "You have been asleep for six hours, Jani, and the aerial-car can travel at speeds in excess of five hundred miles an hour."

"And they will be following us now, in their sub-orbital rocket?"

"The rocket is not as manoeuvrable, and its trajectory is limited – a high parabola from its take-off point to its destination. As such, it cannot *follow* us. However, I suspect it will be making for Tibet in order to head us off."

"Head us off?" She stared at the alien. "The British are still tracking the device implanted in my shoe?"

But Mahran was shaking his head. "I have disabled that device," he said. "No, their pursuit of us is entirely my fault. One of the things I let slip, many years ago when they first incarcerated me, was that the venthas worked in propinquity to the area known as Tibet."

"So they might arrive before us?"

"That is possible – and certainly they will have mobilised the RAF, though Tibet is vast. We might, if our luck holds, evade their attention."

Anand said, "We should be arriving over Tibet in a little over an hour, Jani!"

"And then?" she asked Mahran.

"And then we will place the last two venthas in the ventha-di, and we will be directed to the precise location of the nodal point. When we are within a certain range of it, the portal will open."

"A portal to another world," Alfie said in awe.

Jani touched her stomach. "I think I can feel a certain warmth," she murmured, "or am I imagining it?"

Mahran smiled. "Perhaps the ventha-di senses that we are nearing the nodal point."

"'Senses'?" Jani repeated. "You make the thing sound sentient!"

"It is, like the mechanical hound you named Fido, a Mechanical Intelligence – so, yes, in a way it is sentient."

Jani fell silent and watched the sere landscape roll by far below. She was reminded of the time aboard the *Rudyard Kipling* – what seemed like an aeon ago now – when she had stared down on the foothills of the Hindu Kush with Lady Eddington at her side.

She smiled and said, "I dreamed just now of a friend, Mahran, one Lady Eddington – the fourth member of our little team, without whom we might never have come this far." She shook her head. "I wonder if I will ever see her again?"

"You could always contact her," Mahran said.

"I could?"

Mahran reached out and touched a stud on the control panel, and from a recess in the sloping console before them rose a microphone that resembled the compound eye of a giant insect.

"If you repeat her number to me, I will attempt to integrate the car's logic matrix with the British telephone network."

Jani closed her eyes and summoned the dowager's number, and Mahran tapped the digits into the ship's console.

He vacated the pilot's seat so that Jani could sit down.

She heard the dial tone, and imagined the telephone in the dowager's Mayfair townhouse shrilling its summons. Presently a male voice said, "Lady Eddington's residence. Calling?"

Jani leaned forward, smiling at Alfie. "Mr Dobson. This is Janisha Chatterjee. Is Lady Eddington at home?"

Oh, please let her be, she thought.

"Miss Chatterjee? Her Ladyship has been beside herself with worry. I'll summon her immediately."

"Thank you, Mr Dobson." She turned to Anand and Alfie and beamed her delight.

Seconds later Lady Eddington called out, "Janisha? Janisha – is it really you?"

"Amelia!" Jani said, close to tears. "It is I, and I am with Alfie and Anand."

"My girl! Oh, I've been sick with worry these past two days, with no sight nor sound of you and the Highgate flat deserted!"

"I'm sorry. We had to leave somewhat in a hurry."

"But where are you now? And when can I see you again, my dear?"

"We... we are flying to Tibet in an alien ship," Jani reported, "and I don't know when, if ever, we might be back in London. Maybe one day..."

"Flying to Tibet?" Lady Eddington sounded incredulous. "Aboard an alien ship? But you are safe, my child, and Alfie and Anand too?"

"Quite safe – and in the company of Mahran," she went on, and gave a brief outline of their mission.

"Goodness gracious!" the dowager exclaimed at

last. "Venturing through a portal to another world, no less! Oh, my dear, my wonderful child! How I wish I were fifty years younger and could accompany you!"

"I... *we*... just wanted to say thank you for everything you have done for us, Amelia. We are truly thankful."

"And I am thankful, Janisha, that I have known such true and stalwart friends as you three."

The vessel bucked, as if in turbulence, as something exploded to starboard. Mahran peered through the viewscreen, then gestured to Jani that she should cease her conversation.

"I'd better go now, Amelia. Thank you again."

"God Speed, child!" the old lady sang, and Mahran cut the connection.

"I'm sorry," he said, "but look..."

Directly ahead loomed the bloated envelope of an airship emblazoned with the red, white and blue of the British flag. She saw a puff of smoke issue from a pipe slung beneath its gondola, and something fiery streaked towards them.

She vacated the pilot's seat with haste and Mahran took the controls and slewed the craft to port; the missile and the British 'ship vanished from the screen.

Mahran touched the controls again and the vessel surged, gaining speed. "I'm sorry. I should have been more vigilant. We can outpace such a 'ship with ease, but this indicates that the British are on full alert and are awaiting our arrival."

"How far are we from...?" Alfie began.

Mahran said. "We are entering Tibetan territory now. We should reach the nodal point in twenty to thirty minutes."

"I feel sick," Jani said, touching her stomach.

"The turbulence is unavoidable," Mahran said.

She shook her head. "I don't mean..." she began, but, before she could continue, she felt an intense warmth rising from her stomach.

"The ventha-di," she said.

"Jani?" Alfie said. Anand regarded her with concern.

"I will be fine."

The warmth was like a small flame rising through her torso, cutting a path from her stomach and up her trachea; she was reminded of a double malt whisky she had once sampled, only this time the effect was in reverse.

She felt a sudden constriction in her throat, and then the ventha-di was on her tongue. She slipped it out into her hand decorously, as if it were a plum-stone, and wiped the object on her dress.

Mahran reached out, and she placed the triangular ventha-di, its three circular receptacles bearing just one disc, on his thin palm.

He slipped a hand into the pocket of his prison garb and withdrew the two remaining venthas. "I have awaited this time for so long," he said.

With the ventha-di lying flat on his left palm, he inserted the second ventha, then hesitated and slipped the third one home.

Startled, Jani stood back as something rose from the ventha-di on Mahran's palm.

Alfie and Anand cried out, staring in wonder at the swirling vortex of magenta light that hung in the air before them. Jani made out figures or numerals within the light, though none which she recognised.

"What is it?" she breathed.

Mahran regarded the vortex, his eyes shuttling back

and forth as if trying to make sense of the scrolling figures within the shifting red light. "The operating system of the portal's nexus," he said. "I must issue an authorisation code, as it were, and then it will establish a fix on our bearings and, with luck, grant us access to the world-portal."

He held out a shaking, long-fingered hand and reached into the vortex, his fingertip touching a series of numerals in rapid succession, his long face a mask of concentration. He muttered as he worked, the words alien, as if encouraging himself in his endeavour.

Then he withdrew his hand and, instantly, the swirling ceased and a string of figures hung suspended in the vortex. Mahran smiled. He reached out again, touching a dozen of the floating figures in quick succession, and sighed with relief as they disappeared, and with them the magenta vortex.

"I think," he said, "that I was successful. But come, we should learn within minutes if I am right."

They turned to the viewscreen and peered out.

They were passing over a vast snow-covered valley with rearing mountains on three sides. A storm whipped the air with a pointillistic flurry of snow, and the aerial-car, slowing, rocked this way and that.

Mahran slipped into the pilot's seat and leaned forward. "The portal should establish itself in the centre of the valley far below."

Alfie said, "And this is where the ship came through from Vantissar, all those years ago?"

"Very close to here, yes. We flew it as far south as our fuel reserves would allow, before we came down in the valley in Nepal."

Anand pointed. "What's that?"

Jani followed the direction of his pointing finger and made out, coming through a notched pass in the distant mountain range, the tiny shape of an airship.

"We have company," Alfie murmured.

Mahran nodded. "And another, and another..."

Jani saw two further ships approaching from right and left.

Anand said, "Does the aerial-car have weapons, sir?"

Mahran swung his long head. "It is not an offensive vessel, Anand. We will have to combat the airships with speed and manoeuvrability alone."

"But where is the portal?" Jani said, staring through the viewscreen.

Mahran glanced at Alfie. "How far before the 'ships are within firing range?"

Alfie chewed his lower lip. "The vessel directly ahead is an old Sopwith. It's slow, and I suspect badly armed. The others... The one to our right is a Lysander, faster but not known for its offensive capabilities. The one we have to worry about is the de Havilland on the left. It's a new model, fast and armed with the latest missiles. I should think it could fire on us with accuracy from half a mile."

"Thank you for that," Mahran said. "I'll take evasive action to avoid the de Havilland." And so saying he touched the controls and the aerial-car veered to starboard; the de Havilland slewed away and vanished from the viewscreen.

"That might buy us a little time," Mahran murmured, as if to himself, "but the portal should have established itself by now."

The snowstorm increased; the distant mountain peaks were blurred in the flurry. But for the turbulence, the scene before them might have been no more than an image projected on to a cinema screen.

"How long will the portal be open for?" Jani asked. "And isn't there a danger that the British will simply follow us through?"

"I'm banking on the British erring on the side of caution and not passing through the portal before us," Mahran answered. "The portal will be open and navigable for just three minutes – any longer and the Zhell might be able to detect its presence. I intend to leave our passage through until the last few seconds, so that we *cannot* be followed."

"All this is assuming that the portal does open," Alfie murmured. "Are you sure you have the correct co-ordinates?"

"I have every faith in the car's onboard logic system," Mahran answered. "The portal should open dead ahead of us."

Jani heard a deafening explosion to starboard, and the aerial-car bucked. Mahran adjusted the controls as the vessel slewed through the air like a toboggan.

"And that," Alfie said, "was the de Havilland opening up." He looked at Jani and smiled reassuringly. "A warning shot – they could have brought us down with ease, had they wanted to."

"I am not sure I feel all that reassured," she smiled. She gripped the back of the pilot's seat as the aerial-car rocked.

Alfie pointed. "And what is that, down there to the right?"

Jani, shocked on two counts, could not believe what she was seeing. The fact that the British sub-orbital rocket was sitting on its tail fins, awaiting them, was sufficient cause for concern – but issuing from an arch-shaped exit and marching down a ramp was a seemingly never-ending column of soldiers, the rocket and the ant-like militia reduced to the dimensions of children's toys by the mountains looming on either side.

"They have come in force," Mahran observed, "but with luck their presence will prove futile."

Anand leaned forward, peering intently. "There!" he shouted suddenly, pointing through the viewscreen.

"Well spotted!" Mahran cried. "The portal!"

To their left, far below them in the valley, a series of lights rose from the snowy wastes. Jani gasped as she watched the white lights coil about each other, thick tendrils rising and writhing a hundred yards into the air. It resembled nothing so much, she thought, as a fire of ice – each coiling tendril having the peculiar quality of a flame which rises to its full extent and seems to vanish, yet is renewed ceaselessly from below.

Jani looked back at the rocket, still disgorging its complement of soldiers.

Mahran touched the controls and the aerial-car slanted away towards the portal.

Jani found herself gripping Alfie's hand. They were leaving this world, she thought – and who knew if they would ever return?

They swooped to within fifty yards of the snowfield, levelled out and approached the portal. Jani judged that they were perhaps a mile away. Before them, the portal rose, throwing out a dazzling radiance of ice-blue and white light. Jani told herself that she could make out the image of a landscape beyond the interweaving coils of luminescence: a sandy waste and a distant line of mountains; but then the vision was snatched away and she wondered if she had been hallucinating.

They were perhaps half a mile from the portal when Mahran called out, "Hold tight! The passage is likely to be far from smooth!" And instantly the vessel bucked and turned on its side. Jani was thrown off her feet, falling on Alfie who supported her and reached out to stop Anand from cracking his skull on the wall. Mahran remained in the pilot's seat, wrestling with the controls.

Jani assumed that the turbulence was due to the displacement of air around the portal as they passed through, but Mahran disabused her of the notion. "That was the de Havilland!" he cried. "And they're firing in earnest now."

The next explosion ripped a hole in the flank of the vessel. Where the line of seats had been there was now a great rent surrounded by a ragged crown of metal – with a neat exit hole in the opposite wall. An icy, keening wind filled the ship, freezing them.

"I can't maintain...!" Mahran began, and Jani screamed as the aerial-car lost height and plummeted towards the ground.

She stared through the viewscreen. The white immensity of the snowfield was rushing up to meet them. Mahran hauled on the controls, bringing the car out of its dive. The vessel slowed and levelled out and they ploughed into the snow, spinning like a discus. Jani was thrown to the deck from where she watched her friends tumble outwards with the Coriolis effect and sprawl against the outer walls.

Then the vessel abruptly stopped its dizzy gyre and a weird silence reigned. Jani picked herself up and staggered over the sloping deck to where Anand was sitting, wiping blood from a gash on his forehead. Alfie joined them, holding his left arm. "It's nothing more than a sprain," he said.

Anand wiped blood from his eyes and smiled at them bravely. "I'm okay, Jani-ji!"

"Mahran?" Jani asked, moving across the vessel to where the Morn lay on his back. He struggled to his feet with difficulty, wincing in pain. Jani and Alfie helped him upright.

"Mahran?" Jani said.

"I'll be fine," he said, peering through the viewscreen.

Jani stared. Two hundred yards away, the fiery white portal rose and writhed, filling the car with its icy light.

"Our priority is to reach the portal!" Mahran cried. "I would have preferred to take the car through, but that is no longer possible. We can only have a minute, or two at the most, to reach it, before it closes again."

"And if it does?" Alfie asked.

"Then I must go through the process of opening it again," Mahran said, "by which time the British..."

He was already limping across the rent in the wall. Jani followed, helping Anand. Mahran reached the hole, negotiated the prongs of shattered metal with care, and jumped out into the driving snow.

Jani reached the opening, stepped over the metal shards, and jumped down, her teeth chattering as an icy wind pounced. She wore a summer dress and a cardigan, and her feet were shod in light shoes – hardly the attire for braving sub-zero Tibetan temperatures.

She looked around, peering through the snowstorm for the first sign of pursuing soldiery. To her relief they appeared to be quite alone, for the time being.

Mahran turned and steadied her as she lost her footing in the drifted snow. Alfie and Anand jumped down beside her, and all three stopped and stared up in wonder as the Morn, unfazed by the beauty of the coiling ice-white conflagration before him, stumbled up the icy slope towards the portal.

Tugging Alfie and Anand after her, she slogged through the snow against a ferocious headwind and caught up with the Morn. Ahead, the portal was no longer hanging in mid-air: now its widest point spanned the rise ahead of them for a hundred yards, throwing off sparks and shards of blinding white light.

Jani shouted into Mahran's ear, "It knows where we are and has lowered itself accordingly?"

"Its logic nexus is attuned to the elevation of the ventha-di," Mahran explained, bowing his head against the raging wind.

"How long before...?" Alfie cried, his words ripped away by the wind.

"A minute, perhaps less," Mahran said. Jani looked up; the portal was a hundred yards away.

She trudged on, her every step a terrible effort. Her feet sank into the drifts of snow, and she stumbled every time she tried to lift her foot free of the hole her weight had created. She was helped again and again by Alfie and Anand, and she in turn assisted her friends when they pitched and fell and cried out in desperation.

At one point she felt an urgent tugging on the sleeve of her cardigan. "Look, Jani-ji!"

She turned and looked to where Anand was pointing.

Across the snowy wastes to their right, a column of black-clad soldiers appeared through the snowstorm, the shape of their rocketship looming behind them. She saw tiny explosions of rifle fire, then heard the shots and ducked involuntarily.

Other soldiers knelt beside a silver machine. She heard a deafening report, and something exploded twenty yards to their left. She gagged as the wind blew a sickly cloud of cordite into her face.

Above the keening of the wind she heard an amplified voice boom out. "If you value your lives, stop where you are now!"

The command did nothing but make her all the more determined to reach the portal. She looked up, squinting thought the driven snowflakes. Twenty yards, maybe thirty?

Another shell exploded beyond them, but closer this time. She felt the heat of its discharge and coughed on the resulting cordite cloud.

"Thirty seconds!" Mahran called out.

"I warn you," the desperate voice boomed out. "Stop now!"

They came to the crest of the rise, a matter of yards from the pulsating portal. Mahran reached it first, and turned as Jani, Alfie and Anand drew alongside.

Together they stared down the incline.

"Look!" Anand cried, laughing.

Down below the column of troops was in tatters. Jani watched as a tiny figure sped through their ranks, weaving between soldiers and artillery pieces like a mad mechanical dervish.

"Fido?" she said incredulously. "But how...?"

"There is only one way he could possibly have followed us," Mahran explained. "On the sub-orb rocketship!"

"But how did he sneak aboard?" Anand asked.

"I suspect he concealed himself within a vent or flue on the rocket's carapace," Mahran said, "and hitched a ride."

Having sown confusion and chaos in the ranks of British soldiery, Fido was streaking up the incline towards where Jani stood.

"Come on!" Alfie urged the hound under his breath.

Snow exploded on either side of the racing dog, and gunshots pinged off its carapace. More weapons were brought to bear on the mechanical hound, and great divots of snow erupted in its wake.

It was only fifty yards away now, and rapidly gaining ground.

Jani winced as the artillery found their range and a shell exploded a few yards from the dog. Fido flew through the air, tail over muzzle, landed on its feet and ran on, limping now, towards Jani and her friends.

The mechanical hound raced past them and leapt through the portal. Mahran gripped Jani's arm and they advanced towards the cold, licking flames, just yards away now.

Despite its appearance of monumental ice flames, Jani expected to feel heat as she stepped forward and entered the effulgence. She gasped as her body was gripped by a bone-gnawing cold – far more intense than that of the snowfields they were leaving behind. And then the cold was no more and she felt the warmth of an alien sun on her face.

She turned and stared. Through the coiling tendrils she made out the tiny figures of British troops rushing up the incline, hundreds of them intent on storming the portal. Mahran laughed at the futility of their attempt as the portal disappeared from the bottom up, the flames of ice rising and coiling through the air, reducing to evanescent wisps high above and then vanishing altogether.

She found herself hugging Alfie and Anand to her as they stared down the sandy incline falling away at their feet.

She looked around her. "Vantissar," she said to herself. "But what is that?" she murmured, craning her neck to take in the vast blackened gantry that loomed over their four tiny figures, its spars and girders twisted. It reminded her of the Eiffel Tower, but truncated fifty feet off the ground as if hit by some deadly missile.

"A Vantissarian weapons platform," Mahran said. "Behold."

He pointed, and Jani made out a dozen more stretching across the desert, all of them horribly torqued and twisted. They stood eerily vast and silent, like epitaphs to some deadly conflict.

The flat desert landscape was crossed by arrow-straight canals, fringed with bright green vegetation. In the distance she made out what might have been a great city, its towers and pinnacles – of a design spectacularly alien – blasted and blackened and leaning at every angle.

"What happened?" she found herself asking, before realising that the question was redundant. "The Zhell, am I right?"

Mahran gazed out across the desert. "They destroyed every city and killed millions of citizens. The Vantissarians who survived the slaughter now eke out a living as nomads. They were a once proud, technological civilisation, an ancient, peaceful people, until the Zhell..."

"And the Zhell?" Alfie asked. "Where are they now?"

"They occupy a great city a thousand miles west of here, massing for the invasion of the next world."

"Earth," Anand said.

Jani regarded the long-jawed Morn. "And they can travel from their world to this one with a ventha-di of their own?"

"Something similar, a device that opens the way between the worlds. They were only prevented from accessing your world because of the work of the Vantissarians, who sealed the rift when they passed through. But as Jelch might have told you, for decades the Zhell have been working to breach the rift and access Earth."

"And now we must cross this world to another nodal point, and then enter your homeworld?" Jani said.

The Morn inclined his long head. "That is so. Ideally I would have wished to have come through with the aerial-car. It would have made our onward journey a little easier."

"And how far away is this world's nodal point?" Alfie asked.

"The nodal point giving access to Morn is perhaps five thousand miles north of here. Far enough, but it could have been more. For that we should give thanks." He regarded his friends. "We have many days, maybe weeks, of adventure ahead of us."

"And from Morn," Jani said, "to reach the world of the Meldorans, we must pass through the world of the Zhell?" The thought made her blood run cold.

"We will consider that when we have safely negotiated this world," Mahran said. "but first..."

He reached into the pocket of his prison rags and withdrew the ventha-di. The mechanical dog trotted up to the Morn and sat before him obediently.

Mahran said, "There is a danger, if we keep the ventha-di with us, that the Zhell will detect its presence

– that, I suspect, is how Durga Das was able to trace you all the way from India."

He knelt and touched the back of the dog, and a panel swung open. Mahran inserted the ventha-di into the recess and the tiny hatch wheezed shut. "The recess is shielded. The ventha-di should go undetected."

The hound turned and moved off, limping still, through the sand towards the nearest canal. "Where is it going?" Anand asked.

"Far from here, to the foothills of a mountain range on the north of this continent where, with luck, in time, we will meet it again. But come, we're exposed out here in the open. I see no Zhell for the moment, but it is wise to be wary. We will avail ourselves of the hospitality of the Vantissarians." He pointed across the sand to the canal and the green vegetation that flanked the waterway.

"I wonder if the locals recall the time, fifty years ago, when a vast ship passed this way?" he mused.

Beside Jani, Anand was wide-eyed in shock and wonder, the bloody gash on his brow already drying.

Alfie smiled at her and squeezed her hand. Jani looked into his eyes and smiled in return, her heart swelling.

Together, in the shadow of the derelict Vantissarian weapons platform, they made their way across the sand towards the canal.

CHAPTER
THIRTY

&

Sebastian survives – A dream? –
A voice in his head –
Sebastian is powerless –
"A long, long way from here..."

WHEN SEBASTIAN CAME to his senses he was no longer in
the crypt of St Mary's church.

He was sitting on the bank of the Thames in the shadow
of Battersea Bridge. To his right, dawn was brightening
the horizon and, as the new day commenced, the river
was coming to life. Small boats puttered along its silver-
grey waters and the wakes of larger vessels sloshed
against the pilings at his feet.

He recalled the fat, besuited Indian threatening Jani,
and how the man had fired blue light from his fingertips,
blue light that had hit Sebastian like lightning and filled
him with indescribable pain. He recalled, dimly, lying
on the cold stone floor of the crypt and knowing that he
was dying; he recalled looking up into Jani's ineffably
beautiful, tear-streaked face and pleading with her to
believe him that, this time, he had not betrayed her.

He looked down at his chest, where the pain had
been centred. Not only was he no longer suffering the

searing agony that had consumed him then, but his chest appeared unblemished, and even his shirt and jacket were undamaged. He reached up, tentatively, and touched his right cheek; his fingers encountered only stubble and he shook his head in wonder.

Had it been nothing more than a dream?

But he *had* made his way to St Mary's, he told himself; he had crept down into the crypt, coshed the young Indian over the head and, using him as a shield, confronted the man Jani had told him was a Hindu priest.

He saw again the actinic blue light leap from the man's fingertips, felt again the pain – and he *knew* he had actually experienced the attack.

Then how, he asked himself, had he managed to survive, uninjured?

Because I helped you, Sebastian.

He started at the sound, sat up and looked around him.

He was quite alone on the riverbank.

The voice came again, and this time he realised that the words had emanated from within his own head.

I helped you, Sebastian. I brought you back to life.

"I was dead?" he found himself saying, aghast.

You were very dead, my friend.

"Then how...?"

Because I possess powers beyond your tiny human understanding.

Sebastian was shaking uncontrollably, and it occurred to him that either he was mad or that this time he really was hallucinating. "Who are you? How did you...?"

You may call me Zorkoran of the Zhell.

The Zhell? The name rang a dim alarm bell somewhere deep in his subconscious.

"Why did you bring me back to life?" Sebastian asked, panic seizing him. "What do you want?"

I helped you, Sebastian, because in return I require your help.

"My help?" he echoed.

I need your help in locating Janisha Chatterjee and the Morn. I had employed one Durga Das for this purpose, but he proved useless.

Durga Das... the Hindu priest.

I conferred upon the fool powers undreamt of, but he failed me.

The light that had leapt from the fat priest's fingertips...

That is correct, Sebastian. And, along with the power to kill, the power to heal, to bring the dead back to life. And now, my friend, these powers are yours.

"You left Das, discarded him," Sebastian stammered. "But... but why me? If you wanted Jani and the Morn... why couldn't you have inhabited *their* heads?"

He felt what might have been echoing laughter in his mind. *As powerful as I am, Sebastian, I have my limits. By the time I had recovered from the death of my host, Durga Das, Chatterjee and the Morn had fled, beyond my reach.*

"But I was not beyond your reach," Sebastian said.

Precisely.

"And why do you want Jani and the Morn?" he asked, then answered his own question. "The venthas – of course!"

I think, said the voice in his head, *that you will prove a capable and intelligent host, Sebastian.*

"No!" he cried, jumping to his feet. "If you think I will have anything to do with your schemes to trace Jani..."

He was brought to his knees by an excruciating pain that lanced through his head.

You will do as I say, Sebastian! You will follow my every command to the letter! This time there will be no mistakes, no foolish errors. Come...

Sebastian found himself hauled to his feet against his own volition. He was propelled along the riverbank towards central London, and, try as he might to drag his feet and defy the Zhell in his head, he was powerless to resist.

The Zhell, he thought. The alien race which Jani had told him was bent on invading this world...

He moaned aloud as he was pulled along like a powerless puppet.

"Where are we going?" he asked, distraught.

Again he was aware of the echoing sensation of laughter in his head as the Zhell replied.

Oh, we are going on a journey, my friend; a long, long way from here.